LOGAN COU
220 N
BELLEFO

DISCARDED BY
LOGAN COUNTY LIBRARIES
BELLEFONTAINE, OHIO

Witch Honour

Witch Honour

Narrelle M. Harris

Five Star • Waterville, Maine

Copyright ©2005 by Narrelle M. Harris

All rights reserved.

This novel is a work of fiction. Names, characters, places and incidents are either the product of the author's imagination, or, if real, used fictitiously.

No part of this book may be reproduced or transmitted in any form or by any electronic or mechanical means, including photocopying, recording or by any information storage and retrieval system, without the express written permission of the publisher, except where permitted by law.

First Edition
First Printing: January 2005

Published in 2005 in conjunction with Tekno Books and Ed Gorman.

Set in 11 pt. Plantin by Minnie B. Raven.

Printed in the United States on permanent paper.

Library of Congress Cataloging-in-Publication Data

Harris, Narrelle M.
Witch honour / by Narrelle M. Harris.
p. cm.
ISBN 1-59414-283-1 (hc : alk. paper)
1. Kings and rulers—Succession—Fiction.
2. Witches—Fiction. 3. Women—Fiction.
4. Fantasy fiction. I. Title.
PR9619.4.H365W58 2005
823′.92—dc22 2004057540

Witch Honour is dedicated to:

Yvon, my dear friend,
who was my first inspiration for this book,
Jehni, my soul-sister, who was my second,
And for my beloved Tim,
who never lets me doubt myself.

Prologue

The last leaves had just fallen from the marbletrees when the Witches returned to Tunston.

The townsfolk did not mind so much the healer, Witch Magda, who had been with them for more than four years now. She kept herself to herself in the old fortified hall and dispensed powders and potions and her own strange healing magic which utilised what looked like Arc technology. She was a useful kind of witch—there when you needed her, comfortably out of sight when you did not.

Her young pupil, Tephee Andrieux, they minded only slightly more, but she was one of their own and in some quarters there was guarded sympathy for the girl. Others sympathised more with her hard-pressed mother who, after her husband's death and with five other children to feed, had sent her supernatural daughter out to care for herself. The girl was a witch, after all, and more than capable. It had turned out well, in any case. Witch Magda had taken her in and Tunston had gained the dubious honour of having two resident witches.

And now it seemed that this unwanted distinction would increase twofold.

At the beginning of autumn there had been a fight at the hall. The first the townsfolk knew of it was when poor Aledar, Tephee's mother, had gone knocking at the gate, seeking belatedly after her daughter's health, and on finding her gone had an almighty row with Witch Magda. The next day she had stormed to the gates with a small crowd of fired-up citizens only to find the place abandoned. There was some concern, a little relief, a lot of speculation. Months later, with winter around the corner, Witch Magda and Witch Tephee were back, with two companions.

Aledar the Weaver was in a fine fit about her daughter's abrupt departure and this strange return. By the afternoon she had beaten up quite a froth of indignation among her friends and acquaintances, and a few bystanders who'd been drinking at the inn. Their courage now sufficiently fortified with ale, a delegation was sent to the hall, Swiftfort.

Swiftfort was a large two-storey stone hall with stables set against the western wall, a well, and a gracefully paved courtyard. It had been fortified in some war a hundred years ago with a fifteen-foot, double-layered encircling wall, with only one northward facing gate giving access. It opened onto a road that led down a hill to the small and rarely closed gates of Tunston. The family who'd owned the hall had become extinct when its last child, Haloman Swift, died without issue and it had been empty for years before Magda had claimed it. If anyone had a legal right to it, they hadn't challenged the witch in all the years she'd resided there and during her autumn absence no one had appeared. Except, of course, the rodents and the dust.

Sylvia and Tephee unhitched the horses while Magda and Leenan went to inspect the stables. There was no hay or feed and the stalls were bare, musty, and cold.

"I'll go into town later and get some supplies from Waller Stupps," Magda told her shorter friend. "He might even buy the carthorses off us. They can graze outside the walls for now."

Hobbled, the carthorses and Leenan's bay mare wandered close by and the inspection turned to the hall. It looked little better than the stables. The front doors opened onto a large reception area which was currently home to several nests of birds and winged reptiles and any number of rats, mice, and mauve-skinned hoppers. Doors led from this room to a kitchen, pantry, and various storerooms, and a staircase at the back led to the second floor which housed bedrooms, sitting rooms, and Magda's workroom.

The dragons, Sylvia's cat, Pywych, and Leenan's dog, Alard, were dispatched immediately to clear the hall of rodents. The birds were mostly sensible enough to take off for the trees at first sense of the dragons, but the unlucky rats and hoppers were diligently pursued by hungry predators.

"At least they're good for something," muttered Magda, unloading gear into the front hall. "Do you think we could train them to use brooms and mops on this place?"

Sylvia grinned at her. "Not afraid of a little hard work, are you?"

"Me? Heavens, no. I'm just . . ."

"Lazy," said Tephee helpfully.

Magda looked scandalised. "I've always swept once a month . . ."

"Whether it needs it or not," Tephee completed the old joke for her. "Definitely lazy." She grinned and went out for another armload of furs.

The peal of the bell brought a welcome interruption to the scrubbing in the early afternoon. Magda straightened up her damp and dirty dress and pushed her hair back, leaving dark smudges on her face.

"C'mon, Tephee," she said, "that's probably your mother."

Tephee scowled again. "If it is—which I doubt—I don't want to see her anyway."

"Come on, love, you can't be mad at her forever. She

tried to do what she thought was best . . ."

"She threw me out!" Tephee's voice held a rising pitch, distress and anger combined.

"She did the wrong thing, I know, but she was worried about you. She came to see me after you . . . after you left here. She thought I'd turned you into a frog or something. We can't have her thinking her eldest daughter is a frog, now, can we?" Especially not when the local version of a frog seemed just like the regular kind, but with rows of sharp little teeth and blood-red eyes. They gave Magda the horrors.

"Don't see why not," mumbled Tephee.

"Apart from anything else," said Sylvia, stepping back all sooty from the fireplace, "it doesn't do for people to think that witches would do something so cruel. Go and see your mother, let her know you're not living on a reed clump."

Tephee sighed and stood up. "Okay, okay. But I'm not inviting her in for tea or anything."

"Haven't got any marsh bugs to offer her," Leenan said from atop the stool where she was cleaning down cobwebs. "Ribbit," she added, with an impish grin. Magda threw a grubby cloth at her and left with Tephee, who was at least smiling a little again.

Leenan looked down at Sylvia. "I don't blame her, you know. If anyone ever treated me like that, I wouldn't be in a hurry to forgive them."

"Just as long as she doesn't turn her mother into a frog, that's all I ask."

"She couldn't do that. Could she?" Leenan couldn't always tell when Sylvia was joking, and this time the older woman only smiled her little knowing smile and kept on working.

Magda approached the gate apprehensively, a feeling

largely inspired by the small crowd of agitated people standing just inside the courtyard. Pausing at what she hoped was a safe distance, she waved to them. From within the knot of people a small, stocky woman stepped forward, followed by a slightly taller and fatter man with an air of troubled concern.

"You've been gone a long time, Witch," snarled the woman, "but I haven't forgotten what you did to my girl."

"It was nothing compared to what you did to me." Tephee moved from behind Magda's tall shadow so that she could be clearly seen, whole and unharmed. Her brown hair was longer than when she'd last seen her mother, her hazel eyes bright this time with defiance instead of betrayal. Any remnant of youthful petulance in her grim, forbidding expression was erased by adult pain.

To Magda's relief, the crowd looked sheepishly at each other and then at Aledar with irritation for getting them all worked up over this misunderstanding. Aledar ignored them and rushed forward.

"Tephee, oh, Tephee girl, are you all right?" She tried to touch her daughter's face, but Tephee stiffened and drew back. "Oh . . . it's . . . it's just . . ." Tears sprang to Aledar's eyes. "Oh, girl, if only you knew how sorry I was."

"I don't care how sorry you are. You threw me out. If it hadn't been for Magda, I don't know where I would have gone."

"I didn't know what else to do. So many to feed and your father dead. But it's all right now. I'm married again, this month past. Helman, come closer."

The man behind Aledar straightened and nodded slightly, eyeing the witches with trepidation. "It's true, Tephee. And we've decided that, if you were alive, you were to come home with us. Back to a proper home. Would you . . . would you get your things and we'll . . . we'll go back to town."

Tephee shook her head firmly. "I live here. With the witches. Come and see us if you get ill, but I don't want to see you here for anything else. *Mother*." She strode back into the fort.

Magda watched her for a moment before turning her gaze back to Aledar. "You mean that? You'd take her back?"

"If she'll come. If she really is a witch after all, though . . . maybe . . ." Aledar cleared her throat nervously. "She's my daughter. She's welcome in my house."

"I don't think she'll go back. She has a lot to learn now about herself. Her powers. She needs to be here with us. But I'm sure when she thinks about it, she'll be glad you wanted her. Give her some time to think, that's all." Given that Magda was very nearly the tallest person in Tunston it wasn't strictly necessary, but she stood taller to address the crowd. "Tell the town I'm back. Anyone who needs remedies for sickness can come to me tomorrow. And we need some hay and feed for our horses—someone get Waller Stupps to send it and he'll be paid later. Good day." She turned on her heel and followed Tephee into the building, forgetting that her dishevelled figure made a less than impressive exit. Still, the inn contingent meekly went back home. Helman walked with Aledar, speaking urgently with her as she cried.

Inside the fort, Magda saw that Tephee wasn't in the hall. Sylvia and Leenan both jerked their chins towards the stairs, and Magda trotted up them into Tephee's room. She sat on the bed where the girl lay sobbing, put her arms around her and held onto the girl, soothing and comforting, as Tephee cried her unhappiness and confusion away.

Chapter One

Witch Magda strolled among the tables and tents of Tunston's first market day of spring. Her deep blue eyes held a habitually dreamy expression, which softened her otherwise strong and angular face. She was tall, thin, and moved with economical grace as she wandered through the market, inspecting the goods. Her long bony fingers ran with gentle surety over the fruit and breads, paused over a particular fine piece of dyed bark-lizard leather, held a dazzling crystal necklace up to the sunlight—just another browser in the marketplace.

"Witch Magda!" A woman, thirty-something and plump, rushed towards her through the crowd, holding a basket before her. She pressed this into Magda's hands breathlessly. "Thank you! The dragon bone you gave me has settled my Mershti's lung pox, just as you said. Today she's playing in the yard again, and . . . and . . ." There were tears in the woman's eyes.

Magda smiled warmly and patted her arm. "Well, keep giving her a little with every meal, and make her say the chant too. It will keep the pox out and make sure no more impurity can grow."

"Yes, Witch Magda, I will. Thank you again." With much smiling, tears, and further gratitude, Madam Kullen dashed off to take care of her other chores and Magda peeked into the basket. It was full of gifts—a good yellow cheese, a clay pot of pickled vegetables, a bolt of rich emerald green cloth, shot through with cream and gold thread, and a set of exquisitely carved wooden spoons and forks, made with care by Carpenter Kullen. The dark-grained wood was decorated with intricately detailed flowers and polished to a smooth sheen. There was also a posy of forest flowers, tied inexpertly with a green ribbon. Those were from Mershti herself.

With a happy smile, Magda tucked the posy into the laced bodice of her cream cotton blouse and continued on with a cheerful gait and her long brown skirt swirling around her legs, wondering who the green cloth would suit best. Sylvia, she thought, with her dark hair. Or perhaps Leenan. It would bring out the green in her eyes. No, she thought. Tephee. It might not suit her quite as well, but what a smile it would bring to her face!

Magda stopped by an herbalist's shady stall and selected some fresh cooking herbs, as well as others known more for their medicinal value. Jerd, the stall-keeper, brought her samples of strange plants and fungoid growths which he collected for her in his foraging. She nodded her thanks and moved on. The wine-maker, Seema, who travelled thirty miles from his vineyard every month, exchanged a bottle of catfruit wine for a pot of balm containing dragon's claw for his sprained back. Along the way, Magda purchased items, or more commonly swapped potions and powders and other magical concoctions for the things she needed.

"Witch Magda . . ."

Magda halted on her way past the saddlers as Aledar hurried towards her from a noisy group at a vegetable cart. Aledar the Weaver was in her mid-thirties but a life of hard work and worry had aged her, and her brown hair was already greying at the temples. "How's my Tephee?" she asked, her brow creased in a permanent frown.

Magda stifled a sigh. She felt sorry for Aledar, but she

couldn't like her. After all her promises, she had not sent one word to Tephee for the whole cold season. Tephee had tried to hide her disappointment. "Well enough."

"Oh, she can't be ill . . ."

"No, she's not ill. Not that any of her family have been to visit to find out," Magda said archly.

Stung, Aledar drew back. "It was cold this winter. I had a lot to do, and the other children to care for. And Helman needed me."

Your new husband's a grown man. Tephee needed you more, thought Magda angrily, but she only frowned her disapproval.

The expression wasn't lost on Aledar. "I knew when she went missing from your hall," she protested hotly, "I knew when you'd done something to my girl."

The anger flared in Magda, partly from guilt, because she knew how much she had to do with Tephee running away last autumn. "At least I went to get her," she said, raising her voice.

"I offered her a home back with us, once I had a husband again. I asked her back, but she wouldn't come. She wants to stay with her own kind!"

"You're her *mother.* Her family!"

"You don't know!" Aledar grasped Magda's arms in a strong, biting grip. "You'll never starve, or be cold, or get sick. But it's not the same for us and we don't always have a choice. After Burlh died it was terrible, and Tephee was so . . . so . . ." Aledar noticed suddenly that her fingers were pressed deep into the witch's flesh, and that Magda herself was white with pain, or more probably anger. She released her grip suddenly. The noise of the market seemed distant, the smell of cured leather strong and suffocating. "Six to feed and care for when all I have is an old loom and hands all seizing up. Better Tephee makes her own way in the world than live in that. She's . . . she's different. She's like you." Aledar folded her arms and huddled in on herself. "Maybe if you teach her how to use her power, how to be a witch, she'll never have to deal with mortal pains again."

"It's not the mortal pains that hurt her," replied Magda, but Aledar only stared at her. Magda sighed. She reached into her shoulder-pack for a jar, which she handed to Aledar peremptorily. "Rub it into your hands, every morning, every night. It will help the rheumatism."

"The . . . ?" Aledar reached for the jar before the witch could change her mind.

"The stiffening and pain. The balm contains . . . dragon tooth. While you rub it in, turn twice, clockwise, and say . . ." She leant forward and whispered a word in Aledar's ear. "Say that each time you apply the balm. It will help."

Without waiting for thanks, Magda strode away towards the gates. She heard Aledar's thin voice call out after her: "Tell her . . . tell her I'll visit soon!"

She rushed through the town as quickly as she could with dignity, hiding her blush with the sweep of her long black hair. *Dragon tooth, my eye.* The balm contained no more dragon tooth than any of her other cures contained unicorn horns or eye of newt. Professor Shain at SolOrbit MedCentre would not have been impressed . . . although, Magda relented, old Doc Meredith would have appreciated the skilful use of semantics as a placebo.

Her embarrassed exit from the town was interrupted by a train of colourful caravans entering at the gate. Music, singing, and laughter bloomed out of the train, and a deep male voice called out that Ayman's Players were here to sing, to dance, to entertain, and to inform. It was early in the spring for a troupe to have reached Tunston already, but entertainers were always welcome, and this group livened up the place already.

As Magda watched them clatter down the dusty road and disappear into the market square, with further shouting indicating a space was being made for them there, Leenan NiBreshtan appeared at her side.

"Noisy, aren't they?"

Magda nodded and smiled. "Very."

"Maybe they're going north after this. They could take a letter to Uncle Eli for me."

"We could ask."

"Hmmm." Leenan blinked, thinking, no doubt, of the only family she had, more a father than uncle, so Magda understood. She felt foolishly envious that Leenan had someone to miss.

"Did you get what you were after, Maggie?"

"Mostly. And I got a present from Madam Kullen." She showed the basket of gifts.

"Nice carving work," Leenan commented. "Uncle Eli could have asked a good price for those at the store. Not to mention that cloth."

"How did things go at the stables?"

"Pretty well. I think the foal is all right this time. Won't know for sure until it's born though."

"Waller will be pleased."

"Waller Stupps will only be pleased if it's a colt he can sell."

"You're too hard on him. He's a businessman . . ."

"Uncle Eli's a businessman too. I was trained to help him with the store, and Waller Stupps is a miser and a cheat. I only went over because that mare needed help."

"He keeps you in good supply of oats and hay for Karomi."

"He's trying to keep on my good side because I'm a witch. He knows I'll look after his horses for their sake, not his. He only gives me exactly as little as he can get away with."

Magda only shook her head at her friend's customary forthrightness and Leenan smiled wryly. "Okay, okay. Shall we head back?"

Chatting cheerfully, the two women walked out of the town and up the hill towards Swiftfort.

Leenan and Magda parted in the courtyard—Leenan to the forest outside to bring her horse Karomi in from grazing, Magda into the hall.

Tephee was sitting at the huge table downstairs, studying. She brushed a lock of light brown hair from her eyes, tucking it back behind her ear, and leaned closer over the sheets of parchment on which she was drawing. She looked up from her work with a quick grin of anticipation. "What did you get?"

Magda smiled as she deposited her backpack and Madam Kullen's basket of treats on the table. "This and that. Odds and ends. You know." She laughed at Tephee's evident frustration. "Actually, I've got something here which I'm sure would suit you marvellously. You can sew, can't you?"

Tephee nodded and tried to peer into the basket Magda was opening. Of course, she knew how to sew—it was one thing her mother had bothered to show her when she was little. That thought robbed her of merriment and her pretty round face settled into solemnity once more. Magda ruffled her hair, used to these sudden mood changes, and told her to close her eyes. Then she took the cloth out of the basket and laid it in Tephee's hands. Tephee's eyes flew open.

"Oh . . . Magda . . . it's lovely."

"Isn't it? It'll suit you well, don't you think?" It would certainly be more becoming than the faded yellow dress which Tephee habitually wore over three or four cotton petticoats. The shabby thing had obviously belonged to Aledar for some years before being handed down to Tephee, and it hung like a sack on the girl's still childish frame.

"Oh, I couldn't . . ."

"Yes, you could. You need some new things. You like it, it's yours."

Tephee lifted the material to rub it against her face. "It's so beautiful. Thank you, Magda!" She jumped up to give the older woman an enthusiastic hug, then trailed her fingers across it again. "My mother weaves cloth like this, but she's never given me any."

"Uh . . . about your mother, Tephee . . ."

Tephee looked sharply at her, frowning.

"She asked after you today. She said she'd come to visit soon."

Tephee snorted in disgust. "She probably just wants to make sure I'm not coming home." She couldn't keep the bitterness from her voice, so she gritted her teeth and changed the subject. "I have a present for you too. Sort of."

"It isn't dragons again, is it?" asked Magda, only partially shamming the dread. The first gift Tephee had ever "made" for her was to call up four lizards. It was that first demonstration that magic was real that had frightened Magda half to death last autumn. In the shame of being caught in her make-believe witchcraft, and the shock of realising that this child had real power, she'd said some awful things to Tephee; they had fought, and Tephee had run away. It had taken weeks of searching to find her, living with a hermit-witch on the beach.

She was grateful for that, though. Without Tephee running away and finding Sylvia, Magda would never have known magic was real, here. She would never have found out that she had power of her own.

The lizards, startlingly enough, had grown wings, and protective spinal ridges. They didn't breathe fire—they were only reptiles, after all—but they were getting bigger all the time.

"Nothing like that," Tephee assured her with a giggle. "I've been practicing with Sylvia."

Tephee sorted carefully through the paper on the table and took out a delightful drawing of a flower—very fine and detailed, down to the pink-flushed white petals. One of Sylvia's "doodles." Tephee placed the drawing by itself and stood by the table. She held her hands over the picture, closed her eyes, and concentrated.

The picture began to look more solid, until the flower seemed to rise from the paper. Then it *did* rise. The picture was still there, but above it was a real flower, from the forest outside the fort's walls.

Captain, the bossiest of the young dragons, had been watching this with interest from the rafters. As the flower appeared she flew down to the table. It moved slightly with the faint draft from her colourful wings. Intrigued, she put her forepaw under it and flicked it into the air, right into Tephee's face.

"Captain! No! . . . oh!"

Flowers rained down around them, like fragrant snow. Magda, laughing, turned her face up to the shower. Tephee tried to be cross, but the effect was so beautiful, particularly with Magda there looking like a witchly bride, petals stuck to her long dark hair.

⋆ ⋆ ⋆ ⋆ ⋆

Karomi hadn't wandered far; only down to the creek that ran close to the west wall of the fort. Leenan caught the mare's halter and paused, seeing that Sylvia was just downstream, standing in the shallows and dipping her hand into the water from time to time. It reminded her of the first time she'd seen the older witch. Leenan had heard of a small coven gathering at the seaside and had left her home to join them, giving up at last a lifelong battle to suppress her powers. After some weeks' travel she had come to a place called Blood Rock, named for its red stone, and had seen Sylvia crouched by a rock pool below. She was laughing and dipping her hand into the water while a cream and brown cat stood curiously by.

Sylvia had looked childlike in her unselfconscious attitude. She was squatting like a peasant, balanced on the balls of her feet, with her long black hair swinging over her face, almost trailing in the water. The back of her deep red skirt was pulled up between her legs and tucked into the waistband in front, creating a very mannish pair of pants, not unlike the ones Leenan preferred to wear herself. The woman's slender, sure hands were dipping into the seawater as she alternately crooned and laughed in delight. Karomi, puzzled by the salt air and the strange ground under her hooves, whickered softly. Sylvia had looked up then, and her brown eyes, almond-shaped and up-tilted, showed no surprise as a welcoming smile creased her face. "Hello," she said pleasantly before bowing her head back to her task. Leenan went closer to see what was going on.

At the bottom of the rock pool lay some shells and polished glass, washed up by the last tide. There was also a sea anemone, its fronds wafting in the water. It was this last that the woman found so delightful. As she reached in to pick up the ocean's bounty the sea creature shifted across the sand and tickled her palm with its tendrils. The creature seemed quite determined to play this game with the woman, and for her part the woman was more interested in the game than the trinkets.

The cat, with an inquisitive mew, brought his paw smacking down on the water, sending the creature scurrying for safety. The woman regarded the animal sternly. "Now look what you've done, Pywych." Pywych washed himself.

Leenan had been with them ever since and had joined them in the journey back through Berrinsland to Tunston, where the fort offered better protection for the winter for the four of them than Sylvia's small and overcrowded beach cottage could have done.

Sylvia finally straightened up, smiling a welcome at Leenan.

"What have you been doing?"

"Looking for river crabs," Sylvia said cheerfully, splashing her way back onto the banks. "There'll be some good eating here closer to summer. They're all a bit small now."

They began walking back to the hall, but progress was slow. Sylvia kept disappearing with little cries of delight, only to come back with a stalk, leaf, pod, or root in her mouth. "Try this!" she'd say, handing bits of greenery to her amused friend. "It's sweet" or "It's wild radish—lovely and crunchy" or "This will be wonderful in one of your salads." A walk through the woods with Sylvia was never so much a stroll as a culinary experience.

As they rounded the corner to the north wall and headed for the gates, Leenan noticed again a patch of ground where only yesterday there had been thousands of white paladin flowers. A third of the petals were gone, and Pywych was lying in one of the bare patches.

"Have you been eating paladins again, Py?" Leenan demanded of the supremely uncaring cat. "You know how bad they are for you."

"Don't blame Py," Sylvia told her, "Tephee and I have been practicing a little trick today . . . oh dear . . ." As they spoke, half of the remaining flowers promptly vanished. Sylvia shook her head with a rueful smile. "Either she still isn't focussing properly, or something distracted her."

She glanced sideways at Leenan with a little grin, and Leenan grimaced back. She was never going to live Wefton down. It had been getting cold, on that trip to Blood Rock, and she'd just wanted a blanket to keep warm. She'd closed her eyes and thought of something warm and furry. As a result, almost every warm blooded animal in the village—from the rats to the dogs to the cattle—had leapt fences, or tried to break them down, to get to her.

That was her first lesson in witchcraft—very few witches can create something from nothing. Everything you asked for came from somewhere. She had also ended up hungry from the effort, and not much warmer than when she'd started. That had been lesson number two—magic was like any other kind of work. It made you hungry.

Alard whuffed a gentle welcome as they walked into the courtyard, in time to see a cloud of petals fly out of the front door, and they heard Magda and Tephee laughing from within. Tephee looked sheepishly at Sylvia as they entered.

"Oops," she said.

"Oops indeed. Thank goodness you weren't calling in water from the river to make a water sculpture. You could have drowned us all!"

Tephee giggled at the image and Magda rolled her eyes.

"Hey, Sylvia, Magda says she saw a troupe come into town today!" Tephee looked eagerly at her.

"Really?"

Leenan nodded. "Ayman's Players. I saw them in Scipp about six years ago. Before the plague in the Southern Kingdoms." She had been twenty-one then, and determinedly ignoring her latent powers so that she could help her Uncle Eli with the shop. That was about the time the crockery had begun to intermittently break for no reason, or fly across the room, or disappear. The tiny, unexplained fires hadn't started to appear until years later. "They were pretty good then."

"Do you think we could go see them?" Tephee, who sometimes seemed older than she should, was right now all child.

"I don't see why not. It could be fun."

Ayman's Players were a well known troupe, with a deserved reputation for fine shows. There were bursts of witty commentary on the state of affairs in Berrinsland, the Southern Kingdoms, and even as far as Marin-Kuta; short plays, readings: satire, poetry, and farce; music, song, acrobatics, and dance. Kayla Brittane headed the troupe, and looked to be keeping it as skilled and as profitable as it had been under her late father's care.

The witches went into the town to share in the fun on the first night's performance. Acrobats dazzled the crowd, followed by a silly song about a backwards knight, then Kayla—a tall, willowy woman with long black hair, olive skin, and striking grey eyes—sang a duet with a serious-looking man. Magda thought she hadn't seen anyone who looked less like a troubadour. He had long, dark hair and a scruffy brown beard which filled out an otherwise small chin and, on the whole, made him look like a back-alley thug. His dark brown eyes were hooded and his skin, though pale from winter, was the same olive tone as the woman's. He sang well but self-consciously in a pleasant tenor. With much more skill and pleasure, he played an odd stringed instrument which looked to Magda like a cross between a guitar and a cello. Sometimes he used a short bow, which he drew across the strings, and at other times he plucked and strummed the notes with speed and surety. When he played, he looked less like a ruffian.

Plays followed, bringing news of the overthrow of a king in one of the Southern Kingdoms, squabbles over succession in another, and rumours of all kinds. Before the crowd became too restless, some wondering how all this would affect the trades in southern cloth and spices, others not caring what those southern lunatics did with themselves, there was a roll of delirious music and a wild peasant dance performed by Kayla and two other women which left the crowd breathless and a lot of the men bug-eyed.

A magician came onstage after that. He was slender, mild-eyed, with the same olive complexion as the others, his light brown hair tied back in a ponytail at the nape of his neck with a leather thong wound round with red, green, and blue threads. The style accentuated his high forehead and a hairline that was just beginning to recede, and a slightly darker goatee inexpertly trimmed gave him a raffish air. His rapidly moving fingers were decorated with mismatched rings of silver, obsidian, and wood. A modest ear-ring studded one ear, though he looked as though he would wear something long and colourful with panache. His sleight of hand was perfect, accompanied by rapid banter and convincing pratfalls. He might have been thought incredibly clumsy, except that each time he fell against someone, he had to spend several minutes giving back a handful of their belongings that had somehow ended up in his pockets.

The villagers were impressed and paid generously in coin and goods. Waller Stupps even invited them to set their camp in one of his yards, for a small fee of course, and they looked ready to stay on for at least two more nights.

The witches went home, singing snatches of some of the better-known songs and content in the company of friends.

Chapter Two

It was too bloody early in the morning, thought Tamalan Fingal peevishly, to be not only out of bed, but working. Not that he was working, or that it was even particularly early. He was sitting on a wooden barrel, his feet on its edge and his knees under his chin, arms wrapped around his shins, a position which made him look like a sulking gargoyle. His brown eyes regarded the stableyard before him with a mixture of resentment and concern. From time to time he twisted the rings on his fingers edgily.

Kayla had genuinely been up early, having decided that today was Barber Day, and anyone who wanted a haircut or a shave had lined up outside her caravan and been given the appropriate clean-up with a sharp knife and a deft hand. She'd been doing it for years, she said, and would wrinkle her nose and smile with tolerant amusement at him and Kiedrych when they insisted they were quite happy with their facial hair. Tam shaved irregularly to keep the shape of his goatee, which he'd come to like over the last few months. Kiedrych . . . well, Rych didn't even seem to trust himself with a sharp knife, sometimes, let alone anyone else.

Now that the haircuts and all had been seen to, Kayla was in the yard on one of the horses while Nakamura called instructions to her. Across the yard, Kiedrych Evenahn was watching them with a habitual scowl.

"Remember," Nakamura called out as the horse loped past, "keep that foot in the stirrup. Press it down—that's it.

And hang onto the pommel, not the reins. But don't drop the reins! Okay—now!"

Kayla stood straight up in the stirrups and, while the horse cantered swiftly around, swung almost completely off the animal. Keeping her left foot planted in the stirrup and grasping the pommel with her left hand, she hung onto the side of the saddle. As the animal passed Tamalan he could see what appeared to be a riderless horse.

"Now," called Nakamura. "Up!"

Kayla reached up with her right hand, wrapped it around the pommel, and pushed upward.

"Aaargh! Sh . . ." She failed to get her leg over the saddle and was lying inelegantly across the horse's back. Her left foot was in danger of slipping out of the stirrup.

Tamalan glanced across at Kiedrych, whose scowl vanished as he rose abruptly, but Kayla righted herself and reined in the horse, swearing at her clumsiness. Nakamura ran to take the animal's halter, alternately berating her for losing concentration and anxiously checking that she was all right. Kiedrych settled back in his seat, his expression shuttered.

Tamalan grimaced sourly.

"M-m-mister . . . ?"

Tamalan glanced up. Two boys stood nervously nearby. They'd probably been watching the riding, but Kayla had given up in disgust and, followed by a still-scolding Nakamura, taken the horse for a rubdown in his stall. No doubt the lads had simply turned to the next nearest source of entertainment. Tamalan smiled encouragement.

"We saw you last night," said the bigger boy—blond and chubby, clearly brother to the fat toddler next to him. Tamalan was reminded of his own nephews with a pang. "Do a trick for us?"

and up the hill to Swiftfort.

The fort did not look like he'd imagined it would. No cobwebs. No crumbling towers. Not even any evil smells. In fact, it smelled disarmingly like his mother's kitchen. A horse, hobbled but content, grazed outside. The building was of light brown stone, sturdy but unimposing, and the little courtyard beyond the open gate looked well tended and inviting.

"Can I help you?"

He jumped at the voice, but it was after all only a boy. No—the trousers had tricked him for a moment. A girl. A woman, he corrected again, taking in the short, slight figure with short-cropped dark blonde hair and green eyes that measured him carefully. Her oval face, with a slightly up-tilted nose and expressive mouth, was very pretty, he thought. He smiled charmingly at her. She, unmoved, raised an eyebrow and repeated her question.

"I'd . . . ah . . ." he licked his dry lips, "well, that is, I want to . . ." He began to twist his obsidian ring, then stopped himself.

She nodded impatiently. "Come on in. Sylvia'd be happy to see you, I guess. I'm Leenan." She paused meaningfully.

"Ta . . . Ta . . ." He cleared his throat forcefully and tried again. "Tamalan. Fingal. At your service." He swept an elegant bow to her and he caught a smile twitch at her lips.

It didn't make him any less nervous as he followed her into the hall. She wagged a finger at a dog, black and tan with a white throat and a plumed tail, that sat near the hearth.

"Great watchdog you are, lazy mutt," she chided affectionately. The dog whuffed happily and thumped its tail on the mat.

"Here, take a seat . . . not on the cat! Pywych, move yourself. Just a moment, Mister Fingal."

"T-Tamalan."

"Okay. Hang on. *Sylvia! Teph!* You up there?" She leaned into the stairwell and shouted upward.

"Just . . . oh damn!" A voice drifted back, followed by a reptilian squawk. "Get *off*. Why aren't you out with the others? Out with you."

To Tamalan's considerable startlement, a woman appeared, hanging onto a dragon. Small, true, but a dragon nonetheless. They were rare this far north. Sea green, with golden cats' eyes. Wings. Teeth. Lots of them. The woman deposited the beast into the courtyard and returned.

"Don't know what's got into Greedy," muttered the woman. "He keeps sleeping under Magda's bed, which does not impress the cat," she confided to Tamalan.

He stared at her now. Slightly shorter than Leenan, with long dark hair and sparkling brown eyes set in a lively, friendly face. Her upswept cheekbones made her seem faintly exotic, but about as witchly as the baker's wife.

"Sylvia, this is Tamalan Fingal." Leenan made the introductions. "I guess he wants to ask us something, but he seems a bit nervous." This last thought seemed to amuse her immensely.

"Okay, Tephee's in the stable with Magda, fixing the harnesses. Bring them in and we'll see what we can manage." Then she smiled reassuringly at Tamalan. "Care for a biscuit?"

By the time Leenan returned with the others, Tamalan was munching on his third nut and honey biscuit and feeding pieces of it to the dog.

"Faithless creature," laughed Leenan, plonking down at the table opposite the visitor. Tamalan gave the rest of the biscuit to the grateful animal and brushed his sugary fingers clean on his trousers, in order to greet the others with due respect. The taller woman, slender and angular, had a gentle expression on her handsome, strong-boned face, which was framed with long, wavy black hair. Beside her was a teenaged girl with a round, serious face and light brown hair, cut simply around her face and shoulders. The girl's clear hazel eyes regarded him frankly.

"I'm Tephee. This is Magda," said Tephee.

"An honour," he said, and nodded to them.

"Any biscuits left?" murmured Tephee. Sylvia brought a plate and the five of them sat around the table.

"How can we help?" Sylvia asked.

Tamalan stared down at his fingers, twining round and round themselves in his lap. How could they help? Was it possible for them to help at all? He remembered the card. *What do you want, and will you find it?*

"I need to find someone," he said slowly, "but I don't know that he wants to be found. Or that he's even alive."

"I see."

"But if I don't find him, at least one person will get himself killed. Or kill someone else. He's . . . he's not been right since . . ." He stopped abruptly. He couldn't go on. It'd been a secret for too long. It hurt too much. He felt a hand on his arm and looked into Sylvia's gently inquiring gaze.

"The thing is," he tried again, "he wasn't always right, but he's the King. And he's given up. He can't, you know. He shouldn't." Tamalan rambled on, thoughts bubbling out now, as he made his confession. It felt comforting to say it at last. "I know it was a blow to him. Saebert, after all, hasn't got the right. And he was trusted. Well, I suppose he trusted a lot of people he was stupid to trust, and then the damn fool—excuse me, he's my King, but he's an idiot as well sometimes—but he didn't trust the right people, and trusted all the wrong ones and now he thinks it's *our* fault. Not forgetting her . . . you're not like her at all, you know. She's all broken glass and death and you're all . . . dunno. Cozy, like my mum . . . But it's all such a mess and without him, without him on the throne, it's all wrong. It's going to kill us. Kiedrych, anyway, because he can't trust anyone at all now, and what he lost to save a king who wouldn't trust him is enough to drive any man mad, I suppose, but there you have it. With Armand, we'll probably die, but without him we certainly will. One way or another."

There was a long pause and Tamalan blinked slowly, as though waking up. His sharp glance to Sylvia was acknowledged with an apologetic grimace. "I just helped you to relax," she murmured.

"So how do we find this King?" Magda asked.

Tephee regarded him so steadily that he started to fidget.

"Who's this woman? The one who's 'all broken glass and death.' "

"Well . . . a witch. I guess. But she's not so . . . nice." This embarrassed him, and he looked to Sylvia. "Can you find him?"

"I can try. I need some things, though. Do you have anything that belonged to your King?"

Tamalan frowned and shook his head. "I've got my cards, but that's all I had when we had to run for it. There's . . . well . . ." he paused, struck by an uncomfortable thought.

"There's . . . ?" prompted Leenan.

"Me. I suppose. Well, I'm sworn to him. Jesters are among the first to swear, before the coronation even. I'm sworn, so that makes me his."

Sylvia accepted this and nodded. "Have another biscuit. I'll have to get some things together."

Sylvia had not fetched anything more startling from her room than an aromatic candle—"It's calming"—and a cushion to kneel on. She was kneeling on this now, in front of Tamalan, while the others stood in a rough semicircle around her.

"This may be a little difficult—we don't have much to go on—so if I look like I'm in trouble, take my hand. I may need help to get back."

Her apprentices regarded her with varying levels of concern and curiosity, and Sylvia wished she'd taken time to explain things more fully.

Kneeling before the King's jester, Sylvia took his hands—long, smooth, elegant, with sensitive tapering fingers—into her own smaller, rougher ones. "Relax," she said, "it won't hurt."

This seemed to agitate him further, but her calm flowed into him from her fingertips and he exhaled slowly, sat back.

Her fingertips on his pulse, Sylvia immersed her perceptions in his rhythm. She could almost hear, subliminally, the thoughts of his conscious mind, but she was no mind-reader. Instead, she let her own consciousness float on his, relaxing, allowing the physical anchor of her body to drift away.

The King's jester. Sworn. Bound by duty, by blood? Yes. (Did he know it? Distant cousins, perhaps. Someone's ancestor had misbehaved.) There was the thread, now ravel it, follow it . . . Her perception swept east, south—over the mountains to a dry, flat land. Sparsely green now in spring. Hills, plains. Hot sun to come. And people. A group with horses, living in a . . . goat? No, goat *hair*. A tent. Swathed in cloth, men and women, wrapped against the sand and heat. Among them was the King, but no longer King. Changed, damaged, inside and out. What was this? Something cold wrapped around the thread and . . .

. . . pulled—spinning, rushing, south. Cold curiosity, spite like a blade, like shards of glass, like shards . . . Oh First King, Lords, I'm bleeding . . . dear Lords . . . Tephee?

Abruptly, everything shrank. Everything centred on a point in her chest where breath was dragged in with ragged gasps. Someone held her, gave her water mixed with honey. Her strength returned gradually, and at last Sylvia was strong enough to open her eyes.

Tamalan had slithered to the floor, sobbing with terror, exhaustion, despair. Magda was trying to make him drink, but he, in his fear, fought her until she held him like a child and gave to him what peace she could.

Between them, Tephee sat on the floor. She had strength enough to feed herself biscuits, but looked pale and withdrawn.

"Sylvia? Thank the First King!" Leenan's fingers fluttered down the side of her face. "What happened? Oh . . . don't worry. Later, later. Drink. We'll get food in a minute. You'll be fine."

It was hours before they could talk. First, Leenan and Magda fed Sylvia, Tephee, and Tamalan, who was shivering with shock, and put them to bed to recover. Magda took extra care with Tamalan, heaping blankets on him, propping his feet up, checking his pulse. Leenan regarded her often dreamy friend with surprise as Magda set about her healer's craft with practical determination and not a hint of witchcraft. When the three awoke, they were fed a hastily-prepared broth and more biscuits. Magda had said something about high-energy foods and made them drink some odd-tasting green liquid which she'd fetched from her private workroom. It was unpleasant, but reviving.

It was still dark, in the early hours of the following day, when the whole group was sitting around the blazing downstairs fire, weak but recovering. No one could sleep, and dawn was only an hour away. They all clasped mugs of warm spiced wine and stared into the flames.

"So." Leenan glanced up from the fire to look at Sylvia. A green after-image of fire superimposed itself on Sylvia's face. "What happened?"

"She happened," Tamalan answered, shuddering. "She's been watching him. Oh Lords, we're done . . ." He moaned and huddled into the fur draped around him.

"Who is she?" Sylvia asked him quietly. She spoke calmly but there was a haunted look in her eyes and she was holding her goblet tightly, to keep her hands from shaking. For a moment she thought he wouldn't answer, but after a long pause he drew a shaky breath and began.

"Zuleika Tallan. She's the witch I told you about."

Broken glass and death, Sylvia remembered. Shards of glass and pain and all of her strength bleeding, bleeding . . . She brought herself back to the present with effort.

"She's the one who helped Saebert take Tyne Castle. King Armand's cousin. No right to the throne. No good on it, either. Without Zuleika he couldn't have done it. She killed half the Council in one night, smashed our army at the gates. Some of us . . . we got away. The King fled, and so did we. Haven't been back since." He shook his head and tears spilled down his cheeks. "We're lost. Kiedrych and me. Dead. Now she knows we're here, we're looking."

Sylvia reached out to pat his hand. He had good reason to be afraid. Leaving her hand on his, she turned to Tephee. "How did you get us out?"

"You were in trouble. So I took your hand and went after you."

"I didn't say to do that."

"But you couldn't find your way back. And you were both . . . both dying. So I came after you."

"And brought us back."

"Yes."

So now, Sylvia thought, Tephee knows how strong she is. And what she can do with her strength.

The man rapped once, loudly, on the wooden door before pushing it open and striding into the room. He had to pause for a moment to identify where, among the shadows, Zuleika was sitting.

She was seated in an oversized, cushioned chair with her legs and bare feet tucked under her like a child. Her large, doe-like eyes regarded the sky through the narrow slit of window in the west-facing castle tower, her expression distant. Her wide, sensual mouth sucked delicately on her right index finger, which was sticky from the honey cakes she'd been eating. Long black hair cascaded down the pillows behind her.

"I was told there was some trouble here."

Zuleika looked across the room and smiled, tired but pleased to see him. "Trouble? Not really."

King Saebert Bakar-Cadron of Tyne walked up to the chair where she sat and gathered her right hand up in his, lifting it to his mouth to kiss her sugary fingers. "I'm pleased to hear it." He kissed her palm. "But what happened?"

"Someone was mind-searching for your cousin. When I punished them for their interference, someone else . . . broke them free." Her lovely mouth curled down briefly in displeased puzzlement, then smiled again. "I think the interlopers are sufficiently frightened, however. And if they go looking for Armand . . . well, I don't think that will be a problem either."

"Good." The word was lost in a murmur as he nuzzled her throat. She tilted her head back, brought one long, elegant hand up to run her fingers through his fine brown hair. As her nails raked lightly over the back of his neck, he pulled away. A small disappointed sigh escaped her. Through her drowsy-lidded eyes she watched his face.

"Don't worry," she assured him in a soft voice, "I'll take care of everything."

"The way your cousin took care of things?" There was sharpness in that tone.

"Parsa died for her error in judgement. We didn't need him anyway."

"If it wasn't for her mistake, Armand would be dead now. I don't understand why you can't just kill him."

"For the same reason you haven't sent someone out to see to it yourself. He's too far away, love, and they're on the move all the time. In any case, he's made no attempt to raise an army—he was too badly hurt. We need our strength at home. Why go to all that trouble when even now he is dying?"

Saebert smiled and his lean, aristocratic face became charming, his brown, gold-flecked eyes dancing with laughter. "We can but hope, my jewel." He bent to kiss her again and she wound her arms around him.

Chapter Three

"So these are your virgins, Tam?" said Kiedrych, scowling again, when he saw who Tamalan had returned with. He regarded the four women coldly. Tamalan flinched and Magda touched his hand reassuringly.

"Leave him alone," she chided Kiedrych. "He's already had one bad fright and he doesn't need you to . . ."

"I'll give him more than a *fright.*"

"You'll back off," Magda interrupted sharply. Tamalan gaped at her. Kiedrych, however, found her protectiveness amusing, in his cold way, and did as she told him.

Magda, wishing the man had backed off with more respect than mockery, glanced at Sylvia.

"We need to talk," said Sylvia.

"I don't."

"I don't think you understand . . ."

"I have no wish to understand. To the Red Lord with the lot of you."

"Kiedrych!" Tamalan's voice was a panicked whisper. "By the First King, don't! They're *witches.*"

"Really."

"Yes," said Leenan, her indignation clipping her tone, "really." A faint arc of witchfire hissed between her fingertips. Kiedrych held her gaze steadily. Tephee looked ready to leap to Leenan's defence if need be; Sylvia looked nonplussed to have lost control of events before they'd even begun. Tamalan was pale and his breath was getting shallower. He hardly seemed to notice when Magda took his wrist to check his pulse. Her lips compressed in an angry frown.

"That's enough." Her voice was level, but it carried. She'd used it from time to time in the wards on SolOrbit. It had always grabbed attention then and it didn't fail her now. All eyes were on her.

"If you don't calm down, now," she glared at Kiedrych, "by God, I'll have you pumped so full of relaxant you won't be able to bathe yourself for a week."

The threat, a little lost on the present crowd, was nonetheless delivered with enough conviction to give pause. Magda drew another breath. "Tam here has had enough. You will not give my patient a stroke, do you understand? And don't you dare look at him like that," she jabbed a forefinger at Kiedrych's face. "He was *not* startled by a bogeyman, and this isn't bloody funny." This because Kiedrych was again smiling, albeit sourly, at her.

"Do you expect to frighten me as well?"

"We expect you to shut up and listen," Leenan said coldly.

A deep sigh issued forth from Sylvia, who shook her head. "We've got off to a very bad start."

"We missed you last night, Tam. Good to see you back." A new voice, sounding calm and reasonable. "Do you want to finish this discussion inside my caravan?"

Kiedrych spoke first. "This doesn't concern you, Kayla."

"I think it does. But either way, I don't need a brawl going on outside my window, so you might as well come in and keep it all private, eh?" Kayla strode past them and up the two stairs of the multi-hued caravan that stood behind the small crowd. She ducked inside, then stuck her head out the door. "Come on in, then, there's room enough."

There was room, if barely, for them to sit on the floor,

the bedroll, and the edge of various trunks which contained costumes, props, clothes, and other paraphernalia for living on the road. Magda hunched across to a trunk in one corner and tried to make herself shorter. Kayla sat cross-legged on her bedroll while Tephee, Tamalan, and Leenan ranged themselves self-consciously around her. Kiedrych sat stiffly on the other trunk. Sylvia, short enough to stand straight in the confines of the caravan with a finger-width between her head and the roof, quietly sized up her . . . opponent?

"We've found King Armand," she said.

Kayla drew in a sharp breath. Kiedrych stiffened, but didn't speak.

"In turn, Zuleika Tallan sensed it and tried to kill us."

"Us?"

"Tamalan and myself."

Kiedrych's hands had balled into fists, but he sat very, very still. "Does she know where we are?" He sounded tired.

"No," Tephee spoke up, "I broke the thread. She doesn't know where we are. But she knows we're around."

"I see." He rubbed a hand over his face, wearily. The anger that had erupted on seeing the witches had been suppressed again, but his eyes were dark-rimmed with bitterness and defeat. "What do you want, then?"

"I have to do something about Zuleika Tallan."

Magda found herself searching Sylvia's face for clues to her resolve. Last night, their teacher had told them that she intended to go with Tamalan Fingal to find this witch. None of them had asked for an explanation; each of them had said they would come with her. At the time she had seemed relieved; now she just looked strained and haunted.

"Why? What do you care about one foreign kingdom?"

"To be frank . . . not so much. Not when it's just ordinary human affairs. But Tallan is a witch, and she's using her power to hurt."

"Ah." Kiedrych smiled his sour smile. "A kind of witch police constable. It's your duty to stamp out evil."

Magda saw Sylvia's hands, folded behind her back, clench. She was maintaining her composure with effort. Magda's own hands were twitching with the temptation to shake the ill-tempered pig.

"No," said Sylvia at last, "it's more involved than that. It's nothing so organised as policing. But I've dealt with her type before." A muscle in her cheek jumped. "And she won't stop at one kingdom."

"Ah—it's personal. Now that I can understand."

"Will you help us find the King then?"

"Why?"

"Kiedrych." Tamalan leaned forward and fixed his eyes on Kiedrych's hands, not daring to look up. Those blunt fingers slid over and over the seal of the ring he still wore, despite everything—his seal as Captain of the Castle Guard. "We need him. And he needs us. He's our King. We're sworn to him. If we're with him again, we can . . . we can . . ."

"We can what?" Kiedrych spoke very quietly through clenched jaws. Sylvia thought that if she flicked him with her fingernail, he might shatter.

"We can retake the Kingdom. Restore the King. Make it right."

"Do you believe that?"

This time, Tamalan raised his eyes. "I do. I have to."

"Then you're a fool."

"Of course," Tamalan smiled weakly, "it's my job." He mimed the juggling of three balls.

"If I refuse to go, will you go to him yourself?"

The fool swallowed, and then nodded slowly. Kiedrych turned his face away.

Kayla shifted, and with that small and graceful movement was kneeling in front of Kiedrych so that their eyes were level. "I have to go, too," she said softly. He looked at her. "I'm sworn to him. I have to go, now that I know I can find him. And he's sworn, too, Kiedrych. He's our King and sworn to our protection. He owes us for failing in that. He ought to have a chance at redemption, don't you think? Him and us, both. I wish you'd come with us. I don't know how else we'll stay out of trouble."

She smiled at him, her grey eyes bright, but she didn't touch him or try to coax him in any other way.

"He'll kill us all." He had leaned slightly forward, as though drawn by a magnet towards her.

"We're sworn to die for him."

"And you'd do that?"

"If he's still our King, yes. If he has abandoned us, then—no. I'm not a fool."

"He abandoned us once." He was so intent on her that the rest of them might not have existed.

"We don't know that. We don't know what happened. Until today I thought he might be dead."

"He abandoned us before then, before the battle." There was an awful, angry bitterness when he spoke of it.

A shadow of puzzlement and concern flitted across Kayla's features. "He made mistakes," was all she said. She paused. "Will you come?"

There was a longer pause. He looked away, then nodded, once. "Someone, as you say, has to keep you out of trouble."

"What do you mean, I'm not coming with you?" Tephee's eyes blazed.

"I mean it's not a good idea." Sylvia was trying to remain calm. "You're still very young and inexperienced and this will be very dangerous."

"I'm no more inexperienced than Magda or Leenan. And I'm stronger."

"Strength isn't everything, love, and I don't mean magic experience." Sylvia tried to take the girl's hand but she stepped back.

"You just don't want me!"

"Tephee, it's not that. I worry for you. I don't want you to be hurt."

"I want to go!"

"You can't. And behaving like a child isn't going to make me change my mind."

"I suppose you're in on this as well." Tephee turned her accusing glare on Magda, who shrugged helplessly.

"We thought it would be better for you . . ."

Disgust and scorn twisted Tephee's expression. "So what am I supposed to do while you're gone?"

"Look after the town, practise . . ." began Sylvia.

"And stay by myself at Swiftfort."

"I thought you might like to stay with your mother," suggested Magda with utmost reasonableness.

"My *mother*."

"Aledar said she wanted you to come home. You can stay with her. It won't be forever."

Tephee couldn't find anything else to say. She only stared at them both, outraged, before fleeing up the stairs to her room.

"Oh dear." Magda rubbed a hand over her eyes. "That did not go well."

"No. But it was necessary. We'll be back before autumn, anyway. I hope."

"Autumn? Oh. Well, I don't suppose it'll be a lot of fun. That's why she's staying behind in the first place."

Tephee reappeared on the stairs suddenly, her face puffy with shed tears and an angry pout. "Are you supposed to be taking me back to my mother?" she demanded.

Magda's friendly smile faded under the girl's glare. "If you want me to go with you, Tephee, I'd like to."

Tephee, clutching a small basket overflowing with personal things, walked briskly past her and out the door without answering. Magda cast a helpless look at Sylvia and hurried after her.

"Bye, Teph! Take care and we'll see . . . you . . . soon . . ." Leenan's cheery farewell petered out as Tephee ignored it and half-ran out the gates. Magda was hurrying along behind. Leenan frowned.

Magda finally caught up with the girl at the edge of the old part of town and accompanied her to Aledar's house, though Tephee refused to be drawn into conversation.

At the house, Tephee rapped on the door and waited. Her expression had softened to anxious uncertainty.

Aledar opened the door and stood for a moment staring at her daughter, open-mouthed. "Te . . . Tephee. Dear. How nice . . . how . . ."

"You said I could come home. I'm here."

"Oh . . . yes. I . . . of course." Aledar glanced furtively at Magda, then at her own feet. "Well . . . come in." She stood aside to let the witches enter.

It was late afternoon, almost dinnertime, and Aledar's other children were sitting around the main room of the small house. They stared at their big sister as she walked in.

"H'lo," Tephee mumbled, "I've come home. For a while." Lon, the fourteen-year-old boy at the dinner table, flinched at the sound of her voice. Henny, the four-year-old, started to cry, which set off her three-year-old brother, Daliel.

"Hello, Lonny," Tephee tried again, "I brought you a pres . . ."

"I don't want it," Lon said abruptly as she was reaching into her basket. Then he made a sign with his hand—right hand before him, thumb and middle finger curled to meet, the others sticking out at her. Warding off the witch.

Aledar shuffled nervously past Tephee to gather up the crying baby. "Don't say that to your sister, Lonny. Don't . . ." But it was clear that she wasn't worried for Tephee's feelings. She was afraid for her son's safety.

The ten-year-old twins, Misha and Garik, ran to hide behind their mother then. "When's Pa Helman coming home?" Misha whispered.

"Soon." Aledar's round eyes were fixed on Tephee, a turmoil of conflicting emotions. Guilt and apprehension, mostly, and sorrow, too. "We said you could stay. But that was . . . before winter. I think . . . I think it wasn't a good idea. You belong with witches. You said so. Maybe . . ."

Tephee's brothers and sisters were clustered around their mother, all little reflections of Aledar's round, fearful eyes, her pale skin. In this, her old home—where her dead father's favourite chair was now another man's, her old toys probably burnt on the fire by now, the old smells of her mother's cooking emanating from the walls.

With an inarticulate, sobbing cry, Tephee flung a gesture at them, from which unseen magic arced. The huddle of her family shrank closer together and she fled, dropping the basket of gifts as she did.

"Tephee, no!" Magda wanted to run after her, but first she had to stop what Tephee had started. Bugs were crawling out of all the corners and cracks of the house.

Glitter bugs, cockroaches, glossy-winged stingers—all kinds of household pests called to overrun the dinner table. Magda stopped trying to halt the flow with magic that only tired her. She glared at Aledar instead, who was trying to calm her squealing brood.

"It's your mess," Magda said. "*You* clean it up." Then she ran out after Tephee.

Magda ran through the streets to the square, raked her gaze over and between the market stalls, and thought she caught a glimpse of Tephee's old yellow dress swirling out through the gates. She made her way across the square to the gate and saw Tephee's figure receding up the hill to Swiftfort.

It was fifteen minutes before Magda finally caught up with her. The girl was sitting on a bale of hay in the stable, facing the wall and running her hands over and over Pywych's silky coat as he sat on her lap and butted his head against her tear-damp face.

"Tephee . . . love . . ."

Tephee blinked as she stared at the wall, but said nothing.

"I'm sorry, Teph. She said she wanted to see you. I thought . . ."

"She doesn't want me. She's terrified of me. They all are."

"They just don't understand. That's all."

"What do I do now? Where do I go?"

Magda walked up behind her and placed her hands on Tephee's shoulders. "You'll come with us, of course. We won't . . ."

"Sylvia doesn't want me to go. She . . . she . . ." Tephee clenched her teeth and fell silent, and only tensed her shoulders as Magda slid her arms around them for a comforting hug.

"Tephee, please don't do this to yourself. Sylvia's just worried about you. She thinks this Zuleika Tallan could be terribly dangerous. We talked about it. We both thought it might be better for you to stay here, where you'd be safe, and you could look after . . ."

"I'm the strongest. Stronger than you, and probably stronger than Sylvia too. You need me. Unless you're scared of me too." She started to shake then, but as Magda held her, rocking her like a baby and reassuring her that she was loved, Tephee could not cry.

Chapter Four

It had taken Leenan a little over an hour to pack her things for the journey. It wasn't as if she owned much. She had brought only what she could carry on Karomi when she had left her uncle's home in Scipp. He had told her with a tearful smile that he would look after her things until she could come to see him again, before locking her in one of his great, gentle bear hugs as though the gesture could linger and protect her on her travels.

Leenan shifted the belt around her deep green quilted jacket—Uncle Eli's King's Festival gift to her—and looked towards the hall. Magda deposited a mysterious box in the courtyard, waved, disappeared back inside. Leenan sighed. Anyone would think they were taking half of Swiftfort with them. Shaking her head, she returned her attention to the thick letter she held, ready to give to the players when they met this afternoon. In it, she had told her uncle everything that had happened to her since she'd left home, the things she'd seen and learned. She had, for example, learned how to set fire to things when she meant to, and not simply because she was repressing her powers with her single-minded determination. She hadn't meant to be a witch. She hadn't wanted to be a witch, for the longest time, or so she'd thought, but the desire and the power had tried so hard to surface above her sense of duty and care that eventually she had become too dangerous to Uncle Eli to stay.

She wondered if that was what had happened to her mother: denying herself so hard that the need to be herself leaked out in dangerous ways. Uncle Eli had never told her how the fire that had killed her parents had started, but given her own experiences she could hazard a guess.

She wrote to tell him that she missed him; that she was happy. She did not add that for the first time in her twenty-seven years she finally felt free to be herself.

One of the carthorses stamped impatiently and Leenan ran her fingers down its flanks, imparting calmness with the touch. That made her smile. She should have guessed that her power would manifest itself in a skill with animals. She'd been rescuing animals and bringing home strays since she was four. Alard she had stolen as a puppy from a brute of a neighbour; a whole year's savings for the Lords' Thanksgiving had been spent on an out-of-condition bay mare instead of the starflame necklace she'd been saving for. Uncle Eli had noted more than once that she gave poor dumb creatures more understanding than the people who came to their store. She had countered that animals felt what they felt and that was that, unlike most of their neighbours and customers who, she sensed, had layers of meaning in them and the foremost one was almost never the truth.

"Nearly ready!" That was Sylvia bringing two bags to fling onto the back of one of the carts they had bought back from Waller Stupps, along with their original horses. Just as well they had two carts, Leenan thought. Between the four of them, and with Magda's insistence on bringing those enigmatic boxes with her, they were going to need the storage space.

Kayla took a few hours to sort things out with the rest of the troupe, most of which were taken up with transferring troupe necessities out of Kiedrych and Tamalan's shared caravan, and her own, into other overfull carts and caravans. She handed over the pay accounts to Mikkal, who was one of the few who knew exactly how close her connection to the King of Tyne actually was, and gave him the task of running the troupe while she was away.

"Are you sure you want to go?" asked Mikkal quietly. "I know you're supposed to be the King's Agent, but . . ."

"But nothing," she replied, kissing his dark-skinned cheek. "This isn't just my father's oath. I took one, too. I have to find out what happened. I was there, remember."

"I remember you got out by the skin of your teeth," Mikkal said, then sighed. "I should know better than to argue with you. I used to think Ayman was stubborn."

"He was."

"Don't worry, Kayla." Mikkal's face crinkled in a reassuring smile. "I'll take care of everyone. If you can't make it for the summer circuit at Besgarth, I'll see you for hibernation in Henatith."

"All right." She finally drew back and said her farewells, along with last-minute advice, to the troupe. "Don't get drunk too often, Fonso. Can't have you falling off the stage again, hmm? I've told Salah to slug you one if you do, all right? And Leese, you need to work on that routine with Merri. Piotr . . . where's Piotr? For Lords' sake, Merri, don't start crying . . ."

All told, it took a while for her to say goodbye, and she only left eventually because Mikkal took her by the arm and physically handed her over to Kiedrych.

"Keep her out of trouble," said Mikkal.

"That's the idea," replied Kiedrych, straight-faced. Kayla, fighting back tears at having to leave her troupe, slapped both of them ineffectually on the arms.

"Off you go, kid." Mikkal helped her up to the seat of

her van and handed her the reins. "Take care. We'll see you soon, eh?"

"Sure thing. I've given you everything? You've . . ."

"Yes, yes," he laughed, "everything. Trust me. Now go, it'll be summer before you're out of Tunston."

Kayla smiled ruefully, glanced at Kiedrych, and nodded to him. "Sorry. I'm not usually so . . ."

"Yes you are," he contradicted, but then he smiled. It was so unexpected—he smiled so rarely—that Kayla paused to catch her breath, then smiled dazzlingly back.

"I suppose I am," she agreed. She laughed. "We better get going, then, before I start again."

Mikkal waved goodbye as the horse-drawn caravans moved off. Only Tamalan leaned out of his seat to wave back.

Later in the afternoon, the four carts were still being drawn along roads surrounded by fields and farms. By nightfall they had passed most of the cultivated land and had set up camp behind the trees by the road. Kayla, Kiedrych, and Tamalan had covered caravans to sleep in, so the task of preparing a meal was delegated to them while the witches set up a tent annex against their carts. The dragons went hunting rabbits, but the other creatures waited to be fed.

Kiedrych foraged for fuel, then withdrew. Tamalan took charge of the cooking while Kayla fed wood and bark to the fire. She watched the minor circus of the witches fending off the cat and dog while they tied feedbags to the horses.

"Tephee, could you see to this pair?" Sylvia glanced over to where Tephee was leaning against one of the carts, watching the dragons wheeling overhead.

Tephee, her expression sullen, gestured carelessly. Pywych and Alard bolted into the rabbit meat that had appeared with gratifying speed at their feet. Sylvia's mouth pulled down into a sharp frown and as her gaze met Magda's, she sighed.

"Dinner's ready!"

Even Tephee responded quickly to Tamalan's announcement, and shortly the seven of them were seated around the fire spooning up meat and vegetable stew.

"Good stuff," commented Leenan between mouthfuls.

"Don't look at me," Kayla said, "I'm not much of a cook. I cut up the vegetables but Tamalan put in all the tasty stuff."

"What did *you* do?" Leenan asked Kiedrych.

"Supervised," he replied, deadpan.

"He couldn't boil an egg to save his life," said Tamalan in a stage whisper, and grinned at Kiedrych's glare.

"So, where do we go tomorrow?" Magda gestured towards the road.

Kiedrych gave up pushing his food around his plate. "We have several days to go until we reach the foothills of the Anatacci Mountains, and then we have to find our way through the pass. That's another week. After that, it's up to you. If you," he nodded at Sylvia, "think you can find him in the desert tribes, that is. We go into that land without a clue and we'll probably die of thirst in the flatlands."

"Leave that to me when we get through the pass."

Kiedrych regarded her coolly for a moment, arched an eyebrow at Kayla, then smiled unpleasantly at Tamalan. "Do you realise what it's like out in the flatlands? If she doesn't know where to find Armand, we're dead."

"I . . . I . . ." Tamalan's eyes darted between Kiedrych and Sylvia. "She knows. She'll find him. Won't you?" He ended on a less certain note than he'd intended, and swallowed hard.

Sylvia glared at Kiedrych, but it was only when he noticed Kayla purse her lips disapprovingly that he relented, but only so far as to fall silent.

"You're a mean bugger sometimes," Kayla told him.

"That's what my foster-mother said."

"And Da, and Kunji, and at least three-quarters of the Guard," Tamalan grinned at him. " 'Captain Evenahn is a mean bugger sometimes' will be your epitaph."

"I'd rather hoped it would be: 'Here lies Kiedrych Evenahn, who outlived everyone he knew.' "

"I always wanted to be buried under a tree," Kayla said. "Apple, maybe, or a lenensia tree. All those beautiful blue flowers."

"Don't be in too much of a hurry," said Kiedrych. "There aren't any lenensias in the flatlands."

"Oh, shut up," she punched his arm, "you're giving me the creeps."

For a while there was silence, then Tephee said quietly, "I won't ever die. I don't have to. I could live forever if I wanted."

Sylvia, her voice controlled as she rose, said, "None of us have to die on this journey. And no one," here she looked at Tephee, their eyes meeting, "lives forever. Especially not witches. I think it's time to get some sleep."

Rapidly, with relief, they split up and turned in for the night.

The next day, everyone made an effort to override the tension of the previous night. Kayla sang some of the more cheerful folk tunes, playing on her lute, with Tamalan joining her, and even Tephee was less sullen. She pointed out new plants and landscape features to Magda as they moved through increasingly deserted roads. Only occasionally did they meet another traveller coming the other way. Spring had barely arrived and most of the traders wouldn't start going on the trade routes for another few weeks yet. The dragons, having fed well on rabbits and hoppers, found purchase on the gear in the cart and fell asleep, vying briefly with the cat and dog for position.

They made camp that night without incident or argument and for several days they rode on, the unpleasantness of that first night apparently forgotten—except that Tephee still only spoke to Sylvia when absolutely necessary.

On the fifth night they reached the foothills and found camping space in the yard of a good but nearly empty inn. The cook looked surprised to have seven customers for dinner, plus orders for enough meat to feed a cat, a dog, and four dragons. She managed to feed everyone sufficiently, and even had a good supply of hot mead on hand.

Tamalan looked cheerfully prepared to overindulge. Kiedrych settled a disapproving glare on him and there was a brief, silent battle of wills before Tamalan gave in. He took up a napkin full of cheese scones and fruit pies to compensate and allowed himself to be herded out to the caravans. Kayla watched them leave wistfully, sighed, and downed the last of her cooling mead.

"I suppose I should get some sleep too," she said.

Leenan rolled her eyes and mouthed 'lovestruck' at Magda. Magda grinned. They both sobered suddenly as Kayla's grey gaze swept over them. Then the dancer flushed and looked away.

"Well. Goodnight, then." She left.

Leenan and Magda, still grinning, followed soon afterwards to check the horses and make sure the animals were all bedded for the night. Sylvia and Tephee were alone together for the first time in days. For a few moments they sat in complete silence, regarding each other guardedly.

"We really should talk," began Sylvia. Tephee stared at her, saying nothing. "Tephee, I didn't mean to hurt you. I really felt this journey could be too dangerous for you. I still think so."

"Everyone says that afterwards. No one means to hurt me. But you do." Tephee had shifted forward now, her hands grasping the edge of the table. "I thought I needed you. Mother, Magda, and then you. But I don't. It's the other way around. You need me. Trouble is you're afraid of me. All of you. I'm stronger than all of you put together. It's taken me a while but I've worked it out now." She leaned back again with a cold smile. "I don't need anyone, and I like it that way." *I do,* she insisted to herself, *and I'm not sorry.*

Sylvia sat straight up in her chair, dread curled in her stomach. "I know you're very powerful, but I'm not afraid of you. Neither is Magda or Leenan. But you mustn't give others a reason to be afraid of you. The reason I didn't want you to come was for your protection. You're very young, and Zuleika Tallan is very dangerous."

"I can handle her."

"Maybe. But that's not the point."

"What is?"

"I've met people like Zuleika before. She represents more than physical danger."

"She represents what you're afraid of." Tephee was surprised by Sylvia's stillness, realising suddenly that she had hit the target. "You are afraid, aren't you?"

"Yes. But not of her. Not exactly." Sylvia shifted slightly and looked away.

"I'm not afraid."

Sylvia turned angrily back. "You should be. This isn't a

game, and it isn't everything you think it is. You're still a child, and . . ."

"Child?" The word was nearly lost in the sharp scrape of the wooden chair being pushed back on the stone floor. "I may be young, but I'm more powerful than you can imagine."

"Don't count on it, Tephee. You have a lot to learn." Sylvia had also risen.

The air between them rippled as Tephee raised her hands. The table itself buckled, swelled, grew. The wood raised itself up, shifted, then began to flake apart, the flakes rising and transforming. Legs, antennae, shimmering wings, the wasps hovered a moment, transformed again, and a writhing knot of feyk-snakes hung there. "I can't learn it from you."

The ball of snakes began to change again.

Quietly, Sylvia raised her right hand and a faint ripple spread from her fingers. The snakes froze, solidified into a wooden ball, and sank into the table, the grains separating and reintegrating into the table top. Tephee's magic surged forward, lifted the splinters, but before they changed they flattened out again, and for all her efforts she could not regain control of the magic. Sylvia lowered her hand and stood silent while Tephee, panting and perspiring with the exertion, glared back.

"You don't know anything about me. Or what frightens me, or makes me angry. You don't know what I can do, Tephee."

Without a word, Tephee strode out. She staggered at the door, righted herself, moved on.

Sylvia was sitting again, her head in her hands, when Magda returned. "Is everything okay? I just saw Tephee. She was crying . . ." Magda paused as Sylvia looked up, her own face tracked with tears.

"Why do I keep saying all the wrong things?" She bit her lip, stifling a sob. "I want to help her, to protect her. To stop it happening again. And all I do . . . all I do . . ." She shook her head faintly and sank down again. "All I do is make it worse."

Chapter Five

Zuleika's chamber was dimly lit by a fire which flickered in the hearth. The soft light played over the witch's face, painting her pale skin with a flush of colour. A half-eaten chicken leg dangled from her fingers. She stared into the fire for a long time, then sighed and unfolded from her chair to stand by the window.

In the courtyard below, Saebert was waiting in the shadows. She reached out with her senses and found him by the well. Waiting for Minister Threlfayl. It was a pity about him. She'd rather hoped to keep the old bear on; he was respected—and feared—by his peers and had been useful over past year in keeping the nobles in line, but lately he had started to show disturbing signs of further ambition. It was possible, she mused, that if she and Saebert hadn't removed that fool Armand, Threlfayl would have done so himself.

He wouldn't have succeeded, of course. Despite Armand's ridiculous plans to change the nature of his reign—sending him as a youthful and impressionable ambassador to Berrinsland to pick up populist notions of government had been a bad move by his father—a large number of the Council had actually supported their King, not a full year on his throne since the death of the old one. Still, it had given her the opening she needed. Saebert, her lover even then, had approached her to help him save the country and she had, willingly. For months they had planned and worked quietly in the background, suborning councilmen and influential nobles, planting seeds of dissent.

At last, with the word from Saebert, she made her move, waiting in the gallery at the next Council Gathering and in a burst of power that had left her weak for days, she had burnt to cinders every loyalist Councillor who didn't escape in the first ten minutes. Armand himself had escaped by moments and would have been assassinated on his flight from the castle, had it not been for Captain Evenahn. Who would have thought that he would have stood for the King? That was one seed planted in surprisingly arid soil. Little cousin, Zuleika thought, your power over him was not what you thought it was.

Movement in the shadows below caught her attention. There was Threlfayl now, striding across the courtyard to his quarters after another night call to drum up support for his own bid for the throne. He stopped abruptly as a tall, slender shape appeared in front of him, near the well. She could hear their voices carry through the open glass window.

"Hello, Threlfayl."

"M . . . my Lord." Threlfayl cleared his throat and began more firmly. "Good evening, King Saebert."

"Closer to good morrow, I think, at this late hour, Councillor."

"You know how it is when you're drinking with an old friend, sire. Time gets away from you."

"Oh, I know, Councillor. Perhaps you'd care for a drink with me?"

"It is late, Your Highness . . ."

"Too late," said Saebert, "to drink with your King?"

Put like that, it wasn't really possible to refuse. Threlfayl followed Saebert into the Royal Tower. Zuleika admired the way he strode confidently in—if he was afraid, there was no sign of it.

She quietly left the window and her room to go to Saebert's chamber, through the adjoining passage. There she waited. Moments later, the door opened and Threlfayl was ushered in ahead of his host.

"Take a seat, Councillor. By the fire. Would you care for ale or wine?" Saebert was at his most charming.

"Wine, thank you, Your Highness."

Zuleika shifted out of the shadows, a flask of wine materialising in one hand, a silver goblet in the other. Threlfayl started briefly, then smiled at her. Such a handsome man, too, thought the witch, with his light red-brown skin. Broad and muscular, like a bear indeed. Quite the antithesis of Saebert's ascetic, patrician lines. It really was a shame.

"For you, most noble sir," she murmured, but there was no hint of subservience in her voice. "A fine vintage."

He took the cup and waited as Zuleika poured another goblet for Saebert. The King settled himself in a chair on the other side of the fire, raised his cup in a casual toast, and swallowed a draught of the fine red wine. Reassured as to its safety, Threlfayl followed suit.

It took only a moment for the drug to take effect. Threlfayl's eyes widened fractionally and then he sat rigid while Zuleika lifted a finger and the cup disappeared. Saebert put his own cup down on a low table and moved away.

"The idiots keep forgetting what you can do."

"I expected more from you," Zuleika admonished Threlfayl mildly. "I thought you might at least put up a fight."

There was a faint sound from his frozen throat.

"It would be better for me if you did, in fact. Adrenaline assists the process so well. Still, fear will be enough . . ."

She leant over until her face hovered above his. "I know you don't want to die, but it's all in a good cause. You'll be helping me get stronger. To save the kingdom." She kissed him lightly on his brow. "Goodbye, Threlfayl. I'm sorry it has to end this way. Truly." She kissed him on the mouth this time, and slid her right hand down his shirt to feel the warm brown skin, the mat of curly chest hair, resting her hand at last over his heart. Her left hand caressed his face and stopped, her hand spanning from his throat to his temple.

"It won't hurt," she promised.

It didn't. His energy flowed out of him into her hands, not quickly enough because he was aware of it, and that with each moment he was fading, but there was no pain, only fear, and in a little while not even that. Then it was over and Zuleika stood back and smiled drunkenly. Threlfayl's shrunken body slumped sideways in the chair.

"Put him . . ." she wavered, but when Saebert put out a hand to steady her, an arc of static electricity stung him. Zuleika giggled. "Don't worry about me. I feel . . . fine! In fact, I'll dispose of him myself." With that she flung her right hand out, an energetic but balletic movement, and Threlfayl's husk vanished.

"What will the Councillors think when they realise he's missing?" Saebert asked. He was regarding her cautiously.

"Does it matter?"

"I expect not to you. But I can't rule on your power forever."

"You could, you know. Forever and ever." She stood close by him, pressed her body along his. "I can make sure we do. You and I together, always. Hmm?" She kissed him and the fading electric charge made his lips and tongue tingle. He kissed her back, harder, savouring the sensation.

"King and Queen for Eternity." Saebert bit her fingertips gently and mouthed her palms. "Oh, 'Leika, I like that."

"Come and show me your sabre, Saebert," Zuleika giggled again, then suddenly bit his collarbone. Saebert thrust against her, and they both laughed. With barely a thought, Zuleika's magic stripped them bare and they pulled each other to the floor, biting and laughing.

Chapter Six

Three days into the mountain ranges, the road was becoming considerably steeper, which wouldn't have been so bad except that here, the spring rains came more regularly, and colder, than on the plains. This evening, the travellers had made a shelter by placing their caravans and wagons in a tight semicircle facing a large rock, with a large rectangle of canvas affixed to the top of each one, then drawn across and pinioned into the rock itself, forming a rough kind of tent. The dragons, disliking the rain, had taken refuge beneath the wagons, forcing Pywych and Alard to crawl under the tarpaulins in the back of the wagons. The witches had pitched their tents between the vehicles and under better circumstances it would have been quite cozy.

These were not better circumstances.

They were sitting around the low fire, built near the edge of their makeshift tent so that the smoke could escape, as far as possible from each other without actually being outside its flickering circle of light. Leenan and Magda sat together, conversing sporadically in low tones.

Worse than the silence were the occasional attempts at ordinary chatter, which petered out awkwardly after a few monosyllabic responses to comments on the weather, the meal, the landscape.

Sometimes Tephee would glance surreptitiously at Sylvia. Sometimes Sylvia would glance surreptitiously at Tephee. They never seemed to catch each other at it.

Tamalan looked to his left, where Kiedrych stared

moodily into the fire. Beside him, Kayla also studied the flames, looking wistful and bereft. A choice crowd, he thought, to recover a king and a kingdom.

"I'm for bed," murmured Magda. "See you in the morning."

"Me too, I guess. G'night." Leenan rose.

As though some invisible chain linked them all, the four witches rose and drifted at the same time, but not really together, to their tents to sleep.

"Doesn't look good, does it?" Kiedrych sounded faintly amused by his observation.

"No. It doesn't," said Kayla.

"What's wrong with them?" Tamalan poked at the fire edgily.

"Witch stuff. I don't know. Maybe they can't be trusted after all." Kayla shivered. "Maybe they're just going to join Zuleika Tallan."

"No." Tam's denial was sharp. "Whatever else is going on, it isn't that."

"Ah, the Witchmaster General speaks."

Tamalan grimaced at Kiedrych's sarcastic tone and looked away, but persisted. "You weren't there . . ."

"Where, you idiot?"

"In . . . there . . ." Tamalan fidgeted, kicked at the dying fire, and gestured vaguely at his forehead.

"I should say that you're not there a lot of the time yourself." Kiedrych fell silent at the hooded glare that flashed from the brown eyes, and regarded the jester speculatively. "What do you mean, then?"

"I . . ." He kicked the fire and sparks flew up. "When . . . I went to them . . . we looked for the King. We . . . Sylvia used me . . . went through me to look for him . . ."

"You read her mind?"

"No . . . but I was . . . I don't know. *With* her. With her essence. I don't know how to explain it. But I know she's not on Tallan's side."

Kiedrych, losing his short-lived tolerance and about to make another rude comment, was cut short by a sharp jab to his ribs. Kayla's grey eyes flashed a warning, for which Tamalan was grateful.

"I trust your instincts," she told him, earning a hesitant smile.

"Whatever is going on, let's hope they can get organised enough to find the King when we get through the pass."

Kiedrych found Kayla watching him again.

"So you *want* to find him now?"

He shrugged. "Why not?"

"Not good enough."

"What do you want? An oath of undying fealty to the once and future King?"

"I don't know." Kayla glanced up, but the stars were hidden behind the canvas, so she turned back to the fire, now mere embers. "I want to know what's going to happen. I guess. I want reassurance."

"I can't give you any," Kiedrych said quietly. "I have no more idea of what happens next than you do. If Armand hasn't given up, perhaps what's next is up to him. If he has, perhaps it doesn't matter what we do."

"Maybe . . . we'd be free to do whatever we wanted then. What would you do, Tam, if you were free to choose?"

"I've never thought about it before. I've never been anything else but the King's jester. Go back to the troupe maybe."

"More likely end up with your skull split in some city back alley."

"And where would you be, Kiedrych?"

"Me? A mercenary, I expect." His thumb brushed over his ring, his nail tracing the outline of the seal.

"I hardly pictured you as a farmer, I suppose. For me . . . I'm like Tam. I've only ever been what I am. An entertainer . . ."

"And a spy."

"An agent," she corrected with firmness and some pride. "Maybe I'd just find a husband and settle down. Have babies."

"Anyone in mind?"

Kayla's heart lurched at the question, but there were no hidden nuances in Kiedrych's voice that she could detect. "No," she said faintly, looking at her feet, "not really. I think . . . I'll go to bed now. I'll see you in the morning."

She rose and turned to walk to her own caravan, but stopped as her fingers were momentarily covered by Kiedrych's square, blunt-fingered hand.

"I'll give you this much reassurance," he told her levelly. "We'll find him."

She turned her hand to hold his, squeezed it, then walked on. Kiedrych watched her go until she had pulled herself through the small door set in the side of the van, then turned back to the fire.

"How long have we known Kayla?" Tamalan spoke, trying to sound innocent.

"Three, four years. When she took over as . . . agent, after her father's death. Why?" Kiedrych's eyes narrowed suspiciously at him.

"Quite a long time."

"I suppose so, yes."

"Trustworthy, I'd say."

"Would you?"

"Yes. Pretty, too."

"Anything else to add to her list of virtues?"

Tamalan took a deep breath, steeling himself. "She likes you. And you've known her longer than you ever knew Pars—"

Before he had even finished saying her name, Tamalan found himself flat on his back, blood trickling from his split lower lip and Kiedrych standing over him, his face black with fury. And pain, and humiliation. Better to shut up now.

"She tricked you. Anyone could have been. She was cousin to the witch . . ." He flinched and tried to duck as the captain grabbed him by the shirt front and hauled him up for another blow. "Kayla's not like that. Rych, you've got to let go of Parsa! She wasn't worth . . ." The next blow rattled his teeth and he knew he'd pushed too far. He caught a glimpse of Kiedrych's raised fist, and knew also that he was in for the beating of his adult life. A small whimper escaped him and he covered his head with his arms.

It was a painful but welcome shock to be suddenly dropped onto the ground and left there. Tamalan kept his eyes closed and curled into a protective ball, but Kiedrych stalked away, to their van, leaving the jester bruised and bloodied, but whole. Cautiously, Tam opened one eye, then the other, then sighed in mixed relief and worry.

When it began to rain again, the sound pattering on their makeshift canvas roof, he realised with disgust that he'd have to sleep outside tonight. His timing was terrible.

Leenan, first up in the morning, found Tamalan underneath his and Kiedrych's van, surrounded by animals which had snuggled up for warmth during the night. She noted his face, which was puffy and bruised, without comment. When he woke and disentangled himself from the multitude of bodies (rapidly so, once he realised some of those bodies were dragons), he returned her bland look and told her he'd slipped out for a "quick drink" and kind of forgotten what happened next, a story readily accepted by all who knew him. The good thing about being a jester, his grandfather had always said, was that people always expected you to do stupid things, which was often very convenient.

It was also nice to be fussed over so comprehensively by Magda, who bathed his face and ran her fingers along his bruises and split lip, healing them enough to take away the worst of the pain. He could smile at her now with something of his former cheekiness. He liked the way it made her smile back.

Breakfast was its by now customary uncomfortable experience—Magda and Leenan together, talking quietly; Sylvia picking at her food; Tephee wolfing hers down; Kayla nibbling away and glancing surreptitiously at Kiedrych, who this morning wasn't eating at all and eventually went for a walk. It was a relief when the meal was finished and they could move on.

By the time the sun had fully risen and was burning the last of the night's dampness from the air, they had broken camp and were on their way. It was getting colder in the hills, and wetter, which did nothing for already frayed tempers. The burgeoning spring, evident in green buds, birdcall, and the occasional burst of sunshine through the light cloud cover, was not receiving due appreciation.

"How much longer do we have to do this?" grumbled Leenan, huddled under a fur on the wagon, next to Magda. In the wagon tray, Pywych and Alard crouched under a canvas. The dragons had flown off to hunt. They were often away from the group for hours, trying to find enough meat to fuel their growth, which was continuing steadily. Their shimmering colours and bright eyes made them easy to spot in the distance, and the ridges on their skulls and spines were hardening into scaly shells that spread down their sides and legs. Their wings, still looking translucent at full stretch, were becoming stronger and more leathery. They were still friendly to the humans and the animals that accompanied them, but Sylvia was starting to wonder how long that would last. The dragons were a hand taller than Alard now, and were looking a lot less cute than when they were kitten-sized lizards who ate beetles. If she could have found a way to get rid of them without further hurting Tephee's feelings, she would have done it.

"I'm talking to you," snapped Leenan. "When do we get off this bloody mountain?"

Kiedrych glanced back at her. "Oh, another day to the pass, I believe. From there we travel downhill for three or four days until we reach a valley. Which will be drier, being on the leeward side. Happy now?"

"I'll let you know."

"Do that." Kiedrych turned to look towards Sylvia, riding silently with Tephee. "And you'll be able to find the King?"

"Yes."

"You're quite sure?"

Sylvia returned his look steadily and said nothing. Tephee sat straighter on the seat next to Sylvia and raised her voice. "I'll find him if she can't," she said with a friendly smile.

Kiedrych just nodded and turned back to his horse. Sylvia, her lips pressed together in annoyance, took a moment to calm herself and began to speak quietly while looking straight ahead. "Tephee, you're taking too much on yourself."

Tephee shot a sharp glance at her. She hadn't meant anything by her offer, except to help. Tephee frowned and bit the inside of her lower lip, angrily holding back tears. She didn't want everyone to be so unhappy all the time; she wanted things to be like they used to be. What was it about her that made people dislike her so much? It wasn't fair. Sylvia wasn't being fair. Tephee huffed a disgruntled sigh and looked sideways at her teacher.

Sylvia turned to meet her gaze. "I'm sorry that I hurt you, Tephee. I made some terrible mistakes, and my worst one was not trusting you. You're right, you know. I have been a little afraid. But not of you. Your power frightens me, but not you." Sylvia resisted the urge to reach out to Tephee. Her brown eyes held Tephee's own hazel ones steadily and the girl seemed ready to listen.

"Things happened. It was a long time ago. I find it hard to talk about." Some curiosity showed in Tephee's eyes, at least. "When I was just a few years older than you, there was a witch, like Zuleika Tallan, whose ambition . . . exceeded her mandate. She was prepared to kill to twist the world into the shape that pleased her most, and she came to Besgarth to wield her will. I lived in Besgarth, then. I had a husband. I had a teacher, and fellow students. A very full life. When we were asked to intervene, we thought it was our duty—to protect our city, our reputations." Sylvia's voice wavered. She took a long moment to steady herself. Finally, she lifted her gaze to meet Tephee's.

"Six of us went against Farshee, but she was one of the strongest witches living at that time, and she was using the lives of her followers to give her greater strength. We weren't entirely ready for her, and she also . . . didn't fight fair." She had to pause. Her hands were starting to tremble.

"She killed most of us. She absorbed our power and

used it against us. But I . . . Leroutra, my teacher, had always told me that I was the most powerful student she'd ever had. Stronger than Farshee, if I wanted to be. So I did what I had to do and I k-killed her."

Sylvia, biting her lip until it was white, in danger of drawing blood, shook her head vigorously, denying still the long-past tragedy. Tephee began to reach out to her, hesitated, then placed her hand on Sylvia's and patted it.

Sylvia drew in a shaky breath. "I lost everything. My teacher, my friends, my . . . m-my baby. Four months in my womb . . . never even got to see the sun and the moon, poor thing. I nearly died myself, but I'd . . . I'd used up all my baby's life to win that fight."

She had to stop, and spent a few moments regaining her breath, her eyes fixed on Tephee's hand, patting hers. After a moment she continued.

"My husband left me. The people were too shocked to thank me. I went to live at Blood Rock, and I thought I'd be there forever until you and Magda came. I don't use magic very much now and I am always aware of what it can cost. Our power has a price and we can't forget that." *I can't forget it,* she thought, *this time I'm going to do it right.* It wouldn't bring back her baby, her husband, her teacher, her old life, she knew, but it might atone for her failure.

"Oh, Sylvia . . . I'm sorry. I didn't know." Sylvia saw the relief flood through Tephee's body, the smile return—she thought she saw understanding at last.

"But you don't have to worry," Tephee continued, "I can look after us. You're all my family now and I won't let anything happen. I know I haven't much experience, but I know that I am stronger than you, or Farshee, or Zuleika Tallan. What happened to you won't happen to me. I understand you didn't mean to hurt me . . . it's okay. But,

Sylvia, I'm not going to run away from my own power in fright. I'm not scared by what I am. I'm just . . . hurt, I guess, that others are. But I can do anything and I'll earn their respect in the end."

Sylvia looked up, her eyes wide, and began shaking her head.

"Don't worry about me. I'll look after you when we go after Tallan. I can destroy her without you being hurt again." Tephee smiled brightly at her, sure she was doing the right thing, then turned and swung her legs over the side of the wagon's long seat. Abruptly, she jumped, but instead of falling to the ground or stumbling as the horses trotted along, she hovered, then in two skimming strides came up to the other wagon, took hold of the side boards and pulled herself into the tray. Alard whuffed in surprise as he skittered out of the way and Sylvia saw Magda and Leenan jump with brief alarm as Tephee suddenly appeared behind them on the wagon. The young witch was smiling. It should have been good to see her smiling again, but there was something so arrogant behind her happy confidence. Tephee's voice drifted over to her.

"We've talked. It's okay now. I think she was afraid she wouldn't be strong enough for this, and that I wouldn't know enough to help her. None of you need to worry at all. I'll take care of everything."

Her announcement was greeted with mixed relief and reserve, but the tension broke and they were all smiling again. All but Sylvia, who was clenching the reins so tightly her hands were white.

Chapter Seven

Kiedrych's estimates were accurate, and they reached the pass through a narrow and high-walled trail in the mountains in good time. On the afternoon of the fifth day after the pass, they had made their way to the long valley that led to the desert nomad kingdoms on the far side of the mountain range.

The valley itself was broad and ran seemingly forever eastward under the guard of two long fingers of mountain ranges on either side of it.

The path they were on emerged onto a flat shelf of rock and continued on the northern side as a rough downward trail. That path branched off partway down onto a cliff-hugging pathway which led to a tall stone building. The building was made of a creamy stone highlighted with rose-coloured swirls, and its solid geometrical lines—squares and rectangles topped by triangular lintels—were softened by intricate carvings and tiny alcoves decorated with little statues, and two impossibly tall and thin spires, one at each of the front corners of the façade. The decorations gave the place the grandeur of a cathedral, and its setting, which overlooked the remainder of the downward trail and the valley, gave it the air of a monastery.

"Look!" Kayla was signalling eagerly to the others. "An Arc Temple!"

"Seriously?" Tamalan jumped up to stand on his seat next to Kiedrych and shielded his eyes from the light to see better. "Oh, yeah . . ." his voice drifted into breathy awe.

He turned around to see Sylvia. "A good omen, right?"

"Well, I suppose you could say that. Arc Priests usually allow travellers to shelter for a night or two, which would be nice. I'll need to prepare some things to look for the King . . ." Sylvia looked down the length of the valley. "He's with one of the tribes, somewhere down there." She ignored the look Kiedrych gave her. "And we all need a rest. A day or two there would be good for us."

"Think they'll have any relics?" Leenan asked, avidly noting every detail of the Temple. "I heard that all these Temples had something from the Arc. Isn't this terrific, Magda?"

"Yes, incredible," Magda replied, smiling. *Whatever all the excitement's about.* With all her years in this place, she'd heard of the Arc Temples, of course, though she'd only once seen an Arc Priest pass through Tunston. Even then she'd only known the woman was a priest because of the fuss and feasts that had eddied around her presence for a day. She had seen, though not taken part in, various festivals during the year, the significance of which escaped her. By inference she knew that it was linked to the First King and Lords by which they swore. Occasionally, people would burn incense or place flowers on the small shrine in the town square, or on homemade shrines of earth and stone.

They were welcomed at the great wooden gates by three priests dressed in short grey tunics over pale grey trousers and soft black boots. The tunics were decorated with the symbol of the Arc—on the left shoulder, a golden sunburst flared, rays reaching down the arm and across the torso. Magda thought the pattern vaguely and disturbingly familiar.

The three priests—two men and a woman—showed them where to stable the horses and place their wagons.

Pywych and Alard were bedded in straw in another stall and the dragons took off to hunt through the cliffs. The seven travellers were shown to plain, clean rooms and left to wash up in hot springs.

After first scrubbing off accumulated travel grime at troughs of lukewarm water with the aid of aromatic bars of soap and rough-textured cloths which left their skin glowing, the women, in their own bathing room, lowered themselves into the pool of deliciously warm water.

Kayla submerged herself, revelling in the sensation of her saturated hair floating like a black halo around her face. The water was like a soft hand, a caress, after all that time on the road. She found herself thinking of Kiedrych. What she wouldn't have given to scrub his back for him. . . . Or to get him to scrub hers. Would he do that? she wondered with a barely repressed, wistful sigh. She watched the thin stream of bubbles rise between the tendrils of her hair. He seemed so intensely introverted sometimes, and sometimes he seemed to be clamping down on feelings so passionate that the pressure of them threatened to scorch the air for yards around. She knew he liked her, but what did that mean? It did not necessarily mean he would like to scrub her back for her.

Reluctantly, she surfaced. Damn, this line of thought wasn't getting her anything but frustrated. Forget it, she told herself, and enjoy the bath.

The travellers were reunited when they joined the priests for a plain evening meal in the refectory. Magda sat quietly listening while the others found priests to talk to. It seemed they all had plenty to say. Just not to each other. She pursed her lips unhappily.

"Is everything well, sister?"

"Hmm?" Magda glanced across the table into the bright

blue eyes of a silver-haired man. She guessed that he was in his fifties. His lined face could have been ordinary, but it was lively with humour and intelligence. Her lips twitched in a half-smile. "Oh, I'm fine. Thinking, I guess."

"Always a worthwhile occupation." His smile transformed his face into something enchanting and Magda found herself grinning back at him.

"I'm Magda."

"Sebastian. Perhaps, if you're finished, you'd like to see more of the Temple."

"Yes . . . and I'd like to ask some questions."

"I thought you might. Come along, then."

Sebastian led Magda from the refectory and through a few passages to emerge in a spacious hall, sunlit through tall windows and skylights and filled with benches ranged in front of a platform.

On the platform was a tall section of what looked for all the world like a torn and twisted section of starship fuselage.

Magda stared . . . extended a hand and hesitantly touched the cool surface . . . ran her gaze along its height and breadth, noting the dimmed scorch marks, the jagged tear of the collision-stressed metal. It could have been anything, really. Anything.

Scraps of ancient wiring, hyper-poly-bonded, sprung like technological hairs from the casing.

It couldn't have been just *anything*.

For a dizzy moment, Magda was back on the shuttle, answering the distress beacon with the *Hermes* shuttle pilot. Newly graduated as a Colony Doctor after ten years as a nurse, on her way to her first posting, the *Hermes* had run into interference in hyperspace en route and had popped out into real space to find a distress beacon blaring away.

They had gone to investigate, she with her emergency equipment and Longlife medical units.

Then a wrench, falling, attitude drives and engines dying. The viewscreen image warped and changed, the *Hermes* disappeared, and a strange new world dragged them into its orbit. She'd strapped in. The pilot, Jared Heineger, had not. He brought the shuttle in, anti-grav buffers on maximum, slammed in to the base of what Magda now knew to be the southern end of the Anatacci Mountains. The forward momentum had thrown her so hard against her restraints that she'd passed out. Heineger had been thrown out of his seat against the forward screen to be killed, crushed, instantly.

Sebastian's concerned face swam into view and Magda forced a wan smile to her lips. "My goodness . . ." she managed.

"Amazing, isn't it?"

"It's . . . incredible. How did it get here?"

"It is proof of our past. It is a splinter of the shell that brought the First King and his people to this land. It has been in this Temple for nearly four hundred years, brought here by the founders of this monastery."

Magda's eyebrows shot up. "Four hundred years?"

"Of course, it is much older than that. Theologians date the Arc of Entry some one thousand years ago."

"One thousand years?"

"Well, give or take a century."

"Oh."

"You don't know much about the Arc, do you?"

"Well, no. I've lived . . . a long way from anyone. Until recently."

"I see." He smiled again and gestured around the chamber. "Maybe you should look around at the paintings.

They tell the story of the First King and the Six Lords."

"I will. Thanks."

Sebastian withdrew to a corner, where he turned the pages of a large book filled with calligraphy and beautiful illustrations while Magda took a long, hard look at the paintings.

Fifteen of them, huge, lined the walls, depicting sequentially the arrival and deeds of the First King and his followers, dressed in patterned tunics almost identical to the ones the priests of the Arc wore. Each painting was surmounted by the image of a ball of light at the head of a bright line arching overhead. Arc of Entry. The entry arc, Magda realised, of a ship negotiating planetfall.

The landing flowed on to other events in world-creation myth—the emergence of thousands more people and many animals and plants from the same ball of light, the founding of Paradise, or at least a city. Some kind of split happened next, involving a red-headed Lord and a group of women, all looking demonic with blue light springing from their fingers. The last section of this picture showed the coven driven into exile, leaving the red-head hanging from a marbletree.

Later, the remaining five Lords—three men, two women—were depicted going forth to establish their own cities. It was apparent that a lot of the starship technology was no longer in use, perhaps through lack of raw materials or breakdown of equipment after the crash, though certain elements of the paintings made it clear that they still had electricity and motorised transport. War then swept through the continent and the next paintings showed a dramatic change in the technology of architecture and industry. Another war, an unknown time later, a further drop in technology levels, and finally peace.

There was no way of telling if the events had taken place over thirty or three hundred years, how much was allegory and how much fact. One thing was clear—whether this world on which she had found herself was at the other end of her own universe or part of an alternate one—the humans here had come from her own world.

While she stood in front of the last picture, Sebastian came up beside her once more.

"Instructive?" he asked. His smile was secretive, as though he knew the answer to some harmless mystery and was debating whether or not to share it with her.

"Certainly," she replied, "but I think I have a lot to learn."

"There always is. The Arc Temples are here to try to unravel the past, so that we may see how it guides us in the present." Sebastian turned with a grand gesture that took in the whole sunlit chamber and its holy relic. "This hall, this whole Temple, is dedicated to contemplation of what the First King's great plan was, his reason for bringing life to this world."

Magda suspected that she already knew, and that it was nothing more than the need to colonise a new world. The First King and his Lords dressed in the old uniform of the Colony Fleet—the Fleet's first uniform, back when it was formed in the late twenty-first century. She'd seen the distinctive sunburst in the history books. How this Colony ship had come to this particular reality was as much a mystery as her own arrival had been.

"Where was he from? The First King?"

Sebastian shrugged. "There are many schools of thought, including one that says he came from nowhere at all. What we believe at this Temple is that he came from a Hidden Place, the True World, behind this world but never visible from it." He regarded her with a brief moment of pensive speculation. "It is a place we may one day return to, but not yet."

Kiedrych watched the group split up after the evening meal. Witch Magda had wandered off with the white-haired priest; her colleagues Leenan and Sylvia had found guides of their own. Even the witch-brat, Tephee, was with a Temple priest. Damned child was as moody as Tam's sister Myra had been. Well, Myra had grown out of it (he wondered for a moment if Myra and her family had survived, but that was still an insoluble worry, so he pushed the thought aside)—he supposed the witch-brat might as well.

Thinking of Myra made him think of Tam, and he glanced up to see the jester looking hurriedly away from him. His jaw clenched and he glared at the devious little spy; Tamalan hastily made an excuse to leave.

"I'm just . . . uh . . . you know . . . I drank a lot of wine. Got to . . ." He faltered and paused to look Kiedrych in the eye. "Kayla's just gone out for a breath of air. On the garden terrace."

"Has she?" Kiedrych asked icily.

"She really likes you, you know," he said, then scooted out before Kiedrych could grab hold of him.

Kiedrych frowned at Tamalan's retreating back and sat down again.

Kayla. Maddening woman. After the battle, Kiedrych and Tamalan had managed to join her on her flight from the field. The first thing they had done when they'd stopped for breath is have an argument about where to go next. That she had managed to successfully argue that the safest place for them, for a while at least, was with Ayman's Players, en route up the western coast at the foothills of the

Anatacci Mountains, was attributable as much to her stubbornness as the fact that she was right. Kiedrych, for a time, had been all for going back and murdering Saebert Bakar-Cadron, and then the King, if he wasn't dead already.

Maddening, yes. And stubborn. And unpredictable. She argued with him when she should be taking orders; didn't argue with him when he was prepared for resistance. On a quick mental tally, Kiedrych thought they had probably won about an equal share of their sporadic arguments, although sometimes she didn't lose so much as lose interest. Or she would suddenly change her mind, apologise, and, with an unwarranted and unexpected kiss on his cheek, let him win. Sometimes she didn't, and they'd have to bicker it out to the end. It was difficult to know what she was going to do at any given time. Sometimes that even made him look forward to the argument.

She was also intelligent, organised, and far too perceptive. She disconcerted him, and, strangely enough, calmed him—when he wasn't disagreeing with her. Even more so than Tam, she seemed to have the knack of diffusing his dangerous anger, and even making him smile. Having little in his life to smile about, this was certainly worthy of comment. Kiedrych wasn't sure if he'd come on this journey to claim some kind of restitution from his so-called King, or because he hadn't wanted Kayla and Tam to go without him.

Except that he certainly did want restitution. After what he'd lost . . . after what he'd done for the sake of a craven, faithless . . .

Kiedrych, jaws clenched, shied away from that train of thought, from the image of his wife which those memories conjured. Petite, blonde, beautiful, a voluptuous figure, eyes that sparked with sharp wit and a smile full of secrets. Full of lies.

And then, suddenly, drifting in from the terrace, he heard Kayla laugh, a bright and delighted sound devoid of derision or hidden meaning, and his mind's eye captured an image of long, slender limbs; the gentle sculpture of a dancer's muscles defining those long legs and flat stomach; the curve of her breasts and the hollow of her throat . . .

Kiedrych took a deep breath and held it for a moment. Oh yes, Kayla was beautiful, certainly, and vibrant, and intelligent. But then, Parsa had been all of those things too.

The young Arc Priest had made Kayla laugh with his wry commentary on the monastic life which he had recently taken up, but after dinner he could only step out to show her the terrace for a few moments before he was called back to his duty in the kitchens. Kayla meandered down the terrace and into the vegetable garden to wander between tall rows of bluefruit vines and corn. The sunset cast a brief, pale flush over the far end of the valley before fading into the half-light of twilight. It was pretty and Kayla tried to compose a song about it, but her thoughts were elsewhere and she gave up with a sigh. The sky darkened slowly and as Kayla watched the stars become visible, she heard someone come up behind her.

"Hi, Kiedrych."

"Hello. You have a good ear."

"My father taught me how to listen."

Kiedrych stepped a little closer, stopping just behind her left shoulder. "A pleasant evening."

"Yes. Nice it's not raining for a change."

"Yes."

So here we are, thought Kayla, *making ridiculous small talk about the weather. Just wonderful.*

"We start tomorrow."

"Thought we'd started already," she observed sourly. "I'm exhausted."

"There's worse ahead. One way or another."

"Thanks for the encouragement."

"You're welcome." Another long pause. They began to speak simultaneously, then silence again.

"Kayla . . ." Kiedrych was standing beside her now, both of them looking down the valley below. "Whatever we find, will you . . . stand by me?"

"I'm sworn to the King."

"That's not what I asked."

"If he's failed us . . ."

"Or if he hasn't."

"Stand by you? Follow your decision?"

"Will you?"

She swallowed, nodded. "I'll do that. But you have to promise you'll give him the benefit of the doubt. Give him every chance."

He hesitated, then his lips quirked in a brief smile. "I promise." He heard her sigh, saw her nod again, satisfied. Kiedrych reached out and briefly squeezed her hand, a pressure Kayla returned. Both casually forgot to let go as they kept their eyes on the darkening horizon.

His hand was warm and dry in hers, and she wondered what his palms would feel like against her shoulders . . . her back . . . Kayla began to feel as though she couldn't quite breathe with the agony of wondering. When Kiedrych released her hand and turned to go back inside, brushing against her arm as he did, she breathed in sharply. He stopped again, leaned close to her—she could feel his arm along the length of her own, his hip and leg just touching her, his breath as he spoke softly into her ear.

"Trust me."

"I do."

"Good." His beard was rough against her cheek, and the light touch of his lips on her temple, warm. A moment later she was alone in the garden, a gentle spring breeze ruffling her hair. She wished she had kissed him.

Chapter Eight

"I'd manage this better alone, thank you."

"Not after last time." Leenan's arms were folded and she eyed Sylvia sternly.

"I wasn't prepared for her last time, and I've no intention of using Tamalan for a focus, either. I need some solitude and peace . . ."

"We'll be very quiet," Magda assured her. "We'll stay back here and watch."

"I'll be on hand to help out if you need it," Tephee promised her.

Sylvia's lips compressed into a displeased frown. "Your concern is touching, but I'd ask you to remember that I've been doing this for a lot longer than the rest of you, and I don't need to be coddled."

"We're not going to coddle you. We're going to keep an eye on you." Leenan was being gently stubborn. "That's all. So if you want to get started before sun-up, you'd better start now."

Sylvia sighed and shook her head, acknowledging defeat. "Okay. Just don't interfere, hmm?"

It took her a few minutes to organise herself. First she put a small cushion on the ground and knelt on it, facing out across the valley. The view from this shelf of rock on the cliff face was enchanting. The Arc Temple was above them, the colours of its stone glowing in the first rays of the rising sun. The sun crept over the horizon and fingers of pale gold light reached along the valley and the parallel mountain ranges towards them. Sylvia, her long black hair falling loosely about her shoulders, arranged a few items before her: a lock of Kayla's hair; a drop of Tamalan's blood on a square of white silk; Kiedrych's silver ring, its flat red stone carved with a knot—his seal of rank as the Captain of the Castle Guard. Surrendered only slightly less reluctantly than extracting Tamalan's drop of blood.

Sylvia placed the lock of dark hair on the blood-stained silk, folded the material in half to make a triangle, and wound the ends of it through the ring, finally tying them through the loop of silver, making a small parcel of the items. She held this in her left palm, turned her face towards the sunlight, and dropped into a trance.

The jester's blood was the most important element here—the King's man and his kin as well, even if they didn't know it. This symbol enveloped the hair of a loyal subject, who was under the King's special protection as well, being his agent. The two of these bound and held together by the captain—his duty to the King, and his emotional ties to the others, too—held tight and unacknowledged. With these symbols of their ties to Armand and each other Sylvia could focus, through them, down into the valley and beyond into the desert kingdom where she had previously sensed the vanished King.

As she had done at Swiftfort, Sylvia immersed herself in the task, experiencing the smell, texture, taste, sound, and sight of the parcel in her head and with her blood, before finding the thread. She followed this, strung like gossamer lengthways down the valley. The mountains subsided and became hills. The valley widened into plains. The thread swooped down to a group of tents by the southernmost hills, to the people there, to a man with a scarred face, damaged body, and wounded heart soothing himself with the repetitive task of pounding grain on a flat stone with a sturdy rock, making flour.

The presence she had been waiting for came then. Sharp and bright, like hardened light, it attached itself to the thread that Sylvia was following. Forewarned this time, Sylvia braced herself and, dropping the thread, seized the sharp, bright thing. At first it hurt, but it wasn't real physical pain, after all, and she shrugged off the illusion of it. The texture of the mind behind the presence filtered through to her—outrage was foremost, but behind that were other forces. Ambition. Need. Protectiveness. An enormous capacity for power, but the urgent need to use magic constantly or risk pain, injury, or death from the energy that crackled around her aura. Tallan's strength was also her weakness, like Farshee's had been. But how to use that weakness? Sylvia felt herself being probed in much the same way and sent a buzz of babble into the other's mind—snatches of song and poetry and gibberish of images and sound. She could feel Zuleika's confusion and growing anger and steeled herself for whatever Zuleika would do next.

The attack was so ferocious and came so fast Sylvia was almost taken by surprise. The bright, hard light that represented Zuleika Tallan speared towards her and into the centre of the star of gold light that was her own being on this plane. For a moment it took hold and in one frightening moment began to suck the light away—numb, cold darkness took its place. In the physical world Sylvia let out a brief, startled cry before she recovered and drew her starself into a tiny ball of light. She severed the spearhead of Tallan's probe, assimilated it, then used the extra strength it gave her to dive into Tallan's centre and expand further still, effectively pushing that extraordinary power out, and dissipating it: trying to separate the witch from her power.

Now, Sylvia's awareness thought, for the hard part.

Zuleika, shocked and taken off-guard by the counterattack, was unprepared for the pain when Sylvia's augmented power broke through to the physical world and wrapped her body in arcs of white lightning. She was still screaming, as much in fury as in pain, when Saebert threw the door of her chamber open and ran in, sword in hand.

He stopped abruptly when he saw her, cocooned in a moving network of electricity as she jerked and stumbled across the stone floor. Her long black hair was floating about her head, each hair stiff and alive with white light. Zuleika's dark brown eyes were wide, and her small mouth was stretched wide and round, emitting short, sharp screeches.

"No!" She twitched, jerked herself around and crashed into a wall. "No . . . you . . . don't . . ." Sparks of light were even arcing between her perfect teeth, and these flared as she clenched them. She uttered a shrill grunt, and another, opened her mouth to shout, then abruptly it was over. The fierce energy that had enveloped her vanished and she dropped to the floor amid the smell of scorched skin and hair.

Saebert called for servants to fetch the court surgeon before going carefully to her side and kneeling.

"Zuleika?" Silence. "Zuleika? Can you hear me?"

A dry croak came from her throat and he gave her a sip of water, trying to hold her blistered head without having to actually touch her. Her once beautiful pale skin was red and blistered. She drank a little, coughed.

"Leika, what happened?"

She shook her head, beckoning for more water instead.

"Oo . . . th. Ood," she murmured with her swollen tongue through cracked lips. He flinched and looked away at the sight, and her red-rimmed and lashless eyes burned with the betrayal.

He had recovered an expression of neutrality when he returned with some berries, but it hurt her to swallow. She sipped more water and lay, too exhausted and hurt to even whimper now, on the cold floor until the servant appeared with Craffen, the surgeon.

Saebert had to shift away so that Craffen could kneel beside the stricken witch. Her eyes regarded the surgeon closely as he examined her.

"It's bad," Craffen said, shaking his head sternly. "She's been burnt all over—look at her skin—her hair, for Lords' sake, it's almost all gone. I can't do much for her, you know. I'm no witch."

"What can you do then?" Saebert's voice was edged with warning.

Craffen shrugged his slight shoulders. "I can give her something for the pain. But I'm afraid there's not much hope for her recovery."

"Yes, all right. Do what you can." Saebert waved the servant from the room and checked the door was closed while Craffen knelt beside Zuleika. "Craffen . . . could you just . . ." He hesitated and came to crouch on the other side of her burnt body. "She was important to me. I want you to be sure there's nothing you can do." He took the surgeon's hands and guided them to Zuleika's wrists. "Please, do something. At least see if there is much life still in her."

Craffen clearly would have preferred not to, the way his fingers twitched and pulled away from the red, ruined flesh, but the king he'd chosen to support was watching him. He glanced at Saebert, then down at the witch's face. Her eyes ate into his. He felt her hands move and twist to wrap around his wrists, and tried to look at them, but those fierce eyes held him. A tingle in his arms warned him that something was going on, but he was mesmerised by those eyes, those once-beautiful brown eyes, now without lashes or eyebrows and the creamy skin singed and raw. No, wait. Oh, she had lashes. And her skin . . . not so bad really. Red, but not blistered. Pink, more than red, and quite smooth . . . no . . . pale and lovely. So . . . lovely . . . wicked, evil creature . . . but so . . . so . . .

There was a long moment of silence before Saebert spoke. "Are you all right now?"

Zuleika pushed the husk of the surgeon away from her and sat up smoothly. Her gown was a singed, torn mess, but her body was whole. She tilted her head slightly, first one way then the other, testing herself. She raised her right hand to inspect her fingers, palm, wrist, arm. She ran her hand over her breasts and stomach. Her fingers went to her head and came away smeared with ash and brittle strands of hair. Tears gathered but she forced a smile.

"I feel . . . better." She reached for the berries and saw the remains of a mutton leg, which she began to eat, ravenously.

"Good. What happened?"

She wiped grease from her chin with the back of her hand. "Someone is looking for your cousin." Her smile widened and became predatory. "No need to worry, Saebert." The look on her face brightened savagely. "We can still use that to our advantage."

"Hang on, Sylvia!" shouted Magda.

Ridiculous thing to say, Sylvia thought, under the circumstances. But her irritation soon ran out as she clung onto the cliff face. She wished she'd just killed Zuleika outright instead of attempting to burn out her witchcraft. That consideration for the witch's life had given her the opportunity to lash out and use the last of her strength to wrench Sylvia's body forward. If she'd been in a room, she would have been smashed against a wall, with bruises and a bloody nose but not much more to show for it. Instead, she had been flung over a cliff top and had found just enough remaining power to swoop against the cliffside and find foot- and hand-holds. After that, her strength left her and she simply had to hold on as she heard Leenan, Magda, and Tephee running across the rock to look over the edge. Magda had then given her a priceless piece of advice.

"I told you that you should have let me do it."

"Later, Tephee." *I haven't the breath for this. I'm going to fall . . .*

When her feet slipped on the narrow support, her hands refused to hold on any longer. It didn't feel like falling. More like floating. If only she could float all the way to the bottom, instead of plunging, smashing . . .

Her descent stopped abruptly as she felt a sharp tug on her shoulders and upper arms. Opening her eyes, she saw taloned feet hanging onto the cloth of her rough dress. One dragon at each shoulder, another flying above and coming in to take hold of the material at her waist, the last snagging at her hem. She managed to raise her head to see what was going on at the cliff top.

Magda had her hands outstretched, exerting all her energy to keep her teacher in the air. Beside her, Leenan seemed to be directing the dragons in their actions and yelling at Tephee at the same time.

"You've proven your point, Teph. You're the strongest and we need you, okay? Now do something, will you? I don't think the dragons can hold on forever. *Damn* you, help us!"

Tephee gestured towards her teacher, and Sylvia felt the downward pull lessen and her body drifted back to the cliff. Neither Magda nor Leenan, she noticed dimly, dropped their concentration for a moment. A moment later she felt cold stone under her and the dragons released their hold and flew off to the Temple walls. She could hear the others arguing.

"What was the point of all that, Teph? You could have killed her."

"I wouldn't have let that happen."

"Tephee," Magda was both weary and angry, "it was a stupid way to prove a point. It was childish and irresponsible. You want to show us how good you are—this isn't the way to do it."

"I wouldn't have let anything happen to her."

"You frightened her. And us. That's not how friends treat each other."

"I didn't mean to . . ."

"Not good enough, Teph," Leenan snapped. "You're not a kid anymore. Stop behaving like one."

Sylvia wished they'd stop fighting and give her something to eat. She was starving.

"Is he here then?" Kiedrych did not look at all impressed by the sight of three witches eating leftovers in the otherwise empty refectory. They were all pale, particularly Sylvia.

Sylvia nodded. "He's at the end of the valley, near the plains. Zuleika knows we've found him."

"Well, now, that presents a problem."

"I don't see that it does. She must have known for a long time where he was, roughly speaking."

"If she had no reason to act before, she does now."

"I don't believe that's her intent. I felt nothing in our contact that suggested it."

"You don't believe she does." Kiedrych frowned sourly at her. "That is a comfort."

Sylvia glared back. "Keep it to yourself, Captain. I've had a bad morning and I'm in a bad mood. Take your ring," she tossed it to him and he slipped it back onto his right hand, "and go. Pack the wagons or throw yourself off the mountain, but leave me be for a while, hmm? I've never turned anyone into a frog before, but you're tempting me."

Kiedrych waited long enough to give his departure some dignity. Kayla grinned at him as she was passing the door, tut-tutted, and waggled a finger. "Shouldn't make them cross, you know. I don't expect a frog would last long in the flatlands."

He favoured her with a hard stare, but she only smiled.

"Besides," she added, "I like you just the way you are."

"Oh, I don't know," he responded, his expression softening into a smile at last. "I think I look rather good in green."

Kayla's eyes sparkled, foolishly happy that she had made him smile. Once he'd gone on his way, she stuck her head into the room. "You asked if I'd seen Tephee," she said to the witches. "She's just gone up the western tower. She didn't look happy." She paused a moment and then, with the air of someone not sure if they've understood a joke, said: "You wouldn't really turn him into a frog, would you?"

Sylvia's mouth quirked mischievously. "No, of course

not. Pywych likes to catch them. But I do think he'd make a fetching cat."

Startled and no wiser, Kayla withdrew.

Tephee sat cross-legged on the eastern wall of the Temple as she regarded the view before her. *Magda's right. I was being childish. I was so mad with Sylvia for not taking me seriously. Not that anybody does.* She'd wanted to help: she was strong enough to do it, but no one would trust her. That hurt. Tephee sighed miserably. She didn't mean to keep making a mess of everything, but somehow that's all she did.

She frowned again. Surely it wasn't all her fault. Magda used to be on her side but now she spent all her time with Leenan; so now, like Leenan, Magda thought she was childish and silly. Sylvia wouldn't trust her. She didn't have any friends left.

Tephee heard the soft footfall on the steps but did not turn to face the intruder. "Have you come to lecture me again?"

"Not this time. Not much, anyway," said Sylvia. "Kayla saw you coming up. She said you looked unhappy."

"Bright lady."

"Want to talk to me about it?"

"No."

Tephee tracked the sound of Sylvia's footsteps to the wall a little way up on her left, and for a panicked moment wanted to call out for her to come back, that she was sorry and she did want to talk, but her pride seized her throat. For a short while, neither spoke. Tephee realised that Sylvia wasn't walking out on her after all.

"I didn't mean to scare you this morning, Sylvia," she said in a quiet voice.

"Yes, you did. I was just too exhausted to be properly frightened. If I hadn't been so drained, though, I could have saved myself."

"I wouldn't have let you fall. Not all the way."

Tephee was surprised to hear Sylvia laugh, and turned to look at her. She was smiling.

"Not all the way? Thanks a heap."

Tephee smiled sheepishly back. "Anyway, I'm sorry."

"You frightened Magda and Leenan more than me, you know. They're not as strong as we are. They thought they couldn't hold me."

"They did, though. I thought Leenan was terrific with the dragons."

"Animals are her special skill. Did you know that was why we're stronger? Many witches can do most things reasonably well, but usually have one particular skill. Leenan's is animals; Magda is a healer. You and I aren't restricted like that. We can do it all."

"Why don't you then? You hardly ever use magic, except for your water sculptures or unimportant things. Or the really big things. Even then, only if there's no other way to do it."

"That's not exactly right but, no, I don't use it much. I don't like to."

"Because of what happened with Farshee?"

A brief hesitation, then: "Yes. Because of what it made her become. There's a . . . a danger in becoming too reliant on power. There's a temptation to use it not only to do things but to make things happen. Selfish things." Sylvia drew in on her rising anxiety, calmed herself.

"The other reason is that it costs a witch to use her powers. It tires us. Sometimes it takes more energy to use magic than to do a thing the conventional way. The third reason is important too. We are witches, but we must never forget we are also mortal . . ."

"That's not what I was told."

"By whom? Your town elders? Your mother? There are an awful lot of myths about us that even witches can come to believe. We're just people, like everyone else, and more likely to die fairly young from wearing ourselves out with constant use of magic than to live as long as ordinary folk do. When we use magic all the time, it's easy to forget that before we were witches we were just people."

"People hate us." Tephee recalled vividly the look of naked fright with which her mother and siblings had regarded her, the last time she'd seen them. From her father's death, when her powers had first begun to show, her family and neighbours had come to look on her with increasing distrust and anxiety. She had come to hate that look. It hurt. But she couldn't change who or what she was; and she didn't want to. She liked having power. She liked being a witch. If people couldn't love her for who she was . . . well, Red Lord damn them, anyway.

"People don't understand us, and every time a witch uses her power to control or hurt others, we give them more reason to distrust us."

"I thought you said you weren't going to lecture me."

"Much."

"Hmm." Tephee unfolded herself and stood on the wall, glanced back at Sylvia, then stepped off the wall into space and dropped out of sight.

"Tephee!"

"Here." Tephee, arms hanging by her sides, rose up slowly from below the wall and hovered there. The wall was an armspan in front of her and the ground a long, long way below. In her eyes was a mixture of defiance and entreaty.

"We're not ordinary folk, Sylvia. I don't want to make them frightened, but I can't help being what I am."

"What are you?" Sylvia was unimpressed by the display, and felt her annoyance at Tephee's refusal to listen growing again.

Tephee sighed, almost inaudibly, and her mouth set in a hard line. "I'm just . . . me. Just Tephee." *No one special, to anyone.* She floated higher and stepped back onto the wall.

Chapter Nine

Magda stood at the back of the great hall she had first visited with Sebastian, listening to the service in progress. The priests stood in a horseshoe, facing the twisted relic which presided over them. Their chanting echoed from the vaulted ceiling and marble walls, high and low voices merging together to make a beautiful, incomprehensible sound. Sunlight shone through the skylights and high windows on each side of the Temple and all the Temple priests in their white tunics made her think of an old cathedral she had once seen. She could see Sebastian in the midst of the worshippers, his lined face sober and serene. She wished she'd had more time to talk to him.

The service finished and Sebastian came straight up to where she was waiting by the main door.

"I was hoping to talk to you again before you left," he said as he took her by the arm and walked her out into the courtyard.

"So was I, but I'm afraid we're about to leave. I just wanted to say goodbye. I hope I can see you again. I have a lot of questions for you."

"I'm sure you do. I have a lot myself. I feel . . ." He paused and tilted his head to one side as he looked at her. "I could be wrong, but I feel you may have much to teach us about the First King and the legend of the Arc."

"It's . . . possible."

Sebastian smiled knowingly. "You see," he expanded,

"from time to time the First King sends a visitor from the True World."

Magda blinked. "Visitors?"

"There are legends of two people from the True World who have come to us here, centuries apart. For what purpose, only the First King knows." He eyed her speculatively again. "Perhaps it's to do with your being a witch. Maybe you are meant to resolve the betrayal of the Red Lord at last." A crooked smile lightened his sombre expression. "Your presence here could be a vindication of this Temple's theology of forgiveness and acceptance." The puzzled furrow on his brow made the smile self-deprecating. "Well, I shall simply have to contain my curiosity until you pass this way again."

As always, his bright smile below sparkling blue eyes and silver-grey hair made her smile in return as she regained her composure. "The others say that you can pray for us," she said, changing the subject.

"We can ask the First King to watch over you and guard your journey."

"We need as much help as we can get."

"Perhaps. This man you're searching for, Armand Bakar-Tyne, is, by twists and turns, descended from Lord Tarek El Assad's line. One of the First King's Lords," he added at her blank look.

"Oh?"

"Indeed. It is one of the things that mark him as the rightful King. His cousin is of a different line."

"How do you know all this?"

"As the priests of the Arc, it is our business to know who carries the bloodline of the First King and his chosen Lords. We are secluded, but not uninterested in the world. We know what has happened in Tyne. We've been waiting for someone to come back and set it right."

"Will we do that? Will we succeed?"

"Only the First King knows for sure."

"Well," Magda stuck out her hand and shook Sebastian's warmly, "thank you for your hospitality. I'm . . . uh . . . I don't think I am what you think I am. I mean, I . . . I don't . . ." She was flustered. Her past had been such a strict secret, for fear of how others would react, that Sebastian's certainty that she came from the True World was disconcerting.

Sebastian reached out and patted her hand soothingly. "Your secrets are your own, Magda. Whatever the truth, I would like to speak with you again."

Magda smiled uncertainly. "I look forward to it, Sebastian."

"Safe journey."

Sebastian stood in the centre of the paved courtyard in the late morning sunshine and waved as Magda walked under the high-arched entrance to meet the others on the narrow roadway. She turned to wave back as she climbed into the wagon with Leenan, then all four carts began to wind their way down the path to the valley floor.

On reaching the valley, the first thing they did was to head south, along that arm of the mountains. Water wasn't yet scarce, but it wouldn't take long for the few rivers on this side of the range to dry up or disappear underground, and it was easier to find springs alongside the mountains. Kiedrych judged that it wouldn't take more than a few days to reach the campsite where Armand was currently living.

"The tribes here and in the flatlands were once allies of Tyne," Kiedrych explained to Sylvia as they travelled. "Armand's father, King Graym, was considered a friend by many of the local chiefs. I imagine they are giving the King shelter and protection at the moment. Whether or not they'd follow him into battle against the Witch and Saebert is another matter."

"I'm not sure he's fit for leading an army into battle," Sylvia told him. "He's badly scarred. I sensed other, greater injuries . . ."

"He was burnt the day Zuleika attacked the Council," Tamalan said, shuddering in memory. "Then he got an arrow in the arm and a . . ." He stopped abruptly, looked at Kiedrych with frightened eyes, and fell silent. Kayla arched an eyebrow inquiringly at him, and he shook his head. Kiedrych said nothing, but his eyes were dark with fury.

Kiedrych's reaction to such discussions discouraged open conversation, but as they journeyed towards an uncertain future, the more Kayla worried at the past—all those unknown things; the hidden things that would make sense of Kiedrych's anger and Tamalan's uneasiness.

Tamalan grew more nervous and Kayla often noticed that he became less inclined to speak to Kiedrych at all, merely watching him with furtive anxiety. As counterpoint to Tam's withdrawal, Kayla sat with Kiedrych whenever they stopped to rest, eat, or make camp. She rarely spoke to him—he hardly responded anyway—but as the Captain grew more and more taciturn, Kayla would simply reach out and touch his hand or lay her own briefly on his shoulder, and some of the black anger in him would subside.

Once, Tamalan sidled up to Kayla and muttered: "Maybe this wasn't such a bright idea, looking for the King. Kiedrych's going to skin him alive when we get there."

"A bit late for that now, isn't it?" she responded sourly. "You should have thought of what it would mean to him when we were back in Tunston."

"I did. I mean, I thought I did. He's been a mess for a long time . . ."

"And whose fault was that?"

"Strictly speaking, his wife's."

"Parsa was killed by the witch. How is her death . . . ?"

"That's not exactly what happened."

"She . . . uh . . ." a worrying thought occurred to her, "she's not still . . . alive . . . is she?"

"Oh, no, but Tallan didn't kill her, it was the night the King . . ." and here Tam faltered and became evasive, despite Kayla's best attempts to wheedle the story out of him.

"What were you two talking about?" Kiedrych appeared unexpectedly behind her when Tam had gone, and his cold suspicion made her curious.

That it should have alarmed her never occurred to her. She shrugged one shoulder gracefully. "At this stage, he's getting cold feet."

"It's a little late for that."

"Exactly what I told him. But . . ." Kayla took a breath and smiled up at him. "Damned if he isn't actually worried about you."

Kiedrych's grim expression didn't alter. "What else did he say?"

"Not much."

"It took him a long time to say it." Kiedrych's jaw was clenched, his whole face set rigidly.

Kayla regarded him steadily as fire flared in her own eyes. "You said I should trust you. I do. But if you can't trust me, or him, after all these months, then don't waste my time."

"What did he tell you?"

"Are you listening to me?"

"I want to know . . ."

"Fine," she interrupted fiercely, "Tam said he was afraid you'd hurt Armand. I tried to find out why and he wouldn't tell me. He didn't do or say anything else, and he was only thinking of you, you selfish, suspicious-minded, pig-headed bastard." She jabbed him in the chest with a long forefinger. "And if you could, for just one moment, forget how much you hate Armand, you might notice that Tam's your friend. Lords only know why, because you treat him like dirt."

"I do not . . ."

"Yes, you damn well do. Do you honestly think I didn't know you'd hit him—stop it! Don't," she jabbed the finger towards his nose as he made to interrupt her, "don't you dare. I don't know what it was about, and I expect you'd tell me it's not my business. But you do that to him, and he sticks by you, and you don't even have the sense to treat him as well as you'd treat your horse."

"Have you finished?"

"No." She caught the light of a smile in his eyes. "Yes. What's so damned funny?"

"Tam Fingal and I have a long history. We know where we stand with each other."

"Sure. You standing up, and him on the ground with a tooth knocked out."

"Oh, he still has all his teeth."

"This isn't funny, you know."

He sobered suddenly. "I know." Gently, he traced a line from her temple to her jawline with his thumb. "He knows I'll make it up to him. I get angry, but I look out for him."

"I don't understand the two of you."

"That's all right," he smiled faintly, "no one does."

Kayla swallowed, but her gaze did not waver from his.

"Kiedrych . . . what are you going to do to the King?"

He stiffened, but there was as much pain as anger in his voice when he spoke. "That depends on him."

"Remember your promise."

"Remember yours."

"I will. I may think you're a bad-tempered brute, but you've never let me down."

"I think you'll find Tam shares your opinion."

"Not of everything," she murmured. Now that she wasn't yelling at him, she found his proximity heady. Kayla experienced a sudden and overwhelming urge to lay her head against his chest and listen to his heartbeat.

She closed her eyes as his hand caressed her cheek and his fingers swept her hair back from her face. She felt his lips against her brow and leaned into the kiss. "Kiedrych . . ."

Their lips met, and for that short moment she savoured the sensation, until he drew back and walked away, leaving her breathless.

The valley had widened out into a grassy plain—vegetation was sparse, but recent rains had left the flat vista dotted with tender grass shoots and small plants. Off to the south, the hills shrank away to nothing and beyond that lay the true flatlands of desert. Overhead, the sky was a sunwashed blue with few clouds to divert the eye.

"Is that the camp?" Kayla shielded her eyes against the glare of the sun and tried to make out the details of the shapes ahead. The collection of tents and makeshift corrals was teeming with people and livestock, but from this distance it was hard to identify the group.

"I'm sure," Sylvia said.

"Wh . . . what now?" Tamalan had lost nearly all of his

earlier determination to find King Armand and was sitting as far away from Kiedrych as possible, almost curling in on himself.

"Now," Kiedrych said, his tone clipped, "now we go and see if our sworn King is worth all this trouble."

Kayla gazed ahead a moment more, then put down the reins and climbed down from her caravan. "Here, Tamalan, you take over for me. I want to sit up there."

Tam took her up on the suggestion with only the briefest glance darted towards Kiedrych. Kayla took his place next to the Captain and suffered his fierce glare.

"Remember your promise," she said quietly.

"There's nothing wrong with my memory," he snapped under his breath.

"I never said there was. I'm with you, Kiedrych," she reached out and rested her hand on his wrist, "whatever you decide. But you can hardly make an informed decision if you tear out his throat with your teeth on your first meeting. However much he deserves it."

He was surprised to note the steel behind that comment, and when he looked, he saw that her expression was as stony and grim as his own.

"All right. I'll give him one chance. Then I go for the throat."

She simply nodded, once.

Chapter Ten

The sun felt hot on his back and arms, but not unpleasant. The tickle of sweat collecting on his brow, under his dark curly hair, was distinctly more irritating, but Armand Bakar-Tyne derived a certain pleasure even from that. He was alive after all, and there were days when that still took him by surprise.

Armand was busy kneading bread dough, skilfully mixing water and flour, separating the portions, working them into flat disks over a convex metal pan to be put in the oven by old Hattie beside him. It was women's work, really, but he felt content with the repetitive but necessary task. Making bread didn't call for any special skills, and if he made it wrong, well, it was usually still edible.

El Ashraf Darem had once more suggested he join the men on the next hunt. Maybe he'd go this time. It had been nearly a whole cycle of seasons since . . . since he'd lost his crown (abandoned his kingdom, failed his people) and surely by now he should be physically up to it. Hattie's granddaughter, Dell, had even managed to restore some of the sight in his left eye, though she seemed to think the scarring would be permanent. Obviously she wasn't the witch that Zuleika Tallan was. That thought made him frown.

"Faster, 'Mand," admonished Hattie from behind the brightly coloured scarf that hid her face and hair from the sun and sand. "Lots to do. No time for dreaming, hmm?"

"Sorry, Hattie. Things on my mind."

"No doubt, but it's easier to think when there's enough to eat, eh?"

He smiled at her from behind his own headscarf, and her old blue eyes crinkled back at him.

The work was interrupted again ten minutes later when Darem's youngest boy scampered into view. "El Ashraf Armand . . ."

"Just Armand, Roli."

"My father says you're a chief like him."

"Once, maybe, but not now."

The boy shrugged his skinny shoulders and plucked at the slightly-too-big robe that promptly slid down his arm. "No matter to me, Armand, but Papa said you were to come. There are some people coming, and he wants to know if they are friends of yours."

"My friends are all here, Roli." Armand's solemn comment was spoilt by Hattie, who lobbed a round of bread dough at him.

"Don't be so bad-tempered," she scolded. "Poor little friendless Armand. Bah. Go see who they are. If they are friends, good, you could use some. If they aren't, Darem will slice their heads off. Nothing to lose, either way. Don't stare at me like that, insolent male. Roli, take the fool away to your father." With that she turned back to the breadmaking, ignoring both Armand's offended look and Roli's snigger.

Armand got to his feet with as much dignity as he could muster, teeth clenched against the expected spasm of pain, and followed the boy through the camp and up the gentle slope of the hill nearby, where El Ashraf Darem stood with five of his advisers.

"Out there," said Darem, handing over a telescope. "They look harmless enough—only two men . . ."

"Lords . . ." Armand lowered the telescope to blink, as though the deficiencies of his left eye had transferred to the right.

"What? What do you see?"

Armand raised the telescope again. "Dragons. I've never seen them this far north before. All those women travelling together—witches?"

"Perhaps. Do you recognise anyone?"

He squinted at the riotously coloured caravan, began to smile in recognition, but then he brought the lens to bear on the other covered van. He lowered the scope again, slowly.

Darem waited for Armand to continue, then prompted: "Who is it? I have some men armed and ready to go out to kill them or to bring them in. Which is it to be?"

"I . . . suppose they'd better come in. Tell them . . . to keep their eye on the two men."

"Are they enemies or not, Armand?"

"I don't know," the fallen King admitted. He sounded lost, somehow.

Darem gave the signal and he, Armand, and the advisers watched as the group of twenty rode out to meet the approaching strangers.

Armand hitched his robes more comfortably around his shoulders and adjusted his headgear so that his scars were better covered. "I don't want a guard."

"If they are enemies . . ."

"If they are . . ." Armand sighed. "Leave it to me, Darem. There's at least one there I can trust." Here he allowed himself a brief, self-mocking smile. "I'm just not sure which one." Then he set off down the hill towards the meeting circle, ahead of the camp chief, against current custom but out of an old habit. Darem, far from being insulted, thought it was a good sign.

Armand stood at the back of the meeting circle, his arms loose by his sides, as two of Darem's men guided the visitors into the area. They were on foot now, their wagons and animals held outside the camp by the young boys, who nervously eyed the nearby dragons but held their posts.

Four of the women were strangers to Armand, so he cast a scrutinising glance over them. The youngest, and shortest, had a pretty, round face framed by light brown hair. Her expression was hard to read—suspicion, curiosity, and wonder, among other things, were in her hazel eyes. The next tallest was also the oldest. She had long black hair, tied back, revealing a face made exotic by impish but elegant angles and piercing dark eyes which regarded him steadily. The third had boyishly-cut dark blonde hair and green eyes set in an oval face. She wore trousers and a green quilted jacket which hung open in this heat, revealing a simple white shirt. The attire was mannish, but the woman was not. She was guarded, but curious. The last was tall and lean, angular and graceful at the same time. Her mass of dark, wavy hair softened the sharpness of her cheekbones and her blue eyes gazed in frank curiosity all around her. No immediate threat from that quarter. Good.

Tamalan Fingal was clearly nervous, twisting his rings in a familiar old habit, but just as clearly determined to see this meeting through. Armand wondered if his sly little jester was behind this moment. He hung back behind the others. Tamalan was nearly as tall as the Captain, but somehow contrived to appear both much smaller and weaker than anyone else in the group. Armand didn't know if it was deliberate or a subconscious act that the jester always managed to stand near the tallest person in any gathering. Tam looked leaner and more worried, and had grown a goatee beard. His hair had grown long as well, drawn back in a tail that emphasised how it was starting to recede at the front. He was dressed drably, for Tamalan, in ochre trousers with a blue shirt, but there was some of his former flashiness in the coloured twine that held his hair back. Tamalan's brown eyes watched Armand with equal measure of need and anxiety.

Kayla—Ayman's daughter—looked well. Tall, athletic, her beautiful long black hair falling loosely about her shoulders, and her grey eyes—like Tam's, mixed. Angry, but not wanting to be angry. What was it about him that inspired such confused emotions in people?

He forced his attention back to the Captain, to meet his gaze. The Captain, as always, seemed much taller than he really was by virtue of his stiffly erect posture and the power of his feelings that seemed too large for his body to contain. Kiedrych Evenahn's most striking feature was still his brown eyes, now radiating a kind of heat of their own. He too had changed. His hair had grown long and he'd grown a beard which didn't suit him, but he kept it trimmed. He was dressed all in black, which must have been hot, but he didn't seem to notice; perhaps because his clothes were clearly too big for him. His dark eyes had a bruised look to them, as though he didn't sleep well. Armand knew that his own eyes were like that sometimes.

The eight of them simply stood there for a while, calculating the threat offered, the changes. Armand could imagine what kind of image he presented to them. The skin around his brown eyes lined with pain and fatigue; his formerly stocky body now thin to the point of emaciation. Hidden by the headcloth, his face, which had once been full-cheeked and had carried the hint of a second chin, was now gaunt. Scarred. He put a hand self-consciously to his headscarf, then dropped it, quickly.

Outside the circle Darem and his advisers watched, flanked by most of the twenty fighters. The youngest of the advisers—forty-year-old Aidan—muttered to his chief: "They look at each other like enemies."

"You and your wife look like that most of the time," said Darem easily, but his deep-set eyes were fixed sharply on the scene.

At last, Armand broke the hostile silence. "I hope you haven't come all this way, Captain, just to stare at me."

He saw the muscles in Evenahn's jaw clench, and the skin around his eyes tighten a fraction more. The Captain's silence continued.

"I have other things to do today. Come back when you have something to say." Armand turned his back on the Captain, and knew it for a mistake when he heard the scrape of a sword being drawn. He froze, ready, but nothing further happened. He heard Kayla say something fiercely under her breath, and the sword return to its scabbard. Armand could sense Darem's circle of warriors tense, waiting for his signal.

"We have business, King Armand." Evenahn's first words were ground out, the honorific title full of derision.

"You'll speak to me with more respect, Captain," he warned, turning back.

"When you've earned it."

"Don't you dare speak to me of earning respect. Not after that night . . ."

Both men were rigid with rage, Evenahn reaching for his sword, Armand for the knife he carried in the belt of his robe. Around them, desert warriors were reaching for the hilts of daggers and swords. Kayla and Tam stepped forward at almost the same time.

"Stop this! Highness, Kiedrych, please . . ." began Tam.

"Stop it!" shouted Kayla, striding out between them, but facing the King. "With all respect, King Armand, you owe us an explanation." She did not sound especially respectful.

Neither man moved.

"I said stop," she repeated angrily. "Kiedrych, you promised me. One chance. Let him have it."

Kiedrych's lip curled, blackly acknowledging her unintended double-meaning, but once more sheathed the sword. Darem gestured faintly to his men and they relaxed marginally.

"And you," she whirled to face her King. "Put that thing away and listen. You left us to fend for ourselves. We were ready to die for you!"

Her fury and despair stung him. He swallowed, closed his eyes, shook his head. "Thousands died for me. Be grateful you weren't among them."

"You left us on that battlefield! When we needed you, you weren't there!" Kayla was advancing on him, her fists clenched as her voice began to break.

"I called retreat."

"You ran!"

"I tried to save your lives!"

"You left us *behind*."

Armand was surprised when she struck his chest the first time, and then surprise left him and he stood unresisting as she struck him—chest, shoulders, face—with her open palms, then with fists, again, and again, and again. His scarf fell back, and she slapped his face hard enough to cut his mouth against his teeth. She drew her arm back to hit him again, and struggled when Tamalan grabbed her by the wrist.

"Kayla, no. Stop it . . . please. It's enough."

None of them seemed aware of the circle of warriors, poised once more at their weapons and held at bay by Darem's curt hand gestures.

Kayla was gasping for air between sobs. Finally, as Kiedrych walked up beside her, she looked up. Armand had backed out of the meeting ring and was half-leaning against the corner support of one of the tents. Blood smeared the corner of his mouth and his robes were in disarray. He wouldn't meet her shocked gaze, but stared morosely at the ground.

"Lords . . . Highness . . . I . . . oh . . ."

"It's all right," Armand said quietly. "Even a King is not above his duty. You have a right."

But she shook her head and cried.

"You didn't get that in the fire," said Tam suddenly. He pulled at Kiedrych's sleeve. "Look, Rych. He didn't get that in the fire."

Kiedrych, looking as though he was about to finish what Kayla had started, shook Tamalan off, but cast his glance where Tam pointed. The tip of a livid purple scar could just be seen rising from the King's stomach to his breastbone, where his robes had begun to part. Armand straightened suddenly, pulling the folds closer, and gave them a better opportunity to see his other scars.

The fire which had killed most of the Council had left its mark. The left side of Armand's face, from jaw to temple, was peculiarly misshapen and shiny. His left eye was almost pulled shut by the scar tissue that dragged his brow and eyelid down.

"Who healed that?" Kiedrych asked, lifting a finger idly towards the stomach wound.

"Dell. Afterwards."

"I'm surprised you made it off the battlefield."

"And thrilled. I can tell."

Kiedrych's lip curled in a snarl, but before either could take things further, Darem appeared between them, with his whole entourage. The camp leader made an impressive figure, his robes striped with rich, bright colours and his scarf pushed back from his face, revealing dark, coppery skin, close-cropped red-brown, curly hair and eyes so dark they were nearly black. He smiled, his white teeth giving the expression a predatory overtone.

"Welcome to our camp, Captain Evenahn." Darem recognised him now, though the Captain had changed enormously since their brief meeting many years ago during King Graym's reign. "Now that you have finished paying your . . . respects . . . to your King, you might wish to prepare your lodgings."

Kiedrych, being outnumbered, managed a strained and savage smile. "Of course, El Ashraf Darem."

"There will be a guard nearby," continued Darem civilly, "for your protection."

The Captain's smile widened even more wolfishly. "Better to give him the guard," he said, nodding sharply at Armand. Then he turned on his heel, leaving Tam and Kayla to follow in his wake back to the caravan. Armand watched them go with a mixture of guilt and relief, and allowed Darem to assist him to his tent.

Chapter Eleven

Kayla let herself into Kiedrych's caravan after a brief knock on the door and sat down on a low chest tucked in one corner. Tamalan was sitting on his mattress in the far right corner, his chin resting on his bent knees, hands clasped around his shins. He gave her a fleeting, irritated glance, then turned his attention back to Kiedrych.

Kiedrych was sitting on his own mattress, opposite Tam, his back against the wall and his legs crooked in front of him. He was inspecting the blade of a slim stiletto knife he usually kept in the chest.

The three of them sat that way in silence for some time. Tamalan sighed nervously. Kiedrych slid the blade back into its sheath with a soft "snick." Kayla twisted her long hair around and around a finger. Finally, she built up enough courage to speak.

"I'm sorry, Kiedrych. I . . . lost . . . I lost control."

"So you did." He looked up into her eyes and his tone softened. "We all did. But I thought we were going to give him a chance."

Kayla bit her lip and looked away, ashamed. "I wasn't trying to kill him," she muttered.

"Could have fooled me," snapped Tamalan. His irritation had grown and he glowered at her now. "What do you think you were doing? He's the King. Our King."

"I thought he'd abandoned us!"

"You could have just asked him! That's all. Just 'Highness, what happened? Why did you disappear?' By the First

King, did you see that scar? Did you see it?"

"We saw it, Tam," Kiedrych cut in, abruptly. "So he was cut on the field, called retreat. I presume he was brought here and their witch saw to him. Not much of a witch if the scar is still so . . ."

"Why didn't he try to contact us? Let us know he was alive?" Kayla sounded small and miserable. "Why didn't he look for us?"

"Why didn't we look for him sooner?" Tamalan countered. "We were fit enough. He obviously wasn't, not for a while. We took off and hid and licked our wounds for nearly a year. Why shouldn't he? He lost more than we did . . ." he trailed off and glanced quickly at Kiedrych. The Captain said nothing, but he was fingering the little knife again.

"He lost his kingdom," said Kayla.

"He thinks I helped to take it away," said Kiedrych. He shifted suddenly so that he was on his knee before her, one hand gripping the knife. Kayla nearly shrank from him—the power of his hard-checked anger was bruising. "You said you'd follow me."

She nodded weakly. "Yes."

His hand closed over hers, briefly, before he rose and departed without another word. The afternoon light spilled through the narrow doorframe. Tam's soft, friendly features had hardened into accusation, and Kayla soon hurried out, closing the door behind her.

The tent was as yet unguarded, Kiedrych was unimpressed to notice. When the King's safety had been his responsibility, such omissions had never been permitted. He raised the flap and stepped quietly inside. Armand was propped up against four large cushions, his brooding gaze bent on the interloper.

"Are you feeling better?" He tried to sound calm, conversational. The strain was hardly noticeable.

"Than what?" Armand asked. "Have you come to finish the job?"

A pause, considering. "No. I've come to give you back your kingdom."

"You can't give it to me, Evenahn. It isn't some bauble to wrap in a bow. Thousands died for me to lose it. How many will it take to win it back?"

"I don't think you quite understand. I don't care if you don't want it. I'm going to get it for you."

"How kind."

"You still think I plotted against you."

Armand's scarred face twisted into a snarl. "Of course you did."

"I didn't know what she was doing." Kiedrych's voice was still measured, but the effort required was audible now.

"I can't see how you couldn't have. Your wife was Zuleika Tallan's cousin."

"I killed her to save you." The pretence stripped away and his voice rose.

Armand's voice, rich and deep, boomed back. "I didn't see that. I saw you take a knife and use it against your King." Armand on his feet now and both ready once more to trade blows.

"You accused me of treason!" Kiedrych spat.

"I trusted you!"

"You never, *never,* trusted me."

Armand looked down at the thin-bladed knife that was held at his throat, and managed to look smug and resigned at the same time. "Any wonder?"

Kiedrych hesitated, withdrew the knife as he turned away. Armand watched the hunched back shudder slightly, slowly straighten, rigid as plate armour.

"You're going to get your title back, King Armand Bakar-Tyne," said Kiedrych without facing him. "Whatever it costs, and whether you want it or not. I. Did. Not. Betray. You."

"Parsa Evenahn did."

"She betrayed us all."

And then, Kiedrych was gone.

Armand paused in the sudden silence, then limped back to the cushions and eased himself down. He ached all over and his stomach was cramping up again. He seriously doubted he could sit on a horse for longer than fifteen minutes. Leading an army into battle against the likes of Tallan was not just unthinkable in its human cost—for him it was close enough to physically impossible.

The tent flap swung back again, letting a triangle of sunlight fall into the tent, then the shadows returned.

"I wondered if I might have a moment, King Armand?"

Armand cocked an eyebrow at his latest visitor. Perhaps he would have to get that guard from Darem after all. It was the eldest of the witches—though he could not have guessed exactly how old she was. He gestured gracefully towards the cushions.

"Be my guest. Excuse me if I don't get up."

"You still suffer from a lot of pain, I see." The witch folded easily onto the cushions opposite him. "Magda may be able to help with that. Healing is her specialty."

"I thought it was meant to be Dell's, too." He winced.

"Dell is possibly stronger, but I think Magda is more knowledgeable. I'll send her in later."

"And what's your name?"

"Sylvia." She smiled, inviting trust. "Your Highness . . . what do you plan to do now?"

"Hmph." Armand shifted to a less painful position.

"Perhaps you should ask Captain Evenahn. He seems to have made plans already."

"Oh. Do these plans involve retaking your kingdom, by any chance?"

"They seem to. He hasn't explained how he intends to deal with the witch yet."

"Ah. That's my job."

Armand regarded her coolly, with suspicion. "What are you getting out of this?"

"Peace of mind, perhaps. Future security. Zuleika Tallan isn't going to stop with Tyne. Once she has established her hold, she'll move on."

"And you're going to stop her."

"I've tried stopping her. I'm afraid . . . I'm afraid that I'll have to kill her."

"You'll still need an army."

"King Armand, I'm not asking for your permission, or cooperation, in this . . ."

"You're as bad as Evenahn, then."

"Am I? Maybe I am, at that. I don't know what he's offering you, but I can tell you what I'm doing. I'm going to do something about Zuleika Tallan—if I can do it without killing anyone, so much the better, but I'll do whatever I must. I'm not really interested in what happens next. Once Zuleika is gone, I don't care if Saebert Bakar-Cadron is king, or if you are. Nothing personal," she added at his sardonic look, "it's just that my concern is a witch abusing her power. What the rest of you do is not for me to meddle in."

"So—Evenahn's deal is, ostensibly, to drag me, kicking and screaming, onto the throne. Your plan is to create a power vacuum and let nature take its course."

"I'd say that covers it."

"And with you on our side, it'll be easy."

"Oh, no, King Armand. I never said that. I'll do my best, but I can't protect everyone. As you've just pointed out, we need an army as well as witches, and people will die. But more will die, in the long run, if I don't act."

"You're offering me a choice, then, while my captain gives me an ultimatum."

"Yes."

"I'll think about it."

"Fine." She nodded, apparently happy with the outcome, nimbly unfolded herself, and stood up. "I'll ask Magda to come in. She could use the practice."

Armand wondered how seriously he should take the mischievous grin she gave him before she disappeared outside.

Magda returned to the wagons just before sunset, and carefully stowed the blanket-covered box she held in the cart. "That man is a mess," she grumbled. "He's been stuck back together by a lot of willpower and almost no anatomical knowledge."

"Were you able to help?" asked Sylvia.

"I've started work on that belly wound," she reported, "and regenerated fresh tissues, but it's tricky. I think he's going to need surgery. I don't know yet if I can do it with what I have or if magic would be better."

"I'll do it," volunteered Tephee at once.

"I hardly think that's your field, Tephee," said Magda sharply.

"I was only trying to help. Besides, I can do anything," Tephee protested. She was looking wounded and trying not to pout.

"Terrific. Do it then. All my training is obviously pointless with you around," said Magda tersely. "I'll go and start dinner with Leenan. Unless you want to do that too."

Tephee grimaced at her. "Sure. How about chicken?"

"Tephee, stop it." Magda's blue eyes flared with rare anger. "Stop doing this to us."

"Doing what?"

"Acting like you're . . ."

"Stronger than you are? More able than you are?" She was fuming. They were just jealous of her. That's all.

"Better than we are. Superior. You have more power but it doesn't mean you have to, or can, do everything!"

"I *can* do everything!"

"So you keep saying!"

"Both of you—stop it!" Sylvia did not shout over them, but her quiet anger silenced them both. "By the Lords, I think one warring faction among us is enough, don't you?"

The awkward silence was breached when Leenan appeared with a laden dinner pot and an exasperated expression. "Tephee, thanks for the meal, but I was looking forward to cooking tonight. I can cook you know. No magic required. I like to do it."

"But I can do it so much faster," Tephee tried to explain.

"Doing magic makes you hungry, so you use magic to make food? Even I managed to work out that much math, Tephee. Besides, for some of us, the time it takes is half the fun."

"Oh." Tephee was crestfallen. "I'm sorry. I just wanted to help."

"I know. But you should find out if we need it first."

Tephee nodded miserably. "All right. I'm sorry . . ."

"S'okay. Tastes pretty good, really." Leenan tapped the girl under the chin with the end of the wooden spoon. "But tomorrow you get my cooking, deal?"

"As long as it isn't beans and liver again." Tephee managed to raise a small smile.

Leenan looked wounded. "That's one of my best recipes. Uncle Eli loved it."

"I think," said Magda, relieved that the moment had passed, "your Uncle Eli may have been excessively polite."

After the meal, Magda stopped to see how Armand was faring, but his tent was empty. Occasionally she saw the women of the group, shrouded in large sheets of bright cloth, watching her with a certain amount of scandalised curiosity as they went about their tasks. She must appear a brazen creature, Magda realised with a smile—her ankles and shins showing beneath her skirts, forearms bare to the world, and her hair and face right out there where simply anyone could see. Or maybe they just wondered how anyone could bear to expose her hair and skin to all the damned dust, sun, and sand out here. Considering that both men and women covered themselves up in this climate, perhaps that was the answer. Having to live and work in the sand dunes, where water was much too precious a commodity to actually bathe in, people had to use something to keep the dust and sand away. A strong urge to jump into a river and bathe for an hour gripped her from top to toe.

God, she felt dirty. The one thing she really missed, she decided, more than her music collection, the view from SolOrbit, and even chocolate, was a steaming hot shower every single morning. How sad that she hadn't appreciated the pure luxury of it while hot showers had been available.

"Where were you at dinner?"

"Hmm? Hi Tam. We had our own. Why?"

"El Ashraf Darem wondered where you were. He hasn't offended you or anything, has he?"

"Heavens, no! We just . . . oh dear, we haven't offended him now, have we? I mean, we didn't think!"

Tamalan patted her arm, soothing her agitation. "Just tell him you had secret witch stuff to do."

"But we didn't."

"He doesn't know that. Come on." Tam grinned cheekily at her. "You could say you were brewing up frogs' toes as a good luck charm."

"Or newts' eyes," she laughed, "to ward off evil."

"Dragons' breath and a peddler's kneecap to bring the rain."

"The hair of a man who's seen the sun at night, mixed with dew collected in a desert at midnight . . ." Magda improvised.

"Folded in a silk purse made from cobwebs . . ." Tam added.

"And immersed in the tears of a virgin . . ."

"Lords—it's harder to find one of those than the hair!"

They were both laughing by now. "What's it all for, anyway?" Tam asked.

"Oh, I don't know. A cure for the common cold?"

"Or a love potion."

"Could be. A pretty strange kind of love, if you ask me."

"Yeah, well, a lot of love is, don't you think?"

"Maybe." Magda sobered a little. He really is cute, she thought. He has a nice mouth—always smiling. His eyes are very attractive too. Expressive. So are his hands, come to that. Long, artistic fingers. No wonder he's such a good stage magician. I'll bet he's good at a lot of things . . .

"Magda?"

She shook herself out of her daydreams and smiled guiltily.

"Is everything all right?"

She nodded.

"It's just that you were staring."

"Oh, just thinking. Witch stuff. You know." Magda cleared her throat and rubbed her arms. "I'd better be going. It's getting chilly. G'night."

Magda hurried off, and Tam's brows drew together in puzzlement.

Chapter Twelve

Lamplight flickered within El Ashraf Darem's tent, illuminating the centre but leaving corners shifting in shadow. Darem sat cross-legged on a pile of embroidered pillows and sipped wine from a silver goblet. Opposite him, Armand sat with his left leg crooked in front and his right bent up, his knee supporting his arm.

"You seem in good spirits," Darem commented.

"I am. Witch Magda has been working on me." Armand waved his left hand over the line of his stomach scar. "All respect to Dell—she saved my life—but Witch Magda has surer hands." She also had some Arc artefacts which looked strange in the hands of a witch. She seemed to know what she was doing with them. "At any rate, this is the first night since the battle that I have not felt some kind of pain."

"I am pleased for you. Perhaps she can do something for your sight."

"She suggested she might." Armand shrugged slightly. "I can see well enough, though, and I'm happy simply to be able to share your excellent wine at last." He raised his own goblet and drank from it.

"Do you feel up to speaking of business?"

"I feel up to climbing mountains tonight," Armand grinned. "But business? Oh well, I think I can manage. I take it Kiedrych Evenahn has been talking to you."

Darem nodded, the lamplight casting strange shadows on his face and adding burnished fire to his brown skin. "He claims that with these four witches, he can take back your castle and kingdom."

"With a little help from an army, of course."

"Of course. I said I would be willing, provided the army was led by you."

"What did he say to that?"

"Funnily enough, he agreed, but said it couldn't be counted on. He seemed to think that you weren't interested in taking back your kingdom."

"Let's just say I am reluctant to place my faith in Evenahn." Armand leaned towards Darem. "I admit that earlier today, I was not particularly interested in being Evenahn's figurehead. For all I know, he wants the crown for himself. But since then I have had dealings with the witches."

"You believe the word of a witch over that of your own Guard Captain?"

Put like that, it did seem ludicrous. Still, Armand nodded.

Darem's mouth twitched in disapproval. "It was a witch that took your kingdom in the first place."

"And a witch that saved my life. And now a witch that has freed me from pain. And a witch who has promised me her help. I have had more to trust in witches than I have had in my own military advisers."

"Captain Evenahn strikes me as a capable soldier."

"I expect he does." Armand fell silent. Darem refilled their goblets and waited. Armand sighed. "I can deal with Evenahn and his personal agenda later. He'll help us to regain the kingdom."

"So you do want it back, then?"

Armand paused before replying. "For the first time, I feel that it might be possible. That I might live long enough to make it worthwhile. I still have reservations." He looked up directly into Darem's brown-eyed scrutiny. "I won't ask you all to die for me. Enough have done that."

"There is no need to ask. We offer."

"You don't owe me that."

"No," agreed Darem, "we don't. But apart from the long friendship shared by our fathers, and ourselves," he smiled warmly at Armand, "there is also the distinct probability that Zuleika Tallan and Saebert Bakar-Cadron have no intention of limiting their ambitions to your kingdom. The mountains make it difficult to move south. Resistance from the west would be reinforced by those fanatics on Marin-Kuta. I think they will move north, in our direction. I personally feel it is better to take the war to them while they are still settling their net over Tyne, than wait for them to feel strong enough to come to us."

"You feel so sure of that?" Armand appraised his old friend with wry certainty. "There's nothing else that might be stirring your motivations?"

A knowing grin spread across Darem's face. "Why, what else could there be?"

"That old matter of the Eastern Flatlands and the trade route to Henatith, for a start."

"I'll admit, some help would be appreciated. Those Eastern sand-pirates deserve a drubbing, and we could use the land . . ."

"Naturally." Armand shook his head slowly. "Where do you think I'd find the army for that?"

"The tribes here are willing to wait for Tyne to recover from its misfortunes, of course. The trade routes are another matter, though—trading at the border isn't enough. Our people want the right to travel through Tyne and establish a centre at Henatith itself. We will undertake, of course, the responsibility for the traders' actions. They will not raid the farms and villages on the way through."

"You've put a lot of thought into this in one afternoon, Darem," Armand suggested gruffly.

Darem laughed. "Armand, old friend, I have simply been waiting for you to catch up with me."

"How many of the other Ashrafs have you been talking to?"

"Oh," Darem gestured deprecatingly, "twenty or twenty-five."

"Have I been that slow?"

"Understandable, given your injuries."

"So, how big is our potential army?"

"Two and a half thousand warriors," Darem answered promptly, "all armed and waiting for your word."

A wry grin flitted across Armand's lips. "A guaranteed trade route doesn't pose much of a problem. Perhaps we could discuss the Eastern Flatlands later. You have the strategy at hand, I take it."

"And drawn up," Darem grinned back, producing a large rolled parchment from behind the pillows. "Bring a lamp closer and we'll go over it."

"I really have been slow. Did you know all along I'd be ready for this eventually?"

"Of course. In your heart, Armand, you are a King, not a breadmaker."

They bent over the map and discussed Darem's ideas, until the headache brought on by Armand's bad eye reached the point where he could no longer see out of either one. Darem called for one of his sons to lead the King back to his tent.

"Rest well, my friend. We have a lot to do in the coming days."

Armand nodded gingerly, and allowed the boy, Tamar, to take his hand and lead him through the camp.

⋆ ⋆ ⋆ ⋆ ⋆

Magda had chosen magic over surgery in the end. The equipment she really needed for it had been too bulky to carry on the shuttle, leaving her with only a few pieces of emergency longlifes—an analyzer, the replicator, and a box of handheld diagnostic and first aid units. It was as well the batteries of those were designed to last several lifetimes. The replicator could have produced the necessary drugs and some primitive equipment, but the surgery required would have been both risky and debilitating. In any case, it would be a good clinical test of how much she could do with her power. A strong local anaesthetic had been administered to him, however, just in case.

She submerged herself in the blood and tissues, forcing them back into their original patterns, sometimes with slow deliberation, sometimes with necessary and painful rapidity. It was like unravelling a puzzle, block by block, and she had to withdraw by stages.

"How does that feel?" Magda sat back unsteadily on her haunches.

"Better. What did you . . . ?" Armand pulled himself up to look. His stomach, still tingling with warmth and new skin, showed little sign of the livid purple scar that had run from above his navel to the lower tip of his breastbone. "Oh."

"I . . . think . . . have you got anything to eat?" Magda swayed. Armand was shocked to see that she was about to faint.

"I'm sorry . . ." He fought down the urge to apologise further for tiring her so. "Here, lie down." He helped her down on the cushions and brought her the remains of his largely untouched breakfast. He watched while she ate, her hands shaking and colour gradually returning to her cheeks.

At last he asked: "Are you okay now?"

Magda nodded. "It's a big job," she admitted. "Your internal injuries were incredible. I wouldn't have given you another year, frankly."

"I see." A peculiar blankness settled over Armand's expression.

"Oh god, I'm sorry. Not thinking. You're fine now." Magda struggled to sit up, then paused, panting. "I'll bet you've had an awful year. Must've hurt like hell. Where the blade sliced you, Dell ended up connecting mismatched ends of your intestines . . ." She noted his discomfort once more. "Let's just say she had some of your plumbing in loops. It's all fixed now. I've regrown the severed section of your pancreas, corrected the misalignment of the stomach wall, and . . . you don't really want to hear all of this, do you?"

"I'm not even sure what some of it is," he admitted sheepishly.

"I feel a bit better now. Do you still have that headache?"

"I'll live."

"That you will. I'll see you tomorrow, Armand. You'll be good as new in no time."

The view from the hilltop was spectacular—to one side the hills rose to mountains in a long line, like the jagged back of a great sleeping animal. In the distance a purple smudge indicated the other arm of the ranges extending to the north. Between them, as behind and around, a great flat nothing. The Flatlands.

Leenan felt very small on this great disk of the world, and very exposed. She had come up here to escape the mass of strangers down there at the camp, to find some time and a place for herself, only to find loneliness instead. A sudden longing for Uncle Eli gripped her, for the village of Scipp and all the security wrapped up in the smell of her old room.

Alard whined and heaved himself across her feet and looked up at her with his eyes the very soul of yearning. With a wry, teary smile Leenan tugged on his ears. He thumped his tail happily on the ground and panted up at her.

At first she did not recognise the figure toiling up the hill towards her, but Alard's ears cocked with interest and he barked a friendly welcome. Leenan watched Magda climb the hill, her resentment at the intrusion giving way to relief that she was not, after all, completely alone.

Magda sat beside her and wordlessly offered the flask and some dough-cakes. Leenan took them, breaking the fruit-studded and sun-hardened biscuit dough to share with Alard. She poured water from a flask into the palm of her hand from which he lapped noisily, then wiped it on her trousers.

Magda sighed. "I wish I had an LR-52 Servo-Surgeon with me. That was exhausting."

"A what?"

"Never mind."

Leenan shrugged and returned to her silent scrutiny of the horizon.

Magda started to say something, decided against it, spoke anyway. "Do you want to talk about it?"

Leenan sighed. "Is it that obvious?"

Magda shrugged. "Maybe I can help."

"I doubt it." Leenan propped her chin up on her palm. "I just don't know what we're doing here."

"Sylvia's here to stop a witch gone bad. Tephee's here to

prove that she can do it instead, and probably better. I'm here because . . ." Magda sighed. "Because it seemed like a good idea at the time. Because I thought it might be interesting."

"Because it was an adventure, and a chance to go out into the world and be witches." Leenan snorted her derision. "Because we didn't think an awful lot about it."

"I guess not."

"I keep thinking of Uncle Eli. He doesn't even know I'm here. He sent me off to a coven to be a witch, and now I'm in the middle of a desert with a bunch of strangers, preparing for war. If something happens to me out here, he'll never know."

Magda regarded Leenan with sympathy. "I forget what it must be like for you. I haven't got any family . . ."

"No parents? Cousins?"

"No one." Magda shrugged. "I grew up with the One-Child law. The only relatives anyone had were their parents and grandparents, and all of those died before I was twenty." She cocked her head to give Leenan a crooked smile. "Things are different now, though. Sylvia, Tephee, and you are the only family I've had in a long time. I guess that's why I came, in the end. I didn't want to be left behind and alone."

"You make me feel ungrateful."

"I don't mean to. There's no need to be. There shouldn't be any limit on how many people you can love. I'm sorry that you miss your uncle."

Leenan fidgeted and scratched Alard behind his ears. The dog made little grunts of pleasure and lifted his head so she could scratch under his chin. "I do miss Uncle Eli, but to be honest, that's not all. This battle . . . this witch who keeps attacking Sylvia . . ."

"I know."

"Do you? I keep wondering if I'm going to be much use to anyone. Sylvia and Tephee are both powerful witches."

"You're stronger than I am."

"But at least you're a healer. How much help is someone who can talk to animals?"

"Use your imagination—I'm sure you'll think of something."

"But do I really want to? Maggie—I don't want to kill anyone."

"Neither do I, Lee. I don't think I could. It's against everything that's in me. I'm a doct . . . a healer. It's always been my job to save lives." She slid her arm around Leenan's shoulder and gave her a hug. "So that's what we can do. We can find ways to minimise the bloodshed. You know," she said, straightening up, "there's no reason you can't be a healer too. A little anatomical training, a little knowledge of physiognomy and nerve structures . . . are you a good student?"

"I suppose so. Maggie, slow down."

"In a minute. Can you conjure us some paper and a pen? Thanks. Here, this is the basic human body, okay . . ." Magda swiftly covered the paper with diagrams. Leenan, swept along by her friend's enthusiasm, was soon engulfed in Basic Anatomy, Session One. Engrossed by pictures of parts of the body she had never suspected actually existed, Leenan forgot her melancholy.

"But how," she was asking Magda later in the afternoon, "can you tell the veins from the arteries when you're actually looking at them?"

Magda's answer was forestalled by a commotion down in the valley, to the west of the camp. The women put the paper and pencils on the bare ground beside them and stood up to better see. Alard had leapt to his feet and was poised, sniffing the air, with his ears and tail both erect.

A wall of sand had sprung up out of nowhere, spinning madly around a central point not far from the camp. Among the tents, Leenan could make out the robed women pulling cloth over their mouths and noses before seizing children and flinging them into nearby tents. This action did not dull the sound of their shrill wailing as they ran through the camp, giving their warning and sending the young ones into safety. The flap of the meeting tent was flung violently aside as first Darem, then Armand, followed by Kiedrych, Sylvia, and an assortment of advisers, came out into the daylight. Darem looked into the sky, shook his head, and turned to shout at Sylvia. Sylvia accepted the angry admonishment serenely, but walked away from El Ashraf as it was still in progress.

"Can you see Tephee anywhere?" Magda asked Leenan warily. Leenan's eyes met hers, and they both headed back down the hill at a run.

They joined the gathering crowd at the fringe of the camp to see Sylvia walking towards the sandstorm.

"What's she up to now?" muttered Leenan. Magda simply shook her head and shouldered past the crowd to get a better view.

Sylvia muttered something, raised her hands, and the sandstorm began to abate. As the unnaturally-contained winds died down and the sand settled, a small figure became visible through the flying grains. She wasn't fighting against Sylvia's control, but stood with her arms folded as the world settled to stillness around her.

With silence settling over the camp, Darem strode forward to stand beside Sylvia.

"What was that in aid of?" he growled at Tephee.

"You said you didn't think we could do it . . ."

Sylvia was incredulous. "You were eavesdropping?"

"You left me out of the meeting. I'm involved in this, we all are, and you're excluding us." Defiant; defensive. "You're a damned hypocrite, Sylvia. You keep telling me I shouldn't do it all, even though I can. You tell me and tell me that, but look at yourself! I don't know why we came with you at all, because you want to do this alone!"

"If you want to argue ethics with me, fine, but that doesn't excuse you eavesdropping on our conferences or frightening people half to death. Do you have any idea what a sandstorm means to the people who live here?"

"What better way to show what we can do?" Tephee turned to Darem. "We're strong enough. Plan what you need to around that."

Darem wasn't moved. "So you have power. Have you any control? Can you be trusted? Frankly, you don't inspire me."

Tephee's smile was cold, hardly hiding her disappointment. "We're the best you have."

"Hold your tongue, girl," snapped Sylvia. "Do you honestly think you're helping? Have you ever listened to a word I've said?"

"I'm sick of you telling me what to do! You're not my mother! I'm in charge of my own life, and I'll run it the way I want to. If I want to use magic for everything, I will. If I die young, I die. But it'll be my life, my decision. Keep out of it!"

"If you don't want to be treated like a child, stop behaving like one." Sylvia folded her arms and glared. "Because I'm getting tired of your tantrums."

"Are you now?" Tephee regarded Sylvia coldly, her back rigid, her arms folded in front of her like a shield. "Maybe you'd rather I wasn't with you at all."

"I'd rather you listened to me once in a while. And that you'd take your responsibilities more seriously."

Leenan frowned to hear the two of them. Tephee, she saw, was flushed with anger, but her lip trembled and her eyes shone with repressed tears. *Grow up, girl,* she thought irritably. *There are bigger things than you wanting to strut your stuff.*

"Please, Tephee," began Sylvia, the voice of calm and reason.

"You never wanted me here in the first place," spat Tephee in a voice of hostility and grief. With that, she snapped around and strode away with those distance-eating steps.

Magda tried to follow, only to find Sylvia's hand on her forearm. She turned on her. "Oh, well done," she snapped. "Beautifully handled, oh wise one."

"I never said I was wise," Sylvia shot back. "I never said I was perfect, either."

"She won't listen to reason," interrupted Leenan. "Maybe it's time we stopped coddling her. She keeps telling us she's not a child, so we have to stop treating her like one."

"You don't know what she could become!"

"You don't know what she's been through, Sylvia," Magda replied.

Sylvia looked as though she might add more, but realised belatedly that Darem, Armand, and the others were observing with intense and worried interest. Sylvia took a breath to calm her nerves and turned to the Ashraf. "I think Tephee has amply demonstrated the power at our disposal. She started that storm, I stopped it. Are you convinced?"

"Of that much," Darem said carefully, "yes. I am."

"Good. You can rely on us to do our part. You do yours." She strode away, not quite running, with Magda and Leenan close behind.

Chapter Thirteen

That evening Kayla waited by Kiedrych's caravan, chewing anxiously on her nails. She had been too ashamed to approach King Armand after her outburst, even to apologise. Tamalan still wasn't talking to her, and neither, it appeared, was Kiedrych—though to be fair, he wasn't talking to anyone much. But it was only his silence that made her feel bereft.

A footfall alerted her to Kiedrych's approach, and she sat straighter on the stool. He looked tired and uncommunicative. She smiled anyway.

"Hi, Rych. How is it going?"

He seemed surprised by her presence, and only frowned.

"That good, huh?"

"We leave in a week. Darem claims the tribes need that long to mobilise."

"The King is coming with us? Willingly, I mean."

Kiedrych's mouth drew into a deeper frown. "So it seems."

Kayla rose and stood before him, her hands clasped demurely in front of her and her posture erect. "What do you need me to do?"

"Keep out of the way." Kiedrych pushed past her and strode towards his van. Kayla bit her lip and watched him go. She was still there a moment later when she heard a brief, bad-tempered exchange from within the caravan and Tamalan appeared on the van steps. He was clutching a blanket and his shoes. When he saw Kayla he drew up from his nervous hunch and cleared his throat.

"He wants to be alone."

"I gathered," Kayla replied. She hesitated for a moment, then: "Are you still angry with me, Tam?"

His eyebrows rose in a "who, me?" expression, but at her earnest gaze, his mouth crooked wryly. "Nah. I never can stay mad at anyone for long. It's the secret of my success with Kiedrych." He grinned and stepped down to the ground, trailing the blanket behind him. "Since I'm not mad now, do you want to let me stay in your van tonight? No, no, not with you!" he amended quickly, "I mean, there's a spare bed in there now," he nodded back toward his own van, "and I'm pretty sure you'd be more welcome to it than I am."

Kayla sighed. "Don't count on it. Kiedrych is in a funny mood."

"All Kiedrych's moods are funny. Oh well," Tam sighed theatrically, "looks like I sleep under a wagon tonight. Or maybe the King will let me sleep in his tent. When I was young, just learning to be a jester from my grandfather, I sometimes used to sleep in King Graym's room, by the door. I think," Tam confided softly, "any prospective assassin was meant to trip over me before they got to the King."

"Did anyone ever try?"

"No. Though once a visiting prince's wife got a shock when she tried to sneak in. Without invitation, apparently, or I'd have been sent down to sleep in the kitchen. This was after Armand was sent away to university."

"You've known them both a long time, haven't you?" Kayla said softly.

"Kiedrych and the King?" Tamalan shrugged. "Since we were children, I guess. Though back then I knew Kiedrych a lot better than I knew Armand. As a prince, he was always going off to other courts to learn things. Grandfather said King Graym found it painful to be with him, after Queen Alyce died in childbirth."

"What was Kiedrych like . . . as a child?"

"Pretty much like he is now," said Tamalan, "but less talkative."

"Did he bully you then too?"

Tam's expression hardened. "Rych and me go back a long way. Don't think you know everything about him."

"Oh, Tam, don't get mad again," she admonished him. "I'm in love with the sod, I can't help wanting to find out more about him."

"Like why he's such a sod, you mean? Well, don't ask me. He wouldn't appreciate my talking about it."

"His whole life seems to be like that. It's driving me crazy! Everyone knows why except me!"

"On the contrary, no one knows but me and him. He'll tell you when he's ready. Or maybe I will, after all. Not tonight, though. He's wild enough with me just for bringing us here."

"At least you don't sound surprised. I wish I knew what you'd expected from all this. You started it all, and now you hide all day."

Tamalan shifted uncomfortably and took a moment to fetch up his blanket, dangling in the sand. "They haven't killed each other yet," he mumbled. "That's about what I expected. Better, really."

"You thought Kiedrych would kill him?"

Tamalan coughed nervously and stared at his feet. "Thought he *might.*"

"Lords, Tam, what were you thinking of? What if he had?"

"He didn't. Good job, too. Poor bastard's messed in the

head enough as it is, without that on his plate."

Kayla had never heard anyone refer to Kiedrych as a "poor bastard" before. Coming from Tam, she thought she perhaps hadn't heard it properly. "You feel sorry for him?"

"Wouldn't say that, exactly. I know him too well. It's just," he looked at her, judging whether or not to continue, then shrugged, "he's not at peace with himself. And that business with Parsa, and Armand, just made it all worse."

"I wish you'd tell me what that business was."

The jester cast a quick glance back at the caravan, and his voice dropped to a whisper. "Parsa . . . no one knew much about her, and no one should have trusted her—we didn't find out who she was until too late. Kiedrych was covering the retreat. He saw a bowman waiting as the King was escaping, arrow notched, and he didn't have time to think. He threw his dagger as her arrow flew, and didn't realise until he got to the body that he'd just killed his wife."

"By the First King," Kayla's eyes were wide, "Lords . . . Kiedrych . . ."

"Parsa's arrow had hit the King—cut his arm, nothing too serious—but he found them and jumped to conclusions. He and Kiedrych had always had their differences, but still . . . he took one look and decided that Kiedrych had been conspiring against him."

"Poor Kiedrych," murmured Kayla.

"You can say that again. Kiedrych honestly thought he'd loved that murderous bitch. He . . . was pretty upset. He nearly got his blade into the King before I found them. Kiedrych was in shock . . . I had to help him out of there. Armand went on without either of us. Rych waited all that time to decide he was in love with someone, and it had to be with *her*."

"Why wouldn't you tell me all this before?"

"It didn't seem to be the right time."

"And now it is?"

He nodded solemnly. "Trouble is Kiedrych is getting, I don't know, obsessed, by her, by what happened, since we got back to the King. He needs you . . ."

"He's ignoring me. When he's not simply being rude."

"You said you'd stick by him."

The chill tone took her by surprise. She studied Tamalan's face, and was struck by the seriousness there. He might be the King's jester, but his personal loyalty was to Kiedrych. His fierce protectiveness was astonishing, for any number of reasons, but Kayla found that she shared it. That, like Tamalan, she would always choose Kiedrych above her sworn King.

"I will," she said.

The conviction in those two words was enough for Tam. He nodded, then rearranged his grip on shoes and blanket. "Don't know why we do," he muttered at last. "Oh well. G'night. I'm off to see if King Armand will let me sleep on his floor."

"Goodnight, Tam. And thank you. For telling me."

"You're welcome. But don't tell him I did, okay?"

She smiled faintly and nodded. Tamalan nodded back, and within moments had disappeared into the shadows. Kayla turned back to regard Kiedrych's caravan. Silence.

Quietly, she walked to the door of the van, tapped lightly on it, and pushed the door open.

Kiedrych was sitting in the darkness, still fully dressed down to his boots. He would not look up at her.

"Hi."

"What were you talking about?"

"Who?"

"Don't be stupid."

"Don't be so bloody ill-mannered."

"Tamalan. What were you talking about?"

"You, of course. We always seem to be talking about you."

"What did he say?"

"Can I come in out of the cold?" She batted her lashes at him, but he couldn't see that in the dark.

"What did he say?"

"You're a persistent bastard." She sighed. *Remember what he's been through,* she reminded herself. *Don't lose your temper.* "He's worried about you, but relieved you haven't killed Armand yet. Then he said he was going to sleep on the King's floor. Happy now?" Kiedrych remained silent, and despite her determined caution she began to lose her temper after all. "Look, am I going to have to report every damn conversation I have with him? Because if I do, I'll take a secretary with me to keep notes. What's the matter? Don't you trust me?"

At that, his head lifted and he glowered at her. The distilled bitterness there shocked her, and made her angrier in turn.

"Don't give me your filthy looks, Kiedrych. I'm not the one asking all the bloody questions."

"Go to bed."

"Is that an invitation?" She had meant that to sound sexy, trying to remedy the situation, but she ended up just sounding peevish. He turned away from her. "I'm not a brainless little serving wench," she said, "I won't be treated like this."

"Then go."

"Damn you, Kiedrych! I said I'd follow you, and I have. I will. Whatever you decide, I'm with you. But what did I do to make you act like this?"

His shoulders slumped and his fingers swept briefly through his long, untidy hair. "Nothing." He sighed. "Nothing, Kayla. Go to sleep now. I'll see you in the morning."

He said no more, and so she shut the door quietly and, feeling guilty, confused, and unhappy, went to bed, where she was to get very little sleep at all.

Chapter Fourteen

"Has Tephee come back yet?" Magda raised her voice slightly so that Sylvia, bedding down inside the tent, could hear her. Leenan shook her head on the way past her into the second tent. Magda's lips pressed into a disapproving line, an expression which dissolved into resignation. Tephee could hardly be said to be an innocent victim in all of this. Damn the girl. Damn her wilfulness and her ignorance and all the people who had made her want to have such complete control of everything in her life. One of whom was herself, Magda acknowledged sourly. She wished she'd done the Psych. minor at the Academy—it might have given her a clue as to how to deal with the situation.

"Is there anything left to eat?" A faint voice interrupted Magda's musings. Tephee came out of the shadows, pale and weak, with the haunted, sallow look of a witch who had used too much magic. It looked like she had walked back to the camp from the hills. Magda reached her in two strides and helped her to sit down.

"Hold on . . . here, some chicken, and bread. Slow down, Teph, let me get you a drink." Magda steadied the girl's hand as she drank. Slowly, Tephee regained her strength and Magda stood back to regard her sternly. "What have you been up to, to put yourself in that condition?"

"You were there."

"You weren't this bad when you left. What have you been doing all afternoon?"

Tephee grunted noncommittally and concentrated on her meal. Magda watched her, unblinking, until Tephee held out her cup for more water. The healer poured some for her and resumed her patient, insistent waiting. Finally, Tephee said something under her breath.

"What was that, Teph?"

Tephee jerked her chin up and repeated defiantly: "I said, I tried to find Zuleika Tallan."

Magda's gut clenched for a second. Then: "Did you find her?"

"Maybe. I brushed against something . . . with my mind. I think she noticed I was there, but we didn't connect. Oh, Magda." Tephee's gaze met hers at last, and her brown eyes were shining with awe. "She was so *powerful.* I knew she was strong, but she's so incredibly powerful . . ." A peculiar smile lit her round face. "She's like the sun. It was beautiful."

"Beautiful? Jesus, Tephee, do you know what she is?"

"A witch. Like us, but very strong." The defiance was back. "That's all we know." The memory of that brief contact was still strong; the sense of power, Tallan's surprise and, most amazing of all, the pleasure that had communicated itself fleetingly. Tallan had actually been pleased to find Tephee's presence. If I could be as strong as Zuleika Tallan, Tephee had thought, people would have to be nice to me.

"She's a tyrant."

"So Sylvia says."

"So Armand says. And Kiedrych, and Kayla, and Tam. And everyone else in this camp, if you'd care to ask. She has *killed* people, Tephee."

Tephee swallowed more water, ate more bread, and wouldn't answer.

"Just because she's strong, it doesn't make her right." Sylvia appeared at the tent, her face thin and drawn with fatigue. "She thinks no one can touch her, which isn't true."

Tephee's face screwed into a scowl. "I've had enough of your lectures to last me a month, Sylvia. Spare me."

"Suit yourself. You realise, don't you, that contacting Tallan has given her the advantage. She'll have measured your strength as well. She's very experienced. There's a lot she'll know about you now."

A shadow of doubt passed briefly across Tephee's face, then vanished. "I can handle it."

Sylvia sighed heavily. "Of course you can. Goodnight then."

"Goodnight, Sylvia," said Magda.

The witch nodded and was gone. Magda turned back to Tephee, who was looking better but still pale.

"I'm going for a walk," she said, getting up.

"You should get some rest."

"Later. I want to find more to eat. I'm starving!" Tephee grinned, but sobered quickly when the smile wasn't returned. "You're angry with me too, aren't you?"

"No. Well, maybe a little. Tephee, love, you know how much I care for you. I've done stupid things, I'm not perfect, but you mean a lot to me. You were the first family I'd had in a long time, and I worry about you. But lately . . . you keep pushing me away—all of us—but you want to control everything at the same time. If you could just let go of that, be yourself again . . ."

"Be myself?" Tephee was scornful. "What am I anyway? An outcast, a misfit. From the start, that's all I was. Mama threw me out when she didn't want me any more, and then you did the same . . ."

"Tephee, no! I was . . . I'd never seen magic before.

Never. I'd been pretending all that time, and then you . . ."

"I know you're sorry, but I can't forget it happened. Then Sylvia didn't want me, and Mama lied, and she turned on me again! I don't care how sorry you all are! I can't trust any of you! I can't trust anyone at all." Her eyes were dry, but her voice cracked with emotion. Magda tried to reach out to her, but Tephee was on her feet and backing away. "And you don't trust me either," she said, as though the realisation had only just dawned on her. Before Magda could answer, she turned on her heel and fled from the witches' camp.

Magda began to follow, but soon lost sight of her among the tents and shadows. Defeated, she returned to the camp.

Sylvia was waiting. "I don't think there's much we can do for her."

"How did we make such a mess of things?"

Sylvia joined her in the darkness. "It's not all our fault. At some point, Tephee has to take responsibility for her own actions."

"But she's only a kid."

"She's seventeen now. Young, but not a child. The best thing we can do is to be here to tell her when she's doing well. Or otherwise. Sooner or later, she'll have to realise that strength doesn't necessarily mean safety or happiness."

"And if she doesn't?"

"Then," Sylvia's eyes darkened with foreboding, "she'll probably become another Farshee. Another Zuleika Tallan."

Tamalan had found a reasonably comfortable spot next to the King's tent—His Highness was asleep already, and Tam had thought better of sneaking inside in the dark under the circumstances. The goat hair was scratchy but warm against his back, and he drew the blanket up high over his head, making a cocoon. He was just beginning to drift into sleep, dreamily picturing bright blue eyes in a long, angular face, surrounded by long, wavy black hair, when he heard someone coming. He started guiltily at the approaching footfalls, and only relaxed slightly when he realised that it was the witch-girl, Tephee. She had a mouthful of meat—the remainder of the lamb haunch was in her right hand. Her left contained a pitcher of water. She didn't see him until she had almost tripped over him, and he had to leap up and pound her back to save her from choking. Water sloshed from the pitcher over her shoes, and Tamalan hastily bent over to mop them dry. Tephee jerked back in startlement, got tangled up, and tripped backwards, landing on her rump with a grunt. She glared at Tamalan, who had rocked back in some surprise himself, and he paled. He tried on a winning smile for size, but it came out a little sickly.

"Uh . . . uh . . . sorry. Just . . . uh . . . you know . . ."

Tephee's jaw clenched as tears welled up in her, and she threw the remainder of the lamb at him. The haunch bounced off his arm, leaving a greasy splotch, and Tamalan stared at her in amazement.

"You're frightened of me too," she accused hotly. Her anger was tempered by the tear that spilled down her cheek.

"Well," Tamalan admitted, "I am a bit. But then, everyone frightens me a little." He grinned and shrugged. "That's what comes of always being the smallest."

Her glare hardened. "You're a liar."

"That too. But not *all* the time." Tam's smile widened and he pushed himself up to one knee, sweeping off an imaginary hat and bowing it to her. He peeked up at her from his low bow and said: "This shabby fool begs forgiveness from you, lady." In a swift action, he dropped to both knees and held his hands clasped beseechingly before her. "Can you forgive a clumsy oaf, Lady?"

Tephee bit down on a smile that threatened to start. "I . . . expect I can."

"You are too kind." He suddenly threw himself flat on the ground at her feet in abasement, but arched an eyebrow up at her. "Lady, may I rise? I've just eaten a mouthful of sand." He spluttered and coughed convincingly.

Tephee, managing a small smile now, pushed at his shoulder with her foot. "Oh go on, get up. Idiot."

He bounded to his feet again and offered to help her up. She regarded the elegantly extended hand for a moment, weighing up the options, then gracefully placed her hand in his and allowed him to assist her to her feet. She drew the line at letting him brush the sand off her clothes, so he waited obediently as she did the deed herself.

"You look tired," he commented as she shook sand out of her rough-woven skirt.

She glanced sharply at him, then shrugged. "I guess I've been overdoing it a bit."

"Hungry?"

"Yes. But I've lost my dinner." Tephee stared pointedly at the haunch of lamb that was now half-buried in the sand and attracting insects.

Tamalan spread his old, grey blanket on the ground, folded himself, cross-legged, onto it, and patted the space beside him. "My intentions are honourable," he assured her, "I thought you'd like to share my supper."

"Well . . . it's the least you could do." Tephee sat down a careful distance away.

"So it is, Lady . . ."

"Tephee."

"Lady?"

"My name's Tephee. I'm not a lady. My mother's a weaver."

Tam smiled at her as though he were sharing a secret. "All women are ladies, Lady Tephee. Especially the beautiful ones."

He looked like he was going to pick up her hand and kiss it, and she snatched it away, blushing. Tam didn't seem to mind, or even notice, and reached into his jacket for a small parcel which he placed on the blanket between them and unwrapped. Within it were a dozen strips of dried meat and a handful of nuts and dried fruits. From another pocket he produced a little bag of hard, sweet biscuits, and finally he set down a small water flask.

"Don't gulp that," he warned. "That's not water in there."

Tam offered Tephee first choice, so she gnawed on the tough smoked beef while he popped a few nuts into his own mouth.

"Why're you out here tonight anyway?" Tephee asked around a strip of meat.

"Oh, I love sleeping outdoors! The stars, the moon . . . the sand flies. And I had a fight with Kiedrych."

"Ah."

"We do that a lot. It's because he snores, you know."

"Does he?"

"He'd deny it, of course."

"Naturally."

"And yourself, Lady? It must be getting cold, even for a witch."

"I just wanted to find something to eat. Take a stroll." Tephee glanced at Tam's smooth, accepting expression. "And, uh, I had a fight too."

He smiled, knowing and sympathetic. "Friends can be

awfully difficult sometimes, can't they?"

"I suppose so."

"It's not as if," Tam continued, "they have the answers to everything. Rych seems to think he's always right. But I can't always be wrong, can I? I mean, the odds are against my being wrong *all* the time. Wouldn't you say?"

Tephee nodded. "I know I'm younger than they are, but it doesn't mean I'm stupid."

"Of course not."

"They just don't understand." She turned to speak directly to him. "I just want to have control over my life. I don't want to be at the whim of whoever thinks they know best." Tamalan leaned a little closer, listening with a small smile of encouragement. "If I have control, I . . ."

"Can't be hurt?"

She went red and looked away, but nodded.

Tamalan "hmmed" in sage agreement. "It's a hard old world, isn't it?"

"I used to think it was wonderful."

"Oh, it's wonderful too," Tam said. "It's a lot of everything, really. That's what makes it all so confusing."

"I just wish . . ." Tephee fished for the right words. "I wish they'd trust me."

"It's hard, isn't it . . . when you want to trust someone, but they won't trust you back. Hey . . . don't cry . . ." Tephee sniffed loudly and Tam felt around his pockets for a kerchief.

Tephee wiped her nose on her sleeve instead, and sighed. "I'm not a bad person," she said.

He patted her shoulder kindly. "You're nice."

"Can I have something to drink?" She sniffed again. Tamalan handed her the flask, and had to pound her on the back again after she gulped a mouthful of the contents.

"I said it wasn't water. Oh dear . . . take a deep breath . . . that's it . . ." He began to laugh, and she glared at him for a moment before seeing the funny side herself. "It sure warms you up on a cold night, doesn't it, Lady?"

"Yep," she rasped, then laughed roughly at the rawness of her voice. "Ooh, boy. Here, give me some more."

"Slow down . . . you'd better leave some for me." Tam knocked back a draught of the stuff, wiped the neck of the flask with his palm, and handed it back. Tephee giggled and drank some more.

"What is it?" She hiccupped, and giggled again.

"Potato vodka," he said. They took turns at the flask after that.

"S'good," said Tephee.

"Mmm. M'granny used t' make it. Taught me th' rec'pe. 'Course, she said it was f' cleaning brass."

Tephee tried to focus on him, shook her head to clear her vision, and toppled sideways into his lap. She chuckled at the sight of his four knees.

"Y'kiddin', aren'tya?"

"Who, me? Sure . . . 's my job." He tried to help her sit up, but she grabbed for the flask and lost her balance again.

"Slow down," Tam complained, "won' be anythin' left . . ."

"Yes there will," promised Tephee in a sing-song voice. She wiggled her fingers in his face and a fine blue crackle of witchfire arced between her fingertips and his nose. Tam yelped and clapped a hand to his tingling face.

"Hurts," he mumbled.

"Nah, doesn'," she said. "Tickles."

"Hmm . . ." Tam felt the tip of his nose carefully, then decided she was right. He sneezed. "Oh, sorry."

" 'S okay." She used the hem of her skirt to dry her arm,

then snatched the flask again. She upended it and let some of the vodka dribble out of her mouth and down her throat.

"Whoa! Careful, Lady! Make y'self sick, doin' that. Here . . ." Tam relieved her of the flask and caught her as her eyes rolled and she flopped forward. She coughed a little, then began laughing. That set him off, and the pair of them clung to each other in the darkness in a sodden, drunken tangle. Suddenly, Tephee struggled and Tam collapsed backwards as she threw her head back to gulp down fresh air, before she, too, collapsed. They lay side by side on the old blanket, staring at the stars.

"There's so many of them," breathed Tephee in awe.

"Nah. Same 's usual. You're jus' seein' two'v everything."

"Oh."

They lay there in companionable silence for a minute or so, until Tephee spoke again.

"Wha's she like?"

"Hmm? Wha'? Who?" Tamalan, close to sleep, blinked and tried to wake up again.

"Zu-Zuleika Tallan."

Tamalan shuddered. "Evil."

"But wha' does evil mean?"

"She hurts people."

"Regular people do that," Tephee pointed out reasonably. "Old Tabbot used to beat his wife. Then Gilly, their son, killed Tabbot. Then the town was going to have him hanged, so he ran away. Then there's all those wars. The Explu . . . Explulsh . . . Ex-pul-sion War, an' the Hinter Espan . . . Ex-pan-sion, an' the . . ."

"Tha's different. People killing people is okay. Well, not okay, but, you know, normal. Witches killing people, 's different."

"Why?"

" 'Cause . . . 'cause . . . people can't fight back with magic. 'S unfair."

"Oh. What else is she like?"

"She's . . . beautiful. Very, very pretty."

"Aha. I said she was. Sylvia got mad at me."

"Well . . . I s'ppose . . . she's only beautiful outside."

"Inside, she's strong. No one can hurt her."

"Right 'nough there."

"If she was strong, but she didn't hurt people . . . if she helped them instead, she'd be a nice witch, wouldn' she?"

"Never thought 'bout it. Guess so. She'd be nice." Tamalan rolled his head to one side so that he could see Tephee's face. He smiled lopsidedly at her. "Like you."

That made her smile back.

Within minutes, they'd both fallen asleep.

Chapter Fifteen

Magda was woken by a noise outside. Leenan rolled over in her blankets and Alard, sleeping by the tent flap, lifted his head in a desultory fashion, sniffed the air, and went back to sleep.

"Psst. Anyone awake?" Kayla whispered.

"Hang on," Magda whispered back. She wrapped her blanket around her shoulders, over the cotton nightdress she wore, and stepped over Alard into the crisp quiet of the pre-dawn air. Kayla was standing near the cold fire with a displeased expression and the dead weight of Tephee sagging in her arms.

"Jesus, Tephee . . ." Magda started forward anxiously and felt the girl's face and hands. Pulse seemed good, breathing fine . . . "What happened?"

"She's dead drunk," whispered Kayla, trying not to let her voice carry. "I couldn't sleep so I went for a walk. I found her asleep, with Tam." Kayla blinked at the look Magda gave her. "Kiedrych kicked him out, last night," she said, "so he slept outside. The two of them were snoring their heads off next to the King's tent. I've had words with Tam already."

"Not half as many as I'm going to have," growled Magda. She relieved Kayla of her burden and let Tephee slither to the ground.

"I don't think he meant any harm," said Kayla, losing some of her irritation as the witch grew more agitated. "He said they were just talking. She was hungry and lonely, and needed a sympathetic ear."

"So he thought he'd get her blind drunk, and then . . ."

"Oh, no, he swears he wasn't trying to seduce her. In fact," Kayla smiled, obviously not entirely believing his story either, "Tam says that she reminds him of his sister, Titia."

"I didn't know he had a sister," said Magda coldly.

"He's got lots of them, apparently. This one died of the fever that came through Tyne five years ago. It was a bad year." Kayla frowned, remembering just how bad it had been.

"Hmph."

Tephee groaned and her eyelids fluttered open. She looked from Magda to Kayla, then screwed her eyes shut again. "Think I'm g'na be sick," she mumbled.

"Gee, thanks, kid," Kayla grimaced. Magda swiftly crouched and turned Tephee over so that she could vomit into the sand. Kayla turned away, her nose wrinkling. "She's all yours."

"Thanks a whole heap."

"You're welcome. Should I tell King Armand you'll be seeing him today?"

"Later, maybe. He's all right for now." Tephee began retching again, and by the time Magda had settled her once more, Kayla had gone. Magda sighed, let Tephee lie spread-eagled on the sand nearby, and buried the mess.

She roused Sylvia while trying to get Tephee inside and the two of them managed to put the girl to bed. Sylvia prepared to work magic on her, but Magda said that a good, solid hangover might teach her a lesson. Sylvia looked at her friend curiously for a moment, then conceded to Magda's view. They left Tephee snoring among the blankets.

"If she's sick this time," Magda said grimly, "she can clean it up herself."

When she was told about it over breakfast, Leenan regarded Magda with sympathy and the smugness of someone who has been vindicated mingling in her green eyes. "I told you what he was like," she said.

"Forget it," muttered Magda.

Later in the morning, on her way to see Armand, she caught sight of Tamalan. He was sitting in the shade of the caravan he usually shared with Kiedrych, and she noted with spiteful satisfaction that he was holding his head and looking quite ill. He wouldn't be getting any help from *her* today.

The session with Armand went well, using a compact cell regenerator from her kit to smooth the scar tissue back from the delicate flesh of his eyes, though the shiny patch of unhealed skin still ran down the side of his face. She used magic to correct the damage done to his cornea and retina, but found it more difficult to focus today.

"Sorry," she said shakily. "I must be more tired than I thought. Sorry."

Armand patted her shoulder consolingly and held a goblet of wine to her lips. "You've done more than I could have expected a month ago. Leave it. I'm very grateful for all you've done. I feel like a new man already." He smiled warmly, and despite his scars, painful thinness, and the haunted, ravaged look about his eyes, he radiated sincerity and strength.

When he's well, Magda thought, he must be quite something. As his body, and his confidence, were patched together, the charisma within him was blossoming forth once more. Armand Bakar-Tyne was, or could be, she realised, quite a King.

As Magda was rising to leave, the tent flap was flung aside and Kiedrych stood in the triangle of light. His stillness was so intense that for a second he seemed merely the embodiment of his own black anger. His rage kept driving him here to confront the King. That and his stubbornness. There was a masochistic streak in the Captain's determination to force the King to acknowledge his loyalty, his trustworthiness, and his rights as Captain of the Castle Guard. He seemed oblivious to the fact that the very violence of his emotions worked against him.

"We have things to discuss. Your Highness." His tone was level, ground out of him with such control, they were as cool and neutral as stone.

"I have nothing to discuss with you," Armand countered. "You will receive your orders through Darem when the time comes."

"I am the highest-ranking officer left in your army . . ."

"If you're the best I have left, we are in considerable trouble."

If Kiedrych had had spikes, Magda would have heard them bristle. Kiedrych took the time to calm himself. Magda didn't blame him. So much for the King's charisma.

"I did not betray you, Armand."

"You tried to kill me."

"Do I have to kill myself, to convince you?"

"Perhaps." Armand's lips twitched in a near-smile. "It would certainly make my life less complicated."

That perfect stillness returned to Kiedrych's stance and then he turned on his heel and walked away, too enraged to stay. Magda folded her arms and regarded the King coolly.

"What is it with you two?"

"Don't you start," said Armand wearily.

"I know he's not the most charming man I've ever met—

but he's not the worst, either."

Armand whirled on her, his eyes dark and fierce with fury. "Give me your opinion," he bit out, "when you know the facts."

Magda would not be cowed. "He's come a long way to find you and, as I recall, it wasn't him who tried to break your head first time around. If you keep treating him like a cur, no doubt he'll bite you soon enough."

"No doubt. Goodbye."

"I would have thought a man in your position would have greater subtlety."

"Another man in my position would probably be dead by now."

"If he's as stubborn and unforgiving as you, I wouldn't doubt it."

"You are dismissed!"

"I am not a subject of yours to *be* dismissed. Clearly, if you won't listen to those who came to help you, someone else has got to try."

"Lords!" Armand rolled his eyes and spread his hands beseechingly. "What is it about that man? First Kayla, now you!"

"Kayla?"

"She came this morning to unnecessarily beg my forgiveness—and ended up by begging for his as well."

"Ah. Well, she's in love with him, if that's a help. I'm just a sucker for fair play."

He looked at her in surprise at that. She smiled thinly at him and left.

Over the following days, other tribes began to join Darem's and every person was engaged in preparations for the battles ahead. Old Hattie led the night-and-day activities to organise the food supplies—bread, smoked meats, dried fruit, and the like—while others repaired old weapons or made new ones. In these tribes some families followed behind the army, where they kept busy finding food, making swords and arrows, and later tending those wounded in battle. Sometimes the women went to battle—those who had blood to avenge or simply those who had a mind to it.

The witches had their own preparations to make, but this seemed to consist mostly of eating a great deal and conserving their strength. Only Magda had more to do, and would frequently disappear into her tent, barring Leenan from joining her, and work for hours.

"What are you up to?" Leenan demanded at last.

"I'm . . . making potions. Things to help heal the sick."

"Dung. If you were using magic for all of that, you'd be too exhausted to get up in the morning. Is this to do with those boxes you brought with you from Swiftfort?"

Magda shuffled uncomfortably. "They're . . . magic boxes. All right?"

"I've never heard of a magic box," said Sylvia sternly.

Magda, flustered, flapped her hands in aggravation. "Drop it, all right? I can use it to make people better. Leave it alone."

"It's not magic, is it?" Leenan accused peevishly.

Magda refused to answer and dived back into her tent. She was pulling blankets over the boxes on the floor as Leenan and Sylvia both ducked inside. "For heaven's sake, can't you just leave it be?"

Sylvia looked at her with mixed understanding and irritation. Leenan had her arms folded and her expression indicated she thought Magda was either being unnecessarily stubborn or had been too much in the sun.

"What's this all about?" Sylvia asked. Her tone brooked no argument.

Magda pressed her lips into a thin line and wouldn't answer.

"It's not magic, that much I know."

"Does it really matter?" An edge of desperation entered her voice.

Sylvia sighed. "Does it, Magda?"

"No. It's not important. It doesn't *hurt* anyone, for goodness' sake!"

"It's killing me with curiosity," said Leenan, smiling ruefully. "Come on, Maggie—what's the secret?"

"I can't tell you."

"Spoilsport. Why not?"

"Because . . . because . . . then it wouldn't be a secret."

"You're daft."

Magda sighed. "That's not the half of it."

Leenan grinned and laughed, bringing a smile to Magda's face as well. "You know, Maggie," she said, "sometimes I wonder if witches are quite all right in the head."

"Take a look around you," Magda suggested, "and take a census."

"Hmm." Sylvia scratched her chin thoughtfully. "Based on current evidence, three out of four witches know better than to drink themselves sick on vodka."

"Four out of four talk to animals," said Magda.

"Two out of four fancy court jesters," chuckled Leenan.

Magda pulled a face. "Not any more, after what he did to Tephee."

"Oh, Maggie, it's quite all right to fancy them. Just don't take it seriously."

"Yeah, right, oh sage one."

"That's me—The Love Oracle," said Leenan with a snort of laughter.

With a wry grin, Magda stood up and brushed herself off as the three of them walked back out into the sunshine.

Sylvia paused politely to let Leenan and Magda out first, but as the healer-witch passed, she said quietly: "Don't be afraid what we'll think, Magda. Witches should be tolerant of what is different in others."

Magda drew a sharp breath. "This is . . . very different," she replied softly.

"Arc machines often are," said Sylvia, in a voice so low Magda had to strain to hear it. Then Sylvia smiled and stepped outside. "I think I hear the horsemen complaining about the dragons, Magda. Maybe you should see to them."

Magda blinked, and seemed to mentally shake herself before nodding. "Give me a hand, Lee?"

"Sure. I'll see how the horses are doing while I'm at it."

"Getting fat and lazy, probably," said Sylvia with a laugh.

From the hillside, young Tephee was watching the tribesfolk scurrying like ants. She had recovered from her first hangover with a greater respect for alcohol and a minor grudge against Tamalan Fingal, which had been settled by turning the rest of his vodka supply into vinegar. He'd known better than to complain to her. In fact, after his first wail of despair, he had simply smiled apologetically at her and shrugged.

Tephee saw four dots of colour flashing out among the horses—four dragons, the sun reflecting off their metallic scales, were teasing the horses, who were becoming restless. She'd seen the dragons hunting that morning and knew they weren't hungry, but she supposed she could understand a horse being nervous about a flying reptile with big teeth being so close.

Her pride welled up, that she had made those dragons. They represented the first deliberate magic she'd ever done. That thought was followed by a frown, remembering what had happened afterwards. For years her first teacher had been telling the town she was a witch and, when confronted by someone with real power, Magda had been frightened and, strangely enough, ashamed. Tephee recognised that now. How someone could have this power and not know it still puzzled her, but that was how it was. She had run away, ending up at Blood Rock with Sylvia, still angry, still hurt, until Magda had come to find her.

And there was Magda now, with her preferred friend. Jealousy stained her heart. Magda had dropped her like a prickle bug when Leenan had arrived; Sylvia spent all her time with them, now, too. At the camp, Leenan called the dragons to her, and they swooped down to crouch by her feet. *She can speak to them,* thought Tephee defiantly, *but she can't make them.*

In the distance she could see a cloud of sand, indicating that the last of the tribes was approaching. Once they were here, they would move on, towards the Kingdom of Tyne and Zuleika Tallan. Tephee was looking forward to it.

Chapter Sixteen

The sound of thousands of people marching north made less noise than Magda imagined they would. Perhaps, she thought, it was simply that all the noises merged into a great background noise—stamping hooves and marching feet; horses blowing, their bits jingling as they swayed; voices murmuring low; the creak of wheels and saddles.

If she squinted she could make out Tamalan's caravan ahead of her. Kiedrych was driving the horses—Tam was sitting at the open door, braced against the frame as the caravan rocked, his feet dangling over the narrow steps. He was juggling, catching the flying balls deftly despite the lurching motion. Magda sent a piercing glare in his direction, which no doubt he could not see, because he waved in Tephee's direction.

For her part, although she was cool and aloof with all others, Tephee seemed to have forgiven Tamalan for her first hangover. As far as Magda was concerned, Tam had been much too keen to have Tephee forgive him, bringing her a bunch of flowers he had somehow managed to find in this wilderness, and giving her one of his rings. When he tried the same appeasement on her, Magda refused the gifts, told him what she thought of him, and threatened to turn him into a mouse as a treat for the dragons if he tried it again.

She regretted the latter now. He obviously took her at her word and studiously avoided their camp these days when they stopped on the journey north. Which, Magda told herself, ought to be a good thing. Except that it made her cranky. Leenan just rolled her eyes at the heavens and told her to make up her mind. Sylvia, who might have been more sympathetic, was too busy with Darem, Armand, and the other Ashrafs.

The warriors were all of various tribes, and each tribe was usually split into separate camps. Darem's original camp was only one part of his whole tribe, of which he was, by election, the leader. Each leader who joined him brought not only his own camp of several hundred, but up to fifty other camps all encompassed by the same Ashraf. Not all of them were happy about it, but they all came, with their entourages, food, and water.

Unfortunately, the supplies wouldn't last forever, and with the army massing it was going to become important to find other sources, or to attack as soon as possible, before it became a real problem.

The meeting tent was hot and sweaty with the bodies packed into it. Sylvia sat, quietly observant, behind King Armand and Kiedrych Evenahn, only infrequently offering comment. Clusters of tribesmen sat around on cushions and rugs—a tribal chief at the head of each one, surrounded by the tribe's camp chiefs. They argued a lot among themselves, but fell more or less silent when Armand spoke.

"Swiftness is our only hope," he was saying earnestly. "My cousin and the witch must surely know what's happening here already, and are preparing their own army. The longer we wait, the longer they have to get ready for us."

"But we need time," countered El Ashraf Udan. "Most of us aren't ready for war yet. We are hunters; we fight only occasionally . . ."

"Tell that to El Ashraf Gamre's tribe, Udan!" called out one heckler. "We still don't know who attacked Gamre's camp . . . unless you have some ideas?" There was a threatening pause, interrupted by Darem's deep voice cutting through the tension.

"We can settle our own arguments later. If we do nothing to defeat these usurpers, we will surely face them on our own lands next. We must defeat them now, but we can only achieve that if we work together."

There were grunts of agreement, a few of dissent, but they got back to current business. Kiedrych, his eyes black and bruised with sleeplessness and bitterness, sat to one side of the King.

"There are farms ahead, my lord," he began to say in a low voice. "Some of the crops will be near enough to . . ."

"I will not steal from my subjects."

"Then you will starve. And your army, and all who follow, will die."

"The ends do not justify the means . . ."

"I did not actually suggest you should simply take what you want. It is the most cost-efficient method, of course, but still . . . You can trade with them. If things really are as bad as the reports imply, perhaps your subjects will simply give you what they have. I expect even you are an improvement over your cousin."

"I'll ask for your opinion if I think I need it, Evenahn."

"I am the Captain of the Castle Guard . . ."

"I have no Castle Guard. I have no castle. I don't even have an army, Evenahn. Darem's army is here, fighting in my name. But you you lead a pack of soldiers that no longer exists."

"And who broke it?"

"Traitors like yourself."

"A King who first turned his back on them, and then left them in the field."

"The changes I planned would have made their lives better."

"But not those of the noblemen who paid for them, and it was their support you needed. No wonder you lost your throne so easily."

"You are here on my sufferance, Evenahn. Another word and I shall have you thrown out."

"You trust me so little, you won't even listen to my counsel?"

"No more than I'd take the counsel of a snake."

"Then beware," Kiedrych's voice dropped gruffly, "a cut snake is dangerous."

Armand ignored this, and neither spoke to nor acknowledged Kiedrych's presence for the rest of the day, leaving the man glowering blackly at him. *Let him sulk and stew,* Armand thought. *I won't be deceived twice.*

It was late afternoon before this latest war council broke up, and the participants drifted off to their camps to eat and discuss the outcomes. Sylvia walked with Darem and Armand to Darem's tent, deep in conversation. Kiedrych, his shoulders hunched and expression closed, stalked through the crowded melee of nomads towards his van near the outer edge of the camp. He ignored Tam, who tried to smile a welcome, and went immediately into the darkness of the van.

A movement within caught his eye, and he froze. He did not relax when he saw it was Kayla, kneeling on the floor with a wooden tray laden with food. A carafe of wine was on the floor beside her, and two goblets. She smiled at him.

"I thought I'd make dinner for you. You look tired."

His face was like stone, his expression unreadable. He had to stoop to walk inside, and crouched before her. She held up a plate of salted beef, twisted around spears of pickled vegetables and garnished with olives. He stared at them.

"I made them myself," she assured him. He said nothing. He poked at the food disdainfully, and wiped his finger clean against his trousers.

"Thanks ever so much," she said icily. "What's your problem? Do you think I'm trying to poison you?"

Kiedrych snatched the plate and threw it savagely against the door. Kayla drew back, startled and hurt.

"Get out." She could barely hear him, he spoke so quietly. She stared at him, until he lifted his eyes to meet hers. She had never seen anyone look so wild, and so caged. So near to madness with that anger and pain. He hardly seemed to see her at all. When she didn't move, he snatched up the carafe and flung it at her.

"Get. Out." The carafe flew above her head and smashed, the red wine spilling in a suggestive stain across the floor. Kayla sat up, her heart thumping, feeling sick.

"What's wrong with you, Kiedrych?"

"With me?" He glared at her, only it still seemed as though he was looking through her, at something else. "Nothing." He grinned, a thoroughly unpleasant grin of teeth and sneers. "Trust me."

"*Trust* you?" She stared at him with horror and incredulity, but it was the wrong thing to say. She scrambled for the little door and tumbled outside as the tray with the rest of the meal came hurtling out after her, then picked herself up and ran, sobbing, as far and as quickly as she could.

Within the van, Kiedrych was shaking. He knelt, facing the door, staring at his hands as if they belonged to a stranger, and trembling. His thoughts, disordered, came slowly and drifted without control. Mama. His father, Forster. Parsa. Armand. Each name not a face but a collection of feelings. Love. Pain. Humiliation. Betrayal. Confusion. Anger. He saw Tamalan's face, eyes wide and mouth open in shock and fear. And Kayla's.

He folded his trembling hands into fists, pulled those fists hard into his diaphragm, and tried to breathe properly. The effort brought stinging tears to his eyes, which fell and disappeared into his beard. His rage and pain were an unvoiced howl.

He, like Kayla, did not sleep that night.

A light knock at the door made Kayla jump, and she huddled in her bed with the blankets drawn to her chin. "Wh . . . who . . . ?"

"Only me," piped up a cheerful voice, and Tam let himself in. "I brought you some breakfast. Nothing much." He stood hunched over in the van and handed her a bowl of fruit. He regarded her silently, taking in the drawn and battered look, but noting also that she did not appear to have been physically hurt. "You okay?"

She nodded faintly, gazing at the fruit without interest.

"He didn't mean it, you know."

She stared at him blankly for a second. After that, she simply . . . deflated. Her face crumpled, her shoulders shook, and her body folded over her pain. A low, continuous moan crawled out from deep in her throat. Tam scrambled over to her, hesitated, then drew her into his arms. He patted her hair and rocked her, but Kayla remained knotted up—a ball of barely contained anguish, whimpering like a wounded animal.

"Kayla . . . hush . . . please, don't . . . I know he can be . . . scary. He didn't mean to frighten you. He . . ." Words failed him, and he hugged her close, trying to soothe her. The moan choked off momentarily, only to be followed by a brief, lost wail, which she quickly swallowed again. "Don't give up on him, Kayla. He'll be lost without you."

Kayla struggled to speak, and her voice rasped angrily from a throat tight with emotion. "He's insane."

"He's going through a bad time. Armand . . ."

"I know . . . all about Kiedrych and Armand." Kayla caught her breath in a sob, and fought for control of her voice. "What have I got to do with all of that?"

Tamalan sat close to Kayla, rubbing her back and shoulders, the way his mother had always done when one of her children was distressed. "Everything and nothing, I suppose. Kiedrych has just got used to this idea that people always let him down."

"His p-paranoia doesn't excuse him."

"He thinks that no one trusts him, and that no one else can be trusted. Which, in his experience, isn't too far wrong."

"What?" Kayla managed a snarl, "he's been betrayed by everyone he knows?"

"Everyone that mattered, anyway. Except me. And you."

"So why is he treating me like this?" She shivered, and curled into a ball again. "What did I do?"

"It's not anything you did. He's just confused."

A bitter bark of laughter burst from her. "*He's* confused?"

"He's all caught up in Armand, which involves Parsa. And . . . other things, too, I think. He had a pretty messed-up relationship with his parents. That's how we got to know each other."

"He killed them too?" Kayla's sarcasm was nearly rattled out of her by Tamalan's grip and the fierce shake he gave her.

"Don't ever say that. Ever. It was that brute of a father

of his, Red Lord damn him. He was only seven himself, and he *still* thinks he must have done something wrong."

"You're hurting me, Tam." Kayla spoke softly, and Tamalan released her as though he'd burnt his hand. He mumbled an apology, blushing. Kayla rubbed her arms where he had gripped her, but although pale, seemed in control of herself now. "Tell me what happened."

"Kiedrych's father was a violent, ignorant, ill-tempered whoreson. His mother, now, she was different. Beautiful, intelligent . . ."

"How did she end up with a swine for a husband?"

"The usual way. Two noble families deciding to join their bloodlines. Forster Evenahn was keen enough to marry, but I doubt if anyone asked Naseem how she felt. Kiedrych was born the year before me, and Naseem never had any other children. Mama says she used to go to her, or to a witch, if she could find one, to keep from getting pregnant again." Tamalan's face darkened with anger as he remembered. "She came often enough, too, for treatments for her bruises and cuts. I remember once . . . I was about five, I guess, and I still remember how badly hurt she was. He'd hit her across the stomach with the flat of his sword. Mama would patch her up, give her something for the pain, and swear me to secrecy."

"Why?"

"Stupid reasons. To avoid scandal, and embarrassment. I sometimes wonder if I'd said something . . ." He sighed, shook his head, and resumed his narrative. "She and Rych, though . . . I think she protected him from his father, and from what he did to her. He took after her in most things, except Forster's temper, but she taught him to control that too. If they hadn't been so close, what happened next might not have hurt him so much."

He paused so long that Kayla almost prompted him, but he took up the memory again, his voice full of sadness and regret.

"Eventually, she couldn't take any more. We woke up one morning to Forster tearing up our house, looking for her. King Graym had to have him removed by force. Turned out Naseem and a page named Akram had both disappeared. Poor Rych. He couldn't work out why she'd left without taking him."

"Oh . . ." Kayla breathed.

"Forster rode straight out after them. He came back three days later covered in dried blood. As far as I can figure, he went straight to Kiedrych, beat him so hard that the servants had to intervene, and promptly went to his chambers and hanged himself to avoid the shame of facing his peers. The moron thought it was better to be dead than a cuckold." Tamalan looked away from her at last, to steady his breathing and bring his feelings back in check. "The family disowned Kiedrych—they said he was a bastard, not Evenahn blood. Kiedrych came to live with us, then. We grew up foster brothers. I don't think he ever forgave his mother for leaving like that. Or his father. Or himself. Then Parsa came along." He swore, eloquently expressing how he felt about that particular chain of events.

They sat together in contemplative silence for several minutes. Finally, Tamalan moved to the door and stepped outside. He looked up at her. "Don't give up on him yet."

"I won't," she promised, with a small, wry smile. "Not quite yet, anyway."

"He's not always like this."

"I know. Now get going before he sees you here."

That startled him and his eyes darted over the surroundings before he took off like a rabbit. Kayla nearly laughed, until she realised that, in Kiedrych's current mood, it wasn't at all funny.

Tamalan made his decision on the way back. Taking his courage in both hands—though he felt that his courage was so small that perhaps only one hand would have sufficed—he strode to his caravan.

He flung the door open, checked that Kiedrych was inside, and, taking a deep breath, threw in a whole bucket of water he had picked up on the way. Kiedrych sat bolt upright in his bed, his face and chest dripping, his hand already drawing a knife and his eyes blazing.

"Do that to her again, you thick-witted, foul-tempered, suspicious-minded brute," Tam shouted at him, "and you'll lose her. She's not like me, to put up with this shit forever."

He slammed the door shut and ran before Kiedrych had a chance to catch him.

In the caravan, Kiedrych did not give chase. He regarded the drawn knife with detached curiosity, and held its cold blade against the palm of his left hand; shifted it slightly, so the sharp point rested against the skin. He wondered absently what would happen if he pushed. It would probably hurt. Experimentally, he traced the tip of the knife down his palm, towards his wrist, but only lightly, not even scratching the skin. A quick stab and pull, he realised without emotion, would open him from wrist to elbow. That would hurt quite a lot. How much pain would it take to make up for things?

With an impatient frown, he slid the knife back into its sheath.

Tamalan darted amongst the tents and morning fires, past the people already about their daily business of cooking, eating, gossiping. He liked this new city of tents that travelled with them across the landscape—it reminded him of his own city. He didn't like the little villages and towns amongst which he'd been living. In a city you knew where you were. Not safe, exactly, but surrounded, at least. He missed having lots of people around. He wondered, with a stab of guilt, what his own family was doing. Like him, they had found their own way out of the castle on the night of the fire, but he hadn't seen or heard from anyone since they had fled after the Tyne Rout. He'd just assumed they were all right. Hoped. Prayed.

King Armand was in his tent, finishing breakfast and dressing. Tamalan peeped in to see that he was alone, then darted inside.

Armand arched an eyebrow at him, but smiled. "Ah, Tam! I thought it would be much too early in the day for you!"

"Where do you get off treating him like that?" Tam said hoarsely. Armand's eyes widened in surprise. "You talked so much before about a man's right to justice, and a free and fair society, and then humiliate him in front of his peers! What justice does he get? I never thought you meant to reserve it only for those who *liked* you. You're a damned hypocrite!" The rising torrent of angry words stopped abruptly as Tam stared at his King with a wan face. He added meekly: "Your Highness."

The King did not look amused. "So you're a traitor as well."

"I am not," he denied fiercely, "and if you'd take your fingers from your ears and your thumbs from your eyes, you wouldn't say it." Don't pike out now, Tam told himself, gritting his teeth on his fleeing courage. "You made mistakes the first time—listening to people like Henkle and Threlfayl. Kiedrych didn't agree with you, but at least he said so to your face."

"That bastard tried to kill me," Armand snarled, advancing on his jester.

"Why shouldn't he?" Tamalan surprised himself by walking forward into the King's grasp. "He'd just killed his *wife* for you, you dumb bastard! Then you add to her betrayal by calling him a traitor to his face." He shoved, and Armand fell backward onto a pile of cushions. Tam stood there, breathing heavily, willing himself not to run away. Armand glared at him, stood up, and slapped Tamalan across the face as hard as he could. Tam rocked back a step, his face stinging. *Kiedrych's given me worse,* he told himself, *don't run yet.*

"I could have you executed for that."

Tamalan blanched, but held. "For what? For *disagreeing* with you? Just take me and Kiedrych out at the same time. And Kayla too. Archer squad should be able to deal out your justice pretty efficiently. Just watch out for all the ones who smile and nod. Some of them are the ones with the knife up their sleeve."

Armand looked like he was going to strike Tamalan again, but at the last hesitated. His hands curled into fists and he stood very, very still. Tamalan felt reaction set into his own body as he began to shake.

"Am I . . . as bad as all that?" said Armand quietly.

"N-no, Your Highness. B-but you and Kiedrych n-never were friends. Y-you let that get in the way. We were all f-frightened that night. I know you were hurt." Tam jerked a nod at the faint scarring still surrounding the King's eye. "But so was he. He's no t-traitor."

"And you?"

"N-nor me, Highness."

"Yet you choose him over me."

"I w-would have come to find you m-myself, if he hadn't come with me."

"Would you? I wonder." Armand relaxed a fraction, stepped back to regard Tamalan with grave amazement. "You attacked your King for the sake of him."

"You're killing each other," Tam said after a moment's thought. "You'd get a lot more done, both of you, if you didn't hate so much. Not," he added thoughtfully, "that I think you'd like each other, especially. He's a hard man to like."

Armand snorted, then laughed. "Then why do so many of you love him so much?"

"Not that many, Highness. Kayla, really."

"Not you?"

Tam shrugged. "I'm just sort of used to him, I guess."

"Yes, I suppose you are."

An awkward moment ensued, in which Tamalan and Armand both wondered how they could tactfully end this interview. Tam cleared his throat as Armand approached him, his right hand extended.

"I'll just . . . ah . . ." began Tam.

"I . . . pardon you, Tamalan Fingal."

"You do? Oh. Good. Lords, Highness, I'm sorry . . ."

"I'll think about what you said."

Tamalan considered adding more to his earlier outburst, then decided he'd had a lucky escape twice already today and that he wouldn't push it. He nodded meekly, and bowed low to his King. He backed respectfully away until he reached the tent flap, then turned and fled outside. His breathing was only just returning to normal when a dark-clad figure stepped out of the shadows between the tents and blocked his path. Tamalan's heart lurched sickeningly against his ribs and he had to struggle for the next breath.

Kiedrych looked down at him with a deeply disapproving frown. "Don't," he said, "ever do that again."

Tam nodded, clamping down on a frightened whimper. Kiedrych grunted and strode away. Tam's knees shook and gave out, dropping him to the sand, as he sucked in deep breaths and tried to stop his heart from racing. It hurt.

Chapter Seventeen

Standing on the highest parapet of Tyne Castle, Saebert Bakar-Cadron gazed moodily out towards the southeast. Between the castle wall and the beige-tinged horizon lay acres of land. Flat farmland, for the most part, and sparsely wooded forests, sprawling at last into sand dunes leading to the sea and Henatith, the biggest seaport in his kingdom. Saebert checked his childhood memory of this view . . . he was sure it had been greener then, and that he had seen birds wheeling above the Royal City of Tyne. All seemed quiet now, less vibrant. Perhaps, as the saying went, the having really wasn't as good as the wanting.

Perhaps it was simply Zuleika. Recently her strength had, astonishingly, grown. It struck Saebert that his lover was growing more potent as the people and land around them became more wan and listless. It was as though, not content with the victims she had brought to her rooms to suffer the same fate as Craffen and Threlfayl, Zuleika was feeding her appetite for power from the very lands of Tyne.

Whatever it was, her ambition was outstripping her place in his court. She had begun to tell him what to say and do, how to handle the Council, and who to dispose of when necessary. He was growing irritated and impatient with her fear-based tactics, and resentful of her intrusion into areas that were rightfully his, as King, to command. They had needed her power to begin with—to convince the others that they had the strength to rout the Ki . . . Armand—a weakling and a danger to those around him, Saebert reminded himself—and to hold off his supporters. Strength to keep the Councillors and noblemen in line in the weeks of chaos and reorganisation which followed. It was time to put Zuleika in her place.

Damn Armand, anyway, for his ridiculous foreign ideas. His notions of higher taxes for the nobles, to pay for courts to give the merchant and farmer classes access to judicial appeal and justice; his plans, for the Lords' sake!, to allow those classes *elected representatives* on the Council! Saebert had considered himself as loyal as any other, until Armand returned to preside over his father's funeral and the destruction of the old man's kingdom. It was a pity that Saebert's mother was only a second cousin herself to the long-dead Queen Alyce, or he might have won the right to the throne on his own merit. He didn't even look like a Tyne—his face was too long and thin, chin too narrow, and nose too aristocratically long. His dark hair was fine and straight, not a mass of unruly curls, and his eyes a pale blue. He was better looking than a Tyne, he thought—the royal line carried the physical traits of a blacksmith, whereas the Cadron line—his own—definitely looked more like courtiers. Until Armand, he would have thought the brains were more with the blacksmiths, though.

"I've been wondering where you were." Zuleika's smooth, pleasantly pitched voice startled him, but he was careful to cover it.

"I've come to watch the sunset," he told her.

Zuleika laughed. "What a romantic you are."

Saebert lifted one shoulder in a dismissive shrug. Zuleika stood beside him, and together they contemplated the horizon, admiring the way the sun reflected off the river in a molten silver sheen as it snaked its way to the sea, the pale pinks and yellows of light infusing the few clouds, the sand of the distant dunes.

Saebert thought he remembered the sunsets as being much brighter, in his youth.

"Is there any further news on Armand's army?" he asked after a moment.

"They are nearing the border. Your cousin is quite popular with the desert folk—he has almost four and a half thousand of them at his heels."

"That many? Our own army can't hope to match them."

"Our army doesn't have to. You have me." She smiled sweetly as she tilted her face up to his. The sunset gave her pale skin a honey-coloured flush, and Saebert savoured again her ethereal beauty. Divine creature, and all his, for all her insufferable ambition. He brushed his forefinger along her brow, traced a line down the soft skin of her cheek and across her lips.

"I'd rather you just killed him now, my love," he told her, firmly but without rancour. "Without Armand there is no threat."

"I want the witch that burned me." The music dropped from Zuleika's voice and she scowled, running her fingers through the dark, close-cropped hair that was not growing quickly enough. Saebert swept his hand back through the soft, boyish cut, letting her fine black hair spill through his fingers. He liked this look on her—the elegant structure of her face, no longer obscured by long, silky locks, was truly breathtaking. Her delicately-boned features, her fine little nose, wide sensual mouth, the pointed chin, startling upswept cheekbones, emphasising those huge, dark eyes . . .

She tilted her face up to him and he kissed her. His hands went to her face, traced down her cheek to her long, elegant neck. Slender, fragile. With one sharp twist he could break that neck, or with a sudden blow crush her windpipe. He had done that, once, but she had just been a serving girl. Zuleika would require more subtlety.

He gritted his teeth and turned back to the sunset. "Why not simply kill your rival from here? You know where she is."

Zuleika's puzzled frown dissolved under impatient disdain. "I need more than that to focus me. She is strong. And then there's the other one. The young one. I want them both. Here."

"To what end?"

Zuleika's girlish laugh bubbled in delight. "To drink them both dry, of course. Oh, the power in those two." Her eyes glazed in her anticipation of the drunken glory of it. "With their power absorbed into mine . . . mmm."

Saebert risked a sour sideways glance at her. She was getting more and more unstable. If they simply killed Armand, his army, including his tame witches, would have nothing to fight for. No reason to attack his kingdom. Zuleika was clearly more interested in her vengeance, and her accumulation of magical power, than in the stability and safety of the realm. It was time to do something about her, whatever he thought of her loveliness.

First, however, he would have to do something about Armand.

He glanced back to see Zuleika regarding him through narrowed eyelids.

"I do all of this for you, love," she said quietly. Saebert thought he detected the faintest note of pleading in that. Just like dear dead Helji, and her expression of surprise as he crushed her throat.

But Helji had been a kitchen girl, a nobody, and he needed Zuleika.

"I know you do, my beautiful Leika." He kissed her brow, her eyelids, her mouth, and after the briefest hesitation, she returned the caresses.

Chapter Eighteen

"You look terrible." Magda bent to look into Tephee's eyes with concern.

"Didn't sleep well," the girl muttered. Her "talk" with the witch Tallan last night had left her tired and irritable. She wasn't sure if she had correctly interpreted the mood of that meeting. Had Tallan offered to be her new teacher? She wasn't sure what she'd sensed, though clearly some kind of offer had been made. Tallan wanted Tephee to be with her, that much was certain, and it felt good to know that someone, somewhere, wanted her at all.

As Tephee ate a huge breakfast, she noticed Sylvia watching her with suspicion. *Let her wonder why I'm so hungry,* Tephee thought. *I don't need her, and she doesn't want me. When I'm gone, when I'm with Tallan, she'll be sorry. She'll miss me then.*

When Tephee got up to leave, Magda caught her hand and smiled up at her from where she sat. "Where are you going, Teph?"

Tephee snatched her hand back. "For a walk. Is there something wrong with that?"

Magda stared at her with wounded puzzlement. "Not at all. I was just asking. I thought you might like some company."

"You thought you'd keep an eye on me, you mean. I'm sick of the pair of you," Tephee's angry gaze included Sylvia, "always looking at me like that. You don't trust me. You don't think I can be responsible for my own actions." *You don't even like me.*

"Well," said Sylvia blandly, "you haven't given us much encouragement so far."

"You expect me to trust your judgement, when you have no faith in me at all. The Red Lord can take you both!" Tephee flung her cotton scarf across her shoulders and stumped away.

Leenan emerged from her tent and shook her head at Tephee's rapidly receding back. "Touchy these days, isn't she?"

Magda glanced at the little woven backpack Leenan had hitched over one shoulder. "Are you going to have a tantrum if I ask you any questions?"

Leenan gazed skyward, considering. "Nah," she decided, "depending on how personal you get, of course."

"Where are you going?"

"To the woods. I want to try something."

"Need any help?"

"Thanks, but no. I'll take Alard for protection." Alard, hearing his name from where he lay under the wagon, lifted his head and wagged his tail. Leenan slapped her thigh and Alard trotted obediently to her side.

"There's got to be more to these talents of mine than gently suggesting Karomi not throw me. I thought I might just meditate a bit. Away from people. See what happens." Leenan glanced at Sylvia for confirmation.

"Don't get lost," was all she said.

"I won't," said Leenan, offended.

"I didn't mean in the woods."

"Oh." That was a sobering thought. "Is that a problem?"

Sylvia sucked in her bottom lip as she considered. "Oughtn't be for you. You have a very strong sense of self. It helps, sometimes, to burn incense, or to hold something.

Concentrate on the smell or texture at the beginning, and you can use it to find your way back."

Leenan ducked back into the tent and grabbed a dozen sticks of incense. "I'll light them all," she told Magda, "just to make sure."

"Be careful. If you're not back by sunset we'll come looking for you."

"Okay." Leenan waved a cheery goodbye. Magda watched her go with a sigh, and wished that she was still talking to Tamalan.

It took about an hour for Leenan to reach the woods and then find a place she felt was "right." She could no longer hear the noise of the camp except as a distant mutter of activity, and with a little careful exploration she found the perfect place. Amongst the taller trees of the woods were clusters of large bushes. Inside one of these was a cosy hollow—musky animal smells still clung to it faintly, but there was no evidence of recent occupation. Leenan pushed through the narrow, overgrown channel and sat, cross-legged, in the centre of the den. Alard whined from without, then resigned himself to a few hours of guard duty and flopped across the entrance. With his chin on his paws, he glanced this way and that, then closed his eyes for a nap.

There wasn't much room to move in the hollow, but Leenan managed to empty her backpack and set the items in front of her. A flask of water, a mound of nut cakes, a white silk scarf, a lock of hair from Karomi's mane, another from Alard's tail, a few loose scales from the dragons, and a dozen sticks of incense. The latter she stuck in the ground at her feet. The animal tokens she placed on the scarf in her lap.

She called witchfire to the tip of her finger and lit the incense, and as the delicate scent enveloped her, Leenan closed her eyes and relaxed. Using the techniques Sylvia had taught her, she breathed deeply, cleared her mind, then looked out upon the world with her consciousness.

Leenan sensed herself, a bright point of light, shimmering and shifting with power. She was surprised to see that so much of that power was untapped—she obviously hadn't yet learned how to release her potential energies completely. She'd talk to Sylvia about that later. Cautiously, she reached outward.

A smaller streak of light was nearby, and with it came a mental hum of familiarity. Alard, of course. She sensed his recognition of her. She moved on.

The tokens in her lap helped to guide her. First, she looked for Karomi. Leenan's entranced body shifted so that her fingers rested on the dark, coarse hair she had taken from the animal, and her mind drifted towards the camp.

There were over a hundred oblongs of light around the camp horseyards, but she recognised Karomi without knowing how she knew her.

The dragons were hunting. Leenan abandoned linear thought and immersed herself in the sensations of their sharp reptilian minds. When Captain dived, Leenan sped down with her, exhilarated by the rush of adrenalin, the joy of the hunt. Dragon and bird collided in an explosion of feathers, and Leenan's consciousness expanded to include the terrified bird. It wasn't possible to actually hear its screeches, but its little mind was crying out with insensate terror. Captain bit into the back of its neck and the cry ceased abruptly, leaving only the dragon's satisfaction.

Leenan jerked away, appalled, and for one frantic moment didn't know where she was. She had no body. She was lost. She would have screamed if she had been able to find her mouth, but then the smell of sandalwood and musk and roses. All that incense, and all different types too. Didn't mix well. But that's where she was. The rest of her. The shell, the container for this bright light of her Self. She was fond of that container. Wouldn't do to just let it sit there in the woods and go hungry. There was so much in the world she wanted to do and experience . . . was it raining in the world? She was all . . .

. . . wet. Leenan opened her eyes and was nearly pushed over backwards by the force of Alard's joy. He licked her face enthusiastically, making sure she wasn't going to sleep again. He trampled the incense into the ground, along with half of the nut cakes, but Leenan didn't care. She flung her arms around him, breathing in his doggy smell and drying her face on his long, rough hair, and cried with relief to be back again.

King Armand pushed his empty lunch platter away and lay back on the cushions in a rare moment of contentment. It was a true pleasure to eat a meal and not feel sick after the third bite, or to have stabbing pains in his gut for hours after. He was no longer able to count his ribs. In fact, he was in rather more danger of putting on too much weight. His family had always tended to be stocky, and he'd been such a fat little kid. He laughed ruefully at the memory. Foster families all over the continent had fed him up, knowing he was heir to the throne of Tyne and determined to give the curly-haired and overly solemn youngster the best of everything.

Armand's smile faded as he indulged in the memory. He supposed he'd had a happy childhood, in many ways. He'd seen a lot of the world; learned more in those years away than he had at the university, even. Why was it that, whenever he thought of those years, he mostly saw his father's face, sad and wistful and drifting to the painting of the fragile and beautiful woman that hung in their dining hall? The few months a year he spent at home were filled with perplexed guilt for the death of the mother he'd never known, and for that tragic expression in his father's eyes.

Someone rapped on the wooden post outside his tent, seeking entry. Grateful for the interruption of his melancholy reverie, he rose and called out permission to step inside.

"You asked to see me." Captain Evenahn stood at loose attention just inside. As usual, he was dressed in basic black, his long hair loose about his shoulders and his beard trimmed. His eyes were as black as the rest of him.

Armand's good humour vanished. "That was two hours ago." He'd intended to try to talk to the Captain after Tamalan's lecture, but the man's mere presence filled him with antipathy.

Evenahn shifted in a vague shrug. "I'm here now."

"You're a proud bastard, aren't you?"

Evenahn's steady stance changed, fractionally, so that it was now a stiff, frightening stillness. His face was set in stone, and Armand recalled the stories of the Captain's family. Armand had been fostered for a year in another court at the time and had missed all the details, though he heard enough of the rumours on his return. A ten-year-old could understand only so much, and he'd left to spend another year away soon after. It struck Armand suddenly that his father, King Graym, had always patiently ignored the rumours, had assisted the intense and uncommunicative orphan in his military training, and had promoted Evenahn to Captain of the Castle Guard the year before his death.

"My father," said Armand, "rather liked you, didn't he?"

"It's a pity you're not more like him," replied Kiedrych in a voice full of acrimony and criticism.

Armand scowled. "You will remember that you are speaking to your King."

"I have never forgotten."

"You're a foul-tempered swine, Evenahn."

"So I'm often told. What did you want?"

"I want one reason why I should trust you."

They regarded each other implacably. Finally, Kiedrych answered: "Because I have never lied to you."

"That isn't good enough."

Animation flickered across Kiedrych's frozen features—hatred, anger, resentment, hurt. The shudder of emotion was quickly erased. Kiedrych spoke stiffly. "My word is all I have."

Abruptly, he turned on his heel and strode out of the tent. Armand frowned, at Evenahn and at himself.

Kayla sat on the steps of Kiedrych's caravan, holding tight to her resolve as she watched Kiedrych's approach. He was staring at the ground and hadn't seen her yet. She swallowed, wishing the van was closer to the rest of the camp, but Kiedrych had moved it right to the outer fringes, removing himself from the press of people. In a moment he would step out from among the tents, walk around to the entrance, and see her there. Kayla took a deep breath.

He came to the van, glanced up, halted. "What are you doing here?"

"You know," she said conversationally, "if you keep pushing me away, I'm going to give up and not come back."

"What are you up to?"

"Nothing."

Kayla bit back a squeal of surprise as Kiedrych grabbed

her wrist and hauled her to her feet. His voice was a barely audible growl. "What are you doing here?"

"I stupidly thought I'd like to see you," she growled back. "Let go. You're hurting my arm."

"You're planning something. You and Tamalan. What . . ."

Kayla slapped him with her free hand, as hard as she could. "Lorddamnit!" Kayla's eyes were bright with fury, *"I am not Parsa!"*

They were standing a handbreadth apart and she felt the terrible stillness, the tightening of the already unbearably tight coil of Kiedrych's pain. He still held her wrist, but didn't resist when she snatched her arm back and rubbed the skin to get the circulation back into it. Neither of them moved.

"Kiedrych?" Kayla noticed a smear of blood on his mouth. She really had hit him very hard. "I hope that hurts."

His mouth twitched in a curious smile, then became once more impassive.

"This has to stop, Kiedrych. Look at me."

He continued his heavy-lidded study of the horizon. Kayla took his face in her hands and forced him to turn, to look directly into her face. His face was expressionless, and she nearly walked away then, until she noticed his eyes. His face was like marble, but his eyes were on fire.

"Lorddamned halfwit," she murmured reproach. "What do I have to do to make you believe? I love you."

Kayla pressed her mouth against his. She pressed her body against him, running her hands up his chest and across his shoulders, pulling him closer. *Please,* she thought, *please feel something for me. Wherever you've gone, Kiedrych, please come back.*

For one moment the kiss was simply two mouths meeting, but then Kiedrych stirred, as though waking. The arms that had hung loosely at his sides wrapped around her; one broad, blunt-fingered hand held her tightly against him, and the other buried itself in her beautiful hair. When they finally broke apart, Kayla burrowed her head against his shoulder, and he held her so tightly she almost couldn't breathe. She wasn't about to complain.

"Come on," she whispered, standing back and taking his hands. "Let's go in." She led him inside the caravan and shut the door. When she turned around again, Kiedrych had sat down on the edge of a wooden trunk. He looked pale, shattered. His elbows rested on his knees and his hands were clasped together to keep them from trembling.

"Rych." Kayla laid her hand gently along the side of his face. He looked up into her eyes.

"Give me," he said with a bitter irony she didn't understand, "one reason why I should trust you."

Kayla punched him on the shoulder. "You are the single most stupid man I have ever met in my entire life! I'm in love with you, moron. If I wasn't, I wouldn't have put up with this crap for so long. One more word out of you on that subject, and by the First King, I'll break your heathen jaw!"

This spirited answer both satisfied and amused him, and he relaxed fractionally. With a small grunt of satisfaction, Kayla crouched down until her eyes were level with his and took his fists in her hands. She held them, stroking the back of his hands with her thumbs until the fingers uncurled from his palms and the muscles unclenched. Resting her hands on his thighs, she leaned forward to kiss him lightly, then rocked back on her heels.

"You look awful," she observed.

"I feel awful."

"When did you last eat?"

Kiedrych gestured vaguely. "Day before yesterday. Maybe. I don't remember."

"I'll get you something." Kayla rummaged around in Tamalan's small trunk by the back wall, where she knew he always kept little treats and surprises. She came back with a flask of wine and a leather satchel of dried lamb, fruit, and nuts. She found that she had to coax Kiedrych to eat, by sharing each bite, by urging him: "Just a little more. Try this . . . how about this?" Even so, he couldn't eat much. Kayla put the remains to one side and stood with a hand on each of his shoulders to scrutinise him once more.

"You haven't slept much." She smiled nervously. "Not that I have, either. Do I look as bad as you do?"

She was surprised, but not afraid, when he suddenly clasped her to him, burying his face against her stomach, holding her with near hysterical desperation. Kayla stroked his hair, his shoulders and back, soothingly.

"Shh. Shh. It's all right. Everything's going to be all right now. Don't . . ."

Kiedrych drew her down and kissed her fiercely, then embraced her tightly. She realised his face was wet, and that he was shaking. He rubbed his bristly face against her cheek and in a choked whisper, breathed into her ear: "I'm sorry."

Kayla had never heard Kiedrych apologise to anyone. Ever.

"It's all right," she murmured back. She clung to him as she began to cry, and then laugh. "I love you, Rych." She showered his face with kisses and plunged back into his embrace, still laughing.

"What's the joke?" he asked, with just the slightest and merely half-hearted tinge of suspicion.

"No joke," she grinned, kissing the tip of his nose. "I'm just happy."

The afternoon drifted by with the two of them safely cocooned in Kiedrych's caravan. They ate more of Tam's cache and rested in each other's arms, too physically and emotionally exhausted to do more than indulge in timid, exploratory caresses.

"Are you always this tense?" Kayla asked as she ran the palm of her hand across his back. His muscles felt as unyielding as the mountains.

"Yes."

"Well, I think I can do something about that." She helped him strip off his black suede jacket, then his black cotton shirt and plain brown undershirt. His boots were a tight fit and awkward to unlace, but she yanked those off at last and spent fifteen minutes massaging his feet. Next she loosened his belt and turned him onto his stomach so that she could massage his shoulders and back. Every now and then she would pause to drop a kiss on his warm olive skin.

Kiedrych was still half dressed when he woke the next morning. Kayla was snuggled up beside him, her head on his chest, sleeping peacefully. She had taken off her shoes, but her long colourful skirts and red cotton blouse with its complicated laces were still in place. He couldn't quite believe that they had both actually and simply fallen asleep, but he had to admit he felt a lot better this morning than he had in a long time. He kissed the top of her head and she stirred, waking.

A sharp knock at the door startled them both. The door creaked open to Tamalan's grin—simultaneously cheeky and smug. He nodded to them, sitting up with blankets clutched to their chests.

"About time you two got yourselves sorted out. Does this mean I have to keep sleeping under the caravan?"

Kiedrych arched an eyebrow at him. "I don't know," he

said mildly, "I'll have to ask Kayla."

"Well, ask her soon." There was a note of gentle warning in that sentence. "I brought you some breakfast, anyway." Tamalan pushed a cane tray holding two bowls of cooked oats, flavoured with fruit and nuts, across the floor. "And when you're finished, his Highness asked for you again. A visitor showed up last night. I think he wants your opinion." Tam rolled his eyes in mock disbelief, grinned again, and disappeared.

Kayla could feel the tension coiling through Kiedrych's body again. She leaned forward a little to catch his eye, then placed her fingertips against his temple and cheek. "Tam and I are with you, whatever you do. Never doubt that."

Kiedrych nodded slightly and some of the tension ebbed again. He kissed her briefly, tenderly, and smiled. It had been such a long time since she'd seen a smile grace his features that for a moment she was captivated by the curve of his lips and the way the skin crinkled around his eyes. His face, so often aloof, softened handsomely.

"After breakfast," he said, "tell me where you put my boots."

Chapter Nineteen

Magda was tired of this morning routine where everyone went their separate ways without even eating together first. Sylvia was increasingly involved with Armand and his Council, planning and plotting and, frankly, becoming as intense and uncommunicative as that damned Kiedrych Evenahn. Tephee hardly spoke to anyone any more, and had come back from her walk yesterday even more remote than usual. Then Leenan had returned from her own explorations tired and shaken, had gone straight to bed, and didn't look like waking any time soon.

If I'd wanted to eat breakfast alone, thought Magda with irritation as she stirred a large pot of oatmeal, fruit, and hazelnuts, *I would have stayed at Swiftfort.*

She heard someone whistling a jaunty tune and looked up hopefully. Tamalan was skirting the witches' camp on his way to Kiedrych's caravan.

"Hi, Tam!"

The whistling stopped and Tamalan looked around furtively.

"I'm not going to hurt you," she said, somewhere between encouragement and irritation.

"That's not what you said last time," he replied, looking anywhere but at her.

"I was mad at you last time. I've . . ." she took a deep breath, "I've forgiven you."

"It wasn't all my fault, you know," he said. "I told her what was in the flask. She wanted it anyway. And someone to talk to. We just talked."

"And got blind drunk."

"That was a . . . by-product. That's all."

Magda sighed. "Look, can you come over here and talk to me, instead of shouting all this across the compound? I promise I won't turn you into anything small and edible."

Reluctantly, Tam approached her, and it annoyed Magda that he thought his disobedience might result in becoming a mouse. "Would you stop it, Tam? I was angry, and I said something stupid. I won't turn you into a frog. I doubt I *could* turn you into anything much. I'm not that powerful."

"Suppose so," he admitted warily. He sat down opposite her and leaned across to smell the breakfast she was making. "That looks great. Can you spare any?"

"Plenty. Doesn't look like anyone else is eating today."

"Could I borrow a couple of bowls, and a tray? Couple of spoons as well. I won't be long, then I can come back and have breakfast with you." He treated her to a winning smile and she couldn't help but grin back. Damned if the man didn't know when he was out of hot water. Living with a man like Kiedrych all those years must have developed a sharp sense of survival in him. Magda handed over the tray and bowls, filled them with oatmeal, and watched as Tamalan practically skipped with them over to Kiedrych's van. Tam knocked, opened the door, had a brief conversation with Kiedrych, then closed the door and came back whistling. He dropped to the ground, cross-legged, beside her, looking terribly pleased with himself.

"Do you always bring Kiedrych breakfast in bed?"

"Nope," he said cheerfully, "but today he has company. About time, too."

Ah, Magda thought. Kayla. It was, indeed, about time.

"Is Armand still carrying on about him?"

Tam shrugged evasively. "Maybe. Hope not. Let's have some breakfast, I'm starving!"

Magda sighed, knowing it was almost impossible to get anything out of Tamalan Fingal unless he actually wanted to say it. The man was the most amazing mass of contradictions she had ever met.

"I can't figure you out, Tam," she said. "You're either an idiot or a genius."

"Genius," he said promptly, then grinned and tapped the side of his nose conspiratorially. "But don't let on, okay?"

Magda laughed. "If you don't let on that I can't turn people into frogs, it's a deal."

"My word is my bond," he said solemnly.

"I suppose I should thank you," she said as she dished up breakfast, "for listening to Tephee."

"She needed someone. She's a lot like Rych."

Magda's eyebrows rose in disbelief. "She's nothing like him at all."

"Probably not to you. But they have essentially the same problem."

"Which is . . . ?"

"They feel like the world has let them down. They want someone to believe in, to trust. The trouble is, all that anger and distrust means that no one feels quite safe with them. Which only makes them angrier, because they see themselves as really quite trustworthy."

"You are a very acute judge of character."

The rapidity with which the intelligent concern faded from his eyes, to be replaced by a vacuous, foolish grin, was on its own a fascinating insight into Tam's psyche.

Over breakfast they chatted about him, mostly. His

family, his job. He showed her his deck of cards. She was properly impressed by his grandfather's artwork.

"The Red King . . . that's Armand, isn't it?"

"Yep. He hadn't come to the throne yet, when Grandpop did these cards, but King Graym was already ill and we knew it wouldn't be long." Tamalan sighed. "Poor Graym. I was his jester for the last eight years of his life. I only got to be Armand's for a year. I really made a mess of it."

"How was the King's fall your responsibility?"

"It's part of what I do. I should have known more, learned more, to tell him. The trouble was . . . well, Armand didn't know me very well. He didn't always listen to me."

"I didn't realise that kings were meant to pay much attention to jesters."

Tam looked surprised, then grinned slyly. "No. We're idiots, after all."

"Or geniuses."

"The jesters of Tyne come from an unusual tradition, I guess. We hear things others don't. And sometimes we can . . . ah . . ." Tam wiggled his fingers, covered his right hand with his left, and passed both hands behind her ears. Held delicately in his fingers was her hairclip.

"How did you do that?" she asked, taking it back. "No wait, don't tell me. You devil. I bet you're pretty good with pockets, aren't you?"

He looked genuinely scandalised. "Only in the service of my King."

"Sure. Who's the Red Queen? I didn't think Armand was married."

"He's not. That's a bit embarrassing, really. Grandpop really should have painted someone a bit more generic. Instead, he painted General Kesma's daughter, Jailan."

"Why?"

"She and Armand were sort of . . . friends. They were fostered together one year, when he was about fifteen, I guess. She would have been thirteen or fourteen. When he went away to university, and later to Berrinsland, she wrote to him. They both knew that he, being Heir Apparent, would have to marry someone from a noble house, but Ma—and Grandpop—always felt they belonged together. When Armand took the throne, Jailan went away for a while. I guess she felt they belonged together too." Tam sighed. "Which is why, of course, she wasn't able to talk any sense into him when all the trouble started. She was away, with her sister."

"You lot really are cursed with bad luck, aren't you?"

Tamalan was surprised. "Us? No, I don't think so. We're still alive. Chances are we might even stay that way. Some of us are even finding something better along the way." He nodded towards Kiedrych's van as the door opened and first Kiedrych, and then Kayla, stepped out into the sunlight. Tam's smile was so broad that he seemed to be taking the credit even for the lovely sunny morning. He clambered to his feet. "Gotta go. Thanks for breakfast."

"You're welcome. Hey, Tamalan," Magda grabbed his hand, "I'm glad we're friends again."

Unexpectedly, he raised her hand to his lips and gave a courtly bow. "Me too."

Magda was still gazing after Tamalan's retreating figure when Leenan's derisive snort recaptured her attention.

"You've got that soppy look again," said Leenan from the entrance to their tent.

"He's just a friend."

"Uh-huh. Did your friend leave anything to eat? I'm famished."

"Sure. Come on." Magda ladled the last of the porridge into a bowl and handed it to Leenan as she emerged, dressed in brown cotton pants and a loose blouse. "How are you feeling now? You looked pretty awful last night."

"Felt it too," said Leenan around a mouthful of oats. Magda busied herself brewing a pot of herbs while Leenan ate, then handed her a steaming mug of tea. Leenan took a few sips before steeling herself to answer her friend's unasked questions.

"I don't know that I learned very much," she said.

"You must have found out something."

"I can . . . contact animals. Connect with them. Feel their instincts."

"That's good."

"For what? I can understand animal feelings. Big deal."

"If you can connect with them, you can probably control them."

Leenan shrugged. "Maybe. But what would I want to do that for?"

"You did it once already, when you got the dragons to hang onto Sylvia that day she fell."

Leenan brightened. "I did, didn't I?"

"And I'm very grateful, too." Leenan and Magda both looked up as Sylvia approached them and sat down. "Is there anything left?" she asked, glancing hopefully at the pot.

"Only tea, I'm afraid," said Magda, pouring her a cup. "I'll make you something if you like."

Sylvia shook her head wearily as she took the tea. Her face was drawn and dark circles gave her eyes a bruised, haggard air. Her clothes hung loosely on her already light frame.

"You look terrible," said Leenan.

"There's a lot to do," Sylvia replied tiredly, "and I'm not as young as I used to be. Where's Tephee?"

"Went for a walk early this morning again," Magda advised her.

Sylvia smothered another sigh, but seemed to become even smaller. "I've done rather badly, haven't I?"

"We all have." Magda's self-reproach was evident. "We seem to drive her further away from us all the time."

"Nothing short of letting her get her own way would have kept her here," pointed out Leenan.

The three of them fell into brooding silence, broken eventually by Leenan, who couldn't bear the atmosphere of recrimination hanging over the others. "How are things going on the battlefront?"

"Well enough." Sylvia stifled yet another sigh. "They don't really need me for most of their plans—though they keep insisting that they do. I just need them to keep the opposing army busy so that I can deal with Tallan."

"You don't have to do this all alone, you know," said Magda. "If you'd just tell us what we have to do . . ."

Sylvia shook her head. "I have to do this alone."

"No you don't," Leenan interrupted sharply. "The truth is, you want to do it alone. You expect Magda and me to do our bit with the army, but you don't want us helping you with this."

Sylvia was displeased. "Leenan, I have a lot more experience in this kind of thing. I have to be fully prepared for them . . ."

"Them?"

"I meant Tallan and Saebert."

"No you didn't." Magda's suspicions suddenly coalesced. "You meant Tallan and *Tephee*."

Sylvia refused to answer. She drank her tea, rose, and went to her tent.

"She's right," Magda called back at her. "You don't trust her. And you don't trust any of us enough to help you. I'm talking to you, Sylvia!" The healer was on her feet, already following the older witch.

"Leave it, Maggie," Leenan said. "She's too tired. It's not lack of trust. She's scared."

Magda stopped, stared at the tent where Sylvia had fled, and wondered what that meant for the rest of them.

Chapter Twenty

Tamalan scampered into the meeting tent and dodged his way through the groups of tribe leaders until he reached Armand. "Captain Evenahn will join you shortly, Highness," he reported.

"I trust he won't keep me waiting this time," said Armand grimly. "And what are you grinning at? You were late back yourself."

"Duty called, sire, and a beautiful woman." Tam danced a little on the spot, snatched up three empty wine goblets, and began to juggle. "It's a glorious day, don't you think?"

His exuberance was infectious. Armand and a circle of nearby Ashrafs laughed at him. Delighted to have a full audience once more, the jester performed a few more tricks—sleight of hand with scarves, his cards, and the slickly liberated jewelled daggers and gold rings belonging to those around him. He glanced away when he saw Kiedrych enter and stride towards the King. By the look on his face, Tam had started the celebrations early. There was still the trouble with Armand to clear up.

Tam made his cards, and then himself, disappear. He reappeared briefly beside Kiedrych.

"Where's Kayla?"

Kiedrych spared him a sideways glance. "She went to the river. To bathe."

"Idiot." Tam cuffed the Captain lightly on the arm. "You should have gone with her." He was rewarded by the hint of a smile around Kiedrych's lips.

"You're probably right. But I'm here now."

"So you are. By the way, can you give this back to that fat Ashraf over there? The one with the orange turban—vile, isn't it?—before he misses it and gets mad." Tamalan handed him a wicked-looking stiletto blade, which was considerably more business-like than the ceremonial and decorative arms usually allowed into these meetings. Kiedrych regarded the weapon silently for a moment.

"He'll deny it's his."

"Great. Then we get to keep it. Isn't this fun?" Tam grinned hugely before disappearing again.

Kiedrych approached the King, making sure the knife was clearly seen in front of him. It wouldn't do to have someone else's dubious intentions blamed on him. He was quick to note the fat Ashraf's startled reaction, which was schooled quickly into blankness.

"King Armand," said Kiedrych, to gain his attention. "Tamalan asked me to return this to Ashraf Marek." He turned and presented it to the Ashraf, aware of Armand's eyes on him and the blade. "The jester says he forgot to give this back."

"It is not mine," said Marek staunchly. "He is mistaken."

Kiedrych shrugged, apparently unconcerned.

"I think," said Armand, "that I will take care of it for now." Kiedrych, who had been about to hang the knife from his own belt, paused. Their eyes locked together in a silent battle of wills for what seemed an age. Kiedrych's back was rigid with anger again. Nevertheless, he slowly, slowly, reached out and placed the knife across the King's palm. Armand closed his fist around it. The rest of the circle shifted uncomfortably.

"Tamalan said something about visitors," said Kiedrych,

deliberately leaving off the honorific.

Armand's lips pursed at the slight, but he did not pursue it. "Yes. He says he used to be in the Castle Guard."

Kiedrych's eyes narrowed. "There were a lot of men in the Castle Guard."

"Just so. However, Tam has suggested that you might vouch for the man's . . . credibility. At least confirm if he is who he says."

"You'll take my word?" Kiedrych couldn't hold back that note of incredulity.

Armand stared straight through him. "I'll decide that," said the King, "later." He gestured for someone to fetch the visitor.

Kiedrych clenched his jaws, fixed his gaze on the middle distance, and stood locked in military attention until Darem's men returned with a travel-worn young man between them. He was of medium height and tending towards stockiness, with thinning brown hair and a dark three-day stubble which made him look particularly unkempt. His bearing was a mixture of indignation, awe, and anxiety. When the guards released him, he bowed deeply to Armand, then looked up into Kiedrych's forbidding gaze.

"Captain Evenahn! Thank the Lords. We thought you were dead. Tell the King who I am, Captain. His Highness," the man darted an uncertain look at his King, "thinks I might be a spy."

"Our King is short on trust these days, Malcolm," said Kiedrych drily. He turned to Armand. "This is Castle Guardsman Malcolm Muhsteen. An excellent archer, competent swordsman, but sloppy with maintenance." Kiedrych eyed the man coldly. "I expect you still haven't cleaned the rust from that heirloom sword of yours."

Malcolm Muhsteen was grinning like an idiot at this.

Trust Evenahn, he was thinking, *a hard-nosed bastard and a temper like a cut snake, but he stuck by his men.* "I would have cleaned it, Captain, but I lost it in the battle."

"Careless with his tools, as well," Kiedrych reported.

Despite himself, Armand's lips twitched in a hastily dismissed smile. "All right, Malcolm. Make your report to Evenahn."

"Yes, Your Highness." Malcolm ducked his head respectfully, then made his brief report to Kiedrych. "Some of us survived the battle, after the field broke up, sir. We've been regrouping, waiting for the signal. We have two thousand men, sir—from the Guard and the regular army, ready to join you. They're marching this way, and if His Highness continues north you should meet with them in a few days. The ranking officers will ride ahead, sir, and should be here to meet you this evening."

"Where have you been sheltering?" demanded Kiedrych crisply, his eyes fierce.

Malcolm swallowed. He hated it when the Captain was in one of his moods. "With Jailan Kesma, sir. She sent messengers to us after the battle, when we were in hiding. Once Sergeant Ho heard about it he searched us out. Word spread, and the survivors made their way to her lands by the border, sir."

"Her lands? What about General Kesma?"

"Dead, sir. Jailan and her sister and sister's husband stayed on the General's holdings. They were too far away for the Witch and the Usurper to bother with."

Both Malcolm and Kiedrych glanced across to Armand. The King was studying the hem of Darem's robe, his expression full of doubt and regret.

"Someone else you've kept waiting," said Kiedrych. He was untouched by the hurt, hateful look that Armand cast towards him.

"Enough," Armand dismissed both Captain and Sergeant peremptorily.

"Do you still think he's a spy?" Kiedrych said. He enjoyed the King's discomfiture with a vindictive little smile.

"I believe him for his own sake. Not yours." The King gained a small measure of bleak satisfaction at the way Evenahn froze up again. The Captain nodded a terse farewell, and followed the guardsman out of the tent. He was stopped at the door by Armand's commanding voice.

"You will attend a meal this evening to confirm the identities of these ranking officers, Evenahn."

Kiedrych turned to glare icily at him. Ashrafs and their servants shifted subtly aside so as not to be between these two blazing points of rage. "You should already know your officers. Your Highness."

"Obey your King." The order snapped out, silencing all else.

Into the silence, Kiedrych snarled: "As Your Highness commands." He whirled and disappeared outside.

Tam was dismayed to see Kiedrych all coiled up with animosity once more. He wondered if he should warn Kayla about his mood, decided he shouldn't, changed his mind, couldn't find her, and finally realised that she had taken it upon herself to make sure Kiedrych bothered to eat. In a moment of anxious curiosity, Tam listened outside Kiedrych's (no longer "their") caravan.

Kiedrych was muttering something irritably. Kayla said something rude back about his manners. A plate crashed on the floor. Kayla swore colourfully, another plate crashed, and suddenly she was laughing.

"Lords, Rych, at this rate I'll have to buy a potter's wheel to keep up with the wear and tear. Remind me to bring wooden bowls next time."

To Tam's utter surprise, he heard a low masculine chuckle. "If I stop ducking, will it help?"

"Maybe we just need to change our target," said Kayla, a hint of grimness in her voice. Kiedrych grunted sour agreement, and Tam decided it was high time he left the two of them in peace and privacy.

It was late afternoon when a dozen riders arrived at the camp, their horses worn out with hard riding and the horsemen not much better. All of them had short hair and were clean-shaven in the manner of Tyne's soldiers. Kiedrych watched them critically from the door of his van and rubbed his bearded chin.

"Do you know them?" Kayla, standing at his elbow, peered at the unfamiliar faces.

"Some. Not all. I knew most of the officers stationed near the capital, but some of these are from outlying posts. They've all been waiting for His Highness to return." He considered them for a moment longer, disappeared inside, and returned shortly with a fold-down stool, a mirror, a shallow dish, soap, and a short, very sharp knife.

He scooped up some water from the small barrel he kept by the door to the van, flipped the stool out, and sat down.

"Here." He handed her the water, soap, and the knife. Kayla took them, staring from the knife to his face.

"I need a shave," he said.

She stared a little longer. Two days ago he wouldn't have trusted her with a wooden *spoon* in his presence. Today he hands her a knife and bares his throat. Was this a sign of trust, or a test?

She looked at his face—his eyes were closed, his head tilted slightly back—baring his throat indeed—and there was an expression of anticipation, combined with doubt, and resignation. *Dumb bastard,* she thought, between tenderness and aggravation, *doesn't even know if it's a test himself.*

If she kills me, he was thinking, *Lords, make it quick. I don't want to know about it any more.* He was also thinking: *Fool, she's not going to kill me.*

He wasn't sure which voice he ought to listen to, so he ignored them both.

Kayla soaped up his face swiftly, placed the blade against his throat, and drew it firmly and carefully upward. "Don't sneeze, for goodness' sake," she warned with a laugh, "or we could be in trouble." He didn't reply. She made short work of his straggly beard, then stood back, wiping her hands on her skirt, to survey the result.

"So *that's* what you look like. I'd almost forgotten. It's a definite improvement."

Kiedrych half-opened his eyes to reveal his slightly dented pride. "It was that bad?"

She cocked her head to one side and smiled. "Maybe that's a bit ungenerous of me. But you do look better without it." She leaned forward and gave him a quick kiss on his cheek. Judging by the sudden relaxation in his face, she had passed his unconscious test with flying colours.

"Hang on just a second," she said suddenly, "I have to get you something." She ruffled his hair (he looked at her as though he couldn't quite believe she'd done it. No one had ruffled his hair since he was seven. Except, once or twice, Mother Fingal. Everyone else was too intimidated by him) and ran off to her own caravan. She passed through the witches' camp on the way, to see Leenan heading off with a backpack and her dog up to the river, and Sylvia with Tephee cornered in some serious conversation. Kayla took what she needed from her caravan, and on the way back noticed the others had gone and Magda was scribbling furiously on a piece of paper.

When she got back to Kiedrych, he was busy cutting his long hair to a more soldierly length.

"That's a shame," she said, "I liked it long. Mind you . . . your ears are cute." He arched an eyebrow at her, and she laughed. "Here, put some of this on your face."

He eyed the pot of cream with an ounce of ordinary suspicion, and sniffed cautiously at the contents. It smelt herbal, but not floral, thank the Lords.

"You haven't shaved in a year. Your skin will dry out and feel a bit tender. That should help."

Kiedrych scooped up a little on his finger and looked at it in the light. It was green. He arched that eyebrow again.

"I use it for sunburn," she explained.

A pause. "It's green."

"So it is."

He shrugged and smeared it on his face. He wouldn't admit it, but it did feel soothing. He handed her the knife and got her to finish his haircut while he rubbed cream into his throat and face.

He no longer worried what Kayla would do with the knife.

The sun was setting, casting a rosy glow over the distant mountains from whence they had come. It was a lovely sight, though few people had time to appreciate it. Sylvia only noted absently that it was going to be dark soon.

She walked silently by Tephee's side, both of them striding in a tense, charged silence.

"This was your idea," said Tephee irritably at last. "Say something."

Sylvia rubbed her hand across her eyes. She had seemed

so ageless when Magda and Tephee had first met her, but years were etched into her now. Her face was lined with worry and exhaustion, her shoulders stooped, and she walked with a slow tread, as though the effort were almost too much. If Tephee noticed, she did not choose to comment.

"I don't know what to say," Sylvia admitted. Her voice was low, tired. "I want to say all the right things to you, Tephee. I've said all the wrong things so far. I'm afraid to do it any more."

"Why don't you try being honest with me?"

"I have never lied to you, Teph."

"Sins of omission, then. Or maybe you're just not honest with yourself."

Sylvia sighed. "You're right, of course. It's hard to be honest with yourself. If I try . . . will you promise to try too?"

Tephee bit back a snide reply and nodded.

"I've been very foolish, Tephee. I've come here to become involved in a fight that was not mine, to seek . . . peace, of some sort. Redemption, if you will."

"For your baby."

"For my baby, and my husband and friends and all the choices I could have made and didn't. To be completely honest, I think there is a certain amount of pride involved, too. I beat Farshee at a cost. I wanted to defeat Tallan without paying a price. I have finally realised it isn't possible."

"You don't have to do it alone, Sylvia. You never did."

"I know that. But Magda and Leenan aren't powerful enough to do what has to be done. And you . . . I was afraid for you. That was my biggest mistake. My fear has driven you away from us. It has changed you. And now you've fulfilled my worst fear of all."

Tephee stopped walking and stood very still. She had almost been at the point of apology. She'd wanted to tell Sylvia that she was sorry for all the angry words and hurt feelings, but the tension she felt radiating from the older witch froze her tongue. When Sylvia didn't continue, she prompted: "Which is?"

"I don't . . ."

"You said you'd be honest. Tell me."

"I've made you . . . like them. Full of anger and need. Farshee and Tal . . ." She stopped abruptly as Tephee spun on her heel to face her.

Tephee was incredulous, amazed, wounded, and defensive all at once. "Do you really think I'm so monstrous?"

Sylvia closed her eyes and shook her head wearily. "You're not evil, Tephee. I doubt that Zuleika Tallan thinks that she's evil . . ."

"No, I don't expect she does. She doesn't feel evil, either."

Sylvia bit her lip, holding back tears. "Be honest with yourself, Tephee. Look at what you're doing. What do you want?"

Despite herself, Tephee was crying. "You know what I want."

"You can't get it this way. Not with power."

"The hell I can't."

"Te . . ."

"What *good* is all this power if it doesn't get me what I want?" cried Tephee. "What *good* is it if it terrifies people but won't keep me safe? Damn," she wiped tears from her face with stiff, jerky movements, "denying your power hasn't made you happy, has it?"

"It did, for a long time," said Sylvia sadly.

"And look at you now. A thousand miles from home looking for revenge. Don't tell me what works, Sylvia. You don't know the answers."

"No," Sylvia's brow creased in awareness and loss, "I don't."

They stared at each other in pained silence for a moment longer, before Tephee pulled her shawl closer around her shoulders, her chin jerking up defiantly, began to walk, then broke and ran to the shelter of the woods. Sylvia watched her until the girl had disappeared into the darkness. She hugged herself against a sudden chill in the warm night air, and suddenly was on her knees by the riverside, her face buried in her hands, weeping.

Chapter Twenty-One

The twelve riders turned out to be the five top-ranking officers left in Armand's shattered army and a small escort. Armand had decided to meet them in his own tent, which was smaller and more pleasantly equipped than the giant meeting pavilion.

Captain Evenahn had shown up on time and, what's more, clean-shaven, with a haircut and in uniform. The black pants, piped with silver and gold trim, were baggy and Evenahn had apparently punched a new hole in the black leather dress belt, bearing the Bakar-Tyne coat of arms on the buckle, in order to do it up tightly enough. The richly coloured red shirt was a stunning contrast to his usual black, though the impact was toned down by the black vest, held together with a tarnished chain, and the regulation dress black coat. The Captain's badge of rank was sewn onto the left shoulder, a complicated knot in gold. Despite the too-loose fit, Evenahn managed to wear the outfit with some measure of dignity.

Armand himself had changed out of his nomad robes and into the repaired remnants of the clothes he'd been wearing when forced to leave the battlefield at Tyne. They were similar to the Captain's, but made of richer material, and his shirt was the striking true red of the family colours. The pants were much too big for him now, but like Evenahn he'd tightened the belt, wore a coat to disguise his thinness, and had found time to shave.

Tamalan had not made such a big effort for the occasion, though he'd clearly chosen the best clothes in his wardrobe: a pair of soft lizard-skin trousers dyed an eye-catching shade of green, and a patchwork shirt in a riot of colours. His leather boots were red and his hair was still tied back with a collection of colourful threads. The effect was flamboyant and comical.

Darem and the senior-most Ashrafs of the other tribes had also been invited, and it was a sizable group that gathered on the furs and cushions in the centre of King Armand's tent. Pleasantries were exchanged, Evenahn acknowledging those of the five officers he knew, and asking gruff, piercing questions about their recent activities. Their escort had not been invited and were being entertained by Darem's own soldiers.

One of the five, a tall, lanky Major named Tyrole who Evenahn had known in Tyne, knelt before the King at the beginning of the meal.

"Highness, I would like to present you with a small gift." Tyrole produced a silver and crystal bowl, its lid bearing a simple etching of a tree by a river—typical glassware from the Sharreya region of Tyne. When the container had received due admiration, the Major lifted the lid with a short, elegant motion, revealing the region's other claim to fame—spiced honey dragonflies, a delicacy anywhere in the known world. Armand inclined his head graciously at the exotic and expensive gift.

"A rare gift," he said with proper formality, "and even more so in times like these."

Major Tyrole beamed with pleasure. "Both come from my family's country holding, sire, in Sharreya. It is fitting that these things are delivered to our true King."

Armand dipped his fingers into the crystal bowl and drew out a dragonfly, crystallised and impregnated with delicate spices. Honey dripped into the bowl. Armand was about to eat it when Evenahn spoke.

"Surely, your Most Royal Highness," his formality did not completely disguise the underlying acidity of his tone, "it is my duty to taste this gift before yourself."

Armand narrowed his eyes and gave him a sideways glare. "I think not, Captain."

"Your Highness must know that my duties of Captain of the Guard, in the absence of your personal retinue, include the testing of all gifts. For the safety of your Most Royal Highness." The Captain's voice was icy. If his King demanded an obedient servant, then he was damn well going to get one, right down to the most stringent duty of his post.

Armand was aware that this was a demonstration of will, not fealty. He glared at Evenahn and didn't move.

"I must insist. Your Highness," said the Captain.

There was an embarrassed silence all round, but neither wished to back down. Eventually, Armand stifled an irritated sigh and offered the sticky sweet to the man. Evenahn took it carefully, put it in his mouth, chewed, and swallowed. He maintained an urbane smile, with only a hint of difficulty since he thought honeyed bugs were a revolting concept, and nodded.

"Most excellent, King Armand."

"Your diligence is appreciated," replied Armand through gritted teeth. He reached into the bowl for another dragonfly as Evenahn turned back to face the Ashrafs and officers. Kolett, Hundeline, Nikh, and Morwen avoided his gaze, still embarrassed by the scene, and Tyrole looked . . . afraid?

Captain Evenahn's hand shot out and held the King's arm before he could place the dragonfly in his mouth. Their gazes met, and Armand was startled to see shock and fear blaze for a moment from Evenahn's eyes.

"It's poi . . ."

The first spasm hit Kiedrych as Tyrole leapt at the King, his ceremonial knife drawn. Every other man in the tent dived and tackled the Major, dragging him to the floor, as Armand dropped the sweet, hastily wiping his fingers. Tamalan burst out from the shadows, reaching for the Captain who was doubled over in pain.

"Rych? Lords . . ."

Evenahn tried to speak, but only snatched another breath before doubling up again with cramp. Armand caught him as he fell, and Tam jumped over the pair of them, running for all he was worth outside and down to the witches' camp.

"Magda! *Magda!*" He was shouting before he got there. She was there, by the fire. "Magda . . . quick . . . Rych . . ."

"Slow down, Tam. What is it?"

"Poison," he said between wheezing gasps for breath. "Hurry."

"Kiedrych?" Kayla's voice behind him sounded very small and frightened. Tam turned, but she was already running towards the King's tent.

Magda grabbed his elbow, and he whirled back. She had a strange, square bag slung over one shoulder and her face was grim. "Come on."

They arrived at Kayla's heels. Kayla ran, dropped to her knees, and tried to hold Kiedrych's shoulders as his body shook with spasm. Her face was utterly white. To one side, a thin man was being held down and tied with cotton scarves and Armand had pulled off his jacket and used it to dry the cold sweat beading all over the Captain's face and chest. Magda snapped out orders over the noise as she knelt and opened the square bag.

"How did it happen? Tam, come on," she shook him savagely.

"The dragonflies, he ate one."

Magda was lifting a metallic box from the bag she had brought with her. She glanced up sharply. "Bring it up!"

Kayla returned a desperate look. "How? I . . ."

"Stick your fingers down his throat, woman," Magda growled. "Bugger his dignity. He'll be dead in a minute." She opened the box, pulled open a little door. "Give me one of the bloody things."

Tam hesitated; Armand picked one up and gave it to her. A low moan juddered out of Kiedrych's throat, then the sound of retching, and Kayla, terrified, trying to tell him he'd be all right as she held his head. Magda put the insect into a compartment, flipped up a portion of the box, and peered into a square of peculiar green light.

The spasms stopped for a moment, and Kiedrych crouched on the floor, gasping for breath. His eyes were closed and he leaned into Kayla, kneeling beside him. Part of him was thinking: *This is how much pain it takes, to make things even with the world.*

"Hold on," Kayla was saying, sobbing. "You'll be fine. Please . . . hold on . . ."

The spasms began again. Armand seized him by the shoulders, turned him, and placed a strip of his jacket between the Captain's teeth, to keep him from choking on his own tongue. Their eyes met, and even through the haze of agony and fear of approaching death, Armand could read an "I-told-you-so" there.

"Where are you, goddamnit?" Magda was muttering fiercely to herself. "Isolate this bastard . . . there . . . ah . . ." The structural analyser had found it. The compound.

If she could only . . . yes, take out that element, she could neutralise it . . .

"Magda!" Kayla's scream brought her back. Kiedrych was in cardiac arrest.

"Hold him down . . . *do* it . . ." Magda scrambled over to him, held her hands over his heart, closed her eyes, and reached out with her magic. *Hold on, heart. You're a strong sucker, don't give up. There. Beat. Regular, regular . . . goddamn! . . . too fast . . . shit . . . there's the compound, and there . . . Jesus, it's everywhere. Start here.*

Magda began to separate the compound, pulling out the one element to make it harmless. *Slow work . . . so much . . . too much . . .*

"Tam," she gasped, half emerging from her trance. "Get help. Sylvia, Leenan, anyone . . . I can't do this alone." She closed her eyes again, not seeing Tamalan leap to his feet and disappear once more outside.

The stuff was cleared from his heart . . . stomach, the source . . . okay . . . *god, his respiratory system* . . . With part of her conscious mind, she could hear his laboured gasps for air. Clear the aureoles, then the bronchial tubes . . . god, she wasn't strong enough . . .

"I . . . can't . . ."

Kayla tore her eyes from Kiedrych's waxy, grey face. He was clutching onto her, trying to keep both pain and fear under control, once or twice trying to say her name. She looked wildly at Magda. "You have to! Sweet Lords, not now, don't let him die now!"

"I'm . . . not . . . strong . . . enough. . . ."

"*Find* the strength! Use mine!" Kayla grasped Magda's wrists, forcing them back over Kiedrych's chest. *"Help him!"*

Magda's hands twisted up and over, seizing Kayla's

wrists in return. Strength returned to her. She immersed her mind in the bloodstream of his body, pulsing with it . . . wherever she found the poison, she changed it, drawing out the lethal element and letting the rest filter through his system naturally. No damage to the kidneys . . . good. Clean bloodstream. Clean lungs, and stomach, and heart. All organs and limbs and tissues . . . clean.

God, she was tired.

Someone was talking to her, but it was too much effort to listen. Perhaps she should. It sounded important . . .

The someone had hold of her hands, prising her fingers back. Magda let go (of what? she wondered) and collapsed back into waiting arms.

"Magda? Maggie? Come on, open your eyes . . ."

Magda obeyed sluggishly—it seemed an impossible thing—and Leenan's face swam into view. With a small movement of her head she could see Kiedrych and, beside him, unconscious and barely breathing, Kayla. She remembered . . .

"Oh God," she mumbled, frightened. "What did I do?"

And then Magda, too, slipped into unconsciousness.

Chapter Twenty-Two

As soon as he woke up, he knew that something was not right. The light was too bright. The ground was too soft. It didn't smell right.

He wasn't dead.

Kiedrych's eyes flew open. Above him was the wooden ceiling of his own caravan. The smell was a combination of stale sweat and the lingering acrid stink of someone who'd been sick.

He lay still for a moment, and for that time could feel every tiny cell of his body doing its appointed task. He could visualise the air entering his lungs and filling them completely; his heart beating a steady rhythm against his ribs; his mind clear but at rest. The process fascinated him, and he remained motionless, eyes closed once more, in order to experience it all.

"Kiedrych?" The voice was timid and soft, breaking into his lassitude gently but with a curious anxiety. Kiedrych opened his eyes again. Tamalan smiled nervously down at him. "How do you feel?"

Kiedrych thought about that question. It took him a long time to consider and he fell asleep again while he was doing so. When he woke next time, Tam was sponging his face and chest with a cool cloth.

"You going to stay awake this time?" the jester asked.

"Maybe," Kiedrych replied. He was surprised to hear his own voice sound so indistinct. He tried again. "Maybe."

"Magda says it doesn't matter. You're sleeping naturally

now. Your body has to rest, to get over the trauma, she says."

"Trauma?" Kiedrych's brow creased with puzzlement, then cleared, then creased again with worry. "The King . . . ?"

"He's fine. They lost Tyrole, though. When they tied him up, he just wriggled around till he got near those . . . those Lorddamned dragonflies, and he ate some of the poison. There was no one left to save him. Not as though anyone wanted to anyway. Darem and Armand are pretty sure this is from Saebert, not the witch . . ." Tam trailed off. Kiedrych was asleep again.

The next time Kiedrych woke up, it was Armand sitting cross-legged beside him.

"I didn't think you'd meant that literally, Captain," said the King drily.

"Meant . . . what?"

"When you asked if you'd have to kill yourself, before I'd believe you."

Kiedrych couldn't quite work up a sneer. "Do you believe now?" he asked wearily.

Armand's expression softened, in sorrow and regret and concern. "Oh yes. I believe you now."

"Good." Kiedrych closed his eyes again. After a little while, he heard Armand leave, but someone was still in here with him. He raised one eyelid cautiously, to see Tam regarding him with pursed lips and a glimmer of humour.

"You didn't know that stuff was poisoned, did you?"

"Don't be ridiculous. If I'd thought it was poisoned, I'd have made Tyrole eat it."

"Thought so. The King is impressed, though."

"Hmph." Kiedrych paused and nearly drifted back to sleep. A thought occurred to him, though, and he forced his eyes open again. "Where's Kayla?"

"Oh . . . um . . . she's in her caravan."

Kiedrych detected the worried tone and tried to sit up. "What's wrong?"

"Nothing! Nothing. Magda says she's going to be fine, but she needs more rest."

"Tamalan," snarled Kiedrych through gritted teeth, "what happened?" He managed to lurch onto his side, supported on his elbow.

"I don't know. I don't understand. She helped Magda somehow, and she got . . . worn out. Magda's looking after her."

Kiedrych was on his hands and knees now, ignoring the hesitant attempts Tam made to make him lie back down.

"Shouldn't you be getting more rest?"

Kiedrych made it to his feet and staggered towards the door. He was wearing trousers, at least, which was just as well because he doubted he had the strength to dress himself. He nearly fell down the stairs, but Tam reached down to steady him, and he managed to walk unaided across the space between his van and Kayla's.

Magda saw him coming and stood up, waving away Leenan's helping hands. She caught up to him as he staggered and caught himself on the walls of the caravan.

"You shouldn't be up," she said.

He regarded her thin, ashen face; the dark circles under sunken eyes and the yellowish pallor to her skin. "You look . . ."

". . . abominable. I know." Magda nodded at the van door. "She's asleep."

Nevertheless, Kiedrych leaned over and opened the door.

Kayla was certainly asleep. She was also terribly pale and

still. Beside her bed was a peculiar contraption—a metal frame, holding a transparent bag of fluid. A tube ran from the bag and, attached to a silver needle, disappeared into Kayla's arm.

"It's all right." Magda actually stroked his arm, as though calming an animal. "It's an IV drip. She's not strong enough to eat, but she has to get nourishment. She'll stay on that another day or two. She's not in a coma. She's just sleeping now."

Kiedrych sagged back against the steps and shook his head. "Why do you get to walk around?"

"I expect witch metabolism is more efficient than the usual."

He looked up at her without comprehension.

She rephrased it. "Witches process food into energy . . . strength . . . faster than other people. It'll take Kayla a few days, at least. Don't look at me like that." Magda's anger held at least as much guilt. "If it wasn't for her, you'd be dead, well and truly."

One way or another, thought Kiedrych. When he tried to stand, a wave of dizziness swept over him and he had to sit again.

"You need to eat something yourself," said Magda. "Soup or something. I'll fix it."

She walked away, none too steady on her own feet. Kiedrych waited until the wave of giddiness passed, then made his way up the stairs—hanging onto the door frame for support—and stooped to enter the caravan. At the head of the bedroll, near the farther wall and on the opposite side to the drip, he rested his back on the wood and slithered down to sit on the floor at Kayla's side.

In her sleep, she shifted and murmured something, then was still. He reached down to take her hand, rubbing his thumb gently across the bridge of her knuckles, down her fingers.

When Magda returned with a jug of the peculiar green drink she'd once made for Tam and Sylvia at Swiftfort, Kiedrych had dozed off yet again, still holding Kayla's hand.

It was dark and cold, when Kiedrych woke once more. Someone had pulled a blanket over his legs and bare chest but had left him otherwise undisturbed. It worried him that anyone could have done so without waking him, even under the circumstances.

Beside him was a jug of green liquid, a cup, and a note scrawled in Tamalan's untidy hand saying, "Magda said you should drink this. It tastes like rust and swamp water, but it's got a kick to it. Cheers." Kiedrych poured a glass, screwed up his face at the smell, and drank the lot in one draught.

It was odd, but at least it didn't have any honey in it. Or insects. The memory made him gag, and he pushed the rest of the medicinal drink away. Beside him, Kayla stirred.

Her eyes were open and she was smiling at him. "Hi there." Her voice was weak.

"Hello."

"It's good to see you. Tam said you were all right, but I didn't know if he was just being diplomatic." The effort of saying a whole sentence seemed to tire her out. Kiedrych gave her time to rest.

He thought she was asleep again, realising he'd been doing that to everyone else all day, but when he looked down at her, her eyes were regarding his bare chest contentedly.

" 'S nice," she observed.

"What is?"

"You. Mmmm . . . you're lovely . . ." The last part trailed off indistinctly as, with a smile faintly curving her lips, she finally did go to sleep.

Lovely. No one had described him as lovely before. His lips quirked into a smile at the inconsistency of the image. Hard-nosed, foul-tempered, arrogant, proud, aloof, uncompromising, and dangerous were usual, but not "lovely."

His shoulders and back were getting colder. He should go back to his own van and get some sleep. It wasn't that far, even in the dark and the cold, without shoes. Tam's snoring probably wouldn't even wake him up tonight.

Kiedrych adjusted himself to lie more comfortably on the floor. Kayla shifted to lie closer to him. He pulled the blanket up to his chin, rolled onto his side, draped an arm across Kayla, and drifted back into slumber.

The next morning, Magda had to move Kiedrych's arm so that she could change the drip. He woke suddenly at the movement, seizing her wrist in startled and suspicious reaction. He blinked, confused by his surroundings.

"Let go," Magda shook herself free carefully, "I've got work to do."

He released her and sat up, scrubbing his hands over his face in an effort to wake up. Kayla slept on.

"Did you drink that stuff I left for you last night?"

"A little," he said.

"You've got to drink the lot. I asked Tam, you know, and no one can remember the last time you ate anything. Apart from that damned bug." She sympathised with the look of queasiness that passed across his features. "I take it you don't feel up to eating solids yet."

"The very thought," he admitted, "makes me feel ill."

"If Armand's gag reflex to honey cakes is any indication, anything like that is not going to go down well with you anyway. You need sugars, carbohydrates, and proteins right now, and if you're not going to eat, you have to drink that stuff. Simple as that. Kayla and I didn't go through all that so you could starve yourself to death."

"Hmph." Still, he poured a cup and tossed it back. "Gyaaah. Lords, that's foul."

"Yep. Think of it as punishment for all your misdeeds."

Kiedrych glanced sharply at her, but she was busy making adjustments to her equipment and didn't notice. "I suppose I should . . ." he began gruffly, then halted.

Magda glanced sideways at him. He lifted his eyes to meet her gaze and she was touched to see a humility in his expression she would have thought unlikely a month before.

"Thank you," he said, simply, with feeling.

"You're welcome, Kiedrych. Thank her, too, when she wakes up." She watched as his hand automatically sought Kayla's, closing protectively over her knuckles. "You would have died if she hadn't given me the strength to finish."

"She will be all right, won't she?" All soldierly reserve gone, his voice yearned for reassurance.

"With rest, good care, and your help," she obliged, "there's no doubt of it."

Kiedrych nodded solemnly, as though accepting a vow.

"I'm done here," Magda told him. His eyes were on Kayla. "Don't let that drip get pulled out of her arm," she warned as she was leaving. "And keep her warm."

She left him to the tender intimacy of tucking the blanket close around Kayla's shoulders.

Chapter Twenty-Three

Kiedrych forced himself to drink the rest of the green witch-brew and had to admit he felt much better for it. Taking extraordinary care to see that Kayla wasn't disturbed, he extricated himself from his blankets and made for the door, much more steadily this time. It opened as he got there and Tamalan tossed an armful of clothes inside. He hesitated as he saw Kiedrych staring down at him.

"Figured you needed a change," Tam said lightly.

"I don't need it here."

Tamalan studied him for a minute. "You'd be very stupid to go back to your van just because the rest of us know you'd rather stay here."

"Would I?" Kiedrych stepped outside and closed the door gently.

"Bloody minded, really. Cutting off your nose to spite your face and all. Besides, I've moved back in. I snore. I fart in bed. I look *lousy* first thing in the morning." He was trotting along behind Kiedrych now, ticking his faults off on his fingers.

To Tam's immense relief and considerable surprise, Kiedrych began to laugh. He had a pleasant, deep chuckle which Tam hadn't heard since before Parsa had come along. Tamalan supposed that near-death experiences could do that to a man.

"You were an appalling room-mate even when we were children," said Kiedrych with a smile.

"You were no bowl of roses yourself, mister 'No-ma'am-

I-didn't-put-the-worms-in-the-noodles.' "

"Well, I didn't."

"Okay, but it was your idea. So what are you going to do?"

"I'm going to wash, shave, and take my things back to our caravan. You may be less desirable as a bunkmate, but it would not be appropriate to stay here." However delightful the prospect sounded. Especially considering *how* lousy Tamalan looked in the morning.

Armand met up with Kiedrych down by the river just as the Captain was walking back to the camp. Kiedrych had bathed in the black trousers, which, being too big for him now, sat low-slung on his hips. He'd rolled the cuffs up to his knees, and his hair was damp and spiky. Armand eyed him critically. His olive skin was pale from lack of sun, he was unhealthily thin, he looked tired and hollow-cheeked, he looked very much a bare survivor of what should have been a fatal poisoning—and *damned* if the man didn't actually manage to look relaxed. It was as though by nearly dying, something else poisonous had been leeched from him. Armand wished *he'd* looked that good after the last battle at Tyne.

Kiedrych picked his way carefully up the river bank, mindful of his bare feet. He acknowledged Armand's presence with a nod, but said nothing.

"Captain Evenahn . . . Kiedrych. I wanted to talk with you."

"Fine. Go ahead." Kiedrych walked on past him, pausing briefly in tacit invitation. Armand fell into step beside him.

"How's Kayla?"

"Recovering. Sleeping."

"Ah." Armand collected his thoughts, smiled faintly. "You can't pretend to fall asleep on me today, you know."

Kiedrych cast him a glance of feigned innocence. Armand "hmphed," mostly to disguise the fact that he'd nearly laughed.

"Look . . . I wanted to tell you . . . stop for a minute, will you?" Kiedrych halted obligingly and ran his fingers through his damp hair, making it stick up inelegantly. Armand took a breath. "I'm . . . sorry. I've been a fool."

"Yes," agreed Kiedrych, refusing to be fittingly humble and forgiving of his King, "you have."

Armand was nonplussed by this lack of reaction. He continued. "I have been worse than foolish. I . . . wish to . . . beg your pardon." He knew that it wasn't enough to say, but was at a loss. How could a King apologise for doing what he had done to this man, who he still didn't even particularly like?

Kiedrych straightened his shoulders and gazed directly into Armand's eyes, until the King thought that perhaps his very soul was under scrutiny.

I cannot pardon him, Kiedrych was thinking, *I cannot* . . . but he was still so tired. He couldn't maintain the energy it took to hate someone so much for so long. The sun felt warm on his back, the ground reassuringly solid under his feet, the air sweet in his lungs. It was less effort to forgive. So he did.

"Apology accepted," he said.

Armand was puzzled by the relief that suddenly smoothed Kiedrych's face. He suspected that perhaps the Captain had become slightly unhinged. Lords, the man was even smiling, very faintly, to himself.

"I've arranged for us to hold camp for another day," said Armand, taking refuge in business, "to give yourself and

Kayla time to recover." Kiedrych nodded and they both resumed their walk back to the camp. "Tyrole died."

"Hmm. Tamalan told me. What makes you think it wasn't the witch's doing?"

"I know Saebert. Poisoning is more his style. I'd also have expected Tallan to do something more magic-inspired."

"Yes, she never did like the regular methods. I wonder what Saebert offered him, to do this. I knew Major Tyrole in your father's reign. His family was extremely wealthy; they sided with you in the battle. Blackmail, do you think?"

"Or fear. Saebert probably threatened him, or his family, in some way. My cousin has a penchant for things that suffer. He was a vicious brute as a child."

"You realise this means that she," meaning Tallan, "has got other plans for us. If they killed you now, there wouldn't be much point in continuing this campaign. You have no heirs. Saebert could conceivably be legally next in line to the throne anyway. He wanted to kill you. She didn't. I wonder what she's up to."

Armand revised his opinion about Kiedrych being unhinged. He considered a moment before speaking again. "I know you didn't actually mean to poison yourself."

Kiedrych raised an eyebrow.

"I don't like you very much, Evenahn, but I don't think you're stupid."

"I'm glad to hear that."

"You didn't panic. You intercepted that thing before I ate it. To tell the truth, I was surprised you didn't simply want me to die with you."

"I surprised myself a little on that point. I don't like you very much either, Your Highness. But I told you I was on your side."

"I know. Next time I'll listen."

Kiedrych nodded once, satisfied. "By your leave, King Armand," he said, for the first time with some deference, "I'd like to get dressed."

"Of course. Will I see you at dinner this evening?"

Kiedrych shuddered. "I'd rather not."

"I've forbidden anything containing honey. The sight of the stuff makes me nauseous."

"Then I would be honoured, Your Highness." This without a hint of irony or mockery.

Both decided that was enough, for now, and parted company.

Tephee returned in the early afternoon. She wouldn't tell anyone where she'd been, beyond that she'd taken a long walk, had slept in the woods, and gone swimming. She was tired, but unharmed, and after eating went straight to her tent to sleep.

Sylvia suspected that Tephee had been mentally searching for Tallan, and had probably connected with the witch for a short time. She also suspected that Tallan herself would have kept the contact short. The girl seemed dangerously enamoured of Witch Tallan, and it wouldn't do for her to become too familiar with the older witch's mind-energies—too much of a person could be revealed that way. Sylvia forbore to speak of it to Tephee, though. It wouldn't help, she knew, and would only serve to drive Tephee even further away from them, if that were possible.

When Kayla had the drip removed, Magda declared it safe for her to travel. It took remarkably little time for the tribes to pack up and move, and with a heightened feeling of expectancy they made their way north, to join the remainder of Armand's army. Armand now had a permanent guard—the incident with El Ashraf Marek, followed by Major Tyrole's betrayal, made it prudent.

Whilst feeling remained uneasy and difficult in the witches' camp, the opposite was true of Armand and his subjects. Kiedrych attended the meal, even managed to be fairly charming, and the awkwardness that had long existed between them eased.

Kayla recovered, more slowly than the witch but steadily nonetheless. Kiedrych drove the caravan for her, brought meals for her, helped her to sit in the sun, or in the shade, and made sure she was comfortable each night before he returned to his own caravan to sleep. As she regained strength, Kiedrych settled into a more balanced view of the world. The euphoria of having cheated death dimmed, and he became much more the Kiedrych of pre-Parsa days. Self-possessed, sardonic, taciturn, but with the occasional flash of humour and charm that had always been his saving grace.

Tamalan, for one, was rather relieved. After knowing the man for twenty-five years, a Kiedrych that laughed and was relaxed all the time was nearly as scary as one that was constantly coiled with wounded rage. *This* Kiedrych he knew how to handle.

Within three days the nomad army—consisting of over two thousand warriors, and nearly a thousand people in their families—joined the two thousand of Armand's own broken army who were waiting in a makeshift camp in a field. The nearby village of Fatmah regarded the two armies with anxiety, uncertainty, and a glimmer of hope.

When the nomad army approached the other camp, Darem rode out ahead, accompanied by five of the highest-ranking Ashrafs, taking Hundeline and Nikh out to meet their troops. Morwen and Kolett stayed with the King in the meeting tent, watched closely by Captain Evenahn. The four had been terribly subdued since Tyrole's betrayal and death—suspicion had been cast upon them all and no one knew who to trust, even in their own armies.

Riders from the King's army broke away to meet the nomads. They were led by a woman dressed in elegant and expensive grey leather riding culottes, a finely woven yellow shirt held closed at the throat with a short gold chain, and a flowing grey cotton overgown—when she dismounted the items would hang like a dress. The clothing indicated wealth, if not necessarily rank. The woman herself was sitting stiff-backed in the saddle, her expression severe. Her long blonde hair was swept back from her face and piled high beneath a net of golden thread, which accentuated both her loveliness and her grim determination. With her finely shaped face, her long hands, and her poise, she should have been a noblewoman, and not merely a soldier's daughter. The two groups met and exchanged greetings.

"Where is the King?" asked the woman. Her deep brown eyes were guarded.

"He awaits you, M'lady Kesma," said Darem with a shallow bow.

"Why doesn't he come to greet his army?"

"A recent attempt on his life has made him wary, m'lady."

Jailan Kesma's eyes widened a fraction, and she looked to Hundeline and Nikh for confirmation. Both nodded solemnly.

"It was Tyrole," said Hundeline, still deeply disturbed.

Jailan shook her head sadly. "The First King grant rest to his family, then." She looked at Darem. "He wouldn't say, but I think Tyrole and his family may have been threatened by Cadron's agents. We couldn't find out. I thought perhaps sending him to Armand would have helped him to . . ." Jailan sighed. "A serious error of judgement. Where is Tyrole?"

"Dead, m'lady," and Darem told her the circumstances.

Jailan's lips thinned and her eyes darkened. She nodded. "First King have mercy on them all." She gazed toward the nomad encampment—as big as a village itself, it sprawled across the fields and lands it had appropriated from the local farmers. "Will the King see me, then?"

Darem grinned. "M'lady Kesma, you are the one person who I am sure he *will* see."

Jailan clearly did not share Darem's optimism. She frowned and turned to give instructions to her escort. "Go on back," she said, "I'll talk to him alone." The escort, made up of Sergeants, Lieutenants, and Captains she had known almost all her life through her father, the late General Gerd Kesma, reluctantly obeyed her. "Go on," she reassured them with a tired smile, "I'll be fine." She turned back to Darem.

"You are trusting, m'lady," said Darem.

"If I cannot trust him," she replied emotionlessly, "then everything is finally lost, and it doesn't matter. Does it?" Without waiting for a response, she urged her horse onward. Hundeline and Nikh arranged themselves on either side of her and they followed Darem and the Ashrafs into the labyrinthine tent-village. They dismounted at the meeting tent, and Jailan pushed into the cool shadows within. She paused to allow her eyes to adjust to the change.

Sitting in the centre of the meeting ring on an elegantly carved chair found for the occasion was King Armand, dressed in nomad finery. Behind and to his right was Captain Evenahn, looking as stern as ever, one hand resting on the hilt of his sword. On the left, sitting cross-legged on the floor, was the jester, Tamalan. Jailan rather suspected that even that little fool had a dagger of some description hidden under that ridiculous patchwork shirt of his. Kolett and Morwen sat close by, subdued and unarmed, but clearly mortified about the attack on their King. Her presence relaxed them fractionally. Further back in the shadows stood a woman—small, with long, dark hair and upswept cheekbones. Her bright brown eyes regarded everything around her with alert curiosity. Jailan exchanged a curt nod with Evenahn—they had known each other for some years, too, sharing a grudging mutual respect. She looked back to the King.

It was there again, Armand noted—that look of hope and need tempered with anger, and the not wanting to be angry. Only Evenahn had been unequivocal when they'd met again. Everyone else was torn between wanting to bow to him and wanting to beat him with a club. A small sigh escaped him. To be honest with himself, he sympathised with the desire for the latter.

She was still lovely, too. Still strong and independent. Still everything he wanted, and couldn't have. The Council would never permit him to marry outside the ranks of the nobles. (*What Council?* his subconscious asked.) He gestured for her to come closer, and she did so, leaving Darem and the others ranged behind her. She curtseyed deeply to him, then stood straight again.

"Welcome, Jailan."

She was silent a moment longer, a frown making deep, unhappy lines around her mouth and brow. *Here it comes,* thought Armand.

"Where have you been?"

Armand did not reply. There was more to come, he knew.

"We *waited* for you. We've been waiting for a year. No one knew where you were, if you were alive, if you cared. We needed you, Armand!" Her voice, usually so mellifluous, roughened with rising emotion. She looked like she might either cry or throw something.

"I was afraid," Armand admitted frankly. His eyes were on hers, and for all he cared they might have been alone. She was always the one person to whom he had needed to confess. "I had been attacked and injured in my own castle, by my own people, and I didn't know who to trust. And I trusted all the wrong people. I was stupid, and I let them fool me, and I nearly died. Henkle cut me," Armand gestured vaguely from breastbone to gut, where his scar had once been, "and for three days I wished I *would* die. I deserved it, after all, for my vanity. My stupidity. But Dell wouldn't let me go, and I lived. Thousands died for me, for nothing, and I lived. Just. And then I thought, why start it all again? Because I doubted I'd live more than a year. I have it on good authority," here Armand smiled bitterly, "that I would not indeed have lived another year at all, but I have been healed, and no longer have that as an excuse."

"Are you still afraid?"

"Oh, yes," Armand said, so quietly that she almost didn't hear him. Evenahn and Tamalan both looked at the King. "My reign has been a disaster, Jailan. I took my father's rule and destroyed it."

"Don't be so damned ridiculous, Armand," Jailan spoke harshly. "You made mistakes. Learn from them. Your plans for the kingdom were not bad—King Graym was a fine ruler, but he gave small regard to the rights of his people, for their justice and their stake in the kingdom. Keep to your principles and change your approach. But first, get rid of your Red-Lord-cursed bastard cousin and that black-hearted witch, before they suck the Kingdom dry and leave you—and more importantly, your people—with nothing."

Armand gazed up at her sheepishly. "I've missed you, Jailan."

"You've needed someone to talk some common sense into you, that's why," she said. She was smiling now.

He laughed dryly. "I always could count on you to be honest."

"We know each other too well for anything else. So, King Armand—do you trust *me?*"

His expression sobered. "I have doubted them all, including myself—but never you, Jailan. Never you."

She knelt at his feet, and he took her hands in his. They smiled at each other, oblivious to the others around them.

"Will you lead us?" Jailan asked. "Your people need you."

"For them, for myself, and for those who were betrayed by my foolishness. I'll lead. I'll take back my kingdom. And this time, I'll do a better job of it."

"Good." She kissed his cheek in a charmingly uncourtly gesture, and gracefully rose. "Then I suggest we get down to business. There's a great deal to be discussed."

Chapter Twenty-Four

Kiedrych paused at his caravan on his way to see Kayla, to search for a cloth and a change of clothes, reluctant to descend upon her soiled and sweating from drill practice. It had been a necessary compromise, to march from morning till early afternoon and devote the remainder of the day to preparations. The Guard Sergeant, an outlander named Ho, had devised a punishing training schedule for the fifty-three men who had once been part of an elite unit of three hundred. Kiedrych approved. They needed to be stronger, swifter, better than before. There were no more chances to be had after this.

He found in the trunk a fresh shirt, dark violet, which he recalled suddenly Kayla had given to him last summer, saying the colour would suit him. He'd never worn it. He pulled it on and, running his fingers quickly through his hair, threaded his way among the tents in the growing darkness to Kayla's caravan.

She was leaning against the flank of her gentle carthorse, her wrinkled nose lifted to the air. When she saw him coming, Kayla grinned in delighted recognition. "It does suit you," she asserted.

He grinned back at her. "What's wrong?"

She laughed. "I was wondering what that smell was."

Kiedrych sniffed the air briefly. "That's the armoury at work."

"The armoury?"

"Pigskin. Darem's people use hardened leather plate and

they're making more. It's not much, but it's all most of us will have."

"Oh. Is it . . . all you have?"

"I lost everything but my chain mail and my sword at the Rout." He regarded her soberly. "I've given the mail to the King."

She looked as though she might protest this act of generosity, of duty, but instead she sighed and nodded. "It won't be long now, will it?" Her voice was subdued, unusually timid.

"Not long, no. Maybe a week or two. A group this size doesn't move very quickly. Any surprise we may have had we lost weeks ago."

Kayla stood silent for a long moment, unable to find anything further to say. Kiedrych held his hand out to her; she slipped her own into it and let herself be drawn to his side. He twined his fingers with hers; she laid her cheek upon his chest and he brushed his free hand through her hair.

"Have you eaten?"

"Yes," she murmured.

"You're just tired. Witch Magda says it will pass."

"Yes."

"You should rest."

"Yes."

Puzzled, worried, he walked with her to the steps and helped her inside. Kayla sank onto her bedroll, her expression drawn and pensive.

"Well. Good night."

"Don't go." Kayla drew a sharp breath in on her own urgency, but her eyes were wide and luminous. "Please stay."

Kiedrych hesitated. He wanted to, how he wanted to. But he hadn't made things right yet. He couldn't . . .

He couldn't say no to that look; not when he meant yes, and gladly. He stepped inside and closed the door.

He sat beside and facing her, silent. He took her hand in his, kissed it, held it against his chest so that she could detect the slight bump of his heart. Captivated, she moved her hand across the cloth of his shirt, feeling the weave of the fabric and the shape of his body beneath. Still a little thin, but filling out. He took her hand again, kissing the palm, laying her hand along his cheek.

"You know who I am," he said simply, "what I am."

"I know you. I know I love you."

He nodded, satisfied. Unexpectedly, he thought of Parsa, and how she had fascinated him. He had wanted her because she seemed sexually distant; wanted to know what motivated her, because she had been such a mystery to him. He realised that Parsa had never said that she'd loved him; that, in fact, he hadn't said it to her, either. That, when he'd thought Parsa had shared his sardonic humour, she had been laughing at him. Mocking his pretensions. Was it his love that had been betrayed, or his pride?

"Rych?"

He came back from his reverie and smiled at her. It had been his pride, he decided. Because he had never felt for Parsa the incredible tenderness and affection that he felt with this woman. Even his desire for Kayla felt different from that sexual obsession he'd experienced with Parsa. He leaned forward, gathering Kayla close to him, and they kissed. She murmured his name, kissed his face, throat, lips; moaned softly when his hands ran smoothly down her back, to her waist, then up to cup her breasts through the cotton of her nightshirt. She offered no resistance at all when he began to undress her, though her own efforts to free him of his clothes did occasionally get in the way. He helped her, their efforts punctuated by long, passionate kisses and increasingly bold explorations of each other's bodies, and at last they lay naked together on her bed. Kayla's body tingled with electric warmth wherever their skin touched. Kiedrych pushed her onto her back, his mouth engulfing hers with hard, possessive passion, and with no further preamble rolled on top and entered her, abruptly.

His body reacted before his mind did. He paused, breathing heavily, wondering where the resistance was. Parsa, with mockery in her eyes, had always made him fight for her. Sex with her had been a game of possession and domination: power play, not love. But Kayla, far from fighting him, was welcoming him into her body. She responded not only easily but enthusiastically, wrapping her legs around his waist, her arms about his shoulders, moving her hips against him . . . she wriggled and nuzzled his throat. Kiedrych thrust into her, more gently this time, and she moaned and . . . *giggled.*

Damned if the woman wasn't actually having *fun.* Kiedrych discovered that he liked that idea. A lot. He kissed her, then pulled back to look into her eyes, which were bright and animated with love, lust, and delight. She laughed again, gently nipped his chin, and pressed her body closer to him.

"Don't tease," she admonished him throatily. He found himself laughing softly with her, and resumed a sensual rhythm.

Sex before had always been either relief for a purely physical need or, with Parsa, a struggle to possess and dominate. Having found a new way to experience it, Kiedrych discovered that he liked this way much better. He liked being gentler; he liked taking his time and savouring the scent and touch and taste of his woman.

Kayla had surrendered herself completely to him, and so he couldn't help but to surrender to her in turn. It was a liberating feeling.

Afterwards, both of them sated and grinning with smug contentment, Kayla stayed snuggled in his arms, instead of instantly getting up to wash as Parsa had always done. After that, he banished Parsa from his thoughts, for good. Kiedrych took the opportunity to indulge in kisses and caresses that his earlier haste had denied them. He discovered a small scar on her knee, from a childhood mishap. She found the long scar in his thigh he'd got in training when he'd first picked up a sword, at age twelve, and which Mother Fingal had sewn up with neat, regular little stitches. He discovered that she was ticklish, and that he was not, but was delighted that she had been mischievous enough to try and find out.

They fell asleep, and when they woke before dawn they made love again. Then they lay still in a tangled embrace for a while, letting the rising sun warm the air, listening to the first faint sounds of movement outside.

"I have to go," said Kiedrych, making no move to do so. In fact, he had just begun a close inspection, with his mouth and tongue, of her navel. Kayla hooked her feet around his back and tousled his hair with both her hands.

"I forbid it," she laughed.

"No choice, I'm afraid." He kissed in a line toward her breasts—pausing there for a few minutes of sensual exploration until she moaned and he grinned and continued upward.

"Swine," she muttered, but her heart wasn't in it. She closed her eyes as his mouth reached her throat, then her lips.

"I really do have to leave," he said. He gave her a long, leisurely kiss. Had he any energy left by then, they probably would have made love a third time, but his body wasn't co-operating. Kayla hugged him, kissed his temple, and un-hooked her feet.

"Giroff, then," she laughed, playfully pushing his shoulders back, "you're heavy." Her fingers darted down between them, and Kiedrych found that at some times and in some places he *was* ticklish. He rolled back with a startled yelp. She dived after him, wrestled him to the ground, and sat on his stomach. "Gotcha."

Kiedrych only managed a winded grunt before shoving her off, slapping her rump and, while she collapsed back on the bedroll with a wide grin, rummaging around the room to find his clothes. First he towelled himself clean, then, as he found each item of clothing, he pulled it on. Kayla, lying flat on her belly with her chin propped in her hands, gave him directions towards each of the wayward items and otherwise gazed at him with such intense, smug adoration that in the end, laughing, he picked up a pillow that had somehow ended up across the room and tossed it at her. It caught her on the side of the head, toppling her onto her—he had to admit it—incredibly delectable backside. It didn't wipe off the grin. What the hell—he knew perfectly well he had a matching smirk all over his own face.

"Will you come back this evening?" she asked.

"I might." He looked serious, but his eyes betrayed the laughter within.

"At least come back and say goodnight, hmm?"

"Oh, at the very least." The look he gave her promised a whole lot more than a goodnight kiss, then he opened the door and, after a quick look around, stepped out into the morning sunshine. Kayla sighed blissfully and flopped back on the bed.

Kiedrych sat on a stool outside to pull on his boots, then strolled across the short space to his own caravan, which he'd pulled up near Kayla's. He rapped on the door and waited a moment. Inside there was a muffled curse, followed by several thumps and bumps and the sound of someone tripping over a tangle of blankets and landing against the door.

"Move it, Tam, I haven't got all day."

The door opened a crack and two brown, bleary eyes squinted out. " 'S too early. Go 'way."

"We all have better things to do, Tamalan, but duty calls."

"What're you so damned cheerful ab . . . ? Oh." The eyes blinked and crinkled up with delighted understanding.

"Wipe that stupid look off your face and get out here. The King won't wait all day for you."

The door closed and reopened a minute later with Tamalan tugging his patchwork shirt over his head and his red boots in one hand. He hopped into these as the two of them headed off to the King's tent.

"You going to move out then?" asked Tam.

"No."

"You know you want to."

Kiedrych glanced sideways at the jester but made no comment.

"Come on, Rych, what are you worried about? Your reputation?"

"Not mine. Kayla's."

"Oh."

"She was, after all, a travelling entertainer."

"Well, so were you. And she was the King's Agent, as well."

"But I'm not likely to be pestered by every low-minded soldier in this outfit. Look, I would rather be discreet about this, Tam."

"Then you'd better wipe that grin off your face. You look like the cat that ate a couple of canaries, plus a bowl of cream and a small but tasty mouse." Kiedrych instantly tried to sober his expression, but his eyes still danced. "Anyway, if anyone casts a slur on our Kayla, I'll knock his front teeth out," Tam avowed, all seriousness.

"Hmph," said Kiedrych, in a tone which suggested that anyone being so unwise would have his jaw broken if he said as much in Kiedrych's hearing.

"You could always marry her," Tam suggested thoughtfully.

Kiedrych shook his head. "Not yet. I have to ask the King to clear something up for me first."

They reported to the King, and Kiedrych went on to run through his morning drills with the Guard, leaving Tam as an auxiliary bodyguard—Jailan had been quite correct about the dagger he kept under his shirt. Slowly, the morning progressed, the army packed up and moved on. Kiedrych helped Kayla harness her horse to the caravan, their hands meeting time and again over the same buckles and cinches, both of them laughing at their clumsiness, but he had to leave her to carry on with other duties. He returned to her at night.

For the next fifteen days, the routine varied little. The army moved on; villages were given Royal Notes of Credit in exchange for food stores and any useful items. Young men left home to join the army. The land grew paler, the inhabitants more lethargic.

And in Tyne Castle, the Usurper and the Witch prepared their own defences.

Chapter Twenty-Five

Saebert and Tallan were in the empty Council chambers. Although the rooms had been partly rebuilt, there were still signs of the fire that had killed so many—black sooty stains on the carved and painted ceiling, charred edges on the doors. The Council was rarely called these days, and the few who objected had a tendency to disappear. Those remaining were finally coming to realise it may have been better to have a liberal-minded King than a sadistic, witch-thralled second cousin on the throne. It was, of course, much too late now. When the King's army came, they would have to fight.

Saebert was pacing the stone floor, his hands clasped behind his back and his handsome face dark with turbulent emotion. Zuleika sprawled in elegant disarray across the recently carved and upholstered King's Seat, one long leg slung over the padded arm and the other tucked beneath her. A plate of sweet pastries was balanced on the other chair arm and, as she watched him pace up and down, she sucked sugar from her fingertips.

"We haven't enough soldiers." Saebert was both angry and anxious, mostly at Zuleika's lack of concern. Arrogant little bitch. As soon as this was over, she was going. A drop of blackroot in those sweet little honey cakes she was always eating; it would have to be something fast acting, or she'd be able to magic it away. Not that the blackroot had done the job for Armand. He wasn't sure what had happened there, though Tyrole had died as a result. His wife and son had offered a touch more sport as payback for the Major's failure, but Saebert would have much preferred to be rid of his cousin.

Zuleika's response was sharp and impatient. "I have told you before, *my love,* that you don't need to beat their army."

"My army consists of one thousand infantry and archers, and a mere five hundred cavalry troops. Against their four thousand."

"We don't have to leave this castle, Saebert. The only reason we need an army at all is to keep them distracted while I look after those witches. Once they're dealt with, the army will simply be . . ." Zuleika's lips stretched in a cold, predatory smile, "witch fodder."

"You had better not fail."

"Have I ever?" Her smile was girlishly sweet. "Unlike yourself."

He glared at her.

"Don't think you can fool me, Saebert. I know about Tyrole."

"It makes better sense to kill Armand now. Go chasing after your own causes some other time. Your obsession with that witch is going to make this harder than it need be."

"Is that what you think this is all about?"

"It's what you talk about all the time."

"But don't you see—the nomad tribes are walking right to our door. We can take them now and move into their lands at our leisure. They fight us on our territory, on our terms." She laughed breezily. "You really are terribly short-sighted for a King, Saebert—this way, I get my witch, you get your cousin, and we both get a whole new country added onto this one, for so little effort."

"If," he stressed, "your plan works."

"Of course it will. That silly little girl is fascinated by me. It will be so easy to . . . drink her up." That nasty smile again. The chair on which she was draped changed colour, then shape, then stood: a wooden man holding her in its arms. It set her down, but her feet hovered a little way off the ground, and the man hunkered down and turned into a sheep, then a mouse, and finally into a family of bright purple hoppers—finger-long reptiles that bounded on their tiny back legs around her feet, before being pulled back, squealing, into the original King's Seat. She floated backwards and settled into it again, her cheeks flushed but otherwise unaffected by the incredible amounts of power she had just used.

"By the time I'm finished with them, I'll be able to make this castle *fly*."

Saebert did not ask her why she'd want to do that. It was obvious. She'd do it simply to show that she could. Yes, after the battle . . .

"And don't even consider the blackroot, *dear* Saebert," she said, and he became perfectly still with dread, "I know all of your tricks. I always check my food myself, and if I find anything . . . be prepared to find it in your own dishes as well. My *love*." The repeated bitterness of those endearments, along with that sweet smile of hers, were starting to terrify him. He noticed at last that, although she was lying in the great chair, she was not actually touching it in any place. She simply hovered in it. It occurred to him at last that his plan to take the throne had been ill-considered from the start.

But, like the Councillors, it was much too late for him to back out now.

Chapter Twenty-Six

There was only one approach the King's army could really make to Tyne Castle. Armand knew that, because he knew that his castle and his city had been designed that way by a sensibly wary ancestor. As far as he knew, Armand was the first Tyne monarch to have to attack his own castle from without—a dubious distinction. At its best, it still looked bad.

The castle was perched on a hilltop, at the western-most point of a horseshoe of hills that had made the city nearly impregnable. To the east, where the hills diminished, were farmlands and dunes, but they were all outside the walls of Tyne. It was the city, and the castle, they had to take.

The steep hill on which Tyne Castle sat in its stone inviolability descended onto a flat plain—a good, clear target area for archers firing from the castle walls. A hundred metres to the south was the fortified gateway to the city. If they could somehow force Saebert's army out of the city to fight, they would emerge here, where a shallow incline would allow them to get to the plain without stumbling and breaking their horses' legs.

The plain stretched back for several kilometres, but was divided north to south by a wide, shallow river. It ran briskly enough now, in late spring, but in a month or two would disappear underground, part of a greater underground river which provided the city with its water.

There was only one approach, and both he and Saebert knew it. The outcome of this battle would depend, in the end, on whose witch could outsmart the other. Frowning at Sylvia's careworn features and Tephee's aloof expression, Armand wasn't feeling especially confident.

"Make camp on the western side of the river," he instructed his staff. "Tomorrow, the families can stay there, and we'll cross."

"Magda would like the medical tents to be kept separate," Sylvia told him. "For hygiene. She says they ought to be downriver, and on the castle side."

"Fine," Armand nodded, "see to it."

So the true King of Tyne's army settled itself along the river bank, acutely aware that within the castle, the Witch was watching them.

Magda inspected the med-tents by lamplight. She'd had an extra length of canvas hung up at one end of the main tent, making an alcove that was barred to all except herself. Here she set up her equipment, and all the boxes of medication and syringes she had prepared in advance with the replicator. For the first time in five years, the Longlife unit had registered a drop in the battery metre. She feared it wouldn't be enough, but then, she knew she wouldn't be able to save everyone. That realisation made her angry. If she had Tephee's power, she could do it. Or if she'd had the staff and equipment available at the SolOrbit or CentOrbit stations.

She felt a sudden pang of loss for the life she'd nearly had, as a newly qualified doctor on a colony world. If only her transport ship hadn't received the distress call; if only she hadn't gone with the shuttle pilot to search the planet for a crash site and survivors; if only they hadn't fallen into that . . . vortex, anomaly, whatever it had been . . . and ended up here. If only, if only, if only.

Bugger that. She was here now. Five, nearly six years on this world—it was home. Now she knew where the distress beacon had come from, where these people and Terran animals had come from. She just didn't know how to get back to where she belonged.

"Thought we'd find you here. Is everything okay, or should I give Kiedrych's Guard a scolding and make them come back to fix things up?" Leenan grinned at her. Behind her, Sylvia looked around with interest.

Magda grinned back. *Moron,* she thought, *you belong here.*

"Everything's as good as we can make it, though I'd prefer a concrete floor. And a staff of about fifty. Where they found enough bedding, I'll never know."

"I don't expect the King does, either," said Sylvia with a smile. "I believe he'd rather not know. Kiedrych is very good at getting things done, but his methods can be dubious."

Magda chuckled, but soon sobered. "Look, I wanted to talk to you both. Tell you something, about me."

Both Sylvia and Leenan looked at her as if to say, "It's about time!" and Magda blushed. "I don't know if you'll understand."

"Try us," said Sylvia.

"We're not as dim as you think," Leenan chided her gently.

She took them to her alcove and lit the extra lanterns there. The light flickered eerily over the technological treasures she had kept and tended and brought with her against this need. Leenan stared, wide-eyed—she hadn't suspected this much after all—but Sylvia simply nodded.

"I'm not from around here," said Magda.

"These are Arc machines," murmured Leenan incredulously.

"Not exactly. Though I think the First King came from the same place I do."

Leenan arched an eyebrow at her sceptically. "You come from the True World? You're from *Heaven?*"

Magda smiled wryly. "It was pretty nice in some ways, but it's just . . . another place. A different world. One without magic, and with stuff like this instead. I came here by accident. The vessel I was in crash-landed here. The pilot died, and I took what I could and found Tunston. And here I am."

Leenan continued to study her friend intently. "I always thought you were a little weird."

Sylvia was shaking her head. "I knew you were different, but the True World? I thought you were from an Arc Temple. A priest come to walk the world for a while. Oh well," she shrugged and spread her hands in acceptance and amazement. "At least we can be sure there is a True World after all."

"I guess so." Leenan frowned, then tapped on the top of the replicator. "How does it work, anyway?"

Magda was bemused. She had expected . . . hysteria, maybe? Fright? Incomprehension? Sylvia patted her on the arm, smiling in a motherly way.

"I told you it'd be all right," she said. "Maybe the First King sent you to this place from the True World for a reason."

Magda opened her mouth to reply, thought better of it, and nodded mutely.

"What's this?" Leenan held up a syringe, being careful to keep the wicked-looking end pointed away from her.

"I used to call it a dragon's tooth, but it's just a needle. I'll teach you how to use it. I'll need your help tomorrow."

Leenan held the syringe up to the lantern light and considered it carefully. She gave Magda a sideways glance. "I'll bet that stuff you gave kids wasn't fairy dust either."

"Ah . . . no."

"Didn't think so. I've never seen a fairy in my life. And I started looking for them from a very young age, too." She shook the needle warningly in Magda's direction. "Don't you ever fib to me again. I hate it when I fall for dumb stories." She replaced the syringe, folded her arms, and glared at Magda sternly for a moment before sighing and shaking her head.

"Idiot," she said. "What did you think we'd do? I'm a *witch,* for crying out loud. I've been weirder than nearly everyone I know for most of my life."

"Still are," said Magda. Leenan cuffed her on the ear, and then, laughing, they hugged. Sylvia was pulled into the embrace, and they clung together in friendship, staving off for a little while the fear of the day to come.

Kiedrych came to Kayla's van that night as usual, but they sat fully clothed on the bedroll, arms wrapped around each other, unspeaking.

I will not cling, Kayla told herself resolutely, *I will not cry. I will not embarrass either of us. I will not ask him to stay behind tomorrow. I will not. I will not. Oh, Lords, keep him safe!*

She had already made a shrine to the First King, laid an offering there, and prayed. It was more dignified than flinging herself at Kiedrych's feet and begging him to run away with her. Especially since she was sure he wouldn't. They hadn't come this far for him to abandon the King now.

Kiedrych stroked her hair, sensing the tension in her and knowing why. She said nothing. He was glad of that. He knew what he had to do tomorrow, and that he might die, and a small voice at the core of him was telling him to saddle a horse and ride away with Kayla as far from this madness as possible. It was only a small voice, and he ignored it. There was something else on his mind just now.

"Kayla," he began quietly. How to say it? He felt her eyes upon him. "Kayla, my family is one of the oldest Noble lines of this kingdom."

He felt her stiffen in his arms.

"I am not considered of the true bloodline, by my family, but I am. After this, even if any of the Evenahn line remain, the King has promised that I will be recognised as a full heir to my father's house. By law."

"I see. I understand." Kayla's hands clenched into fists.

Kiedrych glanced at her with a frown. "What is it you understand?"

"I am only a peasant, after all. And a tramp actress to boot." Kayla gave a feeble laugh, then bit her lip. She pulled away, struggling when he tried to hold her.

"Kayla . . ."

"Let me *go!*"

"What's wrong with you?"

"With me? With *me?*" She gave a short, inarticulate screech and tried to knee him in the crotch. Kiedrych intercepted the blow, but didn't quite dodge the fist that came smacking into his cheekbone. Fortunately, she was starting to cry and hadn't put much force behind it.

He grabbed her by the shoulders and shook her, hard. "What the hell's got into you?"

"You bastard," she sobbed and pulled away from him. "What was all this meant to be? What was it all about? What did you have planned for us? If I'm not good enough to be the wife of a noble, I'm still worth more than some tawdry . . ." she gasped for air, "I love you, but I won't be your mistress. I won't. I won't." Even as she denied it, she knew that she would. If he asked. If it was all he offered. She wouldn't like it, but she would do it. She was hunched against the wall of the van and was shivering.

Kiedrych glared at her. "Is that the best you think of me?" he asked.

"You hide," she whispered, "you always look outside before you leave. You don't like people to see you've come here."

He regarded her steadily for a moment, frowned, rubbed his cheek where she'd hit him. "How long has this been worrying you?" She didn't answer and he sighed. "Idiot." It was unclear if he meant Kayla or himself. "Come on." He seized her hand and roughly tugged her outside. She tried to pull back, but he grabbed her firmly and led her into the camp.

"I haven't finished," he told her as he pulled her past the tents and nightfires. "The Evenahn House is not mine to claim yet. I don't have a Noble line to offer you, unless we win, and unless the King can circumvent the Council. I have been disowned by the Evenahns." He stopped before the King's tent and pushed Kayla in ahead of him. Armand looked up in surprise.

Kayla stood rubbing her wrist, glowering at Kiedrych and refusing to meet the eyes of either the King, his bodyguard, Jailan Kesma, or Tam, who were all there, winding up a few last details.

Kiedrych nodded a curt greeting to Armand, who lifted a questioning eyebrow.

"Strictly speaking, Your Highness, I need your permission. And three witnesses," said Kiedrych.

Armand's look of bafflement melted into a grin. "Permission granted. Take your pick of witnesses."

Tam leapt up without invitation, tugging Jailan and Major Hundeline in his wake. Kiedrych nodded and turned to Kayla, who looked stunned and uncomprehending.

"Before the First King and these witnesses I take you as my wife, Kayla Brittane, and attest that you are entitled to all the rights and duties accorded to my rank and—should my birthright be reinstated—my House." Kayla's mouth hung open. *Good,* thought Kiedrych, *I've finally done something to leave her speechless.* Now, however, was not a good time. "Come on."

"I . . . Before the . . . the First King and these witnesses I take you as my husband, Kiedrych Evenahn . . ."

"And attest," he prompted.

"And attest that you are entitled to all the rights and duties accorded to my rank . . . I don't have a rank . . ."

"Station, then."

"Accorded to my station and my House. I don't have a House."

"Neither do I. That was what I was trying to tell you before I . . . proposed."

"That was a *proposal?*"

He shrugged. "Hush. Tamalan?"

Tam, grinning so hard he was nearly all smile, said: "I, Tamalan Fingal, witness this marriage and the promises made between you. You know, Rych, if you'd married her like I told you a fortnight ago, we could have had a party."

"I wanted to spare us all the sight of you, blind drunk. M'lady Kesma?"

Jailan repeated the witnesses' oath, the solemnity of her delivery alleviated by the sparkle in her eye, followed by Major Hundeline.

Traditionally, the couple should give one another a token. Kayla, taken unawares, had nothing on her and it nearly drove her to tears. Kiedrych pressed his lips to her, calming her with a kiss.

"I'll take that, for now," he murmured with a smile, and she laughed meltingly. "I do have something for you," he continued.

He glanced briefly at the King as he removed his ring—the Captain's seal. Armand nodded slightly in approval and, satisfied, Kiedrych took Kayla's hand in his. It was too big for anything but her thumb, so he slid it into place there. The symbol of the only thing he had or could offer. She cupped her hands together and held the ring clasped against her heart, too tearful to speak but the gesture eloquent enough for him.

At the end, Kiedrych grunted in satisfaction and turned back to Armand. "Make sure someone writes this down." Which was the whole point, after all. Victory for the King may still include his own death, and Kiedrych was determined that Kayla be his legal wife and heir, should it come to that. He had to be able to leave her with something, and if his honour was all, then it would have to do.

"I'll see to it."

"Good. See you on the field in the morning."

"And you." Armand wondered if he should caution Kiedrych to get some sleep tonight, then thought better of it. Kayla still looked stunned, but a dazed smile was beginning to curve her lips. Kiedrych took her hand, nodded goodbye to all within the tent, and led her away.

On the way back to her caravan—theirs now, he supposed—he said: "Aren't you sorry you gave me a black eye now?"

"No," she lifted her chin jauntily. "Serves you right for not telling me what the hell you were thinking of." But back in the van, she apologised tenderly and he accepted with passion.

* * * * *

Tamalan, still grinning, watched Kiedrych and Kayla leave before bidding goodnight to the King, Jailan, and the rest of Armand's guard. He made his way slowly back through the soldiers' camp, heading towards the separate area where the nomad tribes' families had set up. The caravan would, without doubt, be entirely his tonight, but he didn't really want to go there. Not alone. Not tonight. Muffled noises drifted around the camp—people drinking, or talking, couples of all persuasions spending what might be a last night together.

He should have felt pleased for Kayla and Rych; or a sense of fellowship with those murmurs in the night; or just plain frightened. Mostly, he felt lonely. Tam wondered where his mother was, and his brother Kunji, and Vi, and Myra and Merri, with their husbands and their squalling packs of grubby and glorious kids. He missed them. He missed the troupe. Right now, he even missed Kiedrych.

What was he doing, he wondered, at thirty-one, without a family of his own? Why didn't he have his own pack of brats, and a lovely, plump honey-eyed wife, with a sweet voice and soft breasts and sense of humour?

Why didn't he have a woman, any woman, just for tonight?

He wandered out towards the periphery of the camp, feeling like a voyeur, listening to all the voices and sounds of the night before battle, hoping to meet someone he could talk to.

"H . . . hello."

Tamalan paused and peered into the shadowed recesses behind the horseyard where he had ended up, figuring at least he could talk to the animals. A shape detached itself shyly, and a young woman smiled nervously at him. Not much more than a girl, really, Tam thought—eighteen, maybe. Pretty, behind the worry and the smudges of dirt and tear tracks.

"Good evening, Lady," he said to her, with a broad grin and a sweeping bow. She giggled. Encouraged, Tam stepped closer. "What brings you here, all alone, on such a night?"

The smile faded from her lips and the worried look came back. "I just . . . I wanted to be here. For a little while. To say goodbye."

"Don't cry, Lady." Tam offered her a silk scarf—normally part of his parlour tricks, but he felt that hers was the greater need. She took the scarf and blew her nose on it, quite daintily. "Say goodbye to who?"

"Oh . . . the horses. My horse. Tamberlaine, the big grey stallion," she pointed. "He's not really mine, but I looked after him. At the stables, at Kesma House. He was always my favourite. He might not . . . might not come back tomorrow." She began to cry again. "I don't mean to be selfish. I know that Major Hundeline may die, or the King himself . . . but I don't know them. I know Tamberlaine."

Tamalan reached out and gave the girl a friendly, sympathetic pat on the shoulder. "It's all right, Lady . . ."

"Felada." Felada sniffed.

"A pretty name, for a pretty lady." Tam smiled gently and stroked her cheek. "It's all right to feel sad for Tamberlaine, you know. He hasn't chosen to be here. He's someone too."

"Yes, he is. Tam's handsome and clever and he loves papplefruit, and he laughs at the other horses sometimes. He loves to be scratched right on his withers, and when I'm brushing him he flicks me with his tail."

"None of which Major Hundeline does, I can bet you."

Felada beamed up at him. "It's so nice to talk to someone who understands."

"Of course I do. You know, he's got the same name as me. Nearly, anyway. I'm Tam, too."

Felada looked at him, blushed, and giggled. He grinned back, perfectly aware of her unspoken comparisons with stallions. He put an arm around her shoulders and hugged her lightly. Felada leaned into him, trembling a little, and sighed. He dropped a light kiss onto the top of her head, and realised to his sudden horror that Felada was about the same age as his youngest surviving sister. Viola was also a horse-lover, and had spent lots of time around the castle stables, cooing over the animals. Kiedrych used to complain about her, but always let her comb and feed his own horse, Amra. Poor Amra, dead on the battlefield. That would have broken Viola's heart. Poor little Vi, as well, wherever she was now.

Tamalan's growing arousal shrivelled into a mixture of deep embarrassment and fraternal concern for a girl out alone in the middle of the night.

"Well . . . goodnight then. Ah . . ." He tried to step into the shadows again, hoping she couldn't see his face redden.

"Don't . . ." She looked very young and very lost. "Don't go," she managed at last, "I'm scared."

"It'll be all right," he said gently, knowing it was not a promise he could swear to. Would Vi have wanted him to lie? Would Ma have expected him to, to protect her? "We have a great army here, and the First King is with us. Everything will be all right."

Felada nodded, obviously trying to believe him. Tamalan gave in to brotherly concern and held out his hand for her to take. She meekly placed her small, rough hand in his and let him lead her back to his caravan. Her shoulders were hunched and tense to begin with, but as he made no unchivalrous move she relaxed. They shared food and the last of his wine while Tam told her about his family. She giggled and told him what it was like living in the service of Jailan Kesma, since Felada's father had been killed at the Tyne Rout.

Eventually, Felada fell asleep. Tamalan covered her with a blanket and sat at the open door, his legs dangling outside. For a long time he stared into the darkness, wishing that he'd spent the evening with Magda instead.

"Let's hope this augurs well for the morning, hmm?" suggested King Armand once the newlyweds had gone.

"Who'd have thought the young dog would have such a romantic streak," Major Hundeline replied with a broad grin.

"He must have got it from his poor mother," Jailan concurred.

"That and his sense of humour," Hundeline agreed. "All he ever got from Forster was a bad temper and regular beatings."

"I intend to see he gets his title, at least." It was a King's promise, that, and if there were no precedents, well, they'd set one. It would square the debt between them.

Hundeline nodded approval. "By your leave, sire," he bowed, "I should get some rest myself." He departed, ensuring the guards were still alert at their posts.

Armand and Jailan stood quite still for a moment, painfully aware of all the guards that were ranged around them just beyond the walls of the tent. Then Armand stretched out his hand, and Jailan took it in hers, and they stood for a while longer.

"When this is over," he said, "damn the Council. I'm going to marry you."

Jailan squeezed his hand. "Is that wise?"

"Probably not. But wisdom was never my strong point." He drew her towards him, wrapped his arms around her, and kissed her forehead. "You are."

They kissed for a long time, until both conceded that she had to leave. They kissed for a while longer, and eventually, reluctantly, Jailan left to go with her escort, Sergeant Ibram, an old family friend, who looked terribly smug and kept casting her congratulatory looks but said nothing of what he might have heard.

A cool breeze stirred around her, lifting the hair from her forehead. Tephee, eyes closed, barely noticed. Her mind was roaming again, seeking that bright light which meant Zuleika was there. She promised so much, and hid so much too, but there was no one left to trust. Zuleika understood her, and that alone was comforting. Tephee didn't think she could turn on her friends—*or,* she thought bitterly, *the people who used to be my friends, before they got sick of me, and frightened of me.* She should just let Sylvia try to do this alone. Fail alone. It would prove that Tephee had been right all along.

What did it matter, anyway, if King Armand lost this battle? Who cared about the petty problems of one kingdom? She knew perfectly well from her childhood in Tunston that normal people hated her; she terrified them, and that made her hate them, too. She used to think there was something wrong with her, to make them feel like that, but she knew now it was their own narrow-mindedness. She despised Sylvia, and Magda and Leenan too, for hiding themselves among them.

If they were afraid of her, and didn't want to be her friends any more, well, that was just fine with her. Zuleika wanted her, and Zuleika was better than any of them. Zuleika would teach her now, and Tephee would be untouchable. No one would ever hurt her again.

Zuleika was right. Witches were more than human. They were better.

Chapter Twenty-Seven

Magda was up at dawn. She was restless, anxious, and wanted to look over the med-tents once more. Tephee had not come back last night and so far there was still no sign of her. Magda was feeling sick with the realisation that Sylvia was probably right—Tephee was no longer with them, in any sense.

The army was already on the move—soldiers were donning what little armour they had been able to find or make; quivers were filled with arrows, swords sharpened and oiled to slide easily out of scabbards. The air was sharp with anticipation and fear.

Everything looked in order within the tents. The stockpile of medications could be renewed if necessary, and pallets and blankets stood in tidy, stark rows in the three pavilions she had set up along the river. Magda had enlisted help from the three nomad witches, and those among the nomad families who had the aptitude, demonstrating how to use a syringe for intra-muscular injections, how to clean and stitch a wound. It was fortunate that True World medicine was so simple to administer. She herself would be kept busy with the more difficult task of judging which medication and what dosage the patients would need.

Magda gave thanks to providence for the Doctorate in Colonial Medicine she had completed, after her many years as a nurse. Colony worlds were often isolated for long periods and modern, technology-based surgery was not always financially viable. All Colony doctors had to know the old ways and have the means of producing the sterile equipment and medication necessary. Thank the Lords most of that equipment had survived the crash.

Movement at the tent flap brought Magda back to the present. She looked up to see Kayla standing diffidently at the entrance. Magda, along with the rest of the camp, had heard of her sudden marriage last night to Kiedrych Evenahn. She hardly looked like a newlywed, Magda thought, but then, her new husband was about to go out and maybe get himself killed. No wonder she looked so grim.

"I thought you might need some help today," said Kayla. She managed a smile. "I figured I could at least mop a few brows."

Anything but wait alone for word of Kiedrych. She fingered his ring, now worn on a chain around her neck. She had found a token for Kiedrych—a small gold coin which had been her mother's wedding token to her father. Ayman had always said it had brought him luck. Kiedrych had wrapped it carefully in a square of silk and placed it carefully inside his shirt, over his heart. For luck, he'd said.

"The more the merrier," replied Magda, trying to smile encouragement. "I could use a hand getting the fires started. We'll need to boil water to sterilise it for bathing wounds. Oh, here's Dell." Magda nodded welcome to the nomad witch. Dell was clearly exhausted—she and others had been working for hours already. After a brief exchange of news, Kayla left with Dell, grateful to do anything at all.

"Got a minute?"

Magda smiled to see Leenan's head poking through the tent flap. "Anytime."

Leenan turned to give a command to Alard and came in

alone. "Sylvia's just heading off to join the King. No sign of Tephee yet."

Magda, hoping for word of her, let go her pent-up breath.

Leenan frowned. "Maggie, do you think . . . well . . . have I been too hard on Tephee? I know she's just a kid."

"She had a bad time of it, Lee, from all of us. But you were right too. She had to grow up and take responsibility."

Leenan still looked unhappy. "She irritated me a lot, you know. I kept waiting for her to see how childish she was being, and she didn't. Maybe if I'd been more sympathetic . . ."

"Maybe. Maybe if I'd been a better friend to her, if Aledar had been a better mother, if people weren't so afraid of her power. We are what we are, and what we've done can't be changed. Tephee's problems aren't all our fault. Maybe we could have handled it differently, but we didn't, and all we can do now is trust Tephee's better nature."

"She's too caught up in her need to be strong and inviolable. She doesn't listen to her better nature any more." Leenan gestured hopelessly, and Magda nodded miserably.

"I know."

The dawn broke on a beautiful clear day, cool and still. As fighting weather went, it was pretty good—soldiers wouldn't overheat just standing in formation, or slip on muddy ground. It was an even better day for much more placid activities. Tamalan would have liked to take Felada on a picnic somewhere, or fishing, like he used to do with Viola. Felada was back in the nomad camp, though, thinking about her two Tams. She'd done a nice job of cutting his hair—she'd said it was like cutting down Tamberlaine's tail before the battle, only not so rough.

Briefly, Tamalan ran his hand through his short brown hair, unused to the feeling of it after so long with a tail himself. Like Tamberlaine, though, one less thing for an enemy soldier to grab onto was a good thing. He was glad he'd kept the beard though. Felada had said it made him look dashing, particularly now that the gold ear-ring in his left ear could be seen properly.

Dashing. Hmph. Felada had hit that one on the head, all right. *Dashing up hill and down dale.* Tamalan scooted up and down the line, delivering messages for the King. If he heard one more brainless, macho moron saying idiotic things like, "Ugh. A fine day to die," he was going to belt the offender over the head with a mace. It was not a fine day to die. It was a fine day to drink wine with a lovely lady and make love under the sun. It was a lousy day to die. He didn't want to die. He didn't even want to be here. To be perfectly frank, he was terrified.

He hated messenger duty. He was vividly aware of the last battle on this field. The King had sent him away with urgent messages for Hundeline and the next thing he knew the army had fallen into retreat; Saebert's forces had begun to overwhelm them all. Kiedrych had literally hauled him out of the midst of the maelstrom by his scruff and dragged him out of there. By the time they had stopped to assess the damage, the King had vanished, the army had either been butchered or fled, and they took refuge with Ayman's Players because there was nowhere else to go.

He scuttled back to the King and quickly reported all the news from the officers down the line. The nomad witches had been trying to scry the Usurper's troops for days now—all three had collapsed in varying states of exhaustion when Zuleika had intercepted them. One had nearly died. The fragmentary reports indicated that Saebert's army was small, but heavily armed. Infantry, archers, horsemen, perhaps two thousand in all, though maybe less. Armand's troops outnumbered the enemy two to one, at least, but whilst well-armed, they were poorly armoured.

The consensus amongst the officers was that they would have to divide Saebert's troops in order to win, to use their superior numbers to overwhelm smaller pockets of the heavily-armed opposition. El Ashraf Darem had offered his own warriors as the first line forward—they would try to wear Saebert's soldiers down by rapid attack-and-retreat sorties, designed to tire a man weighed down with plate and mail.

All very sound and correct military strategies, but only, Armand thought, if the enemy actually bothered to join them on the field. So far, there was no sign of Saebert's army, and Armand flatly refused to make an obviously futile attempt to storm Tyne Castle.

Kiedrych stood to one side of Armand—the King clad in borrowed mail and a steel breastplate which had been commandeered, Kiedrych in hardened leather and a scowl—with the rest of the Castle guard ranged in formation to his right. They had attempted to arrive in their correct field uniform, though it was difficult under the circumstances. Their black pantaloons, pleated and nipped in at the waist by a flat waistband, were often faded and patched, the silver and gold piping down the leg seams frayed. Their red shirts, narrow and tight-fitting on the forearm, were in similar states of disrepair, but only partially visible under an assortment of mail, plate, and leather armour. Sergeant Ho martialled tight formation and cast a glance towards the Captain, who in turn peered across the distance to the castle gates.

As Tam finished passing on his messages, Kiedrych

spoke. "Did you find any armour?"

Tam shook his head. He had his knife, but it wasn't much of a comfort. Kiedrych said something to Ho, who went off and reappeared with a hardened pig-leather set of torso armour. The King watched them silently while Kiedrych helped Tam to put on the front and back pieces over his blue wrap shirt and tie them securely down his sides with leather thongs. Tam readjusted his knife to hang in easy reach at his hip. The armour was a fair fit, and made him feel safer. Tam managed to smile his thanks and Kiedrych nodded curtly.

"Once it starts," said Tam suddenly, addressing Armand but only darting a quick, nervous glance at him, "I'm not leaving you. Send someone else on the errands."

The fierceness behind the anxiety surprised Armand. He smiled wryly at his jester and patted his shoulder. "Let me know if you change your mind."

"Don't tempt me, Highness."

They fell silent for a moment, all of them gazing out towards the castle, wondering where Saebert's army was.

A movement behind made them all turn—the witch, Sylvia, was striding her way through the troops to join the King at last. Kiedrych frowned, unhappy that it had taken her so long to join them, but she merely returned his glare unapologetically, and he held his silence.

Sylvia would make no excuses. She had been looking for Tephee, and not found her. Who knew where she was, or what she was thinking? She hadn't come back to their camp last night, or been seen at all this morning. It was too late now—Tephee would either turn to Zuleika, or she would stay with them. Or, perhaps, go her own way. Sylvia would have to deal with that when the time came. Right now, she had other things to do.

She had twisted her hair into a loose knot to hold it back from her face, but wisps of it still hung across her eyes as Sylvia exchanged a few observations with the King.

"I suppose Tallan will sit there quite happily all day until she has no choice," said Sylvia. "There doesn't seem to be another way in."

"We need to seize the gate," said Armand, indicating what was actually the barred and bolted double gates to the castle. The outer gate was a forbidding cross-hatch of iron bars, studded with spikes that projected into the spaces between bars and out towards invaders. The second gate was a massive, solid piece of heavy timber, entirely covered in metal sheets a thumb-width thick and bolted into the stonework of the city walls by iron rods as thick as a smithy's arm. From previous discussions, Sylvia knew that through the gates was a zigzag path, climbing swiftly upward, branching into two parts—one leading into the castle itself, the other to the city square. It had been designed to keep invaders out, which was a good thing provided you were on the inside.

Sylvia regarded the barrier for a moment, frowned slightly, then nodded. "Give me a little while. Hopefully, they'll come out when I've finished—I don't expect you want to take your lot up that passageway unless you have to."

He agreed with her there. A narrow, twisting path like that was designed so that invaders, should they somehow make it through the gates, would be easy prey for archers and swordsmen within.

Sylvia paused to brush down her skirt, push the wisps of dark hair behind her ears, and rub her nose thoughtfully. This is it, she thought. It starts now. She thought of Magda—come from the True World, perhaps sent by the

First King, whether or not she knew it herself. *A good omen,* Sylvia told herself. She stepped out in front of the King, and further, to stand in front of the army. Four thousand stretched to either side of her—they seemed fragile in the face of those city walls, the gates, that castle, and the witch within. Sylvia took a deep breath, raised her hands, and focussed on the gates.

Had she wanted to show off, she could have changed the metal to a shower of gemstones. She could have made the gates melt and form a paved entry. She could have turned it all into a giant metal stallion and sent it galloping up the path into the castle, invincible for a time. Tephee might have done so, but it wasn't Sylvia's style. She merely reached out to locate the pins and bolts holding the two gates into the walls, and with a push of her will, severed the pins from the gates. With another nudge, the cross-hatched door fell outward, its wicked spikes burying themselves in the ground. The other gate teetered and fell in the other direction, buckling and splitting as it did so, leaving the way clear. The sheer simplicity of it was awesome. The way was open.

A hard, bright light speared towards her, unseen by the thousands around her, and although Sylvia had been waiting for it, still it jolted into her so hard that she was physically picked up and hurled backwards into the front line of troops.

Chapter Twenty-Eight

"I've got her . . ." breathed Zuleika, her gaze distant but fierce. The gate was down, but that didn't matter. Soldiers were easy to deal with. "Send the army down."

"Don't be ridiculous," retorted Saebert impatiently. "We wait. Let Armand's rag-tag lot come through. They are practically unarmoured and we can pick them off as they try to make it through the path."

"I said send them." Zuleika's breath hissed through her teeth. The little witch was starting to fight back. "I . . . need . . . time."

"I said no."

Zuleika's gaze focussed on him for just a second. She raised her hand. Saebert clutched his throat, and blood dribbled from his mouth and nose. Just as suddenly, the pain stopped.

"Do it," she snarled.

Saebert wasted no more time. He obeyed, the taste of his own blood making him feel sick with rage and terror.

Tephee was watching from her vantage point in the woods. She was perched in the high fork of a tree, peering into the distance. She had found that, with a trick of concentration, she could see even distant things with clarity. King Armand's troops were moving slightly in line, waiting for orders. The castle gates had fallen with such ease that it was difficult to comprehend just what an important factor that was.

She had also seen Sylvia thrown backwards into the line of Castle Guardsmen behind her. The King had tried to help her up, but had leapt back as a charge of electricity sparked visibly over his hand. Tephee's heart bumped with fear, which she controlled angrily. She repressed her relief, too, when Sylvia shook her head and lurched to her feet. Faint traces of blue light threaded around her hands and face, and Tephee sensed the air shimmer, like the desert on a hot day, and the battle begin.

Tephee held her breath, her eyes fixed on Sylvia. She had no objections to seeing Sylvia lose this fight—it might teach her a lesson or two—but for the first time the girl realised there was a very real possibility that her former teacher could be seriously—even fatally—hurt. Perhaps she should intervene. If she joined with Zuleika now, maybe she could stop all this before the deaths began. She could get what she wanted, and show them at the same time that her power could be used to help.

A dark blur at the castle gates heralded the appearance of the Usurper's army. The King left Sylvia to her own problems and began issuing commands. A contingent of nomad horsemen broke away from the line, riding hard towards the troops bottlenecked in the gateway. Guiding the horses with their knees, the nomad warriors strung their bows and let their arrows fly as they wheeled past the gate. Some of the enemy fell, dead or wounded, others tried to pull back, but the pressure of the numbers spilling forward down the castle's stone passage to the fallen gate would not let them, so they moved reluctantly outside instead. Mounted archers returned fire and the nomads raced back to the lines, turning in their saddles to fire arrows behind them.

They re-formed, leaving their own scattering of dead and

wounded on the ground. The enemy soldiers, as they emerged from the gates, fanned out ahead, giving their comrades behind cover as they left the safety of the castle.

Tephee leaned forward, trying to see better, and slowly drifted away from the tree. She allowed herself to hover a moment, then slowly she floated out and down. Tephee took great, impossible strides, her feet skimming above the earth, and tried to keep up with the action as she approached the battle lines.

Sylvia's eyes were closed, screwed shut in concentration and against the rivulets of sweat that trickled from her scalp and down her face.

Tallan had grown stronger since the last time they had fought like this. She was taking her power from the lives of all those around her now; and she was trying to latch onto Sylvia in the same way. Sylvia herself was trying to reach Tallan's centre. If she could get into that point, that place, she could . . . *push.* Expand. Separate Tallan from her power. Maybe. But she couldn't get close. Not and keep Tallan from seizing her at the same time. Tallan wanted the same—to separate her from her power, but to absorb it herself, and increase her strength.

There was movement all around her. Sylvia was subliminally aware of the King, Kiedrych, Tam, and the guard all mounting the horses they had brought or commandeered along the way. She was aware of waves of horsemen breaking from the line and tearing past the formidable lines of Saebert's force, goading them into giving chase, trying to wear down the lines of cavalry and infantry who were better-armoured, but more prone to tire quickly as a result.

Mostly, though, she was aware that Zuleika Tallan was winning their battle, and that soon she would falter. Tallan would leach everything from her, because as strong as Sylvia was, she wasn't strong enough.

The sounds of the battle reached them at the med-tents. Kayla paled, but she didn't stop working. Those too seriously wounded to fight but with enough strength to make it back to the King's lines were beginning to arrive. Kayla helped to clean the wounds and hold the men still while Magda injected them with painkillers and antibiotics, then while others stitched the wounds closed. The more serious casualties were still on the field, Kayla knew, too badly hurt to make it back, and too close to the enemy for anyone to risk trying to rescue them, even if they'd had time to spare for it. Occasionally the wind would carry the sound of a distant moan. More often, they could hear the yells and screams of those attacking and those dying. A whining whistle told them when volleys of arrows were flying, but not whose.

Kayla helped where she could. Before long she was lending a hand suturing closed the cleaner flesh wounds; she was a fast learner, and Magda soon had her administering antibiotic shots. Kayla didn't know what they were, but knew it would help, and worked quickly and well, trying to stave off the dread that Kiedrych was one of the wounded who couldn't make it back.

Magda was grateful for the assistance. Besides Dell, Romany was the only other nomad witch recovered enough to offer her services—Yolanta was still unconscious from her encounter with Tallan—but she preferred them to use ordinary medicine, despite begging from those wounded who were in the worst pain. "We can use our magic more effectively later," she'd told them. "There'll be men hurt more badly than this who'll need us more. Save it." She knew she could stay on mortal feet for days, if need be, but to use magic now would debilitate her needlessly. She told herself this repeatedly, but it was hard to accept when all around were people she could heal right now, if she only would. The idea that this bloodshed could only get worse was appalling.

Leenan fidgeted, pacing in and out through the med-tent flaps. Alard paced with her, watching her intently. Magda watched her too.

"I can't stand this," Leenan said at last.

"We're doing what we can," Magda told her gently.

"You are. Maybe I can do something else . . . I just don't know what." Leenan's face was creased with despair.

"Lee," Magda grasped her friend's arm, "it's okay. Help me here. I need you."

Leenan shook her head. "You've got lots of help. We do different things, like you said. You heal. I can talk to animals . . ."

The scream of a wounded horse whipped past them, making them flinch. Leenan frowned, resolution firming in her eyes. "I'll be back when I can," she said. Magda wanted to stop her—she was worried, frightened; she wanted to know her friends were safe. But, of course, none of them were, at the moment. Magda wished she knew where Tephee was; what the girl was thinking. And then more walking wounded arrived, and she had to go back to work.

Leenan, with Alard trotting at her heels, stood regarding the swarming field. It wasn't likely, she knew, that she could do what she wanted without being responsible for some of the deaths that would follow. But to not act would mean even more death. Uncle Eli had always taught her that in a no-win situation, it was best to minimise your losses.

She closed her eyes and took a breath to steady her nerves. Alard was leaning against her right leg, a solid support for her. She let her hand drop so that her fingers touched the dog's head. Leenan let her self . . . *go*. Her consciousness expanded and she could see the world with her mind. Bright points of light. Men and women on the battlefield, their hearts pounding, their minds hard and sharp with determination and courage and fear. Animal minds, too, mostly fearful. She could sense which horses were with the King's army from the minds that were with them. Saebert's army had a different quality. Courage, determination, fear . . . and despair. Most of them the nobles who had sided with Bakar-Cadron, and their armsmen, knowing that whoever won this battle, they were probably dead. They had nothing to lose, or to gain. They were simply going to take as many with them to damnation as they could.

Their horses were, however, just like any other. Poor dumb beasts. Leenan touched each one, lightly but distinctly, and told it to *run.*

And they did, grateful for the excuse.

There was pandemonium in the ranks of Saebert's army as the five-hundred-strong cavalry broke at once, and fled. Riders yelled and cursed and tried to pull their mounts to a stop, but each and every horse had the bit firmly in its teeth. A kindly but urgent voice told them to run, *run, run,* and they had to listen. Some galloped into the opposing line, and kept on running, even after the rider had been killed. A few even turned back and tried to go back through the gates. Most scattered along the length of the army and disappeared north and south.

Other specks of light caught Leenan's attention. Within

the castle, along the walls, were archers, shooting deadly rain from above onto the King's cavalry whenever they approached the walls. But these specks . . . rats and mice, disturbed and startled by the battle. *You're terribly hungry,* she told them. *Hungry. And here's a tasty morsel . . .*

She smiled as she heard the shriek from the distant castle wall, but the smile faded into horror as the shrieks continued—archers being overrun by starving rodents; being bitten and bitten and bitten: being eaten alive. She dived back into the mind-world. *No, no, not that . . .* Just as she had in Wefton, she had failed to focus on what she actually *wanted* to happen. Just a nip, a bite, a distraction. Not slaughter. Lords, not that . . . She found hungry rodent minds and drove them back, crying at them to *stop it.*

Leenan returned to the world, panting, shaking, sick, and sank to her knees, wrapping her arms around Alard and burying her face in his neck. He licked her face and whined.

On the castle walls, the arrows had stopped. So, eventually, did the screaming.

The loss of the cavalry had been a severe blow to Saebert's army, but it was not the end of the battle. A thousand heavily armoured infantrymen were still a formidable obstruction to the castle gates. Kiedrych's Castle Guard were taking their turn in the rush-and-run tactics designed to wear down the opposition, but Saebert's generals had worked out what was happening, and refused to give chase. There was nothing for it now but to rush their lines, and try to break them.

Armand shouted orders, runners delivering instructions up and down the lines. Tam rode on the King's left flank; Kiedrych led the Guard—diminished by a half dozen during the first assault—to take their place on the right and moving to surround the King, his escort, and Tam. Kiedrych sat steadily in the saddle, from which the broken shaft of an arrow protruded, attesting to an early near-miss. A spray of scarlet lent a brighter red to his shirt.

The rapid-fire attacks on the enemy had helped to tire the more heavily-armoured side, but it had taken its toll on Armand's horsemen too. Of the thousand mounted troops, more than a fifth had been disabled through the death or injury of riders or their mounts. The sudden and timely desertion of Saebert's own riders helped, but nearly a thousand of the Usurper's army remained. It took a lot more to get past their armour and kill one of those soldiers than it did for the enemy's arrows and swords to cut swathes through Armand's troops. Pigskin armour only offered so much protection, and most didn't even have that.

One of the three women's units took position on the left flank. Their sex had given them a slight advantage for a moment during their turn at attack, but it hadn't taken long for the enemy to realise that these women were just as deadly, and just as expendable, as male troops. They had been light, and fast, but their losses had been heavy. Their female commander had died, an arrow in her throat, but now Jailan Kesma rode with them, disobeying Armand by being there at all. She was not about to run out after all she had done to prepare for his return. She carried a crossbow, which she used with deadly skill, and her presence buoyed the courage of her adopted unit. All along the line, units of tribesmen, of Armand's old army and the Castle Guard, took their position for the charge.

Sylvia was behind the King, kneeling on the ground with gritted teeth and clenched fists. Blood trickled from her nose, mouth, and ears. No amount of shouting could get her attention. Anyone who tried to touch her was stabbed with an electric shock. Armand hoped that she was keeping

Tallan occupied, that she was winning the battle. With Tallan free to wreak havoc on their army, they would all be dead.

First King be with us, Armand prayed earnestly, *Lords lend us strength. There are more of us, but we're dying faster. Remember the last battle on this field. Don't let it happen again.*

He felt Kiedrych's eyes upon him. An uncanny hush had fallen on the battlefield. Those wounded who could were trying to crawl out of the space that lay between the two armies. Soft whimpering, pain-filled groans, and sobbing rose from the field.

Armand drew his sword and lifted it above his head. He could hear Tamalan's rapid breathing. The jester held his long dagger gripped in his left hand, ready to defend his King to the death. Captain Evenahn and his men were poised, swords drawn, archers' bows taut with notched arrows. Kiedrych's face, grim and fierce, would, Armand thought, frighten the enemy half to death if they got close enough to see it.

Armand turned his head to look down the line. Each unit commander sat tall in the saddle, his or her sword raised above their heads. Waiting. He looked across the field, at those who had betrayed him. He thought he recognised an officer in the Evenahn colours. Kiedrych was the only one of that line who had—despite their misunderstanding—stayed by him. Armand abandoned doubt. It was time.

He sat bolt-straight, drew a breath, threw his head back and with a guttural roar, brandished his sword forward, and kicked his mount into a gallop. Tam was right by him, and the Guard, all yelling and bellowing with frenzied ferocity. The enemy held, for a moment, then they charged—surging forward in a welter of noise and flashing metal.

Where the two armies met, butchery followed.

* * * * *

Saebert paused at the door to the watchtower before entering. All was silent within, but there was a faint glow in the dimness. It was Zuleika. She was crouched on the floor, her short hair floating around her face in a field of static electricity, her skin radiating pale witchfire. Her eyes were only half closed and a savage grin lit her face. Her youthful beauty was lost in that grin. She looked like a gargoyle.

Saebert nearly jumped when she shifted to glance briefly up at him.

"Soon," was all she said, then sank swiftly back into herself.

The little witch was faltering, growing tired. So was she, Zuleika knew, but not for long. Her awareness, stretched wide across the land, drew in, refocused, and found Armand's army. Their bloodlust and lifeblood, already spilling onto the ground, a powerful source for her own needs. She began to drink them up, at the same time bracing for the final assault on this witch who had caused her so much trouble. Then she'd take the young one. And then she would reduce Armand to ash and smoke. That would make Saebert love her again.

Blood trickled from her nostrils, unheeded.

Chapter Twenty-Nine

Leenan didn't know what to do next, and wasn't sure she wanted to try anyway after her last effort, which had shocked and repelled her. She knelt, her right arm still flung around Alard's neck, watching the devastation on the battlefield across the other bank. The two armies were locked together now; Armand's army struggling to break through and divide Saebert's forces, the enemy fighting to keep their line. So far, they seemed even. Closer to the riverbank was a knot of foot soldiers, ranged in a protective circle around someone small and . . . bright. Leenan realised it was Sylvia, locked in her own battle.

Leenan straightened and walked unsteadily towards the battlefield. She had to step past the bodies of the dead, and those still dying. It was awful. She felt ill. Alard whined, hesitated, and followed her. Leenan stumbled and fell halfway across, brushing against a decapitated body. Her hand and arm were covered in his blood and, with a distressed cry, she scrubbed her hand against her trousers. Alard tugged at her sleeve and she staggered to her feet.

Something was wrong. She shouldn't be so tired. She felt like something was pulling at her, from the inside . . .

She realised suddenly what it was, and her eyes widened with fright. Tallan. Tallan was taking the life from her, and not only her. Even her untrained eye could see that things were taking a bad turn on the field. The King's army, on the verge of breaking through, were falling back in bewilderment and exhaustion. Some of Bakar-Cadron's soldiers had recaptured riderless horses and were once more mounted.

Leenan reached out again. She had enough strength, surely, to do something . . . she found Saebert's soldiers, found them easy to identify by their despair and their bitter triumph. However, it was one thing to read these things. Could she influence them? People were not animals.

Or rather, they were not dumb animals. They were more complex, motivated by more than hunger and fear and survival—not much more, true, but she could detect more human notions. Pity. Revulsion. Weariness. The pervading despair. Wherever she found these, she took them, and nudged. With all her remaining energy devoted to this, she didn't see the results of her work. The battle continued, but in places the enemy began to fall back, giving the King's army respite. She wasn't winning the battle for them, but she was giving them a chance. But only if Sylvia could defeat Tallan.

Leenan had to stop at last, hunched over with exhaustion and, surprisingly, pain. Witchcraft had never hurt before. She felt so tired, so cold . . . She sagged to the ground. Alard whimpered and nosed her cheek.

Kiedrych fought with the desperation of a man who knew he was going to die, but like his enemy, was determined to make his death costly. A killing fatigue made his sword arm slow, the sword heavy, but he gritted his teeth and brought the weapon up to ward off another blow. Even his horse was tiring, slow to respond to the drumming kicks he gave it to keep it moving. He shouted orders to his guardsmen, who closed ranks around the King.

Armand's expression was grim and savage, streaked with blood. Impatient at the hampering protection around him, he pushed his horse through the ring of guardsmen and swung a blow at an enemy. His sword bounced off the armour, but for a moment the man hesitated, as though listening to some inner voice, and with a cry, Armand thrust his sword into the man's throat. Blood sprayed in a fount from the severed arteries. Armand had pushed every ounce of his strength into that blow, and the momentum unseated him. He hit the ground with a solid thump and rolled aside as his horse gave a sharp kick, then stood still, head drooping with weariness.

Armand knew he should get up, and soon, but could not find the strength to move. A forest of stamping legs surrounded him and he struggled to sit up.

"Get up, Lords damn you," cursed a familiar voice. Kiedrych swung off his own mount and tried to haul Armand up by his breastplate, but he too lacked the vigour. "Don't give up on us again, you bastard, or I'll kill you myself, I swear by the First King, I will. Get. Up."

Armand made it to his knees. Clutching Kiedrych's arms, he pulled himself to his feet. "That's treason, Evenahn," he muttered, without conviction.

"In my unit, it's called motivation."

The King snorted with bitter humour and stood, swaying. Kiedrych returned to him his sword and the King used it to prop himself up. Around them, the Castle Guard moved and shouted—another assault was pushing them inward. The King and his Captain stood back to back, swords raised before them, ready.

A horseman broke through the ring of Guards, turned to kick at a foot soldier who tried to follow, and rode up to them.

"Get on a bloody horse, for Lords' sake, you pair." Tamalan managed to convey both disgust and anxiety pretty effectively. Behind him, the shouting increased and the strange hesitation that Saebert's troops had been showing seemed to fade. Tamalan pulled his horse around to face the onslaught, managing to lean down and plunge his long-bladed dagger into the neck of a man who was trying to pull him off his horse. He kicked at another, and heard Kiedrych and Armand behind him as they tried to hold their ground.

Tam desperately wheeled his horse around to intercept another attack, thrusting his dagger forward to stop the downward arc . . . he had no strength to hold it. The dagger flew from his grasp. The tip of the sword punctured his leather armour, sliding in and out again, drawing blood and a cry of pain, toppling him from the saddle. He landed heavily, winded, and stared in terror and hopelessness as the sword flashed up again, and down . . .

Another blade intervened, blocked the blow then twisted and arced across, opening the attacker's unarmoured throat from side to side. The man fell backward, clutching at his pumping lifeblood, and Kiedrych moved back again to stand in front of the King. The wound in his side was agony, but Tam reached out for the fallen man's sword and realised suddenly that the pain in his hand, where his dagger had been torn loose, was throbbing in the space where his two outer fingers had been severed. Blood spurted from the stumps.

The Castle Guard drew in around the King and his companions. Kiedrych held his sword in both hands, barely able now to keep it aloft, and snarled. *Typical,* thought Kiedrych, *now that I'm finally getting my rotten life to make some kind of sense, I'm going to die.*

Leenan felt something brush against her hair, and then

the press of bodies around her, and forced her eyes to open. Alard was lying beside her, panting, but others had come too. Pywych, damp and unhappy, was huddled against her side, having crossed the river to answer her subconscious plea for warmth. His bright eyes were round and suspicious, glaring at the dragons that had also answered the call. Captain, Greedy, Buttercup, and Plum rustled their wings from their perch on Leenan's back as she moved. A soft muzzle bent over her and lipped at her short hair—Karomi. *Wefton all over again,* thought Leenan with a breathless laugh.

She tried to sit up, made it only to her knees, and remained there on all fours, catching her breath and trying to see what was going on. Her efforts with the enemy army had briefly helped, but the effect was wearing off. Sylvia, she could see, was hanging in grimly. Tallan had not yet been able to seize her and drain her, but the physical toll of holding her at bay was terrible. Sylvia's face was streaked crimson. The circle of soldiers that had stood around her had, to a man, crumpled. One or two tried to remain vaguely upright, kneeling, but most were prone, too drained to move.

And then, though her ears were ringing with the sounds of defeat, Leenan heard a frightened young voice.

"Dear Lords . . ."

Tephee had finally decided to come back. But to what end? To help them, or to finish them?

The dragons beat their wings. Pywych shivered. Alard licked her chin, and Karomi whickered softly.

Leenan closed her eyes.

Tephee stared around with saucer-eyes, unable to comprehend the levels of slaughter around her. What had seemed clinical and academic from a distance was, up close, a nightmare of blood and noise and acrid, nauseating smells. She could stop all this now. She could wave her hand and make it all stop. Make them go away, safely back to the mountains, all of them, and then Tallan would teach her the secrets that made her strong.

The secrets that made her capable of draining a whole army, a whole land, of all its power.

". . . no . . ." The dry croak cracked from Sylvia's lips, and a renewed trickle of blood followed it.

"The girl . . ." Zuleika's white, drawn face looked freakishly like a skull, coloured by the dark red splash that spilled from her nostrils and over her lips. Damn the little witch for fighting so hard. Stronger than she seemed, or more stubborn. If she took the girl's strength now, while the silly thing was distracted, she could finish this quickly. She would be the most powerful thing in the world. She would destroy the old King and be sure that Saebert would rule.

And if he did not cease to look at her with those cold, distant eyes, if she could not make it like it was, then Saebert be damned.

Her unshed tears burned cold behind her eyes.

Zuleika spread her awareness and shifted suddenly, sensing Sylvia's panicked scream of denial that reverberated through her aura.

Tallan latched onto Tephee's bright centre and drew it towards her.

And then she screamed and lashed out at Sylvia—interfering, stubborn, *dead* little bitch!

Tephee felt three things at once.

The first was the shock as something cold and awful struck at the centre of her self, and began to suck her soul away.

The second was a voice, which she knew partly as her own, and partly as Leenan's, which told her with urgency: *"Trust your instincts. Don't be afraid of us, or be angry any more. Face your fear, your anger. Forgive. You want to love us. Do it. You know we care for you. Trust your heart."*

The third was a pulse of power, which she knew instantly for Sylvia's. It plunged into her centre, and flared bright with a final burst, burning Tallan and Sylvia and herself with the intensity of it. Tephee felt herself freed from Tallan's attack, and saw Sylvia collapse finally, unmoving, amidst her circle of guards.

Tephee took a deep breath and steeled herself for Tallan's next attack, which would certainly come. Like everyone else, Tallan had betrayed her.

Like everyone else. Except that Magda had always stood up for her. Leenan had spoken to her, given her what strength she had. Sylvia had, very probably, died to save her from Tallan's vampiric witchcraft, which was already killing the King's army.

Zuleika Tallan shone, all right, with the brightness of everyone else's strength. The evil in Tallan was nothing more than her selfishness, but that was evil enough when she had the ability to ensure that she got what she wanted, whatever it cost other people. Tephee had indulged in her own share of selfishness, but in her heart she knew what she wanted. She wanted to be loved, and needed and wanted, and ultimately she knew that it was not possible to take those things from other people. The more you tried to take them, the more that people denied them to you. The only way to gain them was by giving them. That was how to turn awe into love, fear into respect.

The decision had, after all, been an easy one. She knew what to do now.

Tephee was ready and focussed when the spearhead of power blasted her a second time. She spread her arms wide, flung her head back, and accepted the power. And then she gave it away.

Chapter Thirty

Jailan's horse had folded beneath her, too tired to carry her any farther, and the soldier's daughter had only had enough strength to roll aside and not be pinned under the massive beast. Her women's unit had drawn back into a knot, fighting back with more and more difficulty. Jailan could see Armand a hundred yards away, surrounded by the Castle Guard, Kiedrych Evenahn standing ferocious guard in front of his King. *Twenty years we've waited for each other,* she thought sadly. *Finally, we can be together, and now this.*

A spear thrust at her and she tried to bring her dagger up to parry the blow, knowing she hadn't the strength, too stubborn to admit defeat yet.

She surprised herself, even more so than the enemy who thought she was done for, when she not only thrust the spear aside, but followed through with the next move, drilled into her by her father, that saw the blade plunge upward under his chin. She tugged the knife free and turned to defend herself again. The weariness was leaving her and in its place was . . . *fire.*

She called her unit to her, and they rallied, bright-eyed, fierce, and strong as warriors.

"To the King!"

They surged forward, cutting a path through the startled enemy ranks to Armand's aid.

He needed less of it than Jailan had suspected. The Castle Guard had been invigorated with the same mysterious revitalisation, and were making up for lost ground.

Someone had recaptured their horses and both King Armand and Evenahn were remounting. Evenahn had lost his sword—it was actually lodged in a dying Ousman noble, through a layer of steel armour, and the driving power that had put it there couldn't drag it free again. Kiedrych simply retrieved another and waved it overhead, rallying his men to his side.

All down the battlefield, the King's men were suddenly rising and fighting back with supernatural force. The King kicked his horse into a gallop and tore down the lines, Kiedrych, Jailan, and their units at his heels, calling order and structure to the attack. Lines reformed, and pushed, and Saebert's army hesitated in the face of the renewed charge, from an enemy they had thought all but dead.

Kiedrych grinned and swung his sword, slamming it into any unlucky enough to be in the way. Gore spattered, flesh opened, limbs were severed, leaving the victims dead, or staring in uncomprehending shock. He felt *invincible.* Armand clearly felt the same—as though the two of them alone could clear this field and take the castle.

Armand's eyes were bright and, for once, clear of the clouds of doubt and responsibility. Here on the battlefield, the choices were unambiguous, and the clarity of their position made Armand stronger. For the first time, Kiedrych experienced the kind of regard and respect for this King that he had always had for Graym. He'd win this castle back for Armand's own sake, and not only because he was King Graym's son.

Zuleika threw off Sylvia's last desperate attempt to thwart her, lashed out, and caught the girl once more. Her bright core was going to be a joy to consume, to make her strong and safe again. Tallan grinned.

Then she gasped and gritted her teeth in anger and disbelief. This child was actually accepting Tallan's power instead of trying to resist it. The damned bitch was holding onto it. Tallan grunted, shifted in her animal crouch, trying to pull back into herself, but Tephee held the witch's power to her own centre and wouldn't let go. Tallan threw more power at the girl, but the child simply . . . took it. But she didn't keep it.

A sharp squeal of frustration and anger escaped Tallan's bloodless lips. She reached out to take more power, she didn't care from where. She was going to kill this upstart and deal with the rest later. She touched the bright lights of ordinary people and animals, and took what she found. Some points of light were nearly out—she had taken from them already—so she found others and drank from them, and threw that power at the girl. It didn't help, and so Tallan searched further, took more, kept trying.

Saebert gasped and staggered against the wall, watching Zuleika with appalled fascination. Blood was pouring from her nostrils again. She looked demonic, mad. Whomever she was fighting, there was no way she was going to give in.

Saebert felt the weakness in his limbs, the weariness in his guts, and knew that she'd kill everyone else, too, if she had to, to kill her enemy.

Damn Zuleika Tallan and her ambition and her childish, ridiculous games that had led them to this. She thought she was so clever, but she was just a selfish fool who happened to be an immensely powerful witch. It hadn't made her smarter, it hadn't made her better. At the rate things were going, it didn't even necessarily make her victorious.

Leenan's mind was drifting. She knew it, because she could see the energy shapes of herself and the animals somewhere "below" her. It was hard to see direction when she was outside herself, but she was aware of her own body, and of other lives around her. She sensed again that well of potential and untapped power that she had seen the first time she had meditated and gone out of her body. She'd never had much chance to talk to Sylvia about it. Poor Sylvia.

She wondered that the power was still there. She felt so weak. She had borrowed the strength to reach out to Tephee, and to help shield her when Tallan's attack came. Yet there was power to be had, if only she could work out how to release it. It seemed locked behind something. A physical barrier, perhaps? Or maybe her own lack of confidence. Maybe she had to learn how to use it first—maybe it was magic for some special skill she hadn't found yet.

It wasn't much use to her as it was. Leenan could see Sylvia's faint, flickering light as she lay dying of haemorrhage and crushing fatigue. She didn't know enough of medicine to help, though Magda would. Magda hadn't much witch-strength, but she was strong in other ways and she knew a lot. If she could get Sylvia to the med-tents, there might be some hope for her, but Leenan knew she couldn't even lift her own head up, let alone drag Sylvia across the field, through the blood and bodies, then up to the tents.

Leenan felt her self tingle and she was tugged towards her body. Tephee? She cast her mind out and felt it brush against Captain's. Dragon minds were intense . . . Leenan had never realised how much power and rudimentary intelligence lay within those reptilian minds until that moment in the mountains, when she had used them to keep Sylvia from falling. What she needed now, Leenan thought blearily, was a giant dragon to fly Sylvia from here to Magda. If she was a dragon, she could do it herself . . .

The tingle in her limbs grew. A surge of energy flooded every cell of her body as Tephee channelled the power thrown at her by the obsessive witch in the castle to those around her, channelling with it some of her obsession. An echo of her intense focus.

If I was a dragon, thought Leenan with a suddenly pinpoint clarity of vision, her mind still touching that of the red-scaled dragon at her side, *I could do it myself. I could . . . do it . . . I . . . can . . . do . . . it.*

The well of power broke open, fractured by Tallan's redirected energy, released by the absolute focus Leenan brought to it. It was indeed a special magic; a skill bound up in all her other skills, but keyed to her understanding of what made people and things who and what they were. A magic held back, before, because she had doubted herself and judged others. To use this magic, though, she couldn't judge; she had to *be.*

Leenan heard, with a sharpness she'd never before experienced, Karomi neigh and stamp back; Pywych hiss and jump aside; Alard bark in wary puzzlement. The dragons she could sense as little fluttering minds nearby, but she didn't sense them in the same way as when she was reaching out of her body. She was in her body, all right, but her body was different.

Leenan spread her pale bronze wings and launched herself into the air. She swooped across the ruination of the battlefield and dropped swiftly, picking Sylvia up in her four outsized claws and, beating her wings faster and more strongly as she got used to them, took her teacher across the field, towards Magda and help.

Landing was difficult, with her hands and feet all full of

Sylvia, and the small group that was standing outside the main tent—mouths hanging open like a bunch of right idiots—were offering no help at all. Even Magda was staring. Well, with reason, Leenan supposed, with a bronze dragon the size of a pony flying down with someone in its grip. She tried to speak, but only strange dragonish squeaks and chirrups emerged. She gave up on the effort and tried to descend slowly. It wasn't easy getting used to being a dragon when you'd been a person for twenty-seven years, but she was getting the hang of it. She let go of Sylvia with her back claws and steadied herself on her back legs before she gently released the dying witch completely and stood back. She tried to speak again.

"Mmmrraaaagh . . . daaaa. Smeeeeee. Rheeeenaaaaaan."

Magda's eyebrows shot up. The shock on her face would have been quite comical if it hadn't been such a grave situation. "*Lee?* Jesus Christ, Leenan, is that you?"

Leenan dropped her snout and breathed over Sylvia's face. Magda dragged her eyes away from the incredible sight and bit her lip.

"Kayla, get some bedding. Good God, look at her. Dell, get me some water and . . ." Magda shook her head and dropped to her knees beside the battered and bloodied woman. The killing fatigue that had already taken the lives of many patients who ought to have lived was fleeing, leaving Magda feeling like she could do anything at all; and it was certain that none of the equipment she had would save Sylvia's life now. She'd have to do it the hard way, and hope she had the strength for it.

Magda, kneeling in the sunshine, in front of the great, beautiful dragon that was Leenan, closed her eyes, plunged her mind into Sylvia's ruptured and dying body, and fought to save her.

* * * * *

Tephee had fallen to her knees, borne down by the sheer weight of the power she was channelling from above. She felt like . . . like a waterfall. That point between the rivers above and below. The point of transition. The energy roared through her, like water thundering down the falls; she took it, and gave it, and the harder the river above tried to flood her, the more she gave to the river below. It felt . . .

Wonderful.

Saebert's army was falling back; trying desperately to rally, but the dreadful weariness that had almost cost Armand the battle had taken hold of them now. Many were stripping off their heavy armour, unable to even stand with such mass pulling them down. Hundreds of the King's army had died, but there were still thousands on the field with the strength of madmen. Where they could, those who had turned on their King now snagged horses and rode frantically away. Others stumbled, crawled, and as long as they were unarmed and did not try to fight, the King's army let them leave.

King Armand led the horsemen towards the gates, where there was still some resistance. Kiedrych, beside him, had a nasty cut on his left arm which he did not seem to notice, though it would need stitching later. The Captain was frowning.

"Where's Tam?" he asked.

The King also frowned, and shook his head. He called Jailan to his side and spoke to her. For a minute she looked like she might argue with him, but changed her mind, nodded, and pulled her horse back, signalling for a handful of others to join her.

"She'll find him," said Armand. Kiedrych nodded, and they moved on.

* * * * *

Zuleika wasn't watching him, was not even aware of him, *which is just as well,* thought Saebert, *or I'd be dead already.* He was edging around the room, using the walls for support as he tried to creep silently behind the witch. In his right hand he held his dagger, afraid that in his weakness he would drop it and all would be lost.

He thought that he probably was dead, anyway, even if he did succeed in stopping her. Either at her hand, or at Armand's, or simply from this terrible weakness. But maybe if he stopped her, there'd be a chance. Maybe Armand would be lenient with him. Yes. Of course. The soft-headed idiot would probably be lenient with him. Exile him, perhaps, or even let him live on in the castle as an untrusted, guarded, but otherwise privileged guest. Yes. Good old pudding-brained Armand would be that forgiving.

But the witch was killing him already, drawing out his life, as he'd seen her do with Threlfayl and Craffen and a dozen others. He'd have to kill her first, if he was to survive to enjoy Armand's mercy.

Zuleika was aware of him only in the last instant, as he reached across her throat from behind and laid his knife blade against her chalky white neck. She screamed inarticulately and spared a little of her power to blast him backwards, but not before Saebert pulled back on the knife, and slashed her throat from ear to ear.

She tried to pull her power back and stop the blood from spraying out like a fountain; she tried to break free and heal the gash before her head tipped back to reveal the gruesome wound, but she couldn't stop. Her power, like her blood, spurted out of her and could not be reclaimed.

In outraged bewilderment at her abandonment and betrayal, Zuleika's cold tears fell at last.

* * * * *

It took a few moments for Tephee to realise that Zuleika Tallan was dead. The power that the witch had hurled at her still flowed for a time, and Tephee continued to push it out again, filling up the cores of those around her, not only restoring but expanding the lifeforce of the King's army. She was hardly aware of anything else now, except that flow of power to and through her to others. It felt good. She'd finally got something right.

When the influx ceased though, she was so steeped in the act of giving that she could not stop. Everything that was in her flowed outward—the river above had ceased to run, and the waterfall plunged wholly into the river below.

Chapter Thirty-One

Leenan stood protectively over Sylvia's unconscious form while Magda sat back to collect herself. Magda's limbs still tingled with the effects of using her magic, and she was amazed that her efforts hadn't resulted in her own collapse as well. She rubbed a hand across her eyes and looked up at the Leenan-dragon.

"I think she'll be okay. I can't detect any brain damage, but I won't know for sure until she wakes."

Leenan nodded, which in her current form was more of a graceful sweeping duck of her head.

"I'll be back in a second," said Magda, pushing herself to her feet. "I'll get someone to help me take her inside. You okay out here?"

The dragon nodded again and, as Magda went inside, Leenan lifted her long neck and head to look around. It was peculiar looking at the world through dragon's eyes. When she tried to analyse it, she became completely confused and all the odd images made no sense at all. An eye on each side of her head did not produce the same depth as her human vision did, and there were two sets of images, but when she relaxed and just let herself see, it was no problem at all.

With one eye she could see a group of female warriors, led by Jailan Kesma, approaching the med-tents. Behind one horse was a kind of litter on which a wounded man was lying.

On the other side, she was looking for Tephee. Finally, Leenan saw a small shape lying huddled on the ground. She stretched her neck higher, trying to see.

"Take her inside, and put her on my bed. Yes, I know it's a dragon. I'll tell you about it later. Lee?"

Leenan bent her head down to meet Magda's gaze. Magda blinked.

"Teeeeeessss . . . ss . . . fs . . . fseeee. Teeefssseee."

"Tephee? Where?"

Leenan lifted a front paw and waved, but Magda clearly couldn't see from her height and with those eyes. She beat her wings in aggravation and rose onto her hind legs.

"You go ahead, I'll follow," said Magda. Leenan whistled through her sharp teeth, nodded, and launched herself into the air. Magda picked her way through the battlefield to where the bronze dragon alighted, hissing at soldiers from both sides to stand clear, which they did with alacrity.

Energy was still pumping feebly from Tephee's core and Magda hurried to kneel beside her. The sudden surge of power she had felt suddenly made sense, and it was equally clear that Tephee was going to die if she didn't stop radiating that power at once. She took the girl's wrists in her hands and felt the charge of energy jump from Tephee to herself.

Gently, she pushed it back. It returned. She pushed again, and again the power came back to her.

Magda shook her head. "Lee, we have to stop her. We can't just feed power into her—she just gives it away again."

Leenan lowered her head and rested it on Tephee's shoulder, breathing into the girl's ear. Carefully, she reached out to brush against her mind. *Poor Tephee,* she thought, *I never liked you much before, but you're a good kid at heart.* The loneliness and fear she found in Tephee's mind made her feel protective; the desire to love, and be loved, endeared the girl to her; but Leenan looked further, for the instinct to survive.

You've done well, Leenan's mind told her, *you did the right thing. We're very proud of you. But it's time to stop now. You'll die if you don't stop, and we don't want to lose you.*

She felt Tephee stir and respond. The wan trickle of outward-flowing energy slowly ceased. Leenan nuzzled Tephee's face and let some of her own power flow into her, and sensed the same coming from Magda.

Tephee was so close to death her skin was already cold and grey. Little by little, colour and warmth returned. The faint, shallow breaths deepened and became more regular. Tephee, however, remained still and unconscious.

Magda was looking pallid herself, now. She had given what she could to Tephee, but she couldn't risk driving herself to collapse as well—there was too much to do. She could see that the battle was all but over. The few enemy soldiers on the field were trying to retreat; a group, led by the King, were at last entering the city gates and making their way into the castle; already men were looking for survivors amongst the bodies and taking them back to the med-tents. The day was not nearly over.

"Lee . . . are you all right? Leenan?"

Leenan was crouched on the ground, her neck and head still lying across the ground, her head resting on Tephee's shoulder. She was relieved that Tephee was alive, but she felt . . . odd. Not weak exactly—just not as strong as she had been a while ago. For a few minutes now she had been trying to change her form back to its proper shape, but the effort was tiring her. It also wasn't working.

She felt something warm and soft against her neck, and realised it was a human hand. It felt strange against her scales, but comforting. She opened her eyes—still green, still Leenan's eyes, though the pupil was slit like a cat's—

and regarded Magda with apprehension.

"Mraaakdaaaa . . ."

"Lee?"

"Ssssss . . . stuuuuuukkkkk."

Magda shook her head, trying to convert reptilian hisses and clicks into human speech. Leenan repeated herself; Magda sounded it out, and blanched.

"Stuck? What do you mean 'stuck'? You can't change back? Leenan, *you can't change back?*"

Leenan wished Magda would stop repeating herself. The problem was worrying enough without useless babbling as well.

"Lords, Leenan . . ." Magda shook her head and rubbed her temples. "Look, we'll deal with it later, hmm? Can you help me get Tephee back? Maybe when Sylvia wakes up she can do something to help you, okay?"

Leenan nodded dolefully.

"Okay." Magda reached across to pat Leenan self-consciously on a dark, scaly cheek. "Here . . . can you carry her on your back? Great . . . just a minute . . . ugh . . . who'd have thought she was so heavy . . . oooooffff . . . there. If you just . . . walk . . . I'll hold her steady."

Working together, they made their way slowly back to the med-tents. "I'm starving," Magda said at length. "You must be famished. I don't know what you should eat. I mean, if you . . . if you want your food cooked or not. I guess . . . I . . . oh, Jesus, Leenan." Magda fell silent, and did not speak again until they reached the tents, where she directed someone to take Tephee inside, then gave orders for water, bread, and meat to be brought to Leenan.

The bronze dragon curled up in a miserable huddle outside the tent. People kept staring, and it wasn't nearly so much fun to be a dragon when she didn't have the option of being human again. Peculiar, alien feelings kept washing over her—Leenan kept thinking of sinking her fangs into a whole, live sheep, which disgusted her, but also made her salivate.

Alard wouldn't come near her, though he lingered a short distance away. He whined and growled and regarded her with unsettled puzzlement. The animals seemed to have recovered from the drain of the energy she had borrowed from them. Someone had taken Karomi back to the encampment. Pywych was being chased out of the med-tent, where he had taken refuge. Only the dragons would come close to her. She could sense their minds, and realised that they, too, were aware of hers, and of how different she was. But they were responding to her distress, flying down to snuggle beside her. Their fuzzy thoughts were warm with reassurance.

How Tam could still be conscious, Kayla didn't know. She wished for his sake that he wasn't. He was silent now, as when Jailan had brought him in, but his face was grey and frozen in a grimace of pain and dread. Kayla sat by him, holding his right hand—his left was mutilated, though the bleeding had finally stopped. When he had first come in, she had tried to cut the armour off him. He had stopped her with a panicked cry, and in a tremulous and horrified voice had told her:

"No. Don't. I think . . . I think it's . . . holding me in."

That was when she'd noticed the puncture in the side of the leather, and the blood, and realised that the belly wound underneath should have killed him. Was killing him. So she had given him a painkiller, bound his wounded hand, held his good one, and waited for the inevitable. The nomad witches didn't know enough to save him. Magda had disappeared with that huge bronze dragon into the field. No one else knew enough about medicine to begin to help. She heard the commotion of the dragon's return, and Magda's voice issuing orders.

"Hold tight, Tam," she whispered, rising. "Hold on. You'll be fine."

She strode in on Magda, scrubbing up in the warm, boiled water in a trough.

"Where the hell have you been?"

Magda looked at her. "To get Tephee."

"That little bitch . . ."

"That 'little bitch' saved our lives. All of us."

"Not all of us. Tam's here." There. That got her attention. "He's dying."

Magda pushed past her and paused in the main tent for a second before spotting Tam and running to him. Kayla was close behind.

"Hold still, Tam . . . let me get this off you . . ."

"No!" Kayla and Tam both cried at once. Magda looked at Kayla, then at Tam's waxy face, damp with perspiration.

"Tam, I have to see what the damage is."

"No you don't," he said, his voice a dry croak. "You can sense it. You're a witch."

"If I use magic for everything, Tam, I won't be able to help many people. But I'm a doctor. I need to see what's wrong, and then I can fix it."

"Please . . ." his voice dropped to a whimper. "Please, Maggie . . . don't. I'm . . . cut up. All cut up inside. It hurts."

"I gave him a painkiller," reported Kayla worriedly, "but he says it hasn't stopped hurting him."

There was a pause, and then, very quietly: "I don't want to die, Maggie." Tam looked like he might cry, if only he had the strength. Magda nodded and drew back to look at the hole in Tam's armour. Just a little magic, maybe, would be all right, she thought. She closed her eyes and felt for the damage with her senses.

By the First King, his Lords, and Christ Almighty . . . he should be dead. Perhaps the energy Tephee had pushed out of herself had kept him alive this long, but now that she had stopped . . . no wonder it was hurting.

The sword had punctured his side and then, as it was drawn out, slit open his belly from navel to waist. The leather armour was all that was holding him intact, and Tam, poor bastard, knew it. Magda swallowed her shock, assuming a professional detachment, and delved deeper.

The main artery rising through his stomach hadn't been severed, or he really would have been dead, Tephee or no Tephee. His insides were a mess. She'd have to do something. Her medicine wouldn't save him—only her magic could.

Magda tried to spare her power, but she had to make sure Tam would survive as well. She mended the severed colon, blood vessels, the ruptured bowel, and internal organs. She cleansed his system of the toxaemia that had begun with the breach of his intestinal tract. She began, but did not complete, the healing process. She mended enough of him that he would survive, and mend himself.

When she opened her eyes, she felt weakened, but knew she could continue for a while.

"It's all right now. Cut off the armour and stitch up the wound."

"But it still hurts, Maggie," Tam sounded a little stronger, but his voice cracked in panic. "Don't leave me like this!"

"You'll be all right, Tam. I promise. Kayla will get me

if she thinks she needs to."

"I need you!"

"A lot of people need me now." Magda knelt and stroked his damp face. "Don't be afraid, Tam. You'll be all right. I promise." She rose and turned to Kayla. "After you've stitched him up, give him a shot of antibiotic and a sedative, okay?" She quickly described how much of each to administer. "Stay with him until he goes to sleep. I'll check on him as soon as I can."

"Can't you . . . ?"

"Kayla, others need me."

Kayla nodded. "Of course. I'm sorry."

Magda swallowed. "I have to go. Get me if he gets worse." Then she turned and went down the rows of injured and dying. Where her medical skills weren't quite enough, she gave a wound a short boost with her magic—sealing arteries and stumps of severed limbs, treating shock. Dell and Romany helped when they could; the others from the camp stitched and gave comfort; many soldiers died anyway. Magda pushed herself, paused frequently to gulp down glasses of her green restorative drink, and hours passed in one long blur of anxiety, blood, sutures, syringes, death, sweat, pity, and exhaustion.

Chapter Thirty-Two

It was nothing at all to take the castle, in the end. Saebert's troops had fled the field in a wild, barely controlled withdrawal. Many of the surviving nobles—those remaining after the five hundred horses had abandoned the field—realised that the chance of escape was too good to miss, found mounts, called their men to them, and made an undignified and hasty retreat. Darem wanted to ride south after them and make sure they never returned—his eldest boy, Kareem, had been killed in battle—but Armand wouldn't allow it. There was too much to do at Tyne first.

Tyne Castle was not quite deserted, but those remaining were the wounded soldiers and castle servants who stayed to greet their King back to his throne. To listen to them, Armand would have thought that not one of them had ever supported Saebert Bakar-Cadron and had merely been biding their time in various plots to overthrow the Usurper. Kiedrych greeted such proclamations with intelligent scepticism and had everyone placed under arrest.

They encountered no resistance as they made their way through the castle, leaving men on guard at strategic points on the way up to the watchtower.

Once there, Kiedrych stood back and let two of his guardsmen kick the door in. The wooden slab swung easily inward and from the dimness within came the sickly odour of death. Armand entered first, sword drawn, with Kiedrych close behind.

"Cousin . . . cousin, how good to see you . . ."

Armand swung to face the voice, his sword raised before him, but he hesitated when he saw Saebert.

Saebert Bakar-Cadron was lying in a crumpled heap against the cold stone wall of the tower. From the way he sat, and the peculiar twisted attitude of his limbs, Armand knew that his cousin's legs and arms were broken in a dozen places, at least.

"Where is she, Saebert?" Armand asked, and was surprised by the pity and compassion in his own voice.

"I killed her for you, cousin. Killed her dead. Not so hard, really, once I tried. Witches bleed just as much as real people do. She was very angry, though. Very . . . angry . . ." Saebert trailed off and blinked owlishly. "Will you forgive me now?" he asked at length, "now that I've killed her for you?"

Armand stared and then turned away. He walked to the chair by the window while Kiedrych took his place, staring down at the thin, crippled wreck of their enemy.

In the chair was the body of the witch. In death, her expression was one of shock and rage. The wound across her throat gaped horribly. The stench of congealing blood was overwhelming.

"I did well, didn't I, cousin?" began Saebert again. Armand would not face him, instead looking out of the watchtower window onto the field below. There were bodies everywhere. From up here the movement of those not yet dead looked disturbingly like maggots on a carcass—Armand gagged and looked away.

Saebert grinned wanly at Kiedrych, who snarled back. "He'll forgive me," confided Saebert in a weak voice. "He's like that. Woolly-headed idiot. He's soft. He'll forgive me." He seemed unaware that the woolly-headed idiot was listening.

Kiedrych glanced up at Armand, waiting for instructions. He rather hoped to just dump the scheming little bastard right out the watchtower window, though he doubted Armand would allow it.

"Take him to the med-tent," said Armand at last.

"You are a woolly-headed idiot."

"Maybe. But I hardly think he's going to be any more trouble. Do you?"

Saebert was grinning and grimacing alternately. His body was literally broken and his mind seemed more than a little cracked as well. Kiedrych pulled a sour face, but he nodded.

"Burn that as well." Armand nodded towards Zuleika Tallan's body. "Today."

Kiedrych issued appropriate orders and waited while Cadron was taken from the room on a stretcher. The soldiers who bore him were not particularly gentle, and Kiedrych stifled his vindictive disappointment that Saebert passed out from the pain before they got him to the door. He left a guard outside and walked over to stand by his King.

They stood together in a long, oppressive silence, which Armand broke.

"A year. Thousands dead. Just to get us back to the start. To restore the status quo."

"You'd better make a good start of it then. Do it right this time."

"I thought you didn't approve of my plans for the Kingdom."

"I don't. But you're the King. I'm just the Captain of the Castle Guard."

Armand shook his head slightly. "I wish I could work you out, Evenahn."

Kiedrych shrugged. "If you ever do, let Tam know. I'm sure he's dying to find out."

"What about Kayla?"

"Oh, I think she might have it. Perhaps she'll explain it to the pair of us."

Armand tilted his head to regard Kiedrych from the corner of his eye. The Captain did not appear to be laughing at him. In fact, he was looking out the window towards the med-tents in a wistful fashion. Armand found himself grinning.

"Let's go and see the Tyne Gate opened," he said. "Then we can get back to the camp."

The Tyne Gate was part of the city fortifications. Tyne Castle stood on its hilltop, surrounded by walls, defending the inner gate to the walled city of Tyne itself. A broad marketplace sprawled between the castle and the enormous gates, which were designed more as an impressive entrance than as a barricade. It still took some time to send someone climbing up the wall and over the other side to release the bolts.

The people of Tyne were overjoyed to see the return of their King, and would have expressed themselves more noisily if they'd been able to. Most were weak and faint from the drain the witch had been making on them for the last few months, and especially in the last few hours. Armand took the scene in with a grim expression and issued strict instructions for food and water to be distributed to those most in need. Kiedrych left the last of the Castle Guard to oversee the regular army in this chore and escorted the King back through the passageways to the fields in front of the castle.

They urged their horses on through the carnage that lay between them and the camp. Periodically, Armand would stop to call the rescuers' attention to a survivor huddled amongst the dead. Soldiers were also picking through the field, scavenging armour, clothing, and valuables from the bodies of both enemy and comrade. None of the King's regular army—not within his sight, anyway—but some of the peasants who had joined them, and some of the nomad folk. Armand frowned but looked away.

They both paused in startlement at the entrance to the first med-tent. A great, shining bronze dragon lay there, eying them balefully.

"Rrrrrroooooo," it trilled. They stared. It flapped its wings and tilted its head to one side. "Ooo roooook . . ." It stopped, flapped its wings again, and thrashed its tail around. Then it snorted and scratched something in the dirt with a foreclaw.

Armand dragged his eyes from the incredible beast to see what it was doing, and his eyebrows shot up in amazement.

It was writing a name. Leenan.

"You . . . are you . . . by the First King, you're a *dragon.*"

The dragon gave him an exasperated glare and snorted again.

Kiedrych began to draw his sword.

"No, no, it's all right." Armand couldn't stop staring. "It's the other witch. The quiet one. Leenan."

Kiedrych regarded her with cool speculation. Leenan felt rather pleased that for once he was viewing her with something like respect. *Darn right, don't mess with me, fellah,* she thought, giving him a steely glare in return, *I'm one helluva witch.* She thrashed her tail again, because she liked how that felt, and grinned an open-mouthed dragon grin at them. She growled experimentally, and a rough rumble emerged from her throat.

She must have looked startling, because both men took

an involuntary step back. Maybe this being stuck as a dragon wouldn't be so bad. In fact, she was starting to enjoy herself again. With a rolling dragon-laugh, Leenan stepped back and let them pass.

Jailan, tending a wounded soldier, looked up from her work to see Armand and Kiedrych step into the main med-tent. Before she even had a chance to rise, she saw Kayla detach herself from Tam's sickbed and rush to Kiedrych's arms. It must be love, Jailan thought with a sardonic grin, because he must stink to heaven of sweat and gore. Maybe she couldn't smell it over the med-tent's similar smells, mixed with odours of chemicals and medicines. The Captain didn't seem to mind either way, and gathered his wife up in his arms and kissed her briefly but energetically. Then he winced and gasped as Kayla jarred his wounded arm.

Armand grinned and gave Jailan a similar embrace when she went up to greet him. He was uninjured, but his clothes were rank and he looked tired, despite the gleam in his eyes.

"You look awful," she said, smiling.

"I think that's what Leenan was trying to tell us," mused Armand.

"Oh. You've seen her then."

"Hard to miss her, really. I think Kiedrych's actually impressed."

"That must be something. How are things out there? I haven't heard much since I brought Tam in."

"We have the castle, and the town. Zuleika Tallan is dead, and Saebert is as good as."

"We know. He was brought in a little while ago. I suppose it was Tallan who smashed him up like that. Magda hasn't the time or witchpower to spare to heal him. As a matter of fact, she seemed angry when she looked at him.

She says that moving him has damaged his back—the spinal cord, she said."

Armand's face darkened. "Tell her to look around her at what he's caused."

"That's what I did, more or less. He's in the corner, anyway—we had to rig a tent wall around him. The other patients kept spitting and throwing things at him."

Armand simply scowled and nodded.

Jailan patted his shoulder. "Here, let me get you out of that filthy armour. I'll send someone to fetch a clean shirt." She helped him to shed the soiled plate, then fetched him a mug of water as he walked amongst the pallets of wounded soldiers, to crouch down and exchange a few words with those able to do so. King Armand wanted to spend some time with the people who had followed him, despite the odds, and brought them all victory.

Nearer the entrance of the tent, Kayla had sat Kiedrych on a stool by Tam's pallet and had stripped off his foul leather armour and shirt to reveal the long, deep gash in his upper arm. She made him sit still while she cleaned it, then jabbed a syringe of local anaesthetic into the muscle.

"Ow! That hurts," he complained. Kayla patted his head, which made him frown. In his right hand, he held the silk-wrapped coin.

"It'll hurt more if I sew that up without it. Hang on a minute." She kissed his brow lightly.

Tam, still under sedation, stirred and moved. He had a drip running from a clear bag into his right arm, giving him the nourishment that he would not be able to eat until his stomach healed. His eyes opened to regard Kiedrych blankly.

Kiedrych looked back, with something akin to guilt shading behind his dark eyes. Kayla arched an eyebrow at him, but said nothing.

"Rych . . . ?" mumbled Tam.

"I'm here."

" 'D we win?"

"Yes. Tallan's dead."

"Good. Hate witches. Don' . . . they don' . . ." But he fell asleep again before he could say what it was they didn't do.

Kiedrych watched him for a moment and when he turned back to Kayla she had knelt down and started stitching his cut closed. "Will he be all right?"

"Magda says so. He'll need a lot of rest, and to be kept still for a week or so. He nearly . . . well, anyway, he didn't. He's fine. He's just mad at Magda for not healing him completely."

Kiedrych's frown deepened. "Why didn't she?"

"There are hundreds here who need help. Hold still, I'll just . . . ah." Kayla cut the surgical thread and regarded her needlework with detached satisfaction. "A nice job, though I say so myself."

He craned his neck to look. "Pretty good," he concurred. Their eyes met and they both sobered. She looked like she might be about to cry. "Hush, love," he said, bending to rest his cheek against her brow. "It's all right."

"I was so afraid." Her voice was small and timid.

"It's over now." He kissed her, gently, and she gave a shuddering sigh and leant briefly against him. He encircled her shoulders with his good arm and hugged her.

"I'm sorry," she muttered, "I'll be all right in a minute. I just . . . I was just . . ." She bit her lip. Kiedrych stroked her hair and murmured reassurances. Presently, she pulled back, drying her face, and smiled ruefully. He held her hand and kissed her fingers.

"Kayla . . . love, will you sit with Tam for me? There are

men from the Guard here. I should see to them."

She nodded, swallowed, and gave that little smile again. "Okay. Just don't get yourself stabbed again."

"Ah, I see you have an idea how my men feel about me." He grinned and she laughed. "I promise to duck."

"Good." Kayla kissed his cheek, his mouth, then let him go. After a moment's consideration, he tucked the coin into the band of his trousers, unwilling to relinquish it, even to Kayla.

She watched him as he moved through the tent, going from man to man and addressing those he knew by name. Mostly he was berating them for letting their guard down long enough to get injured. One man he lectured about having lost two swords in a row. He also made sure each had fresh water to drink, and a grudging word of praise for a successful day's fighting. Generally, the soldiers seemed properly chastened by the rebukes and grinned to each other when he'd moved on, saying what an arrogant old bastard the Captain was, but he sure looked after his own. Marriage, they said, had mellowed him, but not by much.

As Kiedrych left to go on to the next tent, he was surprised by a deep growl in the early evening dusk, followed by the peculiar throaty rumble of a great bronze dragon laughing at him. He scowled.

"Don't try that too often, Leenan," he warned, though not as sternly as he might. "I have a notoriously bad sense of humour."

She actually stuck her tongue out at him, then launched herself skyward, a small honour guard of dragons flying behind her. Leenan had decided to go upriver for a bath, and maybe a spot of hunting. Her human self shuddered at the idea, but she had used a lot of magic today, and her dragon body was hungry again.

Chapter Thirty-Three

That night, Jailan stayed with Armand in his pavilion. If anyone noticed, which was doubtful considering their own celebrations, no one chose to comment. He was the King, after all, and rumour had it that the General's daughter was soon to be Queen in any event. The soldiers heartily approved of his choice—General Kesma had been a great man, and his daughter had proven herself resourceful, capable, courageous, and handy with a crossbow. If Armand Bakar-Tyne really meant to continue with his plans to reform the kingdom, he had chosen exactly the right woman to help him.

Survivors celebrated in their various ways, and mourned as well. The nomads had already begun to claim their own dead and had built a great funeral pyre to the north, to burn the bodies of those who had passed on to wait with the First King for return to the True World. Another pyre burned outside the fallen gates. Many of the soldiers and their families passed by, just so they could spit into the flames. Zuleika Tallan's body turned to ashes and not one person asked the First King to take her soul and prepare her for the next world.

In the morning, the people of Tyne would emerge and search for their own loved ones amongst the rows of the dead. Despite magic and medicine, more died during the night and were added to the lines of blanket-wrapped corpses. Magda worked as long as she could, but she had to use small bursts of magic here and there to give some horrifically wounded soldier a chance, and soon she was moving on willpower alone. Finally, Dell put her to bed and went on the rounds of the three tents herself. She nodded to the young girl sitting by the jester's bed on her way out.

Felada watched the nomad witch leave and turned back to the sleeping Tamalan. She had come an hour or so ago, freeing Kayla to take her husband away for a much-needed bath and some sleep.

Tamalan stirred again—he was restless, and still in pain, despite the regular injections. Perhaps, Felada thought, when Magda had regained her strength she would finish the healing. Maybe she could even do something about poor Tam's hand. He had woken up once, crying out with fear that his hand had been cut off. His relief had been short-lived, and he had cried again, saying that a jester without even two of his fingers was hardly qualified for the job. She had hushed and soothed him back to sleep, but his distress was genuine and wouldn't be soothed. Exhaustion sent him back to sleep in the end.

"K . . . Kayla . . . ?"

Felada brushed her fingers against his face. "No. It's me, Felada."

"Felada . . . oh. Hi." A wan smile appeared, then faded.

"How are you feeling now?"

Tamalan's face creased in a deep frown, and she was sorry she'd asked. His eyes closed and she thought he'd gone back to sleep, but then he looked at her again and even tried to smile once more.

"Is your Tamberlaine all right?"

She beamed. "Oh, yes. He's tired, and he's got a small cut in his chest from an arrow, but it wasn't anything serious. When Major Hundeline brought him back, the first thing he did was butt me in the chest."

"Major Hundeline?"

"No, silly," Felada laughed, "Tamberlaine."

"Oh," said Tam, trying to look sage, "of course." Then another wave of pain gripped him, and he lay there with his teeth gritted and panting shallow breaths until it passed. Felada sponged his face with cool water and murmured reassurances until he relaxed again.

"You'll be all right," Felada promised him. He nodded and let her hold his good hand, and swore he'd never speak to Magda again for letting him go through this.

Magda woke well after the sun had risen, bright and warm. She blinked in the dimness of her separate room and paused to assess her condition. She felt tired, but well enough. There was still a lot to do—she needed to check on all those who required medication, and hopefully have the strength to give one or two patients a boost.

Which made her think of Tamalan, and the angry and accusatory glares he had given her through pain-bruised eyes. She'd see to him first. Maybe then he'd speak to her again. Tamalan's anger was an unexpected thing, and it made her feel like she'd deliberately hurt him instead of saving his life. He ought to be grateful, she thought, feeling like she might cry.

She stopped to check on both Sylvia and Tephee, who were lying on low cots in the same partitioned area as her own bed. She had rigged up drips for them both, and as yet neither had regained consciousness. Magda paused, decided against further witchcraft just yet, and stepped out into the main hospital area.

Tamalan's little friend from last night was asleep on her stool and Magda pettily hoped she would wake up with a stiff neck. Her own jealousy surprised her, but did not relieve the spiteful wish. Tamalan, however, was awake.

"Hi, Tam." She smiled warmly at him. He regarded her coldly. Her smile faded. "Have you had your injections this morning?" He nodded. "Good, good. Let me . . ." She kneeled beside him and placed her hands over his stomach—Kayla had done a very tidy job of stitching it up—and briefly, she immersed herself in the wound, accelerating some of the knitting tissues. She opened her eyes again to see Tamalan looking more relaxed. She tried smiling again, but he scowled at her and brought his left hand up.

"What are you going to do about this then?" The stumps of his lost fingers had been treated and expertly wrapped, though little dots of scarlet spotted the white bandages.

She shook her head regretfully. "There's nothing I can do, Tam."

"Horseshit. You're a witch. Fix it. Put them back."

"I can't. Tam, I'm not God. I'm just a witch, and not a very powerful one at that." Her voice held apology for all her failings.

"I thought you cared about me."

"I do . . ." She was puzzled, wounded by his tone.

"Why did you leave me, then? It *hurt,* Magda."

"You weren't the only one hurting, Tam," her guilt at last gave way to irritation, "you weren't the only one who needed me. You're alive, and you can damn well be grateful for it!" She rose and strode out, her impressive exit impeded somewhat by the simultaneous arrival of a large group of city folk. A woman in her mid-fifties, plump, matronly, and efficient, led the crowd of young men and women, who were in turn surrounded by a mob of small children, into the tent and raked her sharp brown-eyed gaze over the inhabitants.

"There you are!"

"Mama?" Tamalan looked surprised, then relieved and thrilled. "Mama! Vi! Felada, wake up . . ." The rest of his words were lost in the hubbub of Tam's entire family descending upon his sickbed, all chatter and felicitation and sympathy for his injuries.

As she walked out, Magda heard Mama's distinctively loud voice override all the other noise with: "Nonsense, boy—your great-great-grandfather Geddin only had one arm and a limp, and he was one of the court's greatest jesters!"

Magda walked across the open space in front of the med-tent and stopped to consider where to find some breakfast, which she desperately needed. To her right, yesterday's battlefield was today a morgue and graveyard. The people of Tyne moved slowly among the bodies, finding their dead sons and cutting a lock of hair to be placed in a shrine to the First King. As each body was identified, teams of workers took them away to the mass pyre that had been built on the north side of the plain. A horrible task, but it had to be finished soon, or the day's heat would make it nearly impossible to bear, and from Magda's medical point of view, an unacceptable health risk as well.

She didn't have much of an appetite after watching them for a few moments, but Magda knew she had to eat something before she could go back to work. She paused at the riverbank, then sighed and waded into the shallow, fast-flowing stream of cold water which went up to her knees.

The witches' camp was deserted except for Pywych and Alard, both of whom protested at the lack of breakfast. Magda rummaged around the stores and munched on a handful of nuts while she found enough dried meat to go around.

Breakfast of plain oatmeal was bubbling gently over the

fire when Magda heard the soft trilling sound from underneath the wagon. She ducked her head to look, and a scaly head peeped out from underneath.

"Leenan!"

The dragon trilled again, then stretched out her long neck along the ground in dejection. Magda, not knowing what else to do, went to kneel by her friend and pat her reptilian head.

"It's okay, Lee. We'll think of something. When Sylvia wakes up, she'll be able to change you back, I'm sure." Leenan rolled her head onto its cheek and looked at Magda with such human intensity that it took a second for her to realise that the dark stain around the dragon's muzzle was blood. Leenan blinked when she saw the realisation strike home, and heaved an enormous sigh. Magda patted her nose.

"I shouldn't cook the meat, huh?"

A confused image appeared in the healer's mind—Leenan was getting better at this mind-communication, and managed to convey both the thrill of her new dragon-hood, and the utter self-disgust she felt at having, last night, hunted for the first time. It had been exciting and wonderful to hunt; to descend like lightning on the prey; to snatch up the cat-sized wood-lizard in her jaws and bite; to feel the hot blood in her throat. It was only afterwards, when her human self had realised what had happened, that she began to feel frightened.

Magda retrieved some water and a cloth and sponged the dragon's face clean. "Don't feel bad," she said, scratching Leenan's chin. Leenan gave her a strange look, but moved her head to give Magda a better angle. "I expect . . . it's what dragons do. It's not a bad thing. Just dragon nature, hmm?"

Of course it's dragon nature, Leenan's mind retorted impatiently, *it's just that I am not a dragon.*

"Not entirely, anyway," Magda amended for her. She sighed. "Leenan, can you still do magic, like that?"

Leenan lifted her head and exhaled gently. A little ball of orange fire drifted out from between her teeth. She grinned her dragon grin, snorted, and the pot of oatmeal, which had been about to burn, was suddenly on the ground beside them. Magda lifted the ladle up and blew on the oatmeal to cool it.

"I wonder what the problem is, then?" she wondered aloud, taking a mouthful of breakfast.

All the power is locked up inside, Leenan's essence made itself understood in Magda's head. *Tephee opened it up for a while. I think Tallan's drive came through with her power and helped me to focus on the change, but now . . . Now I can't get back at all that locked-up power and I'm not strong enough without it.*

Magda tapped the wooden ladle thoughtfully against her lower lip then dipped it back in the pot. "I don't suppose," she said, "you could become a vegetarian until we get it sorted out."

Leenan snorted, but didn't say she couldn't. *If it wasn't for the killing,* she indicated, *I could quite enjoy all of this.* There was a meditative pause. *Then again,* Leenan continued, *it's only dragon nature. And I'm considerably more dragon than human now.*

"But still Leenan."

Yes, she concurred, *still me. But dragon-me likes to hunt. Human-me eats meat anyway. This bears thinking about.*

Leenan crawled out from under the wagon, shaking her wings out after their cramped confinement. Magda finished eating and, with Leenan flying lazily along behind, returned to the med-tents. Leenan's mind was broadcasting a mischievous desire to give Kiedrych a morning fright.

A breeze had begun to blow in from the east, and Magda arranged for the sides of the tents to be rolled up to let in the light and air for the patients. A good number of her helpers from the nomad camp expressed horror at this notion—they knew that a wounded man had to be kept swathed up in the darkness, where his fever could be cooled, the germs contained, and the sand kept out—but Magda overrode these objections firmly.

Armand returned from early morning rounds of the castle and was a most satisfactory target for Leenan's humour, as she dropped screeching from the sky to land in a flurry of wings, claws, and teeth in front of him by the river. He froze in his tracks, grimaced, and said: "Witch-Leenan, one day you will do that and I will slice off a wing-tip before I see that it's only you." She laughed at him. "If you'd like to do me a favour," he continued, laughing with her, "you could scoot up to the watchtower and tell Captain Evenahn to join the other commanders in my tent for a conference. Just don't scare him off the battlements!" he called out after her as she took off. "I need him in one piece!"

Leenan reflected, as she beat her powerful wings, that she rather liked King Armand. He was a plain-speaking man, straightforward, perhaps a little too honest for his own good. It had taken him a lifetime to learn the arts of diplomacy, and the necessary grey areas of those skills did not sit comfortably with him. He was, she realised, a lot like herself that way. Maybe, now that she was a dragon, she wouldn't have to worry so much about diplomacy.

Her sharp eyes saw Kiedrych in the watchtower, through the open shutters of the window there, and she grinned to herself with puckish glee. She screeched as she tilted her wings back and swung her hind legs towards the window sill.

Kiedrych saw her coming, however, and was becoming impervious to her mock-ferocious attitude. She perched on the watchtower window—a tight fit—and rolled a long "hello."

"Rrrrroooooooo."

Kiedrych raised an eyebrow at her and regarded her with a mixture of curiosity and coolness. "You're not going to growl at me today?"

Leenan shook her head. "Aaarrrrrmaaaan ssssaaaaay m . . . mn . . . mnoooo."

"Ah. Well, that was considerate of him."

Leenan switched to mental communication. It seemed to suit the dragon mind—she'd noticed that Captain and the other dragons communicated with her and each other through pictures and impressions in the same way. It was easier with some people—Magda especially—than with others. Kiedrych clearly didn't like the contact very much and glared sourly at her as she tried to convey the King's message. Because she mind-spoke in images and feelings, rather than actual words, it wasn't easy—as she'd discovered when earlier today she'd tried to tell someone she was thirsty, and the poor nomad child had fled in terror, thinking she wanted to eat him.

"A conference. All right. When?" She shook her head and Kiedrych frowned and shuffled nervously. "No, don't start again. I'll go down now, will I? Good." He left in a hurry, and Leenan thought that maybe she shouldn't talk in his head again.

Kiedrych was interrupted on his ride back to the camp by Kayla, waving cheerfully outside the med-tents. He reined his horse in and dismounted. "How is he?"

"Better today, but he's still confined to bed. He's got a lot of visitors."

Uh-oh, thought Kiedrych.

The Fingal family often had that effect on him.

Before he could remount and get away, there was a joyful cry of "Rych!" from the tent and a young woman of about nineteen ran out and flung her arms around him. He patted her back but tried not to encourage her over much.

"Hello, Vi," he said. "Have you met my wife?"

"Your . . . ? Oh." The young lady drew back and gave Kayla an appraising stare. "Oh."

Kayla smiled in a way both kind and smug. "How nice to meet you."

The family resemblance was very strong. Young Viola was unmistakably Tamalan Fingal's sister, whom he'd mentioned from time to time. He'd never said that the child had an obvious crush on her foster-brother. Vi pouted and turned back to Kiedrych.

"I heard about Amra, Rych. I'm sorry."

"Me too. He was a good horse. Look Vi, I have to go . . ."

"Oh, don't go yet . . . MAMA!" Vi turned to shout over her shoulder and grabbed Kiedrych by the shirtsleeve, tugging him towards the tent. Kiedrych cast Kayla a helpless glance, but allowed himself to be towed along. Kayla followed, bemused.

Kiedrych was surrounded by Fingals, all expressing how nice it was to see him, where in the First King's world had they been for the last year, and why hadn't they been invited to the wedding? Tam was grinning at Kiedrych's discomfiture—Rych hated crowds, and crowds of Fingals doubly so. He complained that they were too noisy, touched him too much, stood too close, and that there were far, far too many of them.

Mother Fingal rose from the midst of them, her bulk much reduced by the months of privation, but her personality making up for much. She was still impressive. "Hello, boy," she said.

Kiedrych held his ground, but nodded respectfully. "Mother Fingal."

"Is this her?" She nodded towards Kayla, who felt the piercing, appraising glance she received, and didn't wonder that it made Kiedrych just a little uncomfortable.

"My wife, Kayla Brittane. Kayla, this is Madam Fingal."

Kayla smiled and held out her hand. Madam Fingal took it, then turned it over and inspected the palm so hard and for so long that Kayla began to wonder if there was something wrong with it. She looked to Kiedrych for rescue, but he only shrugged helplessly. Finally, Ma Fingal looked up at her with a warm, mischievous, and altogether marvellous grin.

"Pleasure to meet you, Kayla, dear. You're an improvement on the last one, that's a fact."

"Uh . . ."

"Mind you, don't let his temper get the better of him. He's a moody beggar, and no mistake."

Kayla's glance darted to Kiedrych again—he was glaring at Ma Fingal's back, but when she turned towards him, his eyes had turned up to inspect the ceiling.

"And you," Mrs Fingal continued, jabbing a finger at Kiedrych's nose. "I asked you to look out for our Tam, and look where he ended up."

"I know." Kiedrych's gaze dropped to meet his foster-mother's. He was sober, and contrite. Ma Fingal regarded him sternly for a minute, then relented and patted Kiedrych on the cheek, as though he were still the little boy who had come to live in her house twenty-five years before.

"Oh well," she said kindly, "no harm done."

"No harm??" protested Tam. "What do you mean, 'no harm'?" He did not have to overly exaggerate his debility—he was still drawn with exhaustion and a chronic ache in his belly.

"Hush up, lad," his mother told him. "You'll live." Her austere expression softened and she smiled, fussing over her ailing son once more. "It's nice to have you home again, my boys."

"Madam Fingal . . . Ma, I have to go. The King is expecting me."

"Well, of course he is. Off you go then." Mother Fingal kissed him on the cheek, and waved him off. "We'll see you after a bit . . . perhaps your lovely wife can stay with us a while."

"Yes," Kiedrych grinned, a certain amount of mischief in the expression. "I don't think she has any other plans for the day. Do you, Kayla?"

Kayla grinned back. "Nothing at all. I'd love to get to know your family."

"Viola, child, stand back and let him through. Merri, get your little ones out of the way . . ." There was organised pandemonium once more as Kiedrych made his way out of the whirlpool of Fingals to his horse. As he rode on to the conference, he had the sudden and startling idea that Kayla really was going to enjoy herself with that lot.

And then he smiled. Well, why not?

Chapter Thirty-Four

Magda had stopped for a break when Sylvia at last woke up. She stirred and murmured something unintelligible and then her eyes snapped open. Magda hastened to her side.

"Hi there," Magda said, smiling a relieved welcome as she checked Sylvia's eyes for clarity and focus.

"H-hello . . ." replied Sylvia uncertainly.

"How are you feeling?" Magda continued to check pulse, blood pressure, and reflexes.

"I . . . feel . . . tired. Strange."

"Not surprising." Magda checked her eyes again. Something didn't seem right. "Look right up here, Sylvia . . . to the left. Good. Then right. What's the last thing you remember?"

"I . . . uh . . ." Sylvia screwed her eyes shut, as though blinded by a sudden headache. "I can't . . . remember much."

"Do you know who I am?"

Sylvia nodded cautiously. "You're . . . oh. I . . . know you. I just can't . . . I can't remember your name. On the tip of my tongue . . ." She shook her head slowly. "Does it begin with a P?"

"Not exactly. Here, drink this . . ." Magda busied herself unhooking the drip. Just wonderful. Medically speaking, Magda didn't know much about amnesia. She'd just have to let nature take its course for a while and see how far Sylvia improved on her own before she tried to intervene.

"So . . . uh . . ." Sylvia grimaced as she drank, but swallowed the green stuff anyway. She vaguely recalled drinking it once or twice before, though she couldn't remember when or why. "What *is* your name?"

"Magda."

"That doesn't begin with anything like a P."

"No. Maybe you were thinking of your cat."

"Pywych."

"Yes. That's him."

"I've remembered something at least."

"A good sign." Magda brushed her hair back from her face and sat down on the edge of the bed. Sylvia adjusted herself to face the healer.

"Something bad has happened, hasn't it?"

"Not exactly."

"I wish you wouldn't keep saying that. Can't you be a little more direct?"

Magda smiled. That sounded more like Sylvia. "There was a battle. Our side won, but you were badly hurt, and so was Tephee, over there," she nodded towards the listless form on the other bed. "And Leenan's turned herself into a dragon and can't change back. There's a phenomenal number of dead and wounded, though I suppose that's to be expected with warfare of this kind. Are you with me?"

Sylvia nodded solemnly. The names sounded . . . not familiar, really, but not entirely alien.

"You . . . uh . . . know you're a witch, don't you?"

"Oh yes," Sylvia nodded carefully, "it's not the sort of thing you can *not* know, if you know what I mean."

Magda grimaced wryly. "Some of us can. But that's enough. You still need your rest. Stay here for a while and I'll take you back to the camp later. I'm sure Pywych is missing you."

Sylvia would have nodded again, but she was already drifting back to sleep.

The sun next rose on order emerging slowly from the chaos. The dead had all been committed by fire to the True World and it looked as though the remaining wounded would survive. Many had gone home to their families either in the city or the nomad camp, and those still too ill to walk were gently shifted to fill the one hospital tent.

Tamalan was carefully moved with the rest of them, and he complained loud and long about the discomfort. His family noisily placated him.

Magda, her expression forbidding, pushed among them.

"For Lords' sake, can't you people be *quiet?* There are sick people in here." Her irritation successfully shielded her from Ma Fingal's deeply reproachful glare, but she found herself still vulnerable to Tamalan's.

"Someone's got to look after me," he said acidly.

Magda shoved past and kneeled by his bed to check his vital signs—another few days at the least, she thought. She couldn't let too much activity risk splitting the newly knitted tissues and he still needed a carefully maintained liquid diet . . .

"It hurts all the time," he said, a plaintive note overriding the accusatory attitude.

"*Do* something!" insisted his youngest sister loudly.

Angrily, Magda pushed her hand against his side and plunged herself into the wound.

When her hand dropped away, Tamalan placed his own hand—still two fingers short—over the new skin and marvelled at the absence of pain. "That's more like it," he said approvingly.

Magda raised her head slowly to glare at him. She was pale and dark shadows bruised her eyes.

Tamalan became shockingly aware of where his new-found strength had come from. "Maggie . . . are you all right?" He held out a hand to steady her.

She pulled away. "Get out."

Immediately contrite, Tamalan got up and tried to help her to her feet. Magda didn't want him touching her. She turned her face from him and tried to rise, stumbled against the cot, pulled away again as once more he moved to steady her. Dell appeared and she sagged gratefully into her support.

"I think you should all go," Dell told the hovering group of embarrassed Fingals.

"Maggie, I . . ."

"Get out of my sight," Magda snapped at him.

Tamalan, surrounded protectively by his family, left hurriedly. As Dell put her back to bed, Magda began to cry, because she hadn't really meant it, but he had gone anyway.

She slept most of that day, missing King Armand's brief visit to the wounded. The castle had been cleared and cleaned and King Armand of the Kingdom of Tyne quickly re-established himself in his own castle.

That second night saw the timely announcement of his wedding to Jailan Kesma. It was ample excuse—if any were needed—for preparations to begin for the celebration, and wine, food, and entertainers began to amass in the great courtyard between the castle and the Tyne Gate. All citizens were welcome to attend—an invitation that gave Kiedrych nightmares and stretched his few resources to the limit.

Leenan was trying to decide whether or not to go to the wedding at all. It was meant to be in three days' time, but whether human or dragon, Leenan was not fond of crowds. After everything they'd been through, she felt she deserved a little quiet time. On the other hand, King Armand had specifically asked her and Magda, and of course Sylvia and Tephee if they had recovered by then, to come and witness for him. Maybe he just wanted to be the first king in history to have a dragon witness for his wedding. Magda thought it would be rude not to go. Leenan thought that a witch, particularly one who was also a dragon, could be as rude as she damn well liked, because not many people would be brave enough to gainsay her decisions. Still, she hadn't entirely made up her mind yet. In fact, she was starting to suspect her recent belligerence had more to do with being a dragon than with being Leenan. Meantime, she sat with her tail curled neatly around her feet and her head pushed under the bottom of the tent so that she could see what Magda was up to. Mostly, Magda was sleeping, or just talking to Sylvia and helping her regain her memory.

Then Tephee woke up. She started by muttering, then jerking around in her sleep, and finally, with a shout, sat bolt upright, her eyes wide and staring and breathing in short, ragged gasps. She flinched when Magda scooted over to her, then collapsed into the healer's embrace.

"Magda . . . oh . . ." She sobbed, then mastered herself and sat up straight. "Tallan's dead."

"I know, love," said Magda, smoothing Tephee's light brown hair back from her face and hugging her again. "It's all over. You did it."

Tephee shuddered and clung to Magda, crying again. "I'm so sorry, Magda, for everything. I didn't mean to be so . . . so terrible. I . . ."

"It's okay, Teph. Shhh. It doesn't matter any more. Hush, hush, don't cry . . . it's all right. It's all right." Magda held her and rocked her until the girl was almost asleep again. Leenan wriggled her shoulders and wings further under the tent until she could stretch her neck up to rest her head on the bed.

Tephee smiled sleepily at her and scratched her just on that perfect spot above her eye ridges. "Hello, Lee."

"Rrrrroooooo."

"I felt it when you changed. And when you spoke to me . . . both times." Her lips curved in a simple smile.

You're a good kid, Leenan spoke in her head. *You did well.*

Tephee, basking in all the approval, fell into a gentle, natural sleep.

The next day, both Tephee and Sylvia were back on their feet. A little unsteady, perhaps, but moving under their own steam. Sylvia's memory was still a patchwork, sometimes forgetting things as simple as the words for different vegetables, at other times remembering small details from her life—the dress she had worn on her tenth birthday, or a winter afternoon spent teaching Magda how to skate, in Tunston. Twice she tried to combine her energies with Leenan's, but she seemed to lack the intense focus required to gain access to Leenan's trapped well of power, or to force change upon her.

Tephee tried too, of course.

She was much too stunned to react with anything but a blank stare when she realised that there was no magic left in her with which to effect any changes at all. She could not even produce witchfire. She tried. Regularly. Sylvia guided Magda in meditation to see if, like Leenan, Tephee's power had become trapped, but there was simply nothing there to find.

"It can't just go away," said Tephee dully, sitting with the others in a room they had been given in the east wing of Tyne Castle. "Magic doesn't just go away."

"No," agreed Sylvia, but then she looked confused. "At least . . . I don't think so. I don't remember ever . . ." She sighed. "That, of course, doesn't mean much at present."

"But it doesn't make sense," protested Tephee, her dullness giving way to desperation. "You're either a witch or you're not. Ordinary people don't suddenly become witches. Why should witches suddenly become ordinary people?"

"Some witches, like Leenan there, come into their powers late," Sylvia nodded towards the bronze dragon, curled up comfortably in front of the fire. "Maybe . . . witches can become dormant again. From what I understand, you did what no other witch has ever done . . ."

"That you can remember."

Sylvia grimaced at the girl, but grudgingly agreed. "Still, it was an incredible thing. Maybe you've given all your magic away."

"Maybe she just needs to recuperate some more," said Magda, determined to give Tephee a bit more encouragement. "You've just been through a major trauma, physically, emotionally, and psychologically. I shouldn't expect immediate recovery. Same goes for you," this she directed at Sylvia, "amnesia's not an uncommon condition." Particularly not after the injuries she had suffered, Magda added to herself, with her brain having been cross-hatched with burst blood vessels and ruptured veins.

Personally, she wasn't sure that Sylvia would ever recover completely. But then, Sylvia often surprised her about a lot of things. "Leave it a few weeks. See how it goes then."

"What about Leenan?" Tephee asked.

Don't worry about me, came the practiced emanation from Leenan, *I'm getting used to it. Armand is feeding me, and*

I'm getting to know the world on a whole new scale. A few more weeks won't kill me.

Magda patted Leenan's face affectionately. "I'm getting used to you too. Even Alard is getting the hang of it."

Alard and Pywych were curled as close to the fire as they could manage, whilst still being a good body-length away from the giant dragon. They weren't altogether comfortable, but neither were they hiding under the bed any more. The other dragons had flown out, hunting for the evening, or they would have been curled up next to Leenan, soaking up the heat of the evening fire.

I've been talking to him, Leenan sent. *By the time I change back, he'll be running away from the human-me.*

"So," said Magda, starting on a new tack, "who's going to the wedding?"

Chapter Thirty-Five

On the morning of his wedding, Armand steeled himself to make an unpleasant visit. He refused to allow a guard to come in with him. Saebert Bakar-Cadron was hardly likely to be a threat to him now.

Saebert had been moved to a small room high on the south side of the castle. Magda, unable to enforce her opinion that he should not be moved at all, had insisted he be given painkilling injections at least and Saebert had not felt a thing in his battered body as he was taken, none-too-gently, to his new prison.

As Saebert had surmised, it was a limited but comfortable kind of prison. Pudding-brained Armand had forgiven him after all. He smiled, a vapid and ingratiating expression that did not conceal a childish glee at having fooled dumb old Armand once again, as the King pulled up a stool.

Armand sat, his elbows propped on his knees and hands clasped before him, regarding his cousin with a troubled expression.

"How goes it, cousin?" Saebert asked. His voice sounded faint, and he thought it strange how difficult it was to speak these days.

"Well, Saebert. You and the witch between you didn't quite manage to destroy the kingdom."

"Never meant to destroy it," Saebert wheezed. "Destroyed kingdoms are no good to anyone. It was Zuleika did that. In the last few months. She was a bit mad, I think."

Armand was silent again. He rubbed his hands over his

face then propped his chin in his left hand. "You know, don't you, that you're a problem."

"Me? Oh no, cousin, not a problem. Not now. I killed the witch for you, cousin."

"You're a problem because by rights I should have you executed. If I'd killed you in battle, that would have been acceptable. If you were whole and healthy, I could have it done then. But look at you."

"I'm just . . . I'm just . . ." Saebert struggled to find the right words. He was all right. He just needed to rest. Zuleika had really been very angry, but she'd only had time to knock him back against the wall. He'd be fine, in time.

"It seems . . . unkingly, to execute you now, Saebert. I think you're dying anyway."

Saebert stared. "Oh no . . . not . . . not dying. I've saved the kingdom for you, Armand. I've killed the witch. I made up for my mistakes, see? I only wanted to save the kingdom. You were . . . you were going to change everything. Mess it all up. I . . . wanted . . ." Saebert faded out, breathless, as cold sweat beaded on his pale face. He drew a harsh breath. "You were wrong. I was right. But . . . I did it . . . the wrong way." Exhaustion claimed him, and he fell silent.

"I don't think I'm wrong," said Armand, "I think it's time for change."

Saebert, his teeth gritted, shook his head.

"I won't have you executed. You're a pathetic ruin. Nearly every bone in your body has been broken. I'm grateful that you killed the witch, but you didn't do it for me. Or for Tyne. You killed her for yourself. For as long as you live—which may not be long, I know—it will be knowing that it is only by my will that you do so."

"Woolly . . . woolly-headed . . . p-p-pudding br . . ."

"Think what you like," Armand rose, his face cold and

hard. "But when you wake up to yourself and realise that you'll never walk again; when you soil yourself and rely on my good will to see that you are cleaned and fed; when you need my lenience to see you are given the medication to keep the pain at bay, you won't think I've been so kind."

Saebert's face crumpled and he looked like he might cry. "Cousin . . ."

"I don't know what to do with you," Armand growled at him. "I can't kill you, despite what you've done, in your condition, and to keep you alive is sadism, but it's all I can do."

"I . . . I'm not . . . dying . . . am I?"

Armand sighed. "I don't think I'll be visiting you again, Saebert." He turned to go.

"W . . . wait . . ." Saebert's voice halted Armand, but the King did not turn back. Saebert sneered at his back. "You're marrying the . . . soldier's brat today, aren't you? She's not . . . noble . . . the Council . . ."

"You and the witch burned the Council," Armand snapped over his shoulder, "and those that remained are dead on the field or have fled it. There is no Council, any more, until I rebuild it. As for Jailan Kesma's nobility . . . she has more nobility of nature and bearing than you do. Cousin."

"Y . . . yes . . ." Saebert's agreement surprised him, and the King turned briefly to regard his cousin with grim appraisal. "I . . . dare say . . . you'd think so."

Saebert closed his eyes, either resting, asleep, or unconscious. Armand didn't care to find out which, and left.

King Armand's wedding to Jailan Kesma went perfectly. Jailan, dressed in a gown of ivory, sparingly but stunningly embroidered with red and gold gemstones around the bodice and waist, was as collected as ever, but her happiness radiated from her like sunshine. Armand himself never stopped smiling.

Most weddings required only three witnesses, but Armand was not happy to settle for so few. In the early afternoon, he and Jailan exchanged vows on the eastern balcony of the castle, overlooking the city. Major Hundeline, El Ashraf Darem, and the witches were the main witnesses, but then Armand and Jailan turned to the court, who were gathered around them on the balcony, and asked them to bear witness.

Nearly two hundred voices responded with the oath, though since they hadn't rehearsed it, the sound was an incomprehensible hubbub of cheerful noises.

Finally, Armand turned to the crowd below, raised his arms, and shouted to them: "People of Tyne. I am your King, but only so long as you will have me. I failed you once, when I did not keep the Witch from taking this city. I will not fail you again, if you will have me. Do you accept me as your King?"

The answer was a deafening cheer, which had no need of encouragement from the Castle Guardsmen arranged strategically around the edge of the square, securing the castle itself. Armand raised his hands again to signal for quiet, and the crowd hushed.

"Today, I have married Jailan Kesma. Will you bear witness to this marriage, and accept Jailan as your Queen?"

The roar of approval that met this question was even louder than the first, and served as the witnessing-oath for the whole city.

On the balcony, Tamalan, who was recovering splendidly and regaining his spirits despite his mutilated hand, began throwing flower petals over the newly joined couple.

Within moments, the balcony was a storm of flowers, which cascaded over the edge and onto the front lines of the crowd below.

Kiedrych called the Guard to order and escorted Armand and Jailan out into the streets. Kiedrych hated this part of Armand's plans, but the King had insisted and was supported by his new Queen. For an hour or two, under strict bodyguard, Armand and Jailan walked the streets of Tyne. The people, still thin and faded from the effects of the witch's occupation, were clearly overjoyed at his return. Many pressed small gifts into their hands, when Kiedrych let them close enough, which wasn't often—jewellery, carved boxes, or sometimes simple posies. Kiedrych flatly refused to allow anyone with gifts of food to pass at all, despite Armand's objections—his recent memories were still much too vivid.

Early in the evening they returned, tired but still smiling, and arranged themselves in the main hall for the celebratory feast. Armand marvelled at Jailan's poise, and told her so. She laughed and kissed him. "It's all a matter of posture," she confided. "Father never let me slouch. If he caught me, I'd have to muck out the stables single-handed."

"Does this explain why you're so fond of horses?"

"I'm afraid so. I did spend rather a lot of time with them." Jailan's grin answered his own. The mischievous expression on Armand's face softened warmly and he leaned close to speak very softly to her.

"You are beautiful, my Jailan. I've been an idiot to wait this long."

"Things were different then," she said, laying her hand against his cheek.

"I love you. I always have." He took her hand and kissed her long, elegant fingers.

She smiled and kissed his brow and said in the softest whisper: "I don't suppose we can leave this party early?" She twisted a lock of his curly hair around her fingers.

He sighed and smiled ruefully. "I don't think so. Certainly not before the first course has arrived. I think they'd notice."

"I suppose they would."

"Perhaps . . ." he grinned again and stroked her cheek with his thumb, "we can manage to slip out before dessert."

Jailan chuckled, a rich, deep sound that made Armand think that they might leave even sooner—what was the point of being King if he couldn't sneak out of his own feasts?—when he became aware that they were drawing attention. Indulgent, amused attention, it was true, but embarrassing nonetheless. He drew back to sit less intimately with his wife, and she smiled at him, her eyes sparkling.

The kitchen hands began to bring out the first course of broths, tiny savoury pastries, and a variety of other delicacies. Kiedrych had reluctantly given up testing all the food, by feeding scraps of it to street dogs, when Mother Fingal, who had resumed charge of the kitchen, scolded him for getting in her way. She did it quietly, of course, so as not to embarrass him in front of his soldiers, but when Mother Fingal scolded, even Kiedrych Evenahn listened. He figured, in the end, that not much ever got past Ma Fingal anyway.

The witches had all joined in the festivities, from the oath on the balcony to this great feast, where they were seated to the left of the King and Queen. Leenan had made a point of eating well before she came—she didn't think that anyone would want to watch a dragon ripping up a haunch of raw beef with great fangs like hers when they were trying to eat. She stood behind the others at the table and mind-spoke with them about the goings-on in the hall and all the new things she could see, hear, and smell with her dragon senses. Sylvia, memory loss notwithstanding, was oohing and ahhing and taking little samples of everything offered, stopping to share tidbits with Leenan. She was looking much younger and healthier now that she was not weighted down with worry about either Zuleika Tallan or Tephee. Tephee herself was quiet, shy almost, but she smiled when people stopped in passing to thank her for her part in the battle.

Word seemed to have spread that she had, somehow—the stories were varied and mostly terribly inaccurate—been a deciding influence on the battlefield. She was treated with deference and warm respect, and despite the loss of her magic, it made her feel wonderful.

Magda was fretting about her patients, who had been moved to more comfortable beds in the castle's own hospital, but only a little. Those who were still alive now would survive, except for the King's cousin. She had done what little she could, what little Armand had allowed, but Bakar-Cadron's body was so ruined that it would take a witch-surgeon with a lot more power, knowledge, and will than she had to restore him. That he was alive at all was miracle enough, but his strength was fading daily.

Across the table, a half dozen seats to the King's right, sat Tamalan, taking every opportunity to elicit sympathy from the women around him about his hand. The skin had healed over the stumps and he was adapting already to the loss. Magda overheard him telling the women the story of how they were cut off as he defended the King from certain death. When asked about it by a man, Tam would just laugh and say he had shaken hands with a master thief, and when he next looked, they were gone. *He was adapting all right,* Magda thought sourly.

Tam looked up and caught her eye, and she looked away again quickly. *Damn him,* she thought, *ungrateful, selfish, womanising bastard.*

"Maggie . . . ?"

She looked across the table at Tamalan where he had materialised. He was looking particularly attractive this evening, she had to admit. His multi-hued jester's shirt was spotlessly clean, and the royal-blue trousers fitted snugly in all the right places. He was smiling tentatively at her.

"What do you want?" Magda said tersely.

"To apologise."

"Then do it and go away."

"Magda, please . . . I thought we were friends."

"So did I." She glared at him, angry at herself that tears were starting in the corners of her eyes. *Damn him, damn him, damn him.*

Tam frowned and reached to take her hand in his. She pulled away.

"Magda," he began again, "I . . . think I wasn't very nice to you."

"You *think?*"

He shrugged uncomfortably. "I wasn't. I was selfish and mean." He looked directly into her blue eyes, unblinking. "I was wrong. I'm sorry."

Magda drew a breath against the imminent tears. "Yes, you were wrong. You weren't fair."

"I know."

"I wanted to do more, but I knew I couldn't if I wanted to help anyone else."

"I know."

"I saved your life."

"I know."

"Would you stop saying that!" she snapped irritably. Tam looked at her like a wounded puppy, but kept his mouth tightly shut.

"Uh . . . Magda . . . ?" Tephee touched her arm. Sylvia, on the other side, regarded the jester with interest and puzzlement, trying to place this brightly dressed man. Magda took a deep breath. Tephee continued. "I think he really is sorry, you know."

Magda looked at Tephee, then at Tam, who nodded eagerly.

"I know," she said.

"Can we be friends again?" Tam's eyebrows rose in a boyishly appealing expression, and Magda sighed again. Friends. Just friends. Damn him.

Don't be mad at me, Leenan mind-spoke to her, *but I did try to tell you about him. All right for a mad fling, but nothing else.*

Magda frowned, thinking: *I'm not even going to get a mad fling with him. Just friends. God, Magda, your taste in men is still a disaster.* Aloud she said: "All right, Tam. Friends again."

He grinned and with a flourish produced from nowhere a posy of flowers for her. She laughed despite herself. Tamalan beamed, then turned to Tephee. "And how are you, Lady?"

Tephee smiled. "Not bad at all. I don't suppose you've got your flask with you tonight?"

Tamalan gave her a scandalised look, then with a meaningful glance at Magda said in a stage whisper: "Between us, Lady, I think our friend here would have me hanging from the rafters if I let you get hold of it again."

"Absolutely right," asserted Magda.

Sylvia sat forward suddenly. "I remember you now!

You're the one from Tunston." She gave a satisfied smile that something had fallen into place, then the smile changed to a smug and mischievous expression. Tamalan got the uncomfortable feeling that she knew all sorts of things about him and was only keeping them to herself out of kindness. Sylvia's smile reminded him of his mother's. With that thought, he relaxed, and smiled back.

"I'd better get back . . . you know . . ."

"Yes," said Magda with a resigned smile. "We know."

He promised to talk more later, and went back to his chair.

The evening continued with one course after another, interspersed with music, dancing, magic tricks, and short theatrical acts that had been gathered over the last few days. Kayla, seated between Tamalan and Kiedrych, spoke into a servant's ear and at the next break he brought her a lute from their quarters above the Guards. He had also brought Kiedrych's cello-like instrument. Armand noticed its arrival, remembering that King Graym had seen to it that Kiedrych had learned music as well as swordsmanship. Armand had begun to suspect his father had always meant for Kiedrych to regain his full Evenahn entitlement.

"Come on," Kayla whispered to her husband, "let's play something for the King and Queen. I thought I might dance for them as well."

Kiedrych frowned and shook his head. "No. And you're not to dance."

"Whyever not?"

Kiedrych nodded at the number of people gathered in the room. "This is the court . . ."

"It's a bit late to tell me now that you're ashamed of me," Kayla bit at him. Kiedrych pulled back, looking puzzled. "I'm a dancer and a musician. It's what I've always done. Why shouldn't I dance for the King?" she demanded.

"I'm not ashamed, Kayla. I just . . ." Kiedrych looked very much like he was wondering how to get out of this one.

"You just what?" Kayla folded her arms and glared at him, and when his silence continued she peered into his face. He shifted uncomfortably, and was surprised when she suddenly smiled. "Oh, I see. You're *embarrassed.* Idiot." She slapped his arm fondly. "You were fine with the troupe."

"That was different," he said, "I didn't know anyone there."

"Don't be silly. You play wonderfully. You don't have to sing if you don't want to, though I think you have a lovely voice. Come on, Rych."

He stared at her, and she gazed at him with a mixture of pleading, humour, and adoration, and he knew he wouldn't be able to stop her short of tying her to the chair.

Kayla played a beautiful love song for the royal couple, but it was meant as much for Kiedrych, and he knew it as he sat on the stool, his gitarchelo tucked between his knees and feet as he played it with her. Kayla got some other musicians in to play what sounded to Magda like an altered and rearranged version of a gypsy folk dance.

Kiedrych still wasn't sure he liked the idea of her dancing in the court, instead of dancing for strangers with Ayman's Players, but in the end, she enchanted them all, and he was pleased she hadn't listened to him after all.

Much later, when the meal was almost over and Kiedrych had drunk a little more wine, he sang a duet with her. The Castle Guard responded with such approbation that it was the perfect opportunity for Armand and Jailan to discreetly hold hands and disappear upstairs to their marriage chamber. Any guests who saw them leave just grinned and left them to it.

Over the next few hours, the celebration slowly broke up. Tamalan found a lovely, sympathetic young woman who didn't remind him of any of his sisters, and took her to his small but comfortable room down the hall from the King's. Magda watched them leave, and sighed again.

"I'm going to bed," she announced. Sylvia patted her shoulder sympathetically and Tephee held her hand.

"He doesn't mean it," she said. "I think he's too nervous of witches to ask you."

Probably doesn't want a two-timed witch on his tail, Leenan pointed out.

"Probably," Magda agreed. It didn't make her feel a whole lot better though. The four of them made their way past those few in the corridor who were still celebrating and up to their east-wing room. Leenan curled herself into a snug ball in front of the low fire while the others put themselves to bed.

Silence descended on the room, and each witch lay there, listening to the others not being able to sleep.

Finally, Sylvia spoke. "I'm sorry I brought you all here."

"You didn't bring us," said Magda. "We came. There's a difference."

"Is there? I suppose so."

"We couldn't let you do it alone, anyway."

"I tried to hard enough."

So maybe you've learned something as well, then, spoke Leenan.

"Maybe I have," agreed Sylvia after a pause. Then she giggled. "I should expect you have, too."

Yes, agreed Leenan with an amused snort. *Never turn yourself into something that's going to frighten the horses.*

"You're having fun," laughed Sylvia. "Go on, admit it."

Oh, I admit it. I'm getting to like it a lot. But I don't want to be a dragon forever.

"We'll find a way for you to change back," said Sylvia, "I promise. I remember more every day. Give me a little while."

Tephee, who had been very quiet all this time, cleared her throat. "I . . . uh . . ."

"Yes, love?" said Magda. "What is it?"

"I think . . . I feel a bit funny."

"Funny how? Did you eat too much?"

"A lot. I thought it might help?"

"Indigestion, I bet. Hang on, I'll get you someth . . ." Magda had pushed the blankets back in the dark and was about to conjure some witchfire to help her see when a little ball of blue light appeared in the centre of the room.

Tephee, grinning inanely beneath it, looked around at her friends, bathed in reflected blue light. It cast an odd hue on Leenan's bronze scales and made Sylvia and Magda look rather ghostly.

Magda dived onto Tephee, tangled in her furs, to give her a hug and, laughing, Sylvia tried to get up, tripped over the bedding, and landed on top of them. Leenan burrowed her head in amongst it all and surprised even herself by butting Tephee's face. The four of them lay there, a Gordian knot of furs and limbs and laughter.

The tiny ball of witchfire bobbed uncertainly above them.

About the Author

Narrelle M. Harris says, "I have been writing almost since I could hold a crayon. I spent too many years working for financial institutions, but taught English in Egypt and Poland for a time. For the last few years, I've been a writer with a leading Australian overseas aid agency.

"Besides writing novels, I have written songs and plays. In September 2003, my one-act play, *Stalemate*, was performed by Harbour Theatre and went on to win 'Best Original Play' at the Bunbury One-Act Drama Festival.

"Currently I live in 'the world's most livable city', Melbourne, with my husband Tim and our cat Petra."

FEB 2005

DISCARDED BY
LOGAN COUNTY LIBRARIES
BELLEFONTAINE, OHIO